UNTAMABLE PASSION

Tony leaned closer to her.

"Answer me," his deep voice commanded in a growl of sound.

Annie responded to his question with momentary silence before kicking her horse into action, sending her mare galloping ahead.

Tony was seconds behind her, his big horse easily matching the mare's strides, catching up to her. He grabbed at the reins and pulled the horse up.

"Let go!" Annie exclaimed.

"Not until you answer me," he insisted.

"You haven't any right to question me," she stated angrily, yanking back against the grip he had on the leather.

"While you're living in my house—"

"It's my house too, or have you conveniently forgotten that, *Mr.* Chambers?" Annie snapped, her temper flaring into life.

"I'm the man of the household," Tony stated, as if that was the answer beyond reproach.

"But you're not *my* man," Annie coolly pointed out, "and you never will be."

"If I were," Tony said in an equally chilly tone, "you would most certainly know your place, my dear, I can very well assure you."

"Since you aren't," Annie retorted, "my place is wherever I please."

GAIL LINK

Forsaking All Others

LEISURE BOOKS **NEW YORK CITY**

A LEISURE BOOK®

January 1997

Published by

Dorchester Publishing Co., Inc.
276 Fifth Avenue
New York, NY 10001

With great affection to Pat Ferrarri of Melbourne (my first international fan). For being a great "mate"—a true world-class friend. Thanks for all your many kindnesses to me (especially your willingness to gather info on my favorite Aussie theatre performers!)—and for your help in the research. How I wish that I could have visited your wonderful country personally, but...Hopefully, one day.

ACKNOWEDGMENTS:

To Annee Chartier and Adrianne Ross—for memories and sharing; may the *Music of the Night* live on forever!

To Madeline Baker—for simply being the generous *you* that you are! Your letters are always sunshine. Keep 'em coming.

To the regular gang at the Barnes & Noble "Belles of Romance." Thanks for all the support. It means so much! You're the best.

To Val Kilmer—you gave "Tony" a face (and my VCR a workout). My admiration for your skill and talent as an actor is unreserved.

To my folks—thanks, one more time.

And, to my readers—who take the journey with me.

Forsaking All Others

Prologue
A Dream Denied

Australia, 1888

He would soon be here.

Annie Ross read for a second time the letter she'd just received from the solicitors in Melbourne. There was no mistaking the contents.

She sat alone in the kitchen of the homestead. It was early afternoon, and even though it was late autumn here in the Australian High Country, where nights could be cool, the day was warm. Her cup of coffee sat half empty in front of her, cooling slowly while she digested the news in the missive.

Of course *he* was coming. He would be a fool not to, what with an estate of this size as an incentive.

Annie rose from her chair and emptied her cup in the sink. She looked out into the garden, abloom with the flowers she loved most, roses. Red roses. Cedric had sent for several different kinds from his native England and brought back many others from his visit to the States. They'd spent many a quiet moment in the garden beneath the rose arbor, the trailing blend of red and white twining among the wooden lattice-work.

"Mummy, what's wrong?"

Annie turned around and smiled in her daughter's

11

direction. Fallon stood there, her long hair mussed from her nap, a questioning look on her angelic face.

"Nothing, sweetheart," Annie assured her child, holding out her arms.

Fallon's bare feet flew across the flagstone floor, her tiny arms going about her mother's neck.

Annie carried her daughter back to her seat at the long oak table. She looked into her daughter's big blue eyes, gently stroking the child's pale blond hair. The heat of the Australian sun had bleached it almost white. A smattering of freckles dusted Fallon's pert nose. It was almost, Annie thought, like gazing into a looking glass.

She thanked God once again that her daughter looked nothing like her natural father; the only thing of his that Fallon could lay claim to was the color of her hair. Fallon was sweet, warm and affectionate, the complete opposite of the man who'd fathered her.

"Will you read me a story later?"

"Of course I will," Annie promised.

"I miss Uncle Cedric, Mummy," the child said as she jumped down from her mother's lap when Lady, the border collie who was her constant companion, entered the room. "He was awfully good at telling stories without a book."

Annie watched as her daughter bent down and hugged the animal. She smiled as Fallon stood and picked up one of her favorite toys from its temporary resting place on the dresser, a carved wooden horse with a real mane and tail of horsehair that Cedric had purchased when last they were in Melbourne, and made it gallop on the air to the delight of the dog.

Annie missed Cedric just as much, or more than, her daughter did. She missed Cedric's calm, gentle manner, his worldly-wise wit, and his stong, comforting arms, arms which offered shelter from the storms she'd known in her short life.

But his death months earlier had put an end to that comfort. That stupid riding accident had taken from Annie her closest friend, the man she depended on, the man she'd trusted to always be there for her.

Now, once again, she was alone. The only difference being that she wasn't completely alone this time—she had her child—and she was no longer penniless, thanks to Cedric's overwhelming generosity. She was now a woman of considerable wealth and property, all of which she would be expected to share with this stranger.

And what of the man who had inherited half the same assets she had?

Cedric's solicitors had advised her that they had sent a letter to the other person named as co-heir of Cedric's estate, Cedric's grandnephew, one Anthony Chambers of London, informing the young man of his inheritance.

A little over two months ago, the solicitors had received a reply that Anthony Chambers was coming to Australia to claim his share of the bequest; they promptly informed Annie.

She glanced again at the latest communication from them. It would seem that her co-heir was already en route, anxious to seize his newfound opportunity.

Annie wondered if Anthony Chambers was anything like his great-uncle. Would he be as kind as Cedric? As charming? As warm? Would he share her grief in the loss of so good a friend?

Annie blinked back tears. Or would he be the type of man she hoped never to meet again? Arrogant. Disdainful. A Janus in his dealings with women.

What would he make of her and Fallon? How would he feel about sharing the homestead with her according to the terms of Cedric's will?

Annie realized that she knew little of this man who would soon arrive other than the few things Cedric had fondly mentioned about his grandnephew.

But Cedric hadn't seen the boy for many years. People changed. Tony, as Cedric called him, wasn't a schoolboy any longer. He was now a young man. A member of the exclusive English upper crust. Used to power and privilege as his birthright. Raised to see the world in a particular fashion.

Annie had bitter firsthand knowledge of just what fashion that was—the same one held by all young men of wealth, no matter what the country.

She sighed as she placed the letter back in the envelope. Annie was more than willing, for Cedric's sake as well as her own, to meet this stranger halfway, as long as Tony Chambers understood the rules.

First and foremost, she loved this land. Secondly, she and her daughter belonged here. It was their home now. One they were willing to share. One they wouldn't give up.

If need be, Annie would fight to keep this station and her place on it. With whatever means at her disposal. No one was ever going to try to sweep her and her daughter away again as if they were yesterday's rubbish.

So, she declared silently, let Anthony David Chambers come. Anne Elizabeth Ross was ready for him, come what may.

Part One

A Dangerous Game

Chapter One

He doubted that his uncle's whore would be among the people welcoming him to Australia.

Tony Chambers watched as the gangplank was lowered. Swarms of people milled about the docks of the bustling city of Melbourne.

He narrowed his eyes as he scanned the area. There were whores, to be sure, plying their trade among the sailors and merchantmen that clogged the busy port streets. He watched as several of the women called out encouragement, flashed an ankle or a smile, in an attempt to lure trade.

Moments later the sight of a constable forced the girls to flee to wharfside taverns, seeking a welcoming haven from the law.

A sharp mental picture invaded Tony's mind. He imagined that the woman his great-uncle had left half his vast estate to would have a hard edge to her, if not the same overly painted look to her face as the dockside sluts possessed.

What the bloody hell had Cedric been thinking of?

Or, Tony mused, what organ had Cedric been thinking with?

Tony's full mouth gave a sardonic twist. Not too difficult to figure that puzzle out. His great-uncle had been sixty-two at his death, the woman a year younger

17

than Tony's five and twenty. Cedric, he was convinced, had been skillfully manipulated by a clever seductress bent on furthering her own interests. Tony was certain of that. No real lady, he knew, would ever consider living with a man not her lawfully wedded husband, or would agree to live with yet another if not for gain.

"Your bags are ready, sir."

Tony turned his head in the direction of the speaker, his valet. "Thank you, Alfred."

Alfred Dunner was a stocky Englishman barely above average height, about forty-five, with gray-flecked, short blond hair. He'd been with Tony Chambers for only a short while, happily hired away from the mercurial star of a troupe of mummers playing the touring circuit throughout the western states of America. It had taken Alfred only seconds to thank providence for his good fortune when the unexpected offer from Tony was made. He'd given his notice on the spot. Though Alfred loved the Bard, he loved the security of a well-cooked bird and an occasional bottle more. Safe and steady employment, even if at the bloody end of the world, was fine by him.

"I do believe I see a man on the dock, sir, holding a placard with your name upon it."

Tony swiveled his head and caught sight of a man standing below. The man was dressed in a dark suit, a thick pair of muttonchop whiskers cupping his round face.

With Alfred behind him, Tony departed the ship that had been his home these past long weeks.

"I'm Tony Chambers," Tony announced as he stepped onto the dock, his nostrils catching the mix of dockside scents of water, fish, and stale humans.

"Good day to you, Mr. Chambers," the other man

said, holding out his pale, beefy hand. "I'm Jason Noble, at your service."

Tony recognized the name from the firm of solicitors that had sent him news of his inheritance.

"If you'll step this way," Noble indicated, "I've arranged a coach to take you and your luggage to your uncle's . . . excuse me, sir, to *your* Melbourne residence."

"I would rather meet with you and your partner straightaway, if that is possible," Tony uttered in a tone that demanded rather than requested. "My valet will see to my luggage if you would be so kind as to secure another coach for us."

"As you will, sir." The rotund lawyer gave instructions to the coachman to take the valet and the assorted bags to the address that he quickly rattled off; then he tossed a coin to a grubby street urchin and told the boy to summon another hack.

"I do trust that you had a pleasant voyage, sir," Noble inquired politely.

"Relatively so," Tony replied, watching as his man and bags were whisked away. The vastness of the Pacific Ocean had been overwhelming. Miles and miles of nothing but water, as far as the eye could see. Only once had the voyage from California been broken, when the captain had put into Honolulu harbor for the unloading of several passengers, and for restocking of provisions. In the five days that they were there, Tony had had a chance to explore the exotic island, sampling the native food, taking in the tropical beauty of his temporary surroundings. And he'd discovered another native delight—the stunning women of this Pacific paradise.

Tony's mouth quirked into a small cocksure grin,

19

his eyes crinkling. "Yes, all in all, a very delightful voyage," he said in a pleasant tone. "Whilst traveling here, I had the incredible good fortune to spot some rather fascinating creatures of the sea, whales and dolphins, not to mention," he added, "as we got closer to Melbourne harbor, birds the captain assured me were penguins."

"Just you wait until you get to the homestead then, sir," the lawyer insisted with a trace of a smile. "You'll see animals and such so different as not to be believed."

"Including one grasping she-cat and her get?" Tony asked, his tone suddenly darkening.

The other man cleared his throat. "Are you referring to Mrs. Ross, sir?"

"*Mrs.?*" Tony raised one thick brown brow in skepticism. "Since when?"

The other man looked uncomfortable. "I have no reason to doubt that the lady is indeed a widow."

"Why?" Tony's tone was rife with skepticism. "Because she calls herself one?"

"Of course." He said it with utter conviction.

"So, I take it that you believe her?"

"I have no reason not to, sir." The clip-clop of shod hooves sounded close by. Noble was relieved. He had no wish to start an argument with a client. That would be bad form, and considering the estate this man had inherited, foolish as well. "Ah, here is our coach, sir."

Tony joined the other man in the carriage, his eyes scanning the busy thoroughfares as they traveled through the growing town of Melbourne. He deeply missed London. He missed the familiar sights, the familiar sounds, the familiar scents. He especially missed the life he'd had there. A life he was used to, one he embraced with relish.

He'd left all that behind him now for this. . . . this what? He asked himself. This new world with all its strange smells and rhythms? Strange sights and customs?

Exactly.

And it wasn't as if he would have to be here forever. A few weeks would be all it would take to set this matter to rights, he was sure, and then he could collect all that was due him and be on his way back to his own world.

A satisfied smile kicked up the corners of his mouth.

A frown transformed his face.

"Are you telling me that there is no legal way in which I can get around these conditions?" he demanded.

The older man behind the massive teakwood desk looked at the man sitting opposite him and took a deep breath. "Yes, Mr. Chambers, that is exactly what I'm saying. Your great-uncle was quite specific about the terms of his will. If you try and break it, then you'll lose completely."

"So, to get what's mine, I have to live at this"—Tony sought the correct word—"*station* for the duration of a year? I must *share* this abode with the woman who's been my uncle's *companion*"—the way he said the word gave an indication as to what meaning he placed on it—"whether or not I like it?"

The other man, William Teaneck, cleared his throat. "You are asked to share the homestead with Mrs. Ross and her daughter for a period of twelve months, Mr. Chambers. If after that time you are so inclined, you can return to England, and provisions will be made to send your profits from the share of the station to you there. Or you may offer to buy out Mrs. Ross; or she you, should you both decide on that course."

Tony considered the lawyer's words. "It would appear that my great-uncle was adamant about this."

"He was, Mr. Chambers," Teaneck agreed. "And he left a letter for you that I think may better explain his frame of mind."

"Have you read it?" Tony inquired.

"No," Teaneck assured him, "I haven't. He did tell me that it was to aid you in understanding his motives for the disposition of his property." Teaneck stood up and walked a few paces to the large safe that held his clients' private papers, bent over, and unlocked the door. He withdrew an envelope and relocked the safe.

"Read this," Teaneck said as he handed the thick vellum envelope bearing Tony's name to the young Englishman.

"I shall leave you to your privacy."

"Thank you," Tony said as he broke the wax seal on the back flap and removed the sheets of paper.

Dear Tony:

I hope that you've accepted the conditions that I've set for your inheritance.

Perhaps you think that I am asking a lot from you, but, my dear boy, I strongly believe that the rewards will be great, although you may not think so at the present time.

You've always been my favorite grandnephew (which is not to slight your older brother Terrence); perhaps because I saw some measure of myself in you, even when you were a child. Not having been blessed with a natural son of my own flesh, you have become that for me in all the ways that count.

Maybe that is hard to believe as we haven't kept in close contact over the years, my fault I fear, but I discovered quite young that I possessed a wanderlust that wouldn't let go. I needed to see more of the world than that which was to be found in our England.

In retrospect, I was searching for something that wasn't available to me in my homeland.

I found it here, in Australia, and I hope and trust that you will too, my dear boy. This land is home to me in a way that my native soil could never be. There is wonder here, a beauty of a rare sort to a man with the eyes to appreciate it. It is a land that has blessed me with more wealth, more opportunities, than I ever dreamed could happen.

Regarding Annie Ross: She is the woman that I have waited my whole life for. Each day with Annie is a gift from the Almighty. She brings such joy into my life in ways that I have never believed possible. And her daughter, Fallon, is as precious to me as any child of my own blood would be. You, too, will love the child. Of that I am certain.

When you meet Annie you will understand for yourself just what I found in her.

Tony gave a small snort. He already knew just what his great-uncle had found in the woman. A young body in which to lose himself. A grasping attempt to recapture his youth and vigor, if only for the moments spent in her arms and between her legs. Sweet oblivion—the ability to cheat death and proclaim life in the most elemental way for a man of his great-uncle's age.

Cedric wouldn't be the first, nor the last, man to trod that particular path.

Tony resumed reading the letter.

I love her.

Tony sighed. You poor old fool, he thought. Caught in the oldest trap, the most seductive web.

Lust. Illusions. That's all it was, Tony decided. Love wasn't really an ingredient, except in his great-uncle's imagination. Tony preferred a simpler arrangement—calling what passed between men and women for the truth as he saw it. Pleasure for pleasure's sake. Knowing the rules of the game.

He doubted that this woman had played his great-uncle fair. Well, that could cut both ways.

And, as for Annie, I leave her to your care and protection.

Tony raised his gaze from the pages in his hand. He rolled his eyes at the last sentence. *Protection?* From what? From whom? A lady always deserved his protection. A grasping tart didn't.

Give this life a chance, Tony. That's all I'm asking that you do. Get to know it as I have. I promise you that you will not regret it.

Tony folded the letter and returned it to the envelope, slipping it into the inside pocket of his expensive wool jacket, tailor-made for him by the Prince of Wales's own personal tailor, Henry Poole & Co.

Tony stood up and walked to the window, staring

outside at the familiar trees that lined the avenue below. This part of upper Collins Street, the eastern side, which housed the offices of many of the important professionals in the city, was one of the few places in Melbourne to have trees of any sort. A passenger on the ship to Australia, a doctor, had told him that many saplings had been brought from England and re-planted in Melbourne so that the native Englishmen and women located there could have some little bit of their homeland close by.

He focused on the trees. They had survived the long journey and flourished, sinking their roots deep into the Australian soil, becoming a part of the landscape. Much as his great-uncle had done.

Tony was still at the window several minutes later when Mr. Teaneck returned to his office.

The lawyer waited until the younger man resumed his seat. "In addition to the house in Melbourne and the half-interest in the property in the High Country, your great-uncle left you a considerable amount of money, Mr. Chambers."

Tony looked the other man square in the face, his eyes direct. "How much," he asked, "is considerable?"

"The sum of one million pounds, sir."

Tony blinked in surprise. "Yes," he said, trying to maintain his calm, "that is rather a considerable sum."

"Cedric Chambers was a man of many parts, as I'm sure you're well aware. He made his fortune in gold mining at Ballarat and invested it wisely in several other ventures. Mr. Thomas at the Central Bank will be happy to go over the details of the monetary portion of your inheritance with you, along with the other financial trusts your uncle set up."

"And what other trusts would they be?" Tony inquired, still reeling from the amount the lawyer named.

"Your great-uncle set up funds for the use of Mrs. Ross and her daughter, along with several of his servants and some of his other employees and friends."

"So, Mrs. Ross and her child have their own money?"

"Yes, that's right."

In a cool, direct voice Tony asked, "What did he leave them?"

Teaneck consulted the papers on his desk. "He left Fallon Ross the sum of 25,000 pounds, to be held in trust until her twenty-first birthday. Mrs. Ross was given the sum of 50,000 pounds outright for her own personal use."

"So, in addition to one-half the station as you here call it, this woman inherited a large amount of money from my great-uncle?"

"Yes, sir, that is correct."

"Interesting." Tony rose. "Thank you for your time, Mr. Teaneck."

"I'm sorry that we had to meet under these circumstances, Mr. Chambers. I liked and respected your great-uncle. He was above all a gentleman, sir. One of a rare breed. He will be missed by all who knew him."

As he entered another carriage for the short trip to his new town house, Tony wondered about the lawyer's final words. Would everyone mourn his great-uncle's passing?

Did she?

The driver turned onto the posh address, one of the most fashionable in "Marvellous" Melbourne. Tony handed the driver his fee and paused before the imposing brick residence. It was Georgian in design, an almost visual twin of the Chamberses' house in London.

Tony's glance skirted the street. Many of the homes were replicas of those in the mother country. A thread of connection to the past.

He walked up the stairs and into the house.

"Let me take that for you, sir," Alfred said as he materialized out of a side room, helping Tony shed his overcoat. "If you would care for some tea, cook has some ready."

Tony heaved a deep sigh. "Actually, what I really could really use is a hot bath. And a glass of brandy, if there's any to be had here."

"Your great-uncle has a tolerable wine cellar here, sir, along with some fine spirits. I've taken the liberty of decanting a rather fine old bottle of brandy."

"Good man," Tony said, heading for the winding stairs. He paused on the bottom rung. "Which is mine?"

"To the right, sir, down the hall. The last room. I shall be with you momentarily."

Tony climbed the stairs, eager for a relaxing tub. He opened the door to the master suite and crossed the threshold.

It was a very masculine room, with no sign of feminine fripperies. Thick curtains of burgundy velvet hung to the floor, matching the spread on the massive four-poster bed. He spotted a book on the nightstand, the ribbon marker still in place. Beside it, a silver-framed photograph was evident.

Tony took the few steps necessary to bring him to the bed. He picked up the frame, examining the photograph. It was the formal portrait of a young woman

27

and a child. He had no doubt that it was this Annie Ross and her daughter. The woman was quite different from what he'd pictured. There was an unmistakable softness about her, a teasing hint of vulnerability in the way her mouth curved.

Tony lay the frame face down on the nightstand, dismissing the image from his mind. That's all it was, he was sure. A clever manipulation.

While he was removing his jacket, a soft rap sounded on the door and it swung open.

Alfred entered the room bearing a silver tray that held a snifter of brandy and a pile of envelopes of various sizes. He placed the tray on the marble-top table nearby and handed the crystal glass of liquid to Tony. Then he strode through to the adjoining bathroom, where he proceeded to run his employer a hot bath in the large, claw-footed white tub.

Coming back into the bedroom, Alfred discovered Tony glancing through the now opened envelopes.

"There's more of the same on your desk in the library, sir."

"Parties. Dinners. Balls. Opera. Races," Tony stated. "An invitation to every social event, private or public, held in Melbourne within the next fortnight, I do believe," Tony said with surprise, taking another sip of his brandy.

"It's never too early to cater favor with a man of your standing, sir," Alfred observed, taking Tony's jacket and hanging it in the capacious closet, removing the green silk dressing gown Tony favored. "After all," he said with a twinkle in his eye, "just how much of a choice can there be here? You are, if I may say so, sir, young, reasonably good-looking, single, a man of property, and most importantly, English-born. What else could any matchmaking mama or hostess want?"

Tony's lips curved into a knowing smile as he unbuttoned his white shirt. "So, I'm a very marketable commodity, eh, Alfred?"

Alfred returned his employer's smile. "A *marriageable* commodity, I would suggest, sir."

"Well, if that be the case, then they're in for a rude surprise, Alfred," Tony commented as he shrugged out of his shirt. "I'm not in the market for a bride, or for what passes for a social season. What interests me," he said as he handed the shirt to the waiting valet and headed into the bathroom, "is the property that I've acquired."

"And your new partner in that venture, if I may add?" Alfred suggested as he followed Tony in and turned off the taps.

Tony considered this as he removed the rest of his clothes and eased into the comfortable tub. "Without a doubt, Alfred." He lathered a soft cloth and soaped one arm. "Send my regrets for all of the invitations."

"Then we shall be leaving Melbourne shortly, sir?"

"Yes. Within a day if I can arrange it. I don't want to wait any longer than necessary to see the property, or to meet my co-heir."

"Then I shall attend to the matter straightaway, sir. Would you like me to inform cook as to when you'd like your supper served?"

"Tell her that I would rather have something simple served up here."

"Very good, sir."

As Alfred started to leave, Tony issued him another order. "Bring me some paper and a pen, also. I want to send a note round to my great-uncle's banker and ask him to come here tomorrow if he would, to discuss business."

Later, after a cold supper of roast beef and cheese, Tony prowled around his room. Restless energy vibrated through him. If he were in London, he would have gone out and visited his club, or gathered several friends together for a night of gaming. Or possibly passed the time in the arms of whichever woman was his current mistress.

But he wasn't in London. Bloody héll! He wasn't even in Texas, where he'd enjoyed the hospitality of his old friend Rafe Rayburne, or that of the Earl and Countess of Derran, Rhys and Tory Fitzgerald Buchanan.

He was alone.

But not for long.

As he began his letter to his cousin Georgie, Tony wondered what the woman who'd shared Cedric's life so intimately was doing.

He stared off into space, his left hand curled and resting against his mouth. Was she as anxious to meet him?

Annie stood at the open window door to her bedroom, staring at the night sky. The great Alpine mountains loomed in the distance. She gazed at the stars that hung overhead, breathed in the slight chill of the winter air. If she were back home in Philadelphia, it would be the height of summer now. Hot, sticky, and far too warm to sleep. Here, the night was cool and pleasant.

He was here.

The telegram from the lawyers had arrived just after sundown. Mr. Teaneck informed her that Anthony

Chambers had arrived today in Melbourne and would soon be at the homestead to claim his share of the inheritance.

Annie lifted the gold cross that lay against her throat, easing it back and forth against the gold chain. It had been a gift from her mother on her fifteenth birthday. She missed her parents, along with her five brothers and sisters. Philadelphia was so far away, and she'd made another life for herself and her daughter now. A life filled with new demands and new challenges. A life fresh and clean, free from the taints of the past.

But for how long?

That question echoed in her mind as she latched shut the doors and climbed into her bed, turning out the lamp by her bedside. As she eased her body into the soft mattress and snuggled under the blue and white quilt, Annie let her thoughts drift to the man whose coming would change her well-ordered life.

What kind of change, she wondered, would it be?

Chapter Two

Tony sipped the strong tea that his hired guide had just brewed. It was strong and sweet, as he liked it, although there were no lemons to be had out here on the trail.

Finally, after almost three days, Tony was within miles of his great-uncle's property.

With an ironic twist of his lips, Tony realized that he had to correct himself: It was *his* property now. Well, that wasn't quite correct, he chided himself; he shared it with that Ross woman.

At least for the time being.

Tomorrow after daybreak they would make the last leg of the journey to the sprawling station that prided itself, he'd been told, on its fine beef and horses.

Tony stood on the small open porch of the stockman's cabin, having politely refused the offer earlier that day of a bed and meal at the Ruranga station's main homestead. He'd wanted to push on, though he did gratefully accept the station owner's second offer of one of the Ruranga stock cabins for the night.

He hadn't been in the mood for either the well-meaning company or hospitality of strangers. It was odd enough to travel with the taciturn man hired to show him the way.

Tony smiled at the thought. The man was hardly

more than a boy and looked it. A wiry lad, born it would seem in the saddle, with a keen sense of direction, which Tony was indeed grateful for. He had decided against taking the Melbourne-Sydney train partway to his destination and then hiring a wagon to haul his bags and the other items he'd bought in Melbourne to make life bearable at this wilderness outpost. Instead Tony chose to do his traveling by horse. He wanted to see close up as much of this country as he could. He wanted to get a sense of what made it so special for his great-uncle.

He breathed in the crisp early evening air as his eyes scanned the area. This land was so vastly different from his England of gently rolling hills and country estates, of small villages and sweet meadows. This land was raw and untamed, aggressive even. The sights, sounds, and smells were as unique as the landscape. It was a world far removed from what he'd known, from what he'd loved.

As they'd made their way slowly across the countryside, leaving the polish and sophistication of Melbourne behind, Tony paid careful attention to the changes in the landscape, from pastoral to woodlands. He observed the many varieties of the gum, or eucalypt, trees. He saw the color and lushness of the grass, the woodland flowers, some hearty species still in evidence even in this winter season.

A strong wind picked up and thunder rumbled. A coming storm had darkened the afternoon sky, and, not wanting to be caught in whatever might come, they'd chosen to spend the night rather than push on to the homestead in the dark.

Tony was glad. He wanted to see the property, and its occupants, in full light. No shadows and no illusions to cloud his judgment.

He put the battered tin cup on a windowsill and withdrew a monogrammed silver cigar case from the inside pocket of his jacket. He flicked a match and lit up one of the slim cheroots, sucking in the rich flavor of the tobacco. Rafe had given him several boxes of Cuban cigars as a going-away present when he'd left Texas, along with a fancy Colt pistol, now safely tucked away in his luggage.

He'd almost wished for the pistol last night when they'd made camp. He and Alfred were treated to their first sight of one of this country's wildly improbable creatures, a six-foot gray kangaroo.

Jack Hollings, their guide, had laughed at their startled reactions to the wandering 'roo that he chased off. Still chuckling, he produced a stockman's whip from his saddle gear and told them it was made of kangaroo hide, snapping it with an expert's touch. He'd even admitted a sneaking fondness for 'roo meat, much to Tony's chagrin and Alfred's obvious distaste.

Why had Cedric chosen this place, above all others, to live? Granted, it was unique. Different. But what was it that had taken an Englishman and changed him forever?

The door to the cabin squeaked open and Alfred emerged. "Jack says we'll be at your *estate* by sometime early tomorrow afternoon. I'm looking forward to that," he said with obvious relief, rubbing his posterior, "as my bum is sore from all this riding about."

"Sorry about that, old man," Tony said, exhaling a thin ribbon of smoke.

"Strange country, this is," Alfred commented.

"Very," Tony agreed.

"Will you have to be staying?"

Tony took a long drag on the cigar. "Longer than I'd planned." He slid a sideways glance at his valet. "I do appreciate your taking this on."

"It's my job, sir."

"Still, it isn't what you were used to."

"I've learned to be adaptable, sir," Alfred stated with a quirky raised brow. "Working with a troupe of actors has taught me well."

Tony gave a brief nod of his head as he tossed the remains of the cheroot to the wooden boards, grinding it out with his boot.

Alfred collected Tony's empty cup and went back into the cabin, leaving Tony alone with his thoughts.

Adaptable. That wasn't a prominent word in Tony's vocabulary. From the grave, it would seem that his great-uncle was telling Tony it was a word that he would have to incorporate into his life if he wished to get by in this new land.

He wasn't sure that he fancied that idea.

Head stockman Jim Winters made his way to the kitchen door of the homestead. A rider had just come from the neighboring Ruranga station with a message.

He knocked on the door and waited for permission to come in.

That granted by a female voice, Jim proceeded inside.

Annie sat at the table sipping her third cup of morning coffee, the account books for the station in front of her. She wanted to make sure that everything was in order should her new partner wish to inspect them today. Cedric had shown her his system of entry, and in the last two years, it had been her responsibility to see that all entries were logged. This Anthony Chambers should be quite pleased, she thought; the station had continued to make quite a tidy profit, as did Cedric's other investments.

She glanced up, saw Jim standing there, and greeted him warmly. "Good morning, Jim."

"A message from Ruranga station just came in, ma'am," he said, "and I thought you'd want to know that Mr. Chambers, along with his man, should be here soon."

"Thanks, Jim."

Jim Winters stood there for a moment, composing what he wanted to say. He gruffly cleared his throat. "I just want to let you know, ma'am, that me and the lads aren't going to let some Pommy stranger try and run you aside. The old man wouldn't have liked that, nor do we. So, if he tries, he'll have a fight on his hands, you can be sure."

Annie smiled in gratitude for her foreman's professed loyalty. She understood that it meant more than a mere empty token pledge. Here, in a country where male bonds were exceptionally strong, to declare for a woman rather than immediately accepting the new man as head boss was rare. Almost unheard of. "Thank you, Jim. That means quite a lot to me," she answered candidly, "more than you know. I hope that it never comes to a choice, for any of us. Cedric wanted us to be partners, and I want that too, in honor of his memory. If Mr. Chambers doesn't, then we shall have to see what comes of it."

"Still," he offered, "you should know that we're with you, ma'am. All of us."

"Please," Annie said softly, "tell everyone they have my deepest gratitude. I will never forget it."

When he left, Annie sat there for a minute, thinking. She was nervous, waiting for this meeting to take place. She desperately wanted it to go well. Her future, and that of her daughter, depended on it.

She rose from her chair, leaving the comfort of the kitchen, and moved through the house until she came to what used to be Cedric's bedroom. She opened the door and walked in. It had been aired, the floors polished, new paintings hung, canine and horse prints that she thought would please the English co-owner. Crisp, fresh linen graced the bed. All made as ready as possible for Anthony Chambers's arrival.

Of course, she thought, it wasn't as grand as what he was certainly used to. Nothing overly ornate or fancy here. The furniture was simpler, and in her mind, much more welcoming and warm than a more formal, stuffy room.

Annie glanced at herself in the full-length mirror as she plumped the pillows one more time. There was color to her cheeks, a flush of pink to her slightly sun-kissed face. This wasn't the face of a trembling virginal beauty who waited for the arrival of her first beau; instead, she saw reflected there the face of a woman, one who'd known heartache and joy, pleasure and pain, sorrow and laughter.

And what of *him?*

She touched the embroidered counterpane on the bed with a reverent skim of her fingers. She so wished that he would be like Cedric. A younger, softer version of the man who'd given her a new life, a new direction. A man who'd respect her and her opinions as Cedric had.

Or would he be just a cool, callow, arrogant Englishman, interested only in his own concerns?

37

Gail Link

A crooked smile crossed Annie's lips. What was it her neighbor Patrick O'Donnell had said when she confided her fears about the stranger to him just last week? "Sure and he's probably a high-stepping Pommy used to getting his own way in all things. Pure *sandstone*."

Annie understood what Patrick meant by the sandstone reference. He already thought Tony Chambers would be a weak-willed, arrogant fool. Sandstone was a lingering term from the old days of the convict settlers—it was a derisive term for a man who collapsed after a flogging. As a native-born Australian, and the son of a man who'd fled Ireland for a new life, Patrick O'Donnell was a fiercely proud man who distrusted the English—especially the upper-class English. Only Cedric Chambers had found favor in his eyes.

But then again, Cedric found favor, Annie recalled with a bittersweet smile, in everyone's eyes. It was as simple as that. People liked Cedric. Trusted him. Respected him. Loved him. He was that kind of man.

Sadly, there were no personal traces of Cedric in this room now. It was all fresh and new as befitting Cedric's last wishes. He wanted his grandnephew to start his life here on the station with a clean slate.

How strange it would seem to have someone else sleep in Cedric's room now, eat at his table, sit at his desk, read his books, ride his magnificent stallion, Merlin.

Annie sank into a comfortable wing chair, alone with her cherished memories. Time flew by as she thought about all the things she still wished to share with Cedric. Just the simple act of having a conversation about the day's events, or a book she'd read, or something about Fallon, was denied to her. She was starved for the kind of conversations she'd had with Cedric. Talk about hopes and dreams, about love and life, about family. She could, she knew, talk to Patrick O'Donnell and to his housekeeper, Mei, her closest female friend, but even then there were limits. Only with Cedric had she confided almost all the secrets of her heart. He'd known the dark truth of her past and accepted it, never judging her.

In a world where everyone was only too eager and happy to point a finger at what they considered her shame, he'd been a quiet haven of understanding.

"Mama."

A childish voice lifted Annie's thoughts from her flightful reverie. She turned and saw her daughter standing in the doorway.

"Some strange men just rode in."

"They aren't strange, sweetheart," Annie murmured as she stood and scooped up her daughter into her waiting arms. "Remember that I told you," she said softly, "that soon a relative of Uncle Cedric's would be coming to join us here? Well, that time is now. So let's you and I go out and greet him, shall we? Make him feel welcome to his new home."

"Do I have to like him?" the child demanded of her mother.

Annie smiled and bent down to allow Fallon to stand on her own. Her daughter was growing taller with each day that passed. One day she will be taller than me, Annie thought. "You don't *have to* like him, but I hope that you shall, sweetheart. Just as I hope that he likes us."

They quickly reached the veranda, which surrounded the house on all sides, watching from there as two men approached the single-story house from the stable area. Some of the ranch jackaroos were helping unload the contents of a flat buckboard, and another was leading several horses into the barn.

Annie's gaze was captivated by the younger and taller of the two men as he strode purposefully toward her.

Had she actually thought that this man would be a softer version of Cedric?

She was so wrong.

Annie flicked her tongue over suddenly dry lips. Yes, Anthony Chambers was young. She'd have to give him that. But softer? Most definitely not. He was easily six feet, with a lean build and broad shoulders. The sun glinted off his light brown hair, streaked with strands of gold.

As he got nearer, Annie's eyes met his. They were set beneath golden-brown brows, a clear, cool green with a hint of gray. Haughty, proud eyes that looked right through her, as if he could see to her skin.

She broke the contact, her gaze wandering lower on his face to his well-shaped mouth. Beautiful was the first word that sprang to her mind—if one could describe a man's mouth as beautiful.

Tony Chambers possessed such a mouth. Full, bow-shaped lips chiseled as if by a master stonemason. They went well with the rest of his face: the squarish jaw, the fine-bladed nose, the definite cheekbones, and surprisingly, the small brown mole on his right jawbone.

All in all, a fine specimen of a man. Handsome and compelling.

Annie guessed that the ladies of London had loved him, and he, in turn, them.

She took a deep breath to quell the rising tide of

nerves and favored him with her most welcoming smile.

"Welcome to Camelot station, Mr. Chambers," she said warmly. "I'm Annie Ross."

Tony halted before ascending the two wide stone steps that led to the veranda. "Camelot?" he asked.

His voice was low and soft, his accent pleasing to the ear.

Her smile deepened. "It was your Uncle Cedric's idea. For him," she explained, "this land was his dream, his one perfect spot, if you will."

How apt in one very obvious way, Tony thought, recalling the legend. The older, more established man who falls in love with a younger woman, giving her a world of power and privilege, only to see that life crumble when she betrays him with another man, a younger man.

Had she played Guenevere to Cedric's Arthur? he wondered.

Annie offered her hand in greeting.

Tony accepted it, holding it a fraction of a moment longer than was polite, or necessary. Her hand was warm, fitting easily inside his much larger grip. Smooth and soft, but not weak.

He dropped his gaze, taking in her slim, curved body from the crown of her head to her flat-slippered feet. Rich-toned, warm, brown hair was pulled back from her face by two mother-of-pearl combs. It tumbled in waves to her waist. Hair so thick a man could lose himself in it. Her eyes were a deep shade of pure smoky gray.

In place of the fancy gown she wore in the formal photograph, she was dressed today in a much simpler manner. An apron of thin blue and white stripes covered her plain white cotton shirt, as well as the navy blue wool skirt, though the apron ended a few inches above the hem of the skirt. The bottom two mother-of-pearl buttons of the wool skirt were left undone, exposing two white petticoats that peeked from beneath the fabric. White stockings delved into black leather slippers. A shawl of navy blue wool was draped around her slender shoulders.

A tiny gold watch was pinned to the apron, above her heart.

It was, Tony quickly noted, the only jewelry she wore besides the hair combs. No rings graced her fingers, not even a wedding band.

"Hello."

Tony looked down at the child who spoke.

Annie reached out her left hand and stroked the child's long blond hair. "This is my daughter, Mr. Chambers, Fallon Ross."

Tony smiled at the child. He'd always gotten along well with children. Bending down so that he was able to look her in the face, he addressed her as he would an adult, "How do you do, Miss Ross?"

Fallon remembered her mother's instructions on polite conversation. With an engaging grin, she responded, "Very well, sir, and you?"

"I do quite well, Miss Fallon," Tony responded, rising, and looking straight at the child's mother. "Quite well, indeed."

"Please come inside," Annie urged, wanting to get away from all the pairs of curious eyes that were trained on them. "You must be tired after your journey. I've prepared some luncheon for you if you'd like to eat once I've shown you to your rooms."

Coolly, Tony responded, "Yes, after the rough-and-ready food of the past few days, a real meal would be most welcome."

Alfred chimed in, "Ah yes, 'tis a *consumption* devoutly to be wished."

Annie's broad smile revealed even white teeth as she grinned at the older man's *bon mot*.

Tony made the introductions. "This is Alfred Dunner, my valet."

"I'm very pleased to make your acquaintance, Mrs. Ross," Alfred said politely. He had stood aside and silently observed the way his new employer and the young woman had looked at each other upon meeting. The temperature of the cool day had risen several degrees in Alfred's humble opinion.

It might have been better for his employer's purpose and state of mind if the woman had been homely or slatternly rather than comely, and the child a brat rather than sweet-faced.

"Annie," she insisted. "We're not so formal here."

"You're from the States, aren't you?" Tony asked as he stepped onto the veranda, standing a good eight inches taller than her.

"Originally, I came from Philadelphia," Annie answered as she showed them through the door and into the interior of the homestead.

She paused inside. "Fallon, do me a favor, sweetheart."

Her daughter responded instantly. "Yes, Mommy."

"Would you run outside and tell Mr. Winters to see that Mr. Chambers's things are brought in and put in Uncle Cedric's room? When you've done that, you can play with Mary until I call you."

The little girl ran off to do her mother's bidding.

"Sorry," Annie apologized. "I've been so used to calling it Cedric's room that I still occasionally slip back."

"That's understandable," Tony stated.

"If you would follow me," Annie replied, leading the way down the wide hall. She opened one door to the left upon a smaller bedroom. "I thought this would suit you, Alfred, as it's across from Mr. Chambers's room."

It was a small, neat room furnished in solid English pine, consisting of a single bed and dresser, a small desk and chair.

"It'll do me just fine, ma'am," Alfred said with a smile.

Annie stepped back into the hallway and to the door opposite. She turned the brass knob, opening the door to reveal a bedroom almost double the size of Alfred's. It had a large, double-sized sleigh bed made of golden oak. A dresser, armoire, and writing desk completed the set. Scattered Chinese rugs graced the floors. A stone fireplace was set between two large windows that reached all the way to the floor. Sheer white lace curtains hung over them; they were pulled back now to let in the available sunlight. The Alpines, with their majestic snow-covered peaks, rose visibly in the background. Closer to the house was the paddock area, where several horses grazed, seemingly contentedly.

The sound of booted feet echoed on the hardwood floor. Moments later, three men from the station brought in the rest of Tony's things, several traveling bags and a trunk. When they finished, they tipped their hats to Annie and left without a word.

Annie was quick to defend the men in case Tony felt slighted by their taciturn behavior. "You have to give them time to get used to you," she said. "When they know you better, you'll see that they are really rather quite friendly. It's just that you're a stranger."

"Is that a warning?"

Annie stared at him. "A warning?"

"Yes," he said. "If I overstep my bounds, will someone decide that it is their duty to take me to task?"

Annie's gray eyes darkened at the thought. "I can assure you, Mr. Chambers," she said crisply, "that you are safe here on the station. No one would think to harm you in any way. Believe me. These men are good people who respected your uncle because he *earned* that respect. Treat them fairly and they will do the same to you."

She turned on her heel and paused in the doorway, checking the little watch on her apron. "Since it's almost one, I will lay out your luncheon meal now, so that you can relax afterwards. Give me at least ten minutes, if you will, then come to the dining room."

She swept out just as Alfred came in to unpack for Tony.

Why wasn't she the woman he expected her to be? Tony thought as he opened one of the window doors and stepped outside. Why wasn't she sleek and sophisticated, with knowledge of the game evident in her eyes, in the way she moved her body?

He pulled a coin from the pocket of his vest, twirling the copper penny between his dexterous fingers.

Maybe she was clever rather than obvious? Perhaps it was too early for her to show the true colors he believed she possessed?

He'd just have to be on his guard with her, keeping his suspicions close at hand. Already his body was responding to the sheer femininity of hers. Tony attributed that to weeks spent without the comfort of a woman in his bed. A purely understandable physical reaction.

And maybe, he thought, that was the way to discover the truth about her. Lure her to his bed and find her weaknesses. He might be able to use what he learned there to his advantage.

After all, he concluded, tossing the coin into the air and grasping it, all was fair in love and war—or in this case, an inheritance.

Chapter Three

Tony entered the formal dining room. It was smaller than the one in his London town house, but still adequate, he assumed, for the social climate of a rural station in the Australian High Country. It radiated warmth from the highly polished cherry table to the matching sideboard and the thick, dark blue and cream carpet underfoot. Waterford cut-glass bowls were placed around the room, some containing dried flowers; one sat in the middle of the table, filled with wildflowers.

The room had two pairs of glass doors that opened out to the veranda. They were covered with the same delicate lace curtains as in his own room, with heavier drapes of royal blue velvet tied back with a thick cream cord.

From the window, he could see the large stone building that housed the men who worked on the station. A smaller, cottage-style house was nearby; smoke rose from the chimney.

Tony walked back to the table and saw that there was only one place setting for luncheon. An uncorked bottle of red wine was waiting for him, with a single glass that he recognized as also a Waterford. He picked up the bottle and poured the dark ruby liquid into his glass and took an experimental sip. It was a surprisingly good vintage, with a decent bouquet. Hefting the bottle in his hand, he read the label. He was surprised to discover that it was a native Australian wine.

Tony lifted the corner of a piece of ivory linen from a basket to the right of his plate. The scent of warm, fresh sliced bread wafted out. A small blue and white crock next to the basket held chilled butter.

He sat down and almost immediately heard a door opening behind him. Tony turned and saw Annie enter with a steaming soup bowl.

He rose instantly, watching as she set the bowl down onto his plate.

"The housekeeper has set only a single place," he pointed out, still standing.

"Please, do sit down, Mr. Chambers," Annie insisted softly.

Tony complied with her request, curious as to why there was no table setting for her.

"And, as for a housekeeper, I set the table," she informed him.

"You?"

One of her slim hands rested on the chair back opposite him as she explained, "There is no housekeeper here at the station besides myself."

"What about a cook?"

Annie shrugged her slim shoulders. "I'm afraid not. As there were only Cedric, Fallon, and myself here in the homestead, there was no real need for a more formal staff. There is a cook, though, for the men; that's to be expected. She's Nora Winters, wife to Jim Winters, our head stockman."

"So, you do all the cooking and the cleaning in the house?" he asked, his eyes sharp on hers.

"I did occasionally have help if we were entertaining," Annie said, "but yes, for the rest, I did it and was happy to. It was no hardship, I can assure you."

Tony digested this fact. The situation here he was beginning to discover was like a giant jigsaw, with more pieces being added by the minute.

"Aren't you eating, then?" he inquired, his innate good manners forbidding him to start while she was still there, no matter in what capacity.

"Yes," she replied, "I am. Please, don't worry about me." Somehow Annie doubted that he was actually concerned on her behalf. She'd thought about setting a place for him in the kitchen, but had changed her mind after their initial meeting. Tony Chambers wasn't a kitchen man, she reckoned, easy with informality as Cedric had been. There were rules and conventions to his life, certain expectations to be met.

Tony quickly glanced around the rest of the empty table. "Where are you dining?"

She responded, "In the kitchen. I prefer it there."

His question was soft and low, probing, as if he didn't quite believe her. "You do?"

Annie nodded and quickly left him to his meal, shutting the door with a decided click, closing herself off from him, from those penetrating eyes of his.

Tony ate his meal in silence, finding the hearty beef and barley soup to his liking. He broke a thick chunk of bread in two and liberally spread butter onto it. He bit into the slice, tasted a fine blend of herbs blended into the butter, giving it a subtle flavor that mixed well with the soup.

At least, he grudgingly admitted, the wench could cook. Tony had always had a fondness for good food.

Replete, he poured himself another glass of wine.

She could have certainly afforded, as could his great-uncle, a staff of servants to help run this house. Yet they'd lived simply, in a manner of speaking, gazing about the well-decorated room. Why? Money was no barrier. Tony thought she would have been the kind of woman who relished the position of lady-of-the-manor, as it were. Flaunting her good fortune at snagging a rich, older protector.

Instead, she chose to run this house herself.

Granted, it wasn't an English manor house with multiple levels and plenty of rooms and guests galore. But still.

Tony looked into the depths of his glass, as if motivation and answers could be discerned from the contents. Curious.

He finished his food and sighed. Meals were for him a social occasion. Although the fare was good, there'd been no one to share it with. No conversation. No quips traded, no banter and gossip exchanged. It was all so sterile, safe. And, worst of all, boring.

Tony pushed back his formal chair, topped off his glass again, and sauntered through the side door that led, he assumed, into the kitchen area.

Entering, he found her there, seated at the table, talking quietly to Alfred, who it appeared was certainly enjoying the same meal that Tony had just finished.

Annie looked up from her bowl of soup as Tony stood there watching her from across the room. By all the saints, this man was handsome. Why couldn't he have been ugly? Or even plain?

Heat flushed her skin under his somewhat imperious regard.

"Is there something else I can get for you?" she offered politely.

Oh, how he longed to shock her with his retort to that properly asked question so that he could gauge her reaction. What would she do if he were to say, *You could be so kind as to get me yourself*. But now wasn't the time.

"What's that?" he asked, pointing a lean index finger toward the pie cooling on the plain table.

"Spiced apple pie," she answered, "freshly baked."

"I'll have some of that then," he said, coming closer and pulling out a chair, nonchalantly joining them, crossing one dark-clad leg over the other, much to the chagrin of Annie and to the amusement of Alfred.

As Annie made to stand, Tony waved her back down. "No need to hurry, my dear," he drawled in a silky tone, pausing to sip his wine. "I shall be quite content to wait until you've done with your meal."

Annie found that it was difficult eating now with an audience. While she hadn't considered Alfred a distraction, she did think Tony could prove one. She was too aware of this younger man as a man. What was it about him? she wondered as she spooned another mouthful of the soup between her parted lips. Cedric had certainly been a man, and still rather attractive looking at his age. Patrick, in his own way, was also a pleasantly attractive man.

So, what was it about *this* man that made her so instantly aware of herself as a woman?

Was it his intense eyes, his oh-so-wicked mouth, or maybe his long, slim fingers?

Annie hadn't a clue. And that was what bothered her.

Tony sat there drinking his wine while she sipped

at her plain glass of cold milk. He probably thought she was an unsophisticated country bumpkin for not having a glass or two of wine herself.

He didn't know that she wasn't much of a drinker. Never had been. Wine went straight to her head, so she drank it sparingly. She'd only ever been slightly tipsy once in her life, and inescapable memories of that one night made sure she never would be again.

Annie knew, at some deep level, that Tony Chambers would be like wine for her—too large a dose and she'd live to regret it.

Besides, he didn't quite trust her. She could see it in those eyes, hear it in his voice.

Yet there was warmth in his soul. She'd witnessed that with her daughter earlier. Was there enough warmth within Tony to allow him to one day become her friend, as well as her business partner?

Or was that simply asking too much?

Tony stared at Annie, unremorseful that he was doing so. He watched the way she held her spoon; watched the way she buttered her bread; watched the way she drank the contents of her glass. Solid middle-class yeoman stock, he assumed, or whatever it was that passed for such in America. Manners polished and acceptable. A fine, shapely figure; a pretty oval face and a stubborn chin. And a hint of fire in those cool, misty eyes. Banked fires, to be sure, but fires nonetheless.

He could, and would, use that to his advantage. He had to know her secrets; he had to know if his deeply held suspicions were true.

"Very good, madame," Alfred said as he rose and put his bowl in the sink.

Annie responded warmly, "Thank you, Alfred."

"After eating from those wretched tin cans for a few days, it's good to have a meal that someone fixed who can lay claim to the title of cook."

Annie beamed at the valet's praise. "Why, how nice of you to say so. Are you by any chance a cook yourself?"

"No, madame," he answered. "'Tis not one of my particular skills, I'm afraid. I do, however, mightily approve of them that can."

"Would you care for a slice of pie, also?" she asked as she rose and placed her own bowl and utensils in the sink. Opening a drawer in the massive hutch, Annie drew out a knife and several spoons; next she lifted three small plates in the same blue and white Spode pattern as she'd used for luncheon.

Tony recognized the rural scene of the pattern as Annie lay them on the table and proceeded to cut a large wedge of the warm apple pie, dripping a small jug of thickened cream over the top. His mother had a similar set of china in their country house.

"I do believe that I could be persuaded to take a taste," Alfred insisted, taking his seat once more as Annie handed the first slice to Tony.

Annie cut Alfred a slice as well, then one for herself.

She risked a glance at Tony after she resumed her chair. He seemed to be enjoying the pie. It had been her mama's recipe, and was a favorite of her daughter.

"Most excellent, madame," Alfred stated after taking his first bite. "I do think that if I keep eating like this, I may easily gain at least a stone within a fortnight."

"Nonsense," Annie said, savoring the taste of the spices mixed with the apples. "You look fit enough to me."

"Stayed that way because of my last employer," he

said. "I worked for the actor-manager of a troupe of players, and there was never a chance to sit idly by and watch the day pass, or to linger overlong on meals."

"Well," Annie said, "feel free to linger as long as you will here in my kitchen." She said that automatically, without thinking. It wasn't just her kitchen any longer, though she had serious doubts that Mr. Tony Chambers would lay claim to this part of the homestead any time in the near future.

"I'd best be getting Mr. Chambers's clothes unpacked and pressed," Alfred announced, leaving them alone as he went to attend to his duties.

"Very good indeed," was Tony's remark about the pie, and his thoughts on how well she'd won over his new valet with almost minimal effort.

"I'm glad that you found it to your liking," she replied, lingering over her own piece, hoping that he would depart as well. Alfred had been easy to talk to. A friendly man without a hidden agenda. Annie suspected that Tony Chambers had one, if not several.

"I've set out the books for the station in the office. I think," she said, "that you'll find everything in order."

"Don't tell me that you kept the books as well?" he asked with an underlying sardonic tone.

Annie flushed. "Only for a little while. Cedric showed me how, very early on after I came here," she explained, "thinking it was important for me to learn about the business of the station. Ignorance was not a condition that he favored."

"Ah," Tony drawled, "so it would seem."

"You'll be pleased to find that we have a surplus of monetary assets at present, which your uncle always invested back in the station."

"How so?"

Annie put down her spoon and faced him, her tongue snaking out to wet her lips. "He bought more stock, encouraged trying new breeds to the expanding cattle herd. Our beef is some of the best in Australia, shipped both to England and Europe now. Our horses have produced champions for both the raceway and the farm.

"Furthermore," she added proudly, "he paid his men the wages that he believed them worth. Jackaroos come from all over the country applying for work here. Cedric hired only the best. Our men are proud to ride and work for Camelot station."

This woman was most assuredly a vocal proponent of his great-uncle's methods and devices for running a station, Tony thought. She sounded quite genuine in her fervor. But was it a performance to gather favor in his eyes? Put on solely to keep him off guard as to her real motives?

Tony wiped his mouth with a napkin, vowing that he would know all there was to know. And soon.

While Alfred tended to his employer's clothes and Annie was occupied elsewhere, Tony pored over the station's account books, carefully checking all the entries. He'd always been good at sums, and while studying the ledgers and station journals, discovered that his great-uncle had a keen mind for business. Cedric had indeed made savvy investments which had paid off handsomely, far outweighing the few things that hadn't turned out well. Along with the financial portfolio that the banker in Melbourne had shown him, Tony was now better able to appreciate just how many pies his great-uncle had dabbled in.

And if the Ross woman had access to this information, then she knew just how widespread Cedric's financial empire was.

Tony leaned back in the desk chair, amazed at his good fortune. Because of his great-uncle, he now owned one-quarter interest in an opal mine; half-interest in a passenger and freight shipping line that ran the Murray River; various real estate holdings in Sydney and Melbourne, aside from the town house in the latter, and smaller property investments in the States also.

All this was his alone.

The only thing he had to share was this station that his great-uncle had built from scratch and fashioned into a dream.

Tony cupped one hand over the other and brought them to rest against his mouth as he stared blankly at the desk, the top of which was strewn with papers and ledgers.

One thought plagued him. Why hadn't Cedric just given it to the woman outright? There had to be some reason. But what? And why this condition?

Tony was anxious to see more of this property and resolved to meet with foreman Jim Winters the following morning for a tour. He knew from one of the ledgers the number of men the station employed, but not their faces. If he had to stay here for twelve months, Tony believed it best if he made his presence known to the men early on.

Tony pushed back his chair, the well-oiled wheels making no sound as they glided smoothly along the parquet floor. He stood up and ran his hands through his thick hair, pushing it back and away from his high forehead, thinking that it definitely needed a trim.

Tony paced around the room, which was filled with floor-to-ceiling bookcases. He examined several titles, occasionally pulling a volume out and leafing through it, then resumed his pacing.

He was bloody well stuck here—isolated and in exile from his own world for a year.

He could, he knew, just up and leave, return home to England. Leave this station to her. It meant nothing to him.

Except, he thought, taking a deep breath, for family honor. Family responsibility. He owed it to Cedric, his benefactor par excellence. If for no other reason than to make sure this who. . . .

Tony found that he couldn't finish the word that he'd bandied about so freely before.

Annie Ross confused him. She didn't act like a whore. She didn't dress like a whore. She didn't look like a whore.

But looks could be deceiving. He'd lived long enough to know that for a fact. He'd seen angelic-looking strumpets conducting business at some of London's finest brothels, all the while looking as fresh as daisies.

He had to determine whether Annie Ross was in truth a real widow, or if it was all a ruse. Had Cedric known the unvarnished facts? Or had he been a pawn in her schemes?

Time, which was on his side, would tell. He certainly had plenty of that to spare. Twelve months' worth to be exact.

Annie relished the feel of the horse racing under her as she gave the mare her head. The animal swiftly ate up the miles, taking her mistress across the lush valley and through the tall gum trees, far from the homestead.

Annie needed this time to be by herself. To be away from the almost overwhelming specter of Tony Chambers. Leaving Fallon with Jim's wife and son, Annie took off as soon as she'd shown Tony the office, leaving the station for higher ground. Riding deeper and higher into the hills, she felt the change in temperature, saw the mist rising thicker in front of her.

Finally she pulled back on the reins and let her horse rest. Hopping down from the saddle, Annie led the mare to some rich grass to crop while she settled herself on a boulder to think.

Annie heaved a deep sigh.

Tension hung heavy in the air between her and Tony. She could feel it; so must he.

He threw her off balance. She didn't know what to expect from him from one minute to the next. Kindness or curses. Scorn or praise. How long could she maneuver, looking over her shoulder, waiting for him to pounce? Like a tall, sleek, sinuous cat, he was at odds with her belief that he would be simply an affable, tame Englishman.

Yes, he could appear, she admitted, quite domesticated. No doubt about that. Then she would glimpse something in his eyes that made her think there was a hint of the predator beneath the smooth surface. Someone who when provoked could be dangerous.

Annie rose from her makeshift seat and walked slowly around the area, admiring the soul-deep beauty of the land from her high vantage point: the tall trees, the range of the mountains with their snow-covered peaks.

This was hers. She belonged here. And she knew

that it would break her heart if she ever had to leave it.

Annie bent down and dug her gloved right hand into the earth, grabbing a handful of moist dirt. She hefted the weight in her palm and let it slide back to the ground, brushing the remains from her leather gloves.

She'd give Tony six months before he decided to return to England. With all that Cedric had left him, he had no real need of this place. He'd tire of playing the grazier soon enough, realize that this life wasn't for him. Maybe he would even entertain the notion of letting her buy out his half-ownership. The money Cedric had left her could be used for a down payment.

Annie gave a small snort of laughter.

That's what she hoped would happen. There was no guarantee that Tony Chambers would follow the scenario she envisioned.

The mist rolled in heavier and darker than before, signaling to Annie that she should leave now. Getting trapped up here could be dangerous.

Gathering the reins firmly in her hands, Annie remounted her mare and headed back to the station. It would soon be time to see to the evening meal and to her daughter's supper and bath as well. She'd have to change her own clothes. She doubted that the redoubtable Englishman was used to seeing women ride their mounts astride, or wearing pants in which to do it.

Annie was determined to get through each day with him as best she could. Right now, there was no other option for her.

"It would appear that you won't have much need for your more formal clothes, sir," Alfred said as he finished his lengthy unpacking duties. He had to remove the clothes from the one capacious trunk, and the two traveling cases as well, then press those garments that had wrinkled most during the last leg of the journey. The still warm flatiron rested on a small slab of granite to cool while Alfred stacked the ironing board back against the wall.

Tony arched a brow. "I don't intend to rusticate whilst I'm here," he informed Alfred with a smile. "Informality is one thing, but to carry it to extremes is another. I do think that we can at the very least keep dinner civilized."

"How will you propose that with Mrs. Ross? I rather feel that she likes things as they are."

"Simple," Tony explained, as if it were a foregone conclusion. "I will insist on it."

Alfred sagely pointed out, "She may not like that."

"Since I own half of this benighted property, I think I do have some say in the running of it, domestic or otherwise."

Alfred gave his employer a skeptical look.

"Do you know where she is?" Tony asked. "When I went looking for her an hour ago after examining the ledgers, I couldn't find her anywhere in this house."

"I'm afraid I don't know, sir."

A speculative look crossed Tony's face. Was she perhaps meeting with a lover? Was she even now in some man's arms, whiling the afternoon hours away as a nameless, faceless man rode her body to exhaustion?

Tony's hands fisted at his sides.

She damned well better not be.

From the corner of his eye through the etched-glass doors, Tony caught sight of a rider approaching at a full gallop. Stepping closer, he spied the figure and recognized the long brown hair caught in a braid as it flew behind the rider.

Tony opened the door and stepped onto the veranda, watching as the rider drew in the chestnut horse and dismounted with a quick jump, giving the reins to one of the hands, who led the animal away.

It was her. Dressed in a man's trousers and shirt, wearing knee-high black boots, along with a stockman's hat and long coat that flapped about her as she walked.

"Hello."

Annie jerked up her head and saw him standing there on the porch, watching her with those cool, assessing eyes. Obviously, she couldn't avoid him now.

She squared her shoulders and kept walking until she was standing next to him.

Annie removed her hat and brushed back a few loose strands of hair from her braid that had escaped.

"Been *riding* I see," he commented.

Her creamy skin, he noted, was flushed with becoming color. From what kind of ride though?

Why did that sound like an accusation? she wondered.

"Yes," she replied.

"Do you do that often?"

"As often as I can," she said, craning her neck slightly upward so that she could see his face better.

"You ride alone?"

"Sometimes."

She wasn't about to reveal anything more than she had to, he thought.

"Where?"

Annie tilted her chin higher. "Why?"

"Just curious, 'tis all," Tony replied.

61

"I'm used to coming and going as I please, Mr. Chambers, so now, if you'll excuse me, I feel the need of a bath."

All politeness, Tony stepped aside and watched her as she went a few feet further down the veranda and opened the door to what he thought must be her room.

Conveniently, it was only one away from his.

Tony smiled enigmatically as he strolled back into his own room and closed the door.

Annie leaned against her own door and shivered, though not from the cold. It was from the look in his eyes as they'd drifted over her body. Sharp and penetrating. The glance of a man who knew what lay beneath her clothes.

Her pulse was rapid. Her breathing slightly raspy.

Annie's hand went to the cross around her neck, clasping it as a talisman against the creeping tremors of her body.

Stop being so foolish, she chided herself.

But she couldn't stop remembering the way his eyes had looked their fill.

Very well, she decided, stripping off her outer coat and casually tossing it on her cushioned chair. He could look all he wanted. Just so long as he never touched.

Chapter Four

"So, tell me, Annie girl," questioned Patrick O'Donnell, his voice barely above a husky whisper, "what do you think of the *English*man?"

Annie poured her friend a cup of tea from the well-used blue and white patterned teapot. Filling her own cup as well, she added milk and sugar from the matching set.

Smoothing her apron over her skirt, Annie sat down, a somewhat perplexed look on her face. "I truly don't know what to make of him, Patrick," she admitted honestly. "He's certainly not what I expected."

"And what were you expecting?"

"Someone different. Perhaps a bit more of a slow-witted, foppish dandy, I suppose." Annie didn't want to admit out loud, even to her close friend, that Tony was neither the cloying, effete snob she dreaded, nor the gentle, easygoing fellow she'd hoped for. Instead, he was a masculine force to be reckoned with, a man who exuded an undeniable power. Part of that power was confidence. Cedric had possessed it; so did his grandnephew, in abundance.

Patrick took a hearty swallow of his tea before asking her, "So where is *himself* this fine morning?"

"He went out early with Jim Winters again," Annie said, pausing to take a sip of strong tea. "Yesterday, he and Jim rode about quite a bit, taking in a good deal of the station. I believe that today they are covering some of the areas they hadn't a chance to before."

Patrick shot her a sharp look, his bright blue eyes reflecting his concern. "Surveying all of the promised land, eh?"

Annie returned his regard. Patrick O'Donnell wasn't an imposing man, standing perhaps five feet eight inches. It was, she knew, his stocky build and cocky disposition that made him seem much bigger than he was. However, there wasn't the least hint of intimidation about him. His boyishly handsome face prevented that. Patrick had been one of the first people in this district to offer her the hand of friendship when she was newly arrived from America. To Annie, Patrick was the closest thing to a brother she could have found in this new homeland.

"I suppose so," she said with a shrug. "There is quite a lot to see here, and for an outsider, well, doubly so." It hadn't been all that long ago when she herself had been an outsider, new to the glories of this land. She'd absorbed the wonders around her like a sponge, soaking up the changes, reveling in the beauty and the sheer grandeur of the place that was now her home.

"Can't I get you something else to go with your tea?" she offered, recalling fondly Patrick's notorious sweet tooth.

"Ah, Annie girl, thank you, but no," Patrick responded with an engaging grin. "Mei is after making certain that I don't leave the house without a huge breakfast each morning."

"If you're sure?"

"That I am, darlin'." A sudden frown furrowed his

wide brow. "What I'm after worrying about is you, my girl."

Annie reached out her hand and laid her fingers over Patrick's much bigger ones, giving them a short squeeze. "Thank you for your concern, Patrick, but I'm managing just fine," she said, "at least for the time being."

"Has this Englishman said or done anything hurtful to you?"

Annie shook her head, her long waves of hair moving slightly with the motion. "He's not spoken one unkind word to me," she admitted.

"But something's troubling you," Patrick insisted. "I can see it in your face, darlin'."

Annie folded her slim hands in front of her. "I can't deny that Anthony Chambers is a man who most certainly confuses me."

Patrick prompted, "In what way?"

"It's difficult to explain," she said, her eyes focused on the cup in front of her for a few moments before she lifted her gaze again back to her friend. "Sometimes he will be all politeness and charm, a man skillful in his compliments and in his manners. Then, it's as though he's gone somewhere inside himself, withdrawing almost, watching you in somewhat of a detached fashion as if you were an animal in a cage for study.

"And then," Annie stated, her gray eyes getting darker with a slight flash of temper, "there was the edict he saw fit to put forth this very morning. He's decided that dinner here at the homestead should be a more formal occasion, eaten in the dining room instead of the kitchen.

"Well," she said, "I had no problems with that, for I

was ready to serve all his meals in there anyway as I'd assumed that it would be more to his liking. But," she announced, "now he wants me to eat with him as well."

"So refuse him," Patrick suggested.

"I did, at first," she confessed. "That decision didn't seem to sit too well with him, however. He became quite adamant, insisting that as co-owners, we should take time from our daily routine to make the effort to do at least some things in the proper English tradition."

Stuff bloody English tradition, Patrick thought, wishing to vent his thoughts aloud but keeping them to himself. Normally, he would have spoken what was in his heart without hesitation; yet, upon his arrival earlier, he noticed that something was bothering Annie and he didn't want to add to her problems. It was, he thought, just this fancy, puffed-up pommy bastard wanting to get his own way and trying to lord it all over Annie that made him want to teach the man a lesson.

"And?" was all Patrick said, anxious to hear what she'd decided to do.

Annie sighed. "I didn't want to appear churlish about it, Patrick, if for no other reason than he was making a good point," she conceded, "even if I disliked the manner in which he made it. As co-owners, we do need to have time to discuss things that concern the station. Dinner was when Cedric and I usually had the chance to talk the most freely.

"So I reconsidered and said that yes, I would keep the evening meal with him, but that was all."

"So," Patrick asked with an arched brow, "he's too bloody good to eat in the kitchen as Cedric did, eh?"

"Well," Annie countered, "let's just say that Mr. Anthony Chambers has his own distinct ideas about how things are to be done."

"And bother to you if you don't agree?"

Annie shrugged her shoulders.

Patrick flexed his hands, fisting them. "I think that this pommy needs to be taken down a peg or two."

"Not on my account, Patrick," Annie asserted softly, afraid that her friend would insist on having a heated word or two on her behalf with Tony Chambers. "I can fight my own battles, should the need arise."

"I'll not stand idly by and see you come to any kind of harm, darlin'," he stated aggressively.

"It won't ever come to that," Annie said firmly.

Patrick asked, "And how would you be knowing that?"

"Because Anthony Chambers is a gentleman. He'd never raise his hand to a woman."

"Are you so sure, Annie girl?"

Annie smiled. "Yes, I am. Anthony Chambers may be a man of many parts, but an abuser of women isn't one of them. I'd swear to that." Annie didn't know or question where her strong belief came from. It was simply there. A deeply rooted instinct she accepted as the truth.

Changing the subject, Annie asked, "I'd like you to come to dinner on Sunday, Patrick, and meet him. Would you?"

Patrick considered the invitation. He had no real fondness for the few English-born men and women he'd met, persons that had as often as not looked down their snobbish noses at him for being either Irish, or a native-born Australian, or both. Patrick had heard some of the sarcastic taunts and brittle comments from the rich and even the not-so-rich English. It was as if, according to them, he were somehow inferior because he wasn't one of them.

At first, he'd been skeptical of Cedric Chambers as well, until his da had told him that Cedric had once given Jamie O'Donnell a helping hand when he'd needed it in the goldfields. After learning that, Patrick was Cedric's friend for life.

And when Cedric had introduced him to the lovely young American woman and her infant girl whom he'd brought to live with him, Patrick had bestowed his friendship to Annie Ross just as readily.

Patrick loved Annie—doted on her as if she were another of his many sisters. He'd been the youngest in his family, the only boy after four daughters, still unwed, to his mother's chagrin, at twenty-four.

"Oh," he said, coming back to the present, "I'm almost after forgetting, Annie girl, Mei sent something along for you."

Annie's face brightened. "She did? What?"

Patrick handed her the brown paper package that he'd set at his feet on the stone floor when he entered the kitchen. "Open it and see for yourself."

Annie hastily removed the blue yarn ribbon that held the paper together. Inside was a piece of delicate needlework within a thin dark frame. It was a canvas of white on which was stitched a bouquet of blue peonies.

"She said I was to be telling you that the flowers are an ancient Chinese symbol of prosperity and good fortune," Patrick explained.

"Oh," Annie exclaimed, her face aglow with delight at the present, "it is so beautiful." She looked up at Patrick. "Please tell Mei how happy her gift has made me. She honors me once again with her kindness."

Patrick said, "She wanted you to have it as a reminder of her belief that all will be well for your future. 'Tis just her way of making sure, I'm thinking."

"It's so lovely of her for whatever reason," Annie affirmed.

"Ah, yes," Patrick agreed. "Mei is a grand lass to be sure."

"And the best housekeeper a man like yourself could ever wish for," Annie put in.

"To be sure," Patrick said, agreeing wholeheartedly. He rose, draining what was left of his tea. "Now, I'd best be leaving you to get about your own work and me to mine."

"I do appreciate your stopping by, Patrick, and bringing the lambs yourself," she said, indicating the two animals that Patrick had brought. Annie had a real fondness for lamb. When Cedric had discovered that, he had proposed that they get their meat from Patrick, so swaps between the stations of lamb for beef had been arranged and still continued.

"And you will come to dinner, then?" she inquired hopefully.

"Yes, Annie girl," Patrick said with a smile, embracing her. "I will."

He left her standing on the veranda as he strode the short distance to where his able bay brumby was tethered. Mounting, he called out, "Till Sunday, then."

Annie went back into the kitchen as soon as he was gone, pouring the remnants of the teapot into her cup, adding a splash of milk. She drank it all, smiling at Mei's gift as it lay on the table. It was so like Mei to think of others. It had been at least a month or more, Annie reckoned, since she'd visited with Patrick's housekeeper. Annie missed her friend, missed having another woman to talk to, to share things with. She and Mei were close in years, and had many of the same interests. And they both knew what it was like to have scorn and derision heaped upon them for being who they were.

When she finished her cup of tea, Annie picked up the framed needlework, eager to show it off.

She stopped, standing in the long hallway, realizing that she'd been heading toward the station's office to show it to Cedric. Even after all this time, the force of habit, she acknowledged, was strong.

Still, she wanted to share this gift with someone because for her the sharing would make it even more special.

The only person in the house was Alfred, so Annie went in search of him.

She found him in the office-cum-library.

Tony's valet was seated in one of the comfortable wing chairs; in his hands rested a leather-bound volume of Shakespeare's plays.

Alfred glanced up as Annie entered, smiling automatically at the young American woman. He, unlike his employer, had taken to her immediately. There was an easy way about her, the kind of informality that he'd found with so many Americans whilst he'd been in that country. An openness that contrasted to the normally more reserved English.

"Am I disturbing you?" she asked, hesitating to intrude on the valet if he wasn't in the mood for company. Annie realized that she had acted on impulse, not thinking if she was being overly forward, or if he'd even be interested.

"No, madame," Alfred answered, rising, a genuine look of pleasure on his face. "I was just revisiting an old friend," he stated simply, slipping the attached satin ribbon bookmark into the book. "May I do something for you?" he asked.

"Nothing, thank you," she replied, stepping closer. "I just wanted to show you something, if you wouldn't mind." Annie handed the framed piece of needlework to him.

Alfred examined it closely, one finger tracing the pattern of the stitches. "Quite lovely, madame," he pronounced.

Happy that he apparently shared her joy in the work, Annie explained to Alfred the significance of the peonies in Chinese lore.

Alfred said, "This woman is obviously an artist with a needle, madame. The stitches are delicate and sure."

"That she is," Annie agreed wholeheartedly. "As a seamstress, Mei is quite clever. But with her needle plied to more creative endeavors, she is superb. Her work is always unique and so beautiful."

"Mei, is that an Australian name, madame?" Alfred asked, wondering if it was a name associated with one of the native aboriginal tribes that he'd heard about.

Annie shook her head. "It's Chinese."

"Chinese? That *is* interesting," Alfred replied. He'd seen many Chinese people in San Francisco when the acting troupe had performed there. Several of the mummers had paid visits to the section of the city known as Chinatown and regaled the others with their tales of the exotic delights to be found there.

"Mei is the housekeeper at Broken Hill station," Annie informed him.

"And where would that be?" Alfred inquired, handing the framed canvas back to her.

"It's our nearest neighbor to the Northeast, less than

71

an hour's ride away. Patrick O'Donnell's place."

"And does Mr. O'Donnell raise cattle as well?"

"Patrick's is a sheep station."

"Mutton," Alfred said, almost smacking his lips.

"More importantly," Annie informed him, "wool. Patrick is quite successful at exporting his excellent wool to America and Europe. There's a ready market for it."

"My grandfather was a farmer," Alfred confided. "Along with barley and corn, he raised some sheep too, though only enough to feed his family and vary our diet."

"So, you're familiar with farm life then?"

"Some," he admitted. "I was raised there till I was thirteen, then I left to look for employment in the nearest city. After coming to London, I went into service, and I never looked back to the farm. The only thing I've ever truly missed from there was the taste of fresh lamb. It's not always easy to come by."

"Then you'll be happy to hear, Alfred, that we'll be having some of Patrick's best lamb for dinner on Sunday," Annie promised.

"Madame," Alfred intoned theatrically, "if you cook lamb the way you cook everything else, then I am your humble servant for life."

"If that is the case," Annie said with a conspiratorial smile, "then I've a favor to ask of you."

"Ask away, madame."

"Mr. Chambers has informed me that he wants a more formal arrangement for dinner. What I need to know is just *how* formal does he intend?"

"In what regards, madame?"

"Clothes."

Alfred hid a smile. "Mr. Chambers won't be wearing

full evening dress, I can assure you, madame."

"That's a relief," Annie said, crossing that worry off her list. "My wardrobe held no Worth gowns the last time I looked, nor is it likely to in the foreseeable future."

"That is *Monsieur* Worth's loss, madame," Alfred stated gallantly. "You would do his designs proud; better, may I add, than some that I've seen. I am sure that whatever you choose to wear tonight will be quite sufficient."

Color rose to Annie's cheeks with Alfred's words.

My, but she was genuine, Alfred thought as he replaced the volume back on the proper shelf. "Now, if you will excuse me, madame, I am going for a walk while the weather is still fine and before Mr. Chambers returns."

Alfred left through the door to the veranda and Annie made her way to her bedroom, anxious to find a place to hang the framed embroidery and select her dinner ensemble.

After locating the perfect spot for the embroidery, Annie walked to the capacious oak wardrobe that held her clothes. As she opened the doors, the smell of the cedar that lined the inside walls gently assailed her nostrils, softly permeating the air. A selection of clothes hung on padded satin hangers, the insides of which were stuffed with dried rose petals from the garden.

Annie paused, looking briefly at the two dresses that hung there. They were hardly in the fashionable style that a man of Anthony Chambers's class would be used to. Her life here, and before in Philadelphia, had precluded society balls and elegant parties, so there was no real need for her to have formal gowns.

73

Gail Link

Annie's gaze drifted to the row of blouses that hung in the next compartment. Some of these were actually elegant enough for evening wear. Several were Mei's handiwork, who could copy most designs, adding touches of her own to make the clothes unique.

Her hand drifted over one high-necked blouse, soft ivory in color. Kneeling, Annie pulled open one of the wardrobe's drawers, removing one tissue-wrapped bundle, examining the contents.

A satisfied smile kicked up the corners of her mouth. These would do quite nicely.

"I want you to send someone to Mansfield to see to it," Tony said to Jim as they halted their horses near a swiftly flowing stream. They dismounted and let the animals drink of the clear, cold water.

"Have you spoken to Mrs. Ross about this?" Jim Winters inquired.

"There's no need," Tony replied, removing a silver object from his waistcoat pocket. He unfolded the metal with a deft movement of his gloved hands and turned it into a small cup. Bending, Tony placed it into the rushing water, procuring himself a drink to relieve his thirst. A clever invention, the folding cup had been a gift from an old friend.

"I'm thinking that there is, sir," Jim countered with cautionary words of advice, "especially if you're to be changing the order of things in her house."

"May I remind you," Tony stated coolly as he rose, cup in hand, "that it is *my* house as well?"

The foreman looked aggrieved. "Still, sir . . ."

Tony fixed his carefully measured gaze on the other man. "If you won't comply with my instructions, then I'd say that we have a very significant problem, Mr.

Winters." When he finished uttering those words, Tony moved a short distance away to get a better look at one of the brightly colored birds that flitted through the nearby twisted-limbed snow gums.

"It's just that . . ."

Tony interrupted him. "It will be good for her. Why not think of it like that?"

"Mrs. Ross may not see it in that manner," the foreman said.

"Let me worry about Mrs. Ross's reaction, favorably or otherwise," Tony said as he turned back around to face Jim, replacing the now-collapsed silver cup back into his vest pocket. "It's to be my surprise."

Jim's mouth tightened into a thin line under his large, drooping moustache. "All right," he reluctantly agreed.

"Good man," Tony said. "I want it done today."

"As soon as we get back to the homestead," Jim replied, remounting his sturdy mountain horse, "I'll send a man out, sir. I'm sure that it won't take long to find just what you want. There's always people looking for a new opportunity."

Tony smiled lazily as he remounted the gleaming, coal-black stallion that had been his great-uncle's. He could well imagine that the sparks would indeed fly when Annie Ross discovered what he had set in motion.

Why was he doing this? she would demand.

As he and Jim made their way back to the main homestead, their mounts taking the route with an easy gait, Tony pondered the question. Could he supply Annie Ross the answers, when he wondered the same thing himself?

Chapter Five

Annie removed the apron that had protected her clothes from the rigors of cooking the evening meal, draping it over a chair. Being dressed like a fashion doll while preparing the food didn't quite fit, but since she couldn't very well stop and change clothes in the middle of cooking, she'd relied upon the apron to maintain her appearance.

Tonight the table in the formal dining room was set for two, as requested by the new master of the house. The candles and the lamps were lit, and the white wine was chilled to perfection. All that remained was to bring in the food and wait for *his* arrival. Eight P.M. sharp was the agreed-upon time.

She checked her gold watch, which hung on a long, slender gold chain around her throat.

Three minutes till the hour.

As she walked into the dining room, Annie took a deep breath. Fallon was bathed, fed, and tucked in her bed. Alfred was making do with a tray in his room. It would just be the two of them.

Straightening a minute wrinkle in the damask linen tablecloth, Annie wet her lips. The room fairly glowed in the combined warmth of the candles and the oil lamps. Jim had constantly urged Cedric to modernize the homestead with a generator that could supply electric power. Cedric had always refused, saying that he liked the homestead just the way it was. It was enough, he'd said, that the house in Melbourne was equipped with electricity and all the newfangled gadgets.

Would Tony be eager to make changes? Annie wondered as she filled the water goblets.

Tonight's meal was decidedly simple, yet chosen to please his sophisticated palate. Local, fresh-water trout, baked with an herbed sauce and served with wild rice and mushrooms, was the main course.

A fire burned brightly in the small stone fireplace, giving off another source of light to the room. The night was clear and crisp, the stars hung low in the sky, visible through the sheer lace curtains.

Tony stood there between the open pocket doors, watching Annie silently for a minute before making his presence known. Bathed in candlelight as she was, he thought she was quietly stunning. Tonight, she was the kind of woman to make any man with blood in his veins covet her. She was clothed, he noted quickly, from neck to hem, with nary an inch of exposed flesh.

The fact that she was so covered, Tony decided, made her all the more intriguing. Any London belle would have flaunted a good deal more bosom and flesh, even while dining *à deux*, rather than concealing her natural charms. This one hid them, and in the hiding, intensified the curiosity.

The heavy ivory silk and lace blouse she wore was skillfully sewn, making the most of the wearer's full, high-breasted figure. It accentuated her womanly curves without being blatant. The huckleberry blue velvet skirt showed off her small waist and slightly flaring hips, draping around her legs in lush folds as it fell to her ankles.

Her long brown hair was twisted into a knot at the nape of her neck, secured with mother-of-pearl combs and pins.

It was all Tony could do to keep his hands from ripping those pins from her head and scattering them to the floor, letting that glorious waterfall of hair cascade down her back in soft, rippling waves.

Now where had that thought sprung from? he wondered as he said in as polite a tone as he could manage, "Good evening."

Annie's head snapped around at his softly uttered greeting. She'd been so lost in thought that she hadn't heard him enter the room.

One look in Tony's direction and Annie assumed he must have been the one man every London hostess wanted at her table. Even without a title to his name, she guessed that Anthony Chambers was a man who could pick and choose where he dined and with whom. And why not? He was, above all, handsome. Not blandly handsome as some men were. Not tamely handsome either. Simply handsome, compellingly so. As polished as the diamond he wore in his burgundy cravat. A tailor's dream, he wore his clothes well. The silver brocaded waistcoat fit his tall, lean body to perfection, as did the black frock coat and trousers.

How many women had cried themselves to sleep when he left England? she wondered. How many missed that broad chest and those long-fingered hands? How many yearned for his penetrating, moody green eyes and that wickedly curved cupid's mouth?

How many, she speculated, craved the feel of his body beside theirs in bed?

78

Annie damned herself for that last question. It was no concern to her how many unknown women wept at their loss. Her experience had taught her that there was little real pleasure for a woman in lying with a man, and even less in believing his promises. It was all, she thought, borrowing words from Alfred's beloved bard to describe it, "full of sound and fury, signifying nothing."

Her only consolation from her fall from grace had been her daughter. Fallon had been worth the high price she had paid. Worth all the heartache and the agony. Worth the disillusionment and the hurt she endured.

Shutting the doors behind him, Tony sauntered over to the table and held out Annie's chair for her. He could tell that something was going on in her brain. He could see the haunting sadness that had quickly come into her misty gray eyes. Who, or what, was she thinking about? What secrets were locked inside her head? Would it be as easy as taking toffee from a child to discover the answers he wanted?

His hands curved on the wood of her high-backed chair as he suppressed the inclination to reach out and touch her shoulder. That would be much too familiar a gesture for such a short acquaintance.

As he took his own seat, he thought that she should have had a hard, calculating look in her eyes; then he might not be feeling this unwanted twinge of compassion. Or better still, her eyes should have held a limpid, melting quality that promised unparalleled sensual delights. Eyes that were older than time with female artfulness. Eyes that told of knowing, and appreciating, the game.

That was the kind of eyes she should have had—but didn't.

He poured each of them a glass of wine, mentally pushing aside, for the moment, any questions or concerns he had. He sipped and nodded his approval of the selection he'd made.

Tony noticed that Annie didn't immediately pick up her glass.

"You don't like it?" he inquired.

She replied, "I'm afraid that I'm not much for wine, Mr. Chambers."

"Do call me Tony," he insisted with a charming smile, a slight dimple of sorts showing in his right cheek. "After all, we shall be living together—"

Was it her imagination, Annie questioned, or had he drawn out the last two words, weighting them with emphasis?

"—for a year. Why be so formal?" he queried. "You don't mind if I address you by your Christian name, do you?"

She met his glance and accepted what could be a challenge. "No," she said, formally granting her permission, "you may call me Annie if you'd like."

"Good." Tony picked up his glass. "It's rather a nice wine, my dear. You really should try it," he coaxed.

Annie decided that a sip or two wouldn't be amiss. "It is quite good," she said, echoing his judgment after sampling it.

"Thank God my great-uncle had excellent taste," he said, pausing for a fraction of a second, "in wine. He lifted his glass high. "To Cedric."

Annie, perforce, lifted hers as well, joining him in the toast. "To Cedric," she echoed.

"Tell me about yourself," Tony urged, picking up the

platter and helping himself to the fish.

"What would you like to know?" Annie asked, her eyes on his hands as he wielded his knife and fork. They were remarkably capable-looking hands: large without being overly so; pale golden hairs dotting the smooth skin of the back; long, slender fingers with neatly trimmed nails. Hands that bespoke a true gentleman to the manner born.

What would he like to know? Tony's mind echoed.

How many men have you slept with?

Did you love any of them?

Where is your daughter's father? Had there been anything special about him—or was he just another in a long line of males that shared your bed?

"Where you are from?" he asked politely, taking a bite of the trout, enjoying the delicate taste. "I know you are an American," he said, conceding that fact. "That's quite a big country, my dear, so if you wouldn't mind narrowing it down?"

"Philadelphia was my home," she replied, helping herself to the fish.

"Ah yes," Tony replied in a smooth tone, "the seat of revolutionary fervor during the War of American Independence."

Annie smiled proudly. "It has that distinction, yes. Have you ever been there Mr. . . . Tony?" The nickname suited him, she thought.

"Alas, no," he responded. "I haven't had the pleasure of that city. I have, however, visited some of your American West."

"Whereabouts?" she asked with more than polite interest as her curiosity peaked and her guard relaxed. She followed that up with another quick question. "Did you like it?"

Gail Link

"Texas," he answered to the first inquiry. "I have friends who live there; and yes, it was a most enjoyable visit, albeit brief."

"Texas," Annie echoed in a soft voice. "Such a very big place, or so I've been told."

Tony's full lips curved into a smile. "Enormous," he said. "A land that breeds quite exceptional people."

"You mentioned that you had friends there?"

"Is that so difficult to believe?" he asked, fixing her with a razor-sharp glance.

"Why, no," she responded quickly. "I meant nothing untoward by that remark. It's just that I don't imagine one finds many Texans in England."

"You'd be surprised at how many Americans, including Texans, are to be found in England right now," he said. Tony paused, taking another sip of wine. "It's rather like this," he explained. "I have a school friend, Rafe Rayburne, a Texan, who is the foster son of the Earl of Derran, an Englishman, who also just happens to be married to a Texan woman and living there. Before coming out here, I spent some time visiting them at their respective ranches."

Annie paused with her fork midway to her mouth. "So, this English lord actually lives in Texas?"

Tony grinned. "He does, and quite happily so. Rhys and his wife, Tory, have four children. Perhaps," he inquired blandly, "you've heard of their ranch? The Encantadora?"

"My God!" Annie said on a gasp. Who, she imagined, in America hadn't heard of the almost feudal kingdom in Texas called the Encantadora? The Enchantress. It was reputed to be one of the biggest ranches in the West, and the owners among the wealthiest people in the United States. She had read about them even in

Philadelphia, where Victoria Reitenauer Fitzgerald Buchanan had relatives.

"So, you have heard of it, and them?" he inquired.

"Yes, I most certainly have," was her reply.

Good God, Annie thought, her child's paternal grandmother was some sort of distant relation to Victoria Fitzgerald Buchanan, if she recalled correctly.

Tony switched subjects without missing a beat. "I've been told that you're a widow. Was your husband from Philadelphia as well?"

Tony was direct, Annie discovered. She wondered if she should be honest and tell him the truth or continue the charade she'd played for so long.

Annie quickly decided she couldn't tell him the truth, at least not yet. She didn't trust Tony Chambers. Nor did she really know how he'd react when he learned what she'd been keeping from him, though she had a good idea what he'd think if he found out that her child had been born out of wedlock. He'd likely believe her to be a whore, as had a good many others in Philadelphia. He'd probably publicly label her child a bastard before everyone here, ruining her reputation with these people as well.

Annie couldn't take that chance, couldn't press that risk. Not now; maybe never.

"Fallon's father was from Philadelphia, yes," she said. That part was true. The lie that followed fell easily from her lips. "He died before she was born."

Tony looked at her, his eyes fixed on the proud tilt of her chin. "I'm sorry for your loss," he stated civilly. "How very awful for you to lose him especially then, when you needed him most. Such a pity he never got to see his daughter."

Yes, Annie thought, agreeing with him. It was a pity

that Fallon's father hadn't seen the one thing in his life that he could be proud of—but then, he hadn't cared enough about his child to even want her to be born.

Annie quickly spoke up. "Fallon was lucky; Cedric was like a father to her."

"Was he?" Tony questioned, watching her as she sipped her glass of wine.

Annie smiled at the warm memories of Cedric and her daughter. "In all the ways that counted. I met your uncle not long after my *husband* passed out of our lives. Cedric was most kind and generous."

"Your husband had no family?"

"None," she lied again, hating to compound the web of deceit, but knowing that she dare not stop.

"And you?"

"My family had other mouths to feed," Annie explained. "Mama and Papa were teachers in Philadelphia; still are in fact. Their meager salaries only went so far, with my younger sisters and brothers to feed and clothe. I couldn't be a burden to them."

Tony's voice was soft and oddly compelling. "How did you meet my great-uncle?"

It was Annie's turn to smile. "I literally bumped into him on the street as he was leaving the Union Club in Philadelphia. I'm afraid that I wasn't watching where I was going and ran into him." She'd been crying that day, her eyes blinded by bitter tears after the scene she'd had with Hamilton Danvers just moments before, when she'd careened into Cedric Chambers on Broad Street.

"So," he asked pointedly, "how did you come to be here in Victoria with him?"

Annie responded, "I needed a job to support myself and my child." That answer was the truth, whether he believed her or not. "He offered me one."

"And it didn't bother you that this job was in a new country? A place halfway round the world from your family and friends, from the life you'd always known?"

"No," Annie answered without hesitation. "It was what I needed." In more ways, Annie thought, than Tony Chambers could ever know.

"So you became his . . ." Tony let the sentence drift off.

"Housekeeper, for want of a better word," Annie stated quickly. "Also," she admitted, "a companion of sorts. And, most importantly, his friend."

She assured Tony, "I was proudest of the latter."

Blinking back a momentary spate of tears, Annie excused herself, putting her napkin on the table, then removing the dinner plates and taking them to the kitchen.

I can't cry, she told herself, stacking the dirty china aside. *I just can't. Not now, and not in front of him.* It would be all too easy to give in to a sudden onslaught of melancholy. All this talk of the past, and the fact that her monthly courses would soon flow, were combining to make her weepy.

Calmly, inhaling slowly, she gathered her strength and went on with her tasks.

Returning in a minute with a tray laden with cheeses and fruit, along with a few slices of shortbread and two cups of coffee, Annie fulfilled her duties as the perfect hostess.

Tony had decided not to pursue his questions further this evening. He wasn't sure that he believed all Annie Ross had to say, but he suspected that he would get no further if he pushed.

Content with what he'd gleaned thus far, he relaxed

and sampled the cheeses and fruit, finding the buttery-tasting shortbread to his liking also.

Annie yawned over her own slice of shortbread.

Tony saw the gesture. "Why don't you go to bed?"

"I can't," she said, her voice growing slightly huskier. "I still have the dishes to wash."

"Leave them," he suggested.

Annie looked shocked. "I couldn't possibly do that."

"Of course you can," Tony insisted. "They can wait till morning."

Spoken like a man who's never had to wash a dish in his life, she thought. "Leave it and the fairies will do it while I sleep?" she asked.

"Amusing scenario, but I can't promise that," he said in response.

"Then, no, I'd better take care of them now," she said as she rose and yawned again.

"Leave them," he repeated, this time in a commanding voice that was used to getting what it wanted.

She *was* tired. The wine had helped make her sleepy. She glanced at the brass clock on the mantel. It was going on ten-thirty, well past her usual bedtime.

She found herself giving in to his suggestion. "All right," she conceded, knowing that she would regret succumbing to the impulse in the morning. "You win."

"I usually do," Tony said with a faintly ironic smile.

What an arrogant man, Annie thought as she went to check on Fallon before she retired. She should have changed her clothes and done exactly what she had planned. Tony Chambers wasn't her keeper.

But she was tired.

He, however, was probably used to late hours; more than likely reveled in them with abandon.

Annie crept softly into her daughter's room. Fallon slept peacefully.

Lady raised her head from the wicker basket at the foot of Fallon's bed. Assured that the child's mother was no threat to her human companion, the dog went back to rest.

Annie bent and placed a kiss on her daughter's soft cheek. "I'd do everything I've done all over again for you, my sweetheart," she whispered to her child. "All that and more."

Tony snuffed out all the candles, save one branch that he would use to light the way to his bedroom, and turned down all the lamps. He'd poured himself a small measure of brandy and then lit a slim cheroot, the thin trickle of smoke swirling about his head as he stood in the open doorway to the veranda, staring at the multitudinous stars.

His cousin Georgie should paint her. Georgie worked wonders with a brush. He could believe the truth of her work, for she captured the soul of whomever she painted with a clear eye.

Tony swallowed the rest of the brandy and took another drag on his cigar, exhaling another stream of smoke into the crisp air. He could use a little of that clarity himself right about now.

Chapter Six

"Mommy, there's some new ladies in our kitchen."

Annie awoke to the sound of her daughter's voice in her ear. Sleepily, she opened her eyes and blinked.

Fallon scrambled up onto the mattress, under the blankets, and into Annie's arms, snuggling close to her.

"What did you say?" Annie asked, not sure if she'd heard Fallon correctly.

"There are two ladies in our kitchen," her daughter repeated. "One was washing the dishes, Mommy, and the other was fixing breakfast."

Annie scooted up against the headboard, one hand pushing back the hair that fell over her face. "Fallon, are you certain you weren't having a dream," she queried softly, "and *thought* you saw them?"

Fallon's face crumbled, her rosebud mouth pouting. "No, Mommy," the little girl insisted. "It's the truth. I would never lie to you. Never. You said that would be wrong." Fallon pointed to her border collie, resting on the floor of the bedroom. "Lady saw them too."

Annie maneuvered her way off the bed and put her daughter down. Grabbing her robe from the small tufted blue velvet chair nearby, she fastened it quickly. "I'll see about this," she said to her daughter.

She sped down the hall, uncaring that she was barefoot, her hair streaming behind her, still mussed from sleep.

Annie entered the kitchen and paused in the doorway, noting that her daughter had been correct. There *were* two unfamiliar women there. One had her hands wet up to her elbows, scrubbing the remnants of last night's meal off the china and cutlery; the other was removing some sort of muffins from the oven. The tempting smell of freshly brewed coffee hung in the air.

"Excuse me," Annie said in an inquisitory tone, "but just what do you think you are doing? And, if you don't mind my asking," she inquired, her hands on her hips, "who are you?"

The woman lifting the tray of muffins set them down on a wire rack and answered first. "Good morning, ma'am," she said with a warm smile, "I'm Mary Dunmartin, and this here is my sister, Alice Potter. You must be Mrs. Ross. We're your new household staff."

"My new *what?*" Annie demanded, thinking that perhaps it was she who was having the dream.

"Mr. Chambers hired us yesterday, ma'am. We were told that you needed some help here, and"—Mary looked imploringly at Annie—"we could sure use the work."

"Oh, Mr. Chambers did, did he?" Annie asked in a silky tone, her nostrils inhaling the coffee's rich scent and her mouth watering at the sight of the muffins.

"Well, ma'am," responded Alice, wiping her dripping hands on a blue and white striped towel, "it wasn't Mr. Chambers that hired us himself exactly. It was a man sent by your foreman, Mr. Winters, on behalf of Mr. Chambers. This man rode into Mansfield late yesterday afternoon and posted a notice at the newspaper office. I was walking by and saw it, so I went to talk to him. He said that he'd been sent to locate some help for the station. When he told me which one, well"—her raisin-brown eyes lit up—"that made up my mind for me. I fetched my sister and we came straightaway, as your man said it was urgent."

Mary chimed in. "We're both widows, ma'am, and we both want the work. Things are pretty scarce around this area now. If we was to move to the city, well, then maybe we could have found something there in Melbourne most likely.

"But," she insisted, "we'd both like to stay here in the district if we can." Mary took a cup from the hutch and poured Annie a cup of coffee, handing it to her. "This offer seemed like a godsend, ma'am. Cooking and cleaning is what we did all of our lives. We'll work our best for you," Mary promised. "Don't you be doubting it."

Annie took the cup, relaxing her stance, letting her other arm fall to her side. She could see that the two women were sincere; she believed that they did need the work. Her heart went out to them, remembering that it was the kindness of a stranger that had once given her a fresh chance. If not for that, her life would have been so very different.

Annie couldn't resist the siren call of the coffee any longer, adding cream from the jug on the table and sugar. Then she asked, "You were told that this hiring was done on the express instructions of Mr. Chambers?"

Mary answered, her bespeckled blue eyes anxious behind the wire-rimmed lenses she wore. "Yes, ma'am. He was right generous in his offer, too."

"How generous?" Annie inquired, wondering if he'd hired them too cheaply merely because of their willingness to work.

Mary named their agreed-upon monthly wage, and added, "We're to have our own lodging, too, ma'am. We came early last night and settled into one of the smaller houses. It's so lovely; more"—she shot her sister a look—"than we ever expected, isn't it, Alice?"

Alice silently nodded her head.

There were two stone cottages on the property near the main house. One, that closest to the bunkhouse, was inhabited by Jim Winters and his family; the other, slightly smaller, had been empty for some time.

"It's quite cozy and just the perfect place for us," Alice said.

Mary asked, certain that they were now to be at least given a chance in their respective positions, "Would you be liking your breakfast now, ma'am?"

Annie looked down at her daughter, who, along with Lady, had come into the kitchen a minute earlier. "Not for me right this moment," she responded, her left hand reassuringly caressing the little girl's shoulder, "but my daughter, Fallon, will have some milk, a boiled egg, and a bowl of oatmeal if you wouldn't mind."

"That'll be no trouble." Looking at the girl, Mary said, "She's a lovely child, ma'am," giving the little girl a beaming smile.

"Thank you," Annie responded, escorting her daughter to the table, where she hoisted her into a chair. "Eat your breakfast, sweetheart," Annie told the child, quickly introducing the two older ladies to her daughter. "Mommy has got to go and talk to Mr. Chambers right now."

91

Annie straightened and faced the two women, who appeared to be in their mid to late forties, handing her empty cup back to Mary. "Do either of you know where I may find Mr. Chambers?"

"I brought him coffee in the library maybe a half-hour or so ago, ma'am," Mary said, selecting a fresh brown egg to boil for Fallon's meal and pouring the child a glassful of cold milk from the glazed earthenware pitcher at hand.

"Thank you," Annie said, giving Fallon's cheek a light caress with her hand. "Be a good girl now," she told her daughter, "and later we'll attend to your lessons."

Annie left the kitchen, not stopping to change her clothes. She was so determined to speak to Tony that she never gave a thought to her appearance or to the proprieties.

Without knocking, she flung open the sliding pocket door and marched in.

"Just what did you think you were doing hiring those women behind my back?" she demanded. "Of all the arrogant, high-handed things to do!"

Tony leaned back in his chair, not at all surprised by this outburst on Annie's part. He'd been rather expecting it. Smiling slightly, he placed the silver fountain pen he'd been using to write his letters back in its holder, taking his time to respond to her, all the while his gaze fixed on the woman who stood in front of the desk. Her long brown hair flowed in tumbling waves to her waist from the center parting; her gray eyes blazed with an icy hue; her cheeks were flushed with becoming color. She was clearly agitated—and Tony found himself enjoying the picture she made.

"What seems to be the problem?" he asked calmly,

as if he didn't already know the answer.

"You know right well what the *problem* is, Mr. Chambers," Annie declared frostily. "Hiring household staff without my consent or knowledge."

Tony picked up the short brass letter opener from the desk, proceeded to thread it through his nimble fingers, weaving it in and out, back and forth. "I don't need your consent to engage staff," he said. "It's my house as well. That simple."

"No," she shot back, removing her eyes from the dexterous movements of his hand, "it's not. You didn't ask my opinion about this at all. You just went ahead and did it, following your own inclinations."

Tony gave her a boyishly charming smile, a deep groove in his right cheek appearing along with the smile. "Yes," he admitted, "I did."

"You had no right," Annie reiterated.

"There's where you're wrong, my dear," he stated matter-of-factly. "I had every right." His narrowed gaze swept over her figure. Her dressing gown was wool, a rich shade of royal blue that complemented her creamy skin. He could see the white of her high-buttoned nightgown beneath the overlapping folds of the robe. It would only take, he guessed, a skillful pull on the sash and the robe would loosen, revealing what lay beneath.

Just the fact that she'd come here, bearding him in his den as it were, without hesitation for rules or formal conduct, was exciting to him. So much that he could feel the emerging stirrings of desire.

Annie Ross looked quite sensational in the mornings. Fresh. Healthy. Alive. If he hadn't suspected her licentious past, Tony could have sworn she looked like a woman unawakened to passion's pleasures. Had his

93

greeat-uncle been so lacking as a lover that he hadn't made an imprint on the woman he'd shared a bed with?

Of course, he admitted if only to himself, he had no real proof yet that she had slept with Cedric. Chances were a guinea to a gooseberry that she had. It was just a hunch, but under the circumstances, it seemed the logical conclusion, and that was enough for him for now.

She did, however, defy his neat categorization. After all, he expected a tart to look like a tart, at least in some respects. There was nothing provocative about her garb. It served its primary function, except that for some unfathomable reason it made Tony think of long, cold evenings spent in a large, soft, warm bed, a fire blazing in the hearth, and himself lazily discovering all the secrets her woman's body had to offer.

She was direct when the occasion warranted. He'd give her that. And real. Touchingly so. Achingly so.

And she was passionate. It was revealed in her eyes, in her voice. Surprisingly, not a feigned whore's passion as he might have expected. Annie's passion appeared genuine. Born out of anger.

"I think not," Annie responded firmly to his assertion of his right.

"If I had consulted you," Tony insisted, "you would have given me some excuse as to why we couldn't, or shouldn't, have hired some rudimentary kind of staff. Perhaps rusticating"—he drawled out the word—"is what prevailed before at this station; that time is at an end as of now. We need some sort of structure here— for both our sakes—and the lady of the house is not expected to be a domestic drudge."

"A *drudge?*" Annie snapped. "Is that how you view a

woman who cares for her home?"

Tony quirked a brow, replying silkily. "Don't put words in my mouth, my dear. I was simply making a point. You are, after all, co-owner of this station, not a simple *housekeeper*"—if she ever was, he thought— "any longer. My great-uncle saw fit to alter your status. And as such," he paused, rising and coming around the desk to stand before her, "you have another position to assume. That role calls for people to serve *you*. Things have changed here, and we must all adapt to something new, mustn't we?"

His words seemed so logical, so considerate and respectful of her new position, that Annie found her anger at his tactics melting away. What was it about him that had the capability of making her soften toward him just when she wanted to contest his tactics?

It was his seeming affability and concern. That had to be the reason, she judged. No other excuse came to mind quite as readily.

Still—a little voice inside her head nagged—he could have talked to her beforehand.

Annie tilted her head back, looking him squarely in the face. "It would have been nice to have been consulted," she stated.

"If they're not to your liking," Tony offered, maintaining his distance from her even though he wanted to step closer, wanted to pick up a handful of that thick brown hair and lift it to his nose, stroke it against his cheek, "then sack them if you wish. But," he said, "I will have them replaced, make no doubt about it."

Annie lowered her lashes, sheltering her eyes from the power of his intense gaze, which she felt as if it were a living thing against her skin. "They seem okay," she said, "and they told me they do need the work, so I will give them a chance."

Okay—such a peculiarly American expression, Tony mused. It reminded him once again that this spirited mare wasn't an English thoroughbred, but an American—what was the term?—mustang. An original. Maybe just this side of wild.

Ah well, he thought, it mattered little to him the type. He was, he'd been told on numerous occasions, an excellent rider, no matter what the mount.

"They shall remain here then as long as their work is satisfactory, we are agreed?" he asked of her.

Annie raised her eyes again, meeting his. "Yes."

All of a sudden, it felt overly warm in the room to Annie, and far too intimate. She remembered then that she was barefoot, in her robe and nightgown, her hair not properly combed. Tony Chambers, in contrast, was fully dressed in a style that only enhanced both his tall form and his courtly manner.

God, what must he think of her?

Probably that she was wanton, loose, abandoned. How could she have been so foolish as to go to him in her bedclothes? Dear God, what had she been thinking?

The answer to that sprang readily to her mind. She hadn't been thinking at all. She'd been reacting. Letting her indignation get the better of her.

Annie took several steps backwards, away from Tony. "Then we shall see how they proceed," she said in an even tone, mentally pulling her composure around her. "If you will excuse me, I have to get dressed."

Tony watched her turn and walk away. An unexpected longing to stop her assailed him. He resisted the urge to lay his hands on her shoulders and forcibly halt her before she could slip out the door.

If he put his hands on her now, Tony realized, he might lose control—and he couldn't risk that.

At least, not yet.

Annie walked into the kitchen, feeling much better now that she was properly attired for the day. She'd felt vulnerable before with Tony, as if he could see into her very soul. It wasn't a feeling she was particularly comfortable with.

Mary and Alice had already settled into a routine, it would seem, since the dishes were not only washed but put away in the hutch, and Mary was chopping some root vegetables and adding them to a simmering pot of beef stock.

"I could make a pot of fresh coffee if you'd be wanting, ma'am?" the older woman offered, her hands still working the knife against the peeled potatoes.

"No need," Annie insisted, removing the jug of ice-cold milk thick with cream floating on top from the icebox. "I'll just help myself to a glass of this and one of your muffins."

"I hope you don't mind that I started the fixings for soup, ma'am, but since we didn't have a chance to talk about what you wanted for the early meal, I thought I'd better get something together right soon."

"Soup will be fine, Mary, and please, stop calling me ma'am." Annie smiled. "My name is Annie."

Mary grinned back, adding the pile of potatoes to the broth. "I'd be right happy to be calling you that."

Annie took a healthy swallow of the cold milk, enjoying the taste. She sliced one of the thick muffins and smelled the strong fragrance of apples. She bit into it and sighed. "This is delicious."

"Thank you." Mary beamed at the compliment.

"I love apples," Annie revealed as she ate the rest of the muffin. "All kinds, though I prefer the bite of the tart above the sweet."

Mary mentally made a note to herself to fix something containing apples at least twice a week from now on.

"You'll have to bear with me, Mary," Annie explained, "as I've never had an actual servant before. I'm used to doing for myself."

"Well," Mary said, wiping the steam from her lenses with a linen scrap from her skirt pocket, "I've never been a servant before either." She walked closer to where Annie sat. "But I've learnt one thing at least in all my years—and that is that life sometimes takes us where it wants us to go, whether we like it or not."

"I think you may be right, Mary," Annie said with a nod. When Annie was younger, she'd certainly never planned on having a child out of wedlock, nor on leaving her own country to start life over in a foreign land.

"When I married my Ben," Mary said, "I thought we would be old together. How was I to know that he'd get himself killed over a hand of cards and leave me to raise our two boys alone?"

"You couldn't have," Annie stated.

"Right. Things happen for a reason," Mary stated. "I'm convinced of that. Else, would I have this situation now if they didn't? It came at just the right moment."

Annie said, "I hope you'll like it here at Camelot station."

Mary smiled. "I already do." Pulling out a chair, she asked. "Do you mind if I sit down for a few minutes?"

"Of course I don't," Annie assured her.

"Good." Mary removed a folded sheet of paper from her apron pocket, along with a small stub of a pencil. "Now, we'd best be talking about what you'd like me to serve for dinner this evening, and if you've a mind, what else you'd like me to fix come tomorrow."

Chapter Seven

"You've been reading my mind again, Mei girl," Patrick O'Donnell commented, removing his well-worn hat and settling his stocky frame onto one of the comfortable, overstuffed Chesterfield sofas in his parlor. He grinned as Mei set a cup of hot tea, along with a small teapot, in front of him on a small table.

"I simply know what pleases you," the soft-spoken Mei responded as she took a seat in front of the upright piano a few feet away from Patrick. "Would you like me to play for you?"

"I'd love that, darlin'," Patrick responded, half draining his oversize cup. It contained an especially strong blend, steeped as he preferred it. But then, Mei did everything as he liked it. He had only to request, suggest, or ask, and it was done. No questions. No hesitations. That small slip of a lass knew what he wanted sometimes before he did.

Buying her from that Melbourne brothel had been the smartest thing he'd ever done; she was worth every pound he'd spent. It was a decision that Patrick never regretted, and doubted that he ever would.

Mei sat straight on the bench, her slim fingers extended, feathering across the keys, coaxing a lovely sound from the old instrument. Mei knew that her music soothed the man who shared the room with

100

her, allowing him to relax from his cares, if only for a little while.

"I've gotten myself an invitation to dinner on Sunday," Patrick informed her.

Mei continued her playing.

"Aren't you going to ask me where?" he inquired.

"You will tell me if you wish me to know," she replied evenly.

Patrick's grin deepened. "You're a wonder, Mei."

The barest hint of a smile crossed Mei's small mouth. She ceased her playing of the sadly sweet nocturne. Moving off the bench, she came to stand behind him, leaning over the back of the low couch. Mei moved her hands, those same hands that had skillfully brought forth music from the piano, and plied them now to the muscles of Patrick's shoulders. She massaged them slowly, easing the knots of tension she found there. Within an instant, she could feel him relaxing, heard the rhythm of his breathing change as she worked her magic on him.

"Well," he said, "since you must know, I've been invited to break bread with both of the owners of Camelot station."

"So," Mei queried softly, "you will finally meet the new Englishman?"

Patrick nodded, marveling anew at how her gentle hands could seemingly soothe all his cares away. He'd been up most of the night and early morning with a mare who'd been having a difficult birth. Finally, after many hours, the colt had been born, but at the cost of the exhausted mother's life. He was drained, completely worn out emotionally and physically, and in need of a bit of comforting. Mei provided all that he needed and more. She was calm and tranquillity in a

101

natural world that could be harsh and uncaring whenever it chose.

"I'm looking forward to seeing what this pommy's made of," he said in a tired voice.

"The same as you, I would imagine," Mei observed.

Patrick momentarily froze. "No chance of that, Mei girl," he shot back. "He's a stiff-necked fool, I'll wager, with more bloody charm than brains. All puffed up with his own importance and be damned to the rest of us."

"What has Annie to say about him?"

"That she hasn't been able to work out what he's up to."

"Are you so sure that he is 'up to something,' as you say?"

"Never a wee doubt about it, darlin'."

"He could surprise you."

Patrick snorted. "I'd be doubting that."

"He could be a good man," Mei said, putting more pressure on the tight muscles until they relaxed, "and," she emphasized, "good for the station, good for Annie."

Patrick snarled the words, "That Englishman could never be good enough for Annie."

Mei raised her head, taking a deep breath. She knew how very much Patrick O'Donnell cared for the other woman. He loved Annie Ross, making no secret of that fact. Mei had willingly accepted that detail long ago. When one couldn't change what the gods had ordained, her mother had often said, then one must accept and go on as one could. Mei's mother had accepted the fact that the man she'd shared a bed with, and who'd fathered her child, could never marry her, as he was already wed. The only thing she hadn't accepted was the gentle Welshman's death in a mining accident. The spark of life had left her mother's body soon after, and reduced the lovely Chinese woman to a shell, her mind clouded and confused by opium, who sold her body cheaply in order to survive.

Her mother, Mei knew, had loved one man too much and herself not enough. It was simply *joss*. Luck. Fate.

Happenstance had bound Mei to Patrick since that fateful night in the brothel where he'd bid the highest for her at the virgins' auction; love kept the threads woven tightly. Mei loved this sweet young man with the laughing Irish face, had from the first moment she'd laid her eyes on him. Loved him with all the capacity that was in her to love.

But that was her secret, guarded from the world at large. Her private heartbreak she would share with no one else. Mei had a place in Patrick's life, and she was content with that. She had to be.

Mei glanced down. Patrick was asleep.

Softly, so as not to disturb him, she reached out and gently touched the crown of his close-cropped dark blond head, longing to cradle it to her breast, aching to hold him secure in her arms, wanting to give him the comfort he so deserved.

But he'd never asked that of her. Never once had he crossed the line to demand that she yield what he'd paid so dearly for.

Bending close to his ear, Mei whispered in Chinese, "Rest well, love of my heart. I shall forever stand watch and keep the dragons at bay."

Annie waved to the men who were maneuvering herds of sheep along the path as she rode her golden chestnut horse through the gates and onto the main property of Broken Hill station.

A lad with a cocky grin and carrot-colored hair took the reins from her and led the horse away as soon as she dismounted. Annie smiled as she looked at the long series of steps that led up to the main house. The homestead was barely four years old, a copy of one that Patrick had seen in the Blue Mountain region of New South Wales while visiting one of his married sisters. The house was set on a hill, affording Patrick a splendid view of the area, and it was painted in bright shades of white, blue, and plum.

She ascended the first series of brick steps set into the hillside, laughing at the stone leprechauns that greeted her there. Continuing across the warm painted bricks set into the grass, she made her way to the next set of steps that led up to the wrap-around porch and the front door, where a smiling Mei waited.

"How good it is to see you, my friend," Mei said as the two young women embraced.

"It's been far too long," Annie replied, pulling off her riding gloves and tucking them into the pockets of her wool jacket.

"Yes, it has," Mei agreed, "but now you are here and are most welcome." She ushered Annie inside the spacious house to the large parlor. "Will you have tea?"

"I'd love some after that long ride," Annie replied.

"Then please sit and I shall bring it to you."

Annie started to sit down and remembered she'd forgotten something. "Blast. I left the magazines I brought for you and Patrick in my saddlebags. Let me run out and fetch them while you're fixing the tea."

Annie was back within minutes, a stack of well-thumbed magazines in her arms. Sent mainly by her mother, although Cedric had subscribed to one or two, they were issues she'd finished reading and usually passed on to Mei and Patrick.

She piled them neatly on the low table. They ranged from *Frank Leslie's Popular Monthly, Godey's Lady's Book, Harper's Bazaar, and Scribner's* to *Ladies Home Journal.* They provided all sorts of information, from politics and the arts to the latest fashions and recipes. Reading them always made Annie feel closer to her former home.

Mei entered carrying a tray, which she set down next to the magazines, then took a seat next to Annie on the wide Chesterfield sofa covered in deep red velvet. "I see that we shall have something new to read," she said as she poured tea into cups and added sugar and milk. "Patrick will be most pleased."

"And what about you?" Annie asked as she took a satisfying sip of hot tea.

"I am most pleased also, my friend."

"It's little enough that I can do to say thank you for all you've done for me since we've known each other."

Mei gave a slight nod. "Friendship is a mutual gift we have given one another."

As they drank their tea in companionable silence, Annie inwardly smiled at her good fortune in meeting a woman like Mei, a woman like herself in many respects. She knew the secret of how Mei had come to be Patrick's housekeeper; Mei knew the full truth of Annie's "widowhood." Annie suspected that her friend's true feelings for Patrick went deeper than Mei let on, though Annie wouldn't broach the subject out of respect for Mei's privacy. Annie recognized the longing in Mei's black eyes whenever Patrick was near. Annie doubted that Patrick would ever find a better woman more suited to him than the exotic beauty who already shared his house and had made it a home.

Yet she couldn't, or wouldn't, intrude. It was between them.

"Where is Patrick?" Annie inquired.

"He was very tired after being up all night with one of his horses," Mei explained. "A difficult birthing that did not go well, and when he came in just a few hours ago and fell asleep while drinking his tea, I suggested that he go to bed."

"Star's Lady," Annie murmured, recalling the formerly wild brumby. "She was one of Patrick's favorites. Is she all right?"

Mei shook her head sadly. "The mare died."

"Poor Patrick," Annie sighed. "What about the offspring? Did it survive?"

"Thankfully, yes," Mei replied. "Patrick has a new colt."

"Sometimes," Annie observed, "being a female of the species is fraught with risks."

Mei inquired, "You are thinking about your own child's birth, are you not?"

Annie nodded.

"Would you willingly go through that risk again to have another child?" Mei asked her friend. She'd often wondered what it would be like to have Patrick's seed growing inside herself, changing her body as it changed her life. For that experience, Mei knew she would risk anything.

Annie's face took on a sorrowful expression. "To do that I would have to lie with a man, and I cannot fathom the possibility of that ever happening again." Annie kept to herself the memories of the hurried, pain-filled coupling that had produced her daughter. All her romantic, girlish illusions had been shattered to dust that one time with Fallon's father. "I trusted a man once before," she said, "and it led to betrayal."

"You do not want to marry?"

"For what reason?" Annie asked. "I have money and property now, a secure future for my daughter. There is no need."

"What about for love?" Mei prompted.

"I loved a man once," Annie said, "and that was enough. I won't be used that way again."

"From what you have told me," Mei countered, "that wasn't love, at least not on his part. It was selfishness. He took the gift of love that you gave him and threw it away, as a child would do when he is tired of a toy. He wasn't worthy of your honor.

"One day, another man will be," Mei said. "You loved Cedric, did you not?"

"Yes," Annie admitted, "but not in the way that you mean. I cared deeply for him. It was a safe, comfortable love, the kind one feels for a good friend. That was all."

"So, you did not want to share his bed?"

"No," Annie replied. "Though, truthfully, I would have if he'd asked."

"You would have?" Mei inquired.

"If it would have made him happy," Annie responded, "then yes. It would have been little enough to repay him for all the kindness he'd shown me. Charity paid for charity shown. But Cedric never asked. I think he knew how I felt, that my heart wouldn't be involved."

"And you think that it never will be again?"

"Honestly, no, I don't, Mei."

"I think someone will come along to change your mind," Mei said optimistically.

Annie let out a deep breath. "I doubt that very much." As soon as Annie uttered those words, a clear vision popped into her brain—a vision she chose to ignore.

Feeling slightly shaken by the vivid mental picture, Annie steered the subject away from a topic that made her strangely uncomfortable.

"I've invited Patrick to dinner on Sunday night, Mei. Will you come with him?"

"I cannot," Mei responded politely.

"Please reconsider, Mei," Annie entreated her friend. "I would so love to have you there, as I'm sure Patrick would."

Mei would have loved to accept, but she felt uneasy about leaving the station. Here at Broken Hill, she felt protected, safe, in a world where she mattered—a world in which she belonged. Away from Broken Hill, society could be ugly and unforgiving, especially, she knew, to one of mixed race. She'd already experienced life outside the perimeters of the station, and was in no hurry to do so again.

"My place is here," she said quietly.

"Of course it is," Annie agreed, "but it isn't the *only* place."

"It is for me," Mei stated.

"So I can't change your mind?"

Mei shook her head.

"I could have used another ally at dinner," Annie confessed.

"You will do well," her friend insisted.

"Having another woman there would have been very nice," Annie stated firmly, "evening the odds."

108

"Suppose that you and this Englishman—"

"His name is Tony Chambers," Annie interrupted, the mention of his name giving an unexpected leap to her pulse.

Mei nodded in acknowledgment with a smile. She rephrased her question. "Will you and Mr. Chambers come to dinner on the Sunday next? Spend the night perhaps? I'm sure that Patrick would give his approval of the arrangement."

"I'm not so sure about that."

"Now who is hesitating?" Mei asked with a smile as she refilled their cups. She gave Annie a plate with a thin slice of orange bread. "Think about it and I shall talk to Patrick in the meantime."

"I promise I shall consider it. Though," Annie teased, "I'm not sure I should as you've refused my invitation."

"You would not hold that against me?" Mei asked carefully.

Annie laughed softly. "I was just kidding, Mei. Of course I wouldn't," she protested. "I understand your reluctance to leave the place where you feel most comfortable." After all, she felt the same, in a way. Annie only left Camelot station to travel to Patrick's, shunning most of the other numerous offers that came her way to visit other stations for parties and dinners. She was quite content where she was.

Annie tasted a forkful of the still warm bread, and it made her think of something else she wanted to relate to her friend. "I must tell you about the new additions to my household," and she proceeded to fill Mei in on the hiring of Mary and Alice, along with the presence of Tony's valet, Alfred.

"So," she said, "that leaves me with very little to actually do around the house at present."

Mei cocked her head to one side, glancing at her confidante. "How shall you fill your time?"

Annie shrugged her shoulders. "I don't know."

Mei posed a question to her. "Were you trained for any kind of work before you came here?" Training had been a big portion of her own upbringing. Mei followed her mother's example and learned carefully at her side the arts of pleasing a man, of taking care of him.

"I was planning on becoming a teacher, like my parents," Annie said wistfully.

"Can you still pursue that choice?"

"If I lived in Melbourne or Sydney," Annie replied, "perhaps."

A sharp light came into Mei's black eyes. "Suppose that you could still teach from far away."

Annie was puzzled. "What do you mean?"

"Look at the magazines you have brought with you," Mei said, indicating the pile with a wave of her slim-fingered hand. "Do they not feature stories?"

Annie responded in the affirmative.

"Then," Mei suggested, "could you not instruct others in your birth country of what life is like here in your new country? Do you not think that many Americans would be interested in Australia?"

Annie listened thoughtfully, considering Mei's words.

"Have you not told me that your brothers and sisters love your letters, especially when you include your sketches of the plants and animals that live here?"

"Why, yes, they do," Annie replied, "but that's because they're my family. My life here interests them for that reason only."

"Maybe yes, maybe no," Mei pointed out. "It could be because you have a way, Annie, with the telling of the tales, also.

"Have you ever thought about putting some of these things on paper, perhaps for children?"

"You mean," Annie asked, "write an actual book? Try to get it published?"

Mei nodded. She rose and picked up a volume that Annie had lent her on her last visit. "You could be like Jo in this book," Mei said, holding *Little Women* in her hand.

Annie's gray eyes lit up. "I admire Miss Alcott tremendously," Annie said. It was one of the reasons that she'd lent the book to Mei.

"Then," Mei proposed, "why not follow her example, in this way?"

Annie considered the idea, and the more she thought about it, the better she liked it. It would be a way to make productive use of her free time, and maybe earn her own way, thereby proving to her new partner that she wasn't simply a decoration to be brought out at dinner time along with the fine china and crystal.

"There is a typewriter in the office; Cedric bought it just before his death," Annie said. "I suppose I could learn how to use it if I needed to, and I've a sketchbook that I've already made simple drawings in."

Annie paused, thinking for a moment before speaking again. "Oh, Mei, it's such a grand idea. This way, I can share my love for this area with others, if they're curious. Perhaps some of the American newspapers or magazines would be interested in a series of articles."

Gail Link

Mei smiled. "I think you have found what you were looking for."

"I think I have," Annie replied enthusiastically, finishing the cooled tea in her cup. "This is wonderful. It'll give me something to focus on, a goal, if you will. With Mary and Alice helping around the house, I'll certainly have the time to devote to it."

Annie suddenly frowned. "But suppose I can't?"

Mei laughed lightly. "Don't be—what is the phrase—a funny goose?"

Annie laughed. "It's silly goose."

"Silly goose, then," Mei said. "If there is one thing I know about you, Annie, it is that once you put your mind to something, it is done to the best of your ability," Mei stated.

Annie put down her cup and impulsively hugged the other woman. "It's worth a try."

"What's worth a try?" mumbled a distinctly male voice from the doorway.

Glory be to God and all his saints, Patrick thought as he stood there watching the two women. They were surely the most beautiful creatures, each in her own way distinctive. Annie was the warm sunshine of a fine day; Mei was the comfort of a cool evening breeze. Even their looks complemented one another. Annie reminded him of the land, dressed in her hues of the earth, shades of brown and cream. Mei brought to mind the power of fire, clothed in dazzling colors of red, gold, and black.

Both women smiled in his direction—one with affection, the other in love.

"So, would you ladies be minding if I join you?"

"Please do," Annie insisted.

"Would you like a cup?" Mei asked, ready to see to his needs.

"Sit still, darlin'," Patrick said as he came into the room and took a seat on the other Chesterfield sofa. "I'm fine as I am. Now, what was it I heard you two nattering about?"

Annie quickly filled Patrick in on the details.

"I'm thinking that's a wonderful idea."

"You do?" Annie asked.

"Sure and why not? Are you not some good part Irish, my girl?" he asked rhetorically. "We Irish do love the telling of the tales. It's in our blood. Why not make a few pounds, then, for what comes naturally?"

Annie said with a deprecating smile, "That's if anyone cares to purchase what I write, Patrick."

"You'll not be finding out till you try, my girl," he declared.

Annie beamed. "Then I will."

"Good for you," Patrick stated.

Annie checked her watch. "It's getting late and I'd best be heading back to the station," she stated as she rose.

"Mind you be careful as you go," Patrick insisted.

Annie tossed him an arch look. "Aren't I always?"

She and Mei exchanged embraces and then Annie hugged Patrick. "Thank you both," she said, "for your belief in me."

"Anytime, Annie girl," Patrick replied.

They both walked her to the porch, where, in a booming voice, Patrick summoned for Annie's horse to be brought round.

"Till Sunday, then," Annie said as she made her way back down the series of steps where the carrot-topped lad waited with her horse.

"I'll be there, never fear," Patrick answered as Annie mounted and rode off.

"Well, doesn't that just take the bloody cake?" Patrick asked Mei as he followed her back into the parlor, where she was cleaning up the remnants of the afternoon's tea.

"What?"

"He's gone and gotten her a staff."

"I would say that it was considerate of him," Mei observed.

"Something's got to be in it for him," Patrick muttered darkly.

"Perhaps you are being too suspicious," Mei suggested softly.

"I don't think so."

"From what I've learned, he's a rich Englishman, used to having servants about him. Perhaps," she pointed out, "he feels that Annie deserves them as well."

"She does that, I'll willingly admit."

"Then do not look further than that for now."

"I do bow before your calm brand of logic, my girl," he conceded. "At least until I've had a chance to discover for myself."

Mei gave him a quiet smile.

"Now, what's on for supper this evening? I'm so hungry that I think I could eat a 'roo raw."

Chapter Eight

"Where is Mrs. Ross?"

Mary blinked behind her spectacles, startled by the sound of Tony Chambers's deep voice just as she opened the oven door. "She went out just after luncheon, sir," Mary responded, removing several loaves of bread from the oven.

"Out?" he queried.

"Yes, sir," Mary repeated, setting the loaves to cool on the table.

"Where?" he demanded.

Mary cleared her throat, caught off guard by the tone of his voice. "She said she was going visiting over to the Broken Hill station, sir."

"Did she go alone?"

"I believe she did, sir."

Tony strode to the kitchen door and opened it, gazing outside. The sky had darkened with the approach of evening, and the temperature outside had dropped. "Damned fool," he muttered under his breath.

"Excuse me, sir?" Mary questioned, wondering if he was speaking to her.

"Nothing," Tony replied, not bothering to turn around. Annie Ross had no business riding about the countryside alone, without a proper escort. He'd ridden this property and seen the terrain. It was rugged in some spots, and, he suspected, it could be unforgiving to anyone who tried to best it.

"Where's the child?"

"She's with Mrs. Winters, sir."

"Just as well."

Mary wondered if he was going to stand there much longer, letting in the cool air. "Would you like me to make you a pot of tea, sir?"

"No," Tony answered, "I don't have time."

With that remark, he walked out of the kitchen door and toward the stables. He spied Jim Winters walking with two of the men, deep in conversation.

"Winters," Tony called out.

Jim halted. He could tell by the determined look on Tony's face that something was not agreeing with the boss. "Yes, Mr. Chambers?" he replied, dismissing the other men and moving in Tony's direction.

Tony quickened his steps until they met in front of the large brick building that housed the stables.

"Has Mrs. Ross come back yet?"

"Not that I know of, sir," Jim replied.

"Did anyone accompany her?"

"I don't think so."

Tony demanded, "Why not?"

Jim was baffled by the new owner's seeming anger. "Mrs. Ross never takes an escort with her when she rides. Besides," he said, "she was only going to Broken Hill station."

"Which is how far from here?"

Jim replied, "About an hour or so, sir, depending."

"Depending?" Tony asked. "On what?"

"Weather's one thing," Jim stated. "If you've got a fast horse can be another. Of course, you've got to know where you're going, too."

Tony inhaled sharply, his nostrils flaring slightly. "From now on, Mrs. Ross doesn't leave the station without an escort. Understood?"

Jim looked Tony square in the eye. "That's for Mrs. Ross to say."

Tony raised one brown brow. "I beg your pardon?" he drawled.

"It's for her to tell me, Mr. Chambers," Jim repeated. "She's capable of looking out for herself."

"That's beside the point," Tony insisted.

"I don't think so, sir," Jim responded. "Mrs. Ross is a crack rider, and she knows the area as well, or better, than some of the men."

"She's also," Tony pointed out, "a woman, alone."

"That isn't, if you don't mind my saying so, sir, a problem out here. Ladies can come and go as they please."

"I think that it *is* a problem," Tony insisted.

"Then that would be between you and Mrs. Ross to settle, now wouldn't it?" Jim asked.

"And we shall, make no mistake about that," Tony promised. "So, you're not worried that she hasn't returned yet?"

Jim answered honestly, "No, sir, I'm not."

Tony could see that he wasn't going to get the foreman to budge on this particular issue. They obviously saw things in a much different light.

"See to it that my horse is saddled and waiting for me," Tony directed.

A note of disbelief in his voice, Jim asked, "You're going after her?"

"Yes," Tony replied. "Any objections?"

"None, sir," Jim answered, wisely choosing not to

117

say anything more on the subject. "I'd best be riding with you, though."

Tony gave a short nod of consent. "I'll be back as soon as I change clothes," he said and left the foreman standing there, rubbing his chin in wonder.

Back inside the house, Tony made his way down the long hall toward his own room, calling for Alfred.

"Yes, sir?" his valet responded.

"Fetch me my riding boots and my greatcoat."

Alfred raised both bushy brows in concern. "You're going riding now, sir?" His tone conveyed his surprise. "Rather late in the day, isn't it?"

"I hadn't planned on it," Tony said as he removed his shoes and stripped off his more formal trousers, replacing them with a tapered pair of moleskin pants better suited to riding. He fastened the buckle of his leather belt, Alfred handing him his well-polished knee-high black boots, which Tony pulled on.

Tony changed jackets as well, opting for a heavier one over his plain dark waistcoat and white shirt.

Alfred pursued his question. "Is there some urgent reason, sir?"

Tony shrugged into the long outer coat, fastening the closures. "It would seem that Mrs. Ross went out earlier and still hasn't returned."

"Oh."

Tony shot him a sharp glance. "Is that all you have to say?"

"What would you have me say, sir?"

"Perhaps that you find this situation as disturbing as I do," Tony suggested. "Or am I the only person who finds it amazing that a solitary female rides about the countryside by herself?"

"I should think that Mrs. Ross knows this area well,

118

sir," Alfred calmly pointed out, "and she does appear quite capable of taking care of herself."

Tony was getting tired of stating the obvious. "She's a woman."

Alfred smiled, a devilish gleam in his eye. "Yes, I had noticed that, sir."

"You know bloody well what I mean," Tony said, clearly not amused by Alfred's remark. "She's alone. Unprotected."

"And you feel that it's your duty to look out for her, sir?" Alfred inquired.

"It's my responsibility, yes," Tony said, "since she's living under this roof."

"I do see your point, sir," Alfred agreed, his smile deepening. He neglected to restate the obvious, that prior to Tony's arrival, Mrs. Ross had most certainly ridden out alone and had come to no harm whatsoever.

"I should hope so," Tony muttered, exiting his bedroom by the glass doors that opened to the outdoors.

Alfred folded the trousers Tony had removed and set them aside to press later. The valet found this new situation very intriguing, and mildly amusing. A sea-change had already crept into his new employer's attitude toward the young woman he shared the homestead with. Weeks ago, Alfred was certain that Tony Chambers might not have cared a whit if the woman was out roaming the countryside alone, no matter what the time of day. Now, there was an underlying concern about the woman's welfare, whether Tony admitted it or not. Was Tony beginning to care about the American lady? And if he was, how deep did that care go?

Ah, Alfred mused, shutting the doors that Tony had left open, the plot doth indeed thicken.

Merlin was saddled and waiting for Tony, as was Jim Winters.

"Which direction?" Tony asked as he gathered the reins and mounted the stallion, swinging into the saddle with the ease of an experienced horseman.

"Northwest, sir."

"Then let's not waste time," Tony insisted as he put heels to the animal's sides.

The two men rode off to the curious looks of several of the station's hands.

About a half hour later, they saw a horse and rider in the distance, coming over a hill. It was getting darker, so they couldn't make out the identity of the rider at first.

Jim pulled up, squinting his eyes as the horse got closer. "I do believe that that's Mrs. Ross coming now, sir," he said. Sensing that there was going to be a reckoning of sorts, Jim wondered if he should stay or go. "Would you like me to remain, Mr. Chambers, or should I leave you and Mrs. Ross alone?"

Tony halted his own mount and watched as the rider got closer and closer. It was Annie Ross, no doubt about it. "I would like to have a word with Mrs. Ross in private, Jim, if you don't mind. We can find our own way back."

Jim shrugged his shoulders, shifting the reins to the left, tugging on the bit. Turning his horse around, he headed back to the station.

Annie arrived momentarily. She saw Tony sitting astride the big black stallion and immediately reined her own horse in. She was shocked to see Tony there, and her first thought was that something might have happened to her daughter.

"Is Fallon all right?" she demanded anxiously.

Tony responded instantly, recognizing the worried tones of a mother. "She's quite fine, I do believe. She was still with Mrs. Winters when I left the station."

Annie breathed a deep sigh of relief. "Thank God. When I saw you—and that was Jim, wasn't it, I saw riding off?—I immediately thought something might be wrong with Fallon." She paused, catching her breath. "What are you doing out here, then? Were you and Jim taking another look around?"

"No," Tony stated flatly, "we were looking for you."

"You were?" she asked, puzzled as to his motive. "Why?"

"I should think it obvious."

"Well," Annie said, "since it isn't *obviously* obvious to me, would you care to enlighten me?"

Tony's nostrils flared with impatience at having to explain what should be plain to yet another person.

"You've no business to be out and about by yourself," he replied.

Annie stared at him, hardly able to believe what she was hearing. "I beg your pardon?" she asked. "What gives you the right to say that to me?"

"Right?" Tony shot back, moving his horse closer to hers so that only inches separated them.

"Yes, right," she repeated. "You are not my keeper, *Mr.* Chambers. Where I go and what I do are my own affair."

"Affair?" he whispered darkly.

Annie realized that Tony had misinterpreted what she said by the remote look that had come over his face. "That was a figure of speech," she hastened to add.

"In this case, is it an accurate one?"

"What?" she gasped.

"Are you having an affair, *Mrs.* Ross?" he demanded softly. "Is that where you rode off to this afternoon—your lover's house?"

"Lover?" God, if that wasn't so ridiculous a question she would have laughed out loud. That was the last thing she wanted in her life. "Are you joking?"

Tony fixed his green eyes on her, and Annie knew he wasn't kidding. He was deadly serious.

Tony's gaze quickly roamed over Annie's form as she sat still on her horse. She was dressed like a youth—and looked anything but—in dark brown trousers that molded her legs like a second skin. Some sort of soft buckskin, he thought. An old pair of knee-high brown boots, a plain white shirt, and a riding jacket of brown wool completed the outfit. She wore the same type of hat that he'd seen the stockmen and Jim wearing; her long brown hair was pulled back in a single braid.

Had this man O'Donnell ridden between those thighs? Had he reveled in the silky flow of her hair? Had he captured and plundered those tempting lips? Had his hands cupped her naked breasts, the flesh filling his palms? Had he sampled the softness of her skin?

Tony leaned closer to her. Did she carry O'Donnell's scent?

"Answer me," his deep voice commanded in a growl.

Annie responded to his question with momentary silence before kicking her horse into action, sending her mare galloping ahead.

122

Tony was seconds behind her, his big horse easily matching the mare's strides, catching up to her. He grabbed at the reins and pulled the horse up.

"Let go!" Annie exclaimed.

"Not until you answer me," he insisted.

"You haven't any right to question me," she stated angrily, yanking back against the grip he had on the leather.

"While you're living in my house—"

"It's my house too, or have you conveniently forgotten that, *Mr.* Chambers?" Annie snapped, her temper flaring.

"I'm the man of the household," Tony stated, as if that were the answer beyond reproach.

"But you're not *my* man," Annie coolly pointed out, "and you never will be."

"If I were," Tony said in an equally chilly tone, "you would most certainly know your place, my dear, I can very well assure you."

"Since you aren't," Annie retorted, "my place is wherever *I* please, which right now is home with my daughter, if you don't mind."

Their locked gazes heated the air between them. Tony relaxed his grip on her reins and Annie set her horse in motion again.

Tony watched her ride off, his hands curling into tight fists as he held his own leather reins tight in his grip.

Damn her!

Damn him!

Annie pushed her horse to the limit as she made her way back to the station, the mare making short work of the miles.

He was doing it again. Playing the lord-of-the-manor to her, issuing orders and decrees as he saw fit.

Except that Annie knew Tony wasn't playing. It was exactly how he saw his role in life. He was in charge, in total control. No ifs, ands, or buts. For him, there was one law, one order. His own.

"There was no stopping him," Jim said when she dismounted from the chestnut mare.

"I can see that," Annie said, leading the horse into the stable herself and giving the reins to the young lad who served as a groom on the station.

Jim followed her, waiting outside the large doors until she emerged again. "Mr. Chambers was determined to go and find you." Jim rolled himself a cigarette and struck a match across the mellow brick wall of the building. "I tried to talk him out of it, but he wouldn't listen. He's a right stubborn man when he sets his mind to something."

Jim took a deep drag of the tobacco. "Truth is, he was worried about you, Mrs. Ross. There's no doubt in my mind about that."

"Worried?" Annie questioned, pausing. She had seen only censure in Tony's face, heard only rude accusations from his lips. She'd seen no evidence of the worry that Jim believed he felt.

"You're certain of that, Jim?"

"As certain as I am of my own name, ma'am." Jim took another drag, exhaling a cloud of smoke. "Mr. Chambers seemed afraid that something might have happened to you since it was getting late and you hadn't come home yet. His concern was genuine, so I thought I'd best ride with him and show him the way, even though I told him that you'd be fine. It's not as if you'd never ridden between here and Broken Hill station before."

"Thanks, Jim."

"No need for thanks, ma'am. I'm just telling you because I thought you should know."

Annie was lost in thought for a moment, her eyes cast to the ground.

"Mrs. Ross?"

Her head snapped up. "Yes, Jim?"

"Are you all right?"

"Sorry," Annie apologized softly. "I was just thinking," she explained. Her anger with Tony had abated somewhat with the foreman's words, replaced by an even stronger sense of bewilderment regarding Tony Chambers. What was she to make of this man and his conflicting attitudes? Jim was a straight-talking fellow, a man whose loyalty was to her, she knew. Jim saw things as they were, without embellishment. If he said that Tony was worried, then she could take that information to any bank in Melbourne for coin of the realm.

But then why hadn't Tony shown any of his concern to her? Why had he jumped to erroneous conclusions and accused her falsely? Why had disdain flared into those green eyes, coating them with a thin layer of ice?

It had simply never occurred to her that Tony would fret about her whereabouts, or the time she was gone from the station. No one had before.

Did he truly care? Or was it just another way to exercise some sort of control over her?

And why the contemptuous tone when he asked about a "lover"? It all made no sense to her. None whatsoever.

Annie heard someone shout a greeting and turned

her head as Tony rode in through the stone gates. He galloped past her, sitting erect in the saddle, his face a stiff mask of pride, never acknowledging her.

Stung, Annie whirled and headed for the Winterses' cottage to pick up her daughter.

Tony unsaddled the stallion himself, removing the various pieces of the tack, making it quite clear to the stable boy that he wanted to be left alone. Merlin whickered as Tony laid a hand along the horse's neck, absently stroking the thick black mane.

Could he really believe the shock he'd seen in her eyes when he'd flung his accusation at her? Annie's face had gone pale, her eyes widened.

Innocence—or anger at being caught?

Which was it?

Damned if he knew.

Tony inhaled deeply, his head tilted slightly back, his eyes focused on the cross beams in the roof as he contemplated what had passed between himself and Annie Ross. Two words sprang instantly to his mind: cold, hot. The cold ache of uncertainty, the hot flare of desire. Both were mixed in equal measures inside himself toward her.

Why?

Annie walked into the kitchen, her manner calm and collected. She'd made her decision about dinner this evening and wanted to let Mary know her plans.

Alice was finishing a cup of tea at the table, a warm scone topped with thick cream and apricot jam in front of her. Today she'd finished with the parlor, where for the last two days she'd aired the rugs, waxed the floor, and polished the furniture, giving the room a vigorous going-over. Freshly laundered and starched white crocheted doilies, looking like giant snowflakes, lay on the wide kitchen table, waiting to be put back where they belonged.

Mary stood at the stove, stirring something in a large copper pan.

Annie moved closer and examined what Mary was cooking. It was a creamy white soup, fragrant with black pepper and onions.

"Would you care for a taste?" Mary asked.

Annie couldn't resist. She took the wooden spoon and dipped it into the simmering pot, relishing the hearty potato flavor.

She lifted her head and saw Alfred in a corner at the ironing board, busily removing the wrinkles in a pair of pants.

Annie returned the spoon to Mary and smiled. "I'd like it if you shared your recipe for that with me, Mary."

"Of course, ma'am."

"Tonight," Annie said, "there will be a change in the dining arrangements."

"Yes?"

"I want my dinner served in my room," Annie instructed.

"Your room?" Mary asked.

Annie replied, "That's right."

Mary stopped stirring the pot. "What about Mr. Chambers?"

"He will have his in the dining room as usual," Annie stated. "I know that this is inconvenient," Annie began.

"It's no trouble at all, ma'am," Mary hastened to say.

Annie smiled in response. "Fine. Then I would like

dinner when I'm done with my bath, if you would."

"When will that be?"

"In about an hour."

"I will have it ready then," Mary promised.

"Thank you," Annie replied. "Oh, just a bowl of the soup will do me, and perhaps some bread. I don't want anything more."

"As you wish," Mary said.

The trio assembled watched as Annie left the room. They all exchanged swift glances with one another when the kitchen door shut behind her.

"Now," Alice asked, wiping a dab of jam from her fingers with her napkin, "what was that about?"

Mary shrugged. "Who knows?"

Alfred paused to check his handiwork. "There's more here," he said cheerfully, "than meets the eye."

Alice snorted agreeingly. "Isn't that always the way of it when a man and a woman are involved?"

"All that and so much more," Alfred suggested with a smile.

Chapter Nine

Tony drummed his fingers on the table, casting a sharp glance at the brass clock on the mantel. He'd arrived early for the meal, intent on being in the room when Annie arrived.

After the heated exchange that had taken place between them, Tony wanted some time alone to evaluate her mood. He still wasn't sure that she hadn't something to hide in her relationship with O'Donnell.

The door from the kitchen opened and Mary walked in with the first course, a bowl of her potato and leek soup. As she placed the wide china bowl before Tony, Mary realized that she had forgotten to remove the place setting for Annie.

As Mary gathered the dishes and cutlery, Tony asked as casually as he could muster, "Where is Mrs. Ross?"

"She's chosen to have a light supper in her room, sir," Mary explained.

One of Tony's thick brown eyebrows quirked upwards. "Oh, she has, has she?" Why? Guilt? he wondered. Was that the reason she couldn't face him over the table? Or was exhaustion the cause? Riding a horse back and forth over a long distance, coupled with riding a demanding lover to fulfillment, all in one afternoon, could be fatiguing indeed.

"Yes, sir," Mary responded. "Mrs. Ross was quite tired and said that all she wanted was the soup."

Tony pushed back his chair slowly and rose, placing his dark blue damask napkin beside the soup bowl. "We shall see about that," he stated softly.

"*We*, sir?" Mary asked in a small voice, not exactly sure what was going on. She watched as Tony shoved back the pocket doors and strode into the hallway, turning in the direction of the bedrooms. Hesitating a moment, deciding what to do now that he'd left the table without eating a drop of soup, Mary picked up the bowl and returned with it to the kitchen.

"Mr. Chambers decided against the soup then, Mary?" Alfred asked, curious, since he was thouroughly enjoying his portion. Mary was, without a doubt, one fine cook.

"He never touched a drop," she said, pouring it back into the pot simmering on the stove, then rinsing out the bowl and drying it in case Mr. Chambers should change his mind and decide that he was ready to resume his evening meal. "He wanted to know where Mrs. Ross was, and when I told him that she'd chosen to have her meal in her room, he stormed out.

"No, that's a mistake," she corrected immediately. "Stormed out isn't quite what I want to say." Mary paused, hands on her ample hips, reconsidering her words. "Mr. Chambers was very controlled, almost icy in his manner when he quit the room. Quite peeved, actually, I'd wager, and not wanting to let on that he was."

Alfred smiled to himself as he finished the contents of his bowl.

"Now, what's that look about?" Mary questioned when she saw the contemplative expression on Alfred's square face, taking her seat at the kitchen table, her own bowl of hot soup awaiting her.

"Haven't you noticed how it is between them?" Alfred confided, deciding to trust the sisters with his observations, eager to see if they concurred with him, curious if they too had felt the raw energy generated by the couple whenever they were together.

"Vinegar and oil, I'd say they were," Alice stated.

Mary gave a gentle shake of her head, offering a different slant. "More like honey and salt, to my way of thinking," she offered, adding a dash of ground pepper to her soup.

Alfred chuckled as he set down his glass of *vin ordinaire*. "Ah, I think you've hit on it, Mary," Alfred replied, nodding in agreement with her pronouncement. "Sweetness and spice. Perhaps one of the best blends for loving."

"Are you daft?" Alice asked, astonished at the valet's musings.

Alfred looked suitably affronted. "I've quite a long distance to travel before I could be considered daft, my dear woman," he said, defending his statement. "'Tis merely that I've seen, in my long career with several acting companies, most recently Basil Markham's Strolling Players, that human nature being what it is, passion that is born to last is found in men and women who possess both diverse elements in their nature. All sweetness is boring, like a diet of treacle pudding eaten every single day; all spice is overwhelming, leaving one with no appreciative appetite for other tastes."

"So," Mary asked, her bespeckled gaze fixed upon the valet, "you believe that there is something between Mr. Chambers and Mrs. Ross other than the arrangement we've heard put about?"

131

"Indubitably, my dear woman," Alfred asserted, putting down his silver soup spoon.

Alice considered his words with an audible, "Hmmm," while Mary sighed.

"You know, you may be right, Alfred," Mary suggested, calling him by his Christian name as he'd requested she do, pondering his words.

"I have been known to be so on many occasions," he insisted dryly, "and mark me well, ladies, this will be one." He picked up his glass again and took a sip. "Just you wait and see."

Annie sat on a thick Chinese wool rug woven in shades of blue, cream, and rose in front of the small brick fireplace in her room. A quilt was tossed casually across her legs as she leaned back against the small tufted velvet chair. A wooden tray on the floor beside her contained a bowl of soup, a glass of milk, and two thick slices of buttered soda bread.

The wind howled outside her door, vanguard to the approaching rain. It rattled the leaded glass. Splinters of lightning illuminated the sky, visible through the sheer white lace curtains.

The weather complemented Annie's mood.

The fire crackled and burned brightly as she stared into the orange depths of the flames. She couldn't get Tony Chambers out of her mind. The look on his face as she'd ridden up—the chilly scorn in his oh-so-patrician voice when he pronounced the word "lover." The term was like a barbed dart aimed straight for her heart. Or like the precise slash of a stockman's whip. Then, the way he'd ridden into the homestead, proud-as-you-please, as if he couldn't see her; his variation of what she knew the English called the "cut direct."

That had hurt most of all.

Arrogant, pompous ass, Annie thought, tearing off a piece of bread with a savage snap of her teeth, chewing angrily.

Why had Jim insisted that Tony had been worried about her when all indications pointed otherwise?

Annie lifted the bowl closer, spooned out a measure of the thick soup, and swallowed it.

An imp of a smile crossed her lips. She wondered if the haughty Englishman was sitting all alone in the dining room, missing her? Was he angry at being left to his own devices this evening? Was he confused, perhaps? Or would he merely ignore her non-appearance in a very phlegmatic English way?

It would serve him right if he was upset, she thought with a touch of tartness. Treating her like a recalcitrant schoolgirl who needed to be lectured on what was right and wrong; or worse yet, insinuating by look and word that she was a beneath-contempt slattern.

"Annie, darling," her mother had been fond of saying, "keep that temper of yours under control. Don't allow it to make you a prisoner of actions that you will regret later."

Annie wondered if her even-tempered mama would know what to make of someone like Tony Chambers? Her father, who taught the classics as well as Latin, would have chided her with a gentle rejoinder, "*Damnant quod non intelligunt.*" They condemn what they do not understand. Be fair, he'd always warned. Never make a hasty decision if it can be helped.

Oh, Papa, Annie thought as she put the bowl down, the contents half gone, would that you were here to counsel me now. You and Mama both.

Tears formed in Annie's eyes. She sorely missed her

family; missed having the chance for Fallon to get to know her grandparents, along with her assorted aunts and uncles, cousins and what-have-you.

But that had been the heavy price of exile—had she remained in Philadelphia, Annie would have risked bringing shame to all of her family by bearing her child out of wedlock. No hastily pretended, conveniently dead, husband could have been procured for her there for people to readily accept. Like the fictional Hester Prynne, she would have been branded a fallen woman, condemned and scorned for her sin. Certainly not a fit individual to teach other women's children. Rather than a visibly stitched scarlet **A** to be worn on her chest, Annie's mark would be an unseen but still understood **W**. *Whore.* Her daughter would have carried an invisible brand as well—**B** for bastard. All because Annie possessed neither a band of gold for her finger, nor a man's name. That she'd been deceived and lied to, her innocence robbed from her by skillful trickery, mattered little, except to her family. To the outside world, she was considered damaged goods, beyond the pale of decent society.

Sometimes, more so since Cedric's death, Annie felt so alone—and in need of comfort. Even if it were only a smidgen of that precious commodity, it would have been welcome.

There was a knock on her bedroom door, disturbing her chain of thoughts. Thinking it was Mary come to check up on her, Annie wiped away the trace of tears from her eyes. "Come in," she called out, looking up at the door to the tall figure that loomed there, half in shadow.

"Are you ill, Mrs. Ross, or merely sulking?"

As soon as the words left his mouth, Tony regretted

them. As he stepped closer, he could see that Annie had been crying; her gray eyes glistened with tears. Why the bloody hell had she been weeping? Surely not over this afternoon's contretemps?

"Neither, Mr. Chambers," Annie replied to his question. "I am simply tired and desirous of some rest, and," she added, hoping that he would take the hint and leave her alone, "time to myself, thank you."

Her unexpected position, sitting on the floor, surprised him in its childlike simplicity. Annie's legs were tucked to one side, a quilt draped over them. She was dressed for bed, her hair unbound; from what he could see in the light of the single lamp and the glow of the fire, it was damp, tendrils curling about her features. Her strong face looked so much like a freshly scrubbed schoolgirl's; it was somehow hard to believe that she'd borne a child. Her mouth, he noted, looked much too soft and inviting.

Tony ventured further inside the room, his gaze quickly assessing the femininity of the decor. It was soft, comforting, warm. The bed, big enough for two, was turned down; an invitation, he fancied, to take solace there. The pillowcases were edged with lace, as was the pristine white sheet that would cover her body. He could almost feel it sliding against his own naked skin.

Tony came closer.

No male, including Cedric, had ever crossed the threshold of her bedroom. Now Tony was here, in her room. Making it seem smaller by the mere fact of his being. His presence should have been a violation of her privacy. And yet somehow it was more like an affirmation, but of what she couldn't be sure.

Annie scrambled to her feet, dragging the quilt with

her, holding it against her body like a shield. She felt vulnerable—even more so than the other time he'd seen her dressed so casually. Then, anger had fueled her and she had sought him out, regardless. She'd also, she recalled, had on a robe and slippers. Tonight, her feet were bare, her skin covered only by a soft, well-worn nightgown of creamy-hued flannel.

Tony slowly reached out his right hand and softly touched Annie's cheek.

Annie stood still, as if frozen to the spot, not knowing what she ought to do, or how she ought to react, her experience almost negligible.

He stared down at her, locking on her eyes, huge with wariness. Tony's hand curled tightly as he brought it back to his side.

"As you wish, madame," he said so low that Annie had to strain to hear. Turning on his heel, he walked out, shutting the door behind him with a click.

Annie sank into her chair as if the wind had been knocked out of her, her eyes on the closed door.

Why? she asked herself—why had she felt, in that single moment, more intimate with Tony Chambers than she ever had with the man who'd fathered her child?

Tony forgot about eating at that moment, heading for an avenue of escape from walls that seemed too close, too confining.

Opening a door, he moved outside to the veranda, feeling the sharp slap of the wind. Rain began to pelt the roof as he lowered himself into a chair. Chances were he was going to get very wet and he bloody well didn't care.

Tony pulled out his silver cigar case and match

holder from his inside coat pocket. He cupped his hands and lit a slim cheroot, drawing in the flavor of the premium tobacco.

By all that was holy, he wanted her.

Wanted her desperately.

Wanted to take her and make her forget anyone that had come before. Wanted to make himself forget too that he was not the first.

He watched as lightning tore through the night, providing a celestial light show, listened to the ominous rumblings of thunder. He gazed at the towering Alpines in the distance.

What had brought her to tears?

The question plagued him. He wouldn't have thought her capable of crying for no apparent reason. She wasn't, he'd decided, the clingy, weepy sort of female who used tears as either weapons or leverage. He could have easily laid odds on that at his London club without a second thought.

And what of the sadness he'd seen in her gray eyes? From where, or what, did that stem?

Tony took another long draw on the cigar, a curl of smoke leaving his mouth.

What puzzled him was his almost overriding desire to take Annie Ross into his arms and simply hold her, to offer her what comfort he could, to be the strong shoulder she could lean on, much as he had for his cousin Georgie after her recent traumatic ordeal.

"Sir," a male voice cut through the storm-swept night. "Can I interest you in coming inside and having a proper meal before you catch your death of cold?" Alfred asked. He'd assured the two sisters a short while ago that he would see to Mr. Chambers himself so that they could seek their beds without waiting any longer.

Alfred had waited patiently for Tony's return, and when it looked as though he wasn't coming back to the dining room, Alfred got up and went in search of him. Concern for his employer weighed heavily on his mind.

This was surely the last place Alfred would have suspected to find Tony. In the middle of a damnable storm that was sending chills up his own spine, his employer was sitting there as calm as you please, smoking as if nothing untoward was about.

Alfred shook his head in amazement. He could see that the master was in a particular stew about something.

Or *someone*.

Annie Ross, Alfred decided, was the answer.

Tony stood up and pitched the stub of his cigar into a puddle. "I do think I could use a spot of brandy and perhaps a bite to eat, Alfred. Just allow me to change into something a little less sodden." Tony's elegant jacket and trousers were wet from the wind-driven rain.

"Take as long as you need, sir," Alfred replied in a smooth, understanding tone. "I'll see to your repast. Would you like it in your room?"

"No," Tony said matter-of-factly. "I shall have it in the kitchen, actually." He smiled. "Remind me, Alfred, that a raise in your salary is needed, as you seem to be taking on more duties than we'd once discussed in terms of your employment."

Alfred blinked in surprise, both at his employer's choice of where to eat, and at the promise of more money. "As you wish, sir."

*   *   *

Annie hadn't moved from her seat for several minutes after Tony left her bedroom. She'd been thrown into confusion yet again by his actions. When he'd entered, he'd been annoyed. She could tell that from the way he'd spoken to her. Then she could see a change washing over him as he'd come closer to her. It was written in his eyes. Those sharp, sage green eyes that locked onto hers with an eerie connection.

And then he'd touched her.

She ran her own hand over the same spot that he had. His fingers had been so gentle, almost reverent. She could still feel the warmth of his unexpected, tender touch moments later. Flesh against flesh, slow and sure. Tingling. It had raised a new level of awareness between them.

And then he'd left her abruptly, with the oddest expression on his face before he'd turned away from her.

Annie rose, tossing the quilt to the chair behind her. She knelt down and picked up the half-empty soup bowl, placed it on the tray, along with the lukewarm glass of milk and small plate of leftover bread.

Her appetite had disappeared, chased away by the uncertain feelings that had come upon her so suddenly.

Annie stared into the heart of the fire, fascinated by the colorful dance of flames. His touch had been warm, also.

But like fire itself, she didn't doubt that it could prove just as hot.

Rising, Annie straightened her spine, pulled on her robe, and headed for the kitchen, making her way silently on bare feet and without benefit of illumination.

She was surprised to see light spilling into the hall

from beneath the kitchen door. Assuming that it was probably Mary and Alice, she entered the room without hesitation.

"Good evening, ma'am," Alfred said politely.

Annie returned the valet's greeting, and as she did, noticed there was someone else at the table, casually eating his meal.

Her full glance immediately went to Tony Chambers in his relaxed manner. Gone was the arrogant lord-of-the-manor look he could affect with such ease. Here was a man devoid of artifice, resembling, for once, the young man that he actually was. It was partially because he'd changed clothes, she thought. He had on a long, dark green silk robe fastened over a partially unbuttoned white shirt. Gone was the formal silver waistcoat he'd worn earlier.

"May I take that for you?" Alfred offered.

Annie handed him the tray, reluctantly tearing her eyes from Tony. "Thank you," she murmured, deciding that it would be wise for her to leave.

"Will you join me?" Tony asked as Alfred whisked the tray away, keeping discreetly in the background.

She saw the cut-glass decanter in front of Tony. "You're having brandy?"

Tony nodded. "Quite a good bottle, I must say. Care for a glass? 'Tis a wicked night and this might ease your . . . sleep."

Annie stood there for a moment, thinking over the offer. "I suppose that a small glass won't be amiss."

Good God, she wondered, what had made her agree when she'd been determined to go?

"Alfred, if you wouldn't mind, a snifter for Mrs. Ross," Tony requested in a soft voice.

"Certainly, sir," the valet replied approvingly. "I'll be

back in a moment." He made his way through the door and returned less than two minutes later with another glass, which he handed to Tony. "Will that be all, sir?"

Tony nodded.

"Very good, sir," Alfred replied. Before taking his leave of the couple, Alfred paused and spoke to Annie. "A pleasant good night, ma'am."

"You don't have to leave on my account," she insisted, wondering again why she'd agreed to stay. With Alfred as a buffer between them, it hadn't seemed a bad idea. Now, however, with the valet's imminent departure, it seemed ludicrous. Just as unwise as sticking one's hand too close to the flames.

"I'm not, ma'am," Alfred assured her, faking a yawn to add an appearance of truth to his statement. These two, he thought, were like magnets, each pulling toward the other, no matter what, or who, stood in their way. He'd seen it as soon as Annie Ross had entered the room, watched awareness of her flood into his employer as quickly as one of the bolts of lightning had torn through the sky.

"Good night, Alfred," Tony said, pouring a tiny amount of amber liquid into the snifter for Annie, then handing it to her as his valet left them alone.

"What shall we drink to?" he asked.

Annie thought it over for a moment. "How about to the future?" She'd had enough heartache tonight dwelling on the past, she didn't want to waste any more time on it.

"To the future, then," he said, tapping his glass against hers in salute.

Tony watched her swallow the drink. What would her skin taste like, he wondered? Sweet, to be sure. Annie possessed the type of neck that would do justice

141

to one of the Chamberses' family heirlooms: the pearl, diamond, and ruby choker presented as a wedding gift to one of his ancestors by Mad King George himself. With her long hair dressed high on her head, her long, slender throat exposed, she would dazzle anyone, anywhere.

Good God! he thought angrily. What was he doing thinking about dressing her in any of his ancestral jewels? They were reserved for the properly wedded brides of the family, not the suspected former mistresses.

"We will be having company for dinner this coming Sunday night," Annie informed him, her voice a whisper in the dimly lit room.

"Who?" Tony asked, though he had a feeling he knew the identity of the guest.

Annie wet her lips with a flick of her tongue. "Our neighbor, Patrick O'Donnell." She waited for Tony's reaction.

"The man at whose station you were visiting today?"

"Yes."

Tony half closed his eyes. "Was he a guest in this house whilst my great-uncle lived?"

Annie put down her glass. "He was."

"Regularly?"

"At least once a month the last year of Cedric's life. They were good friends."

"How very charming," Tony stated in an outwardly casual manner, though inside he brooded with nagging questions.

"I don't know if *charming* quite describes it," Annie said. "But it was comfortable, yes. We all felt close, and he and Cedric played cards most times after dinner. They both loved poker."

"So, O'Donnell's a gambling man, is he?"

"No more than Cedric was, I'd say."

"Were large sums involved?"

Annie chuckled at the memories. "Shillings."

Tony tossed back the contents of his glass. "Shillings? You're certain?"

"I didn't observe every game they played," she answered, "but, yes, it was definitely for small amounts only. They both played for the game, not the money. The challenge of the cards, as Cedric once said." Annie cocked her head to one side. "Do you play also?"

Tony thought of the money he'd wagered over the years, vast sums he'd won and lost on a turn of the cards. "Occasionally," he admitted.

"Then perhaps you and Patrick might use a game to get to know each other better. He'd like that."

Tony arched a brow. "Would he?"

Annie realized that she was stretching the truth somewhat, but she deemed it necessary and for a good cause. "Why not?" she asked. "You're new to the district, and after all, Patrick's been a very good and trusted neighbor of this station for a very long time." She waited to see if Tony would challenge her claim.

He took a sip of his brandy. "Is Mr. O'Donnell married?"

"Patrick's unwed at present."

He could have guessed as much, Tony thought. "Is his a small property?"

Annie laughed.

Tony leaned closer to her. "What's so amusing?"

"The judgment of what constitutes small," Annie responded. "Here in this area, we live on what we think of as large stations. Much bigger, I'd wager, than some actual states back home in America," she pointed out, "or anyplace in your own country. In Victoria, though, size is relative to what part of Australia you live in. I've heard of stations to the north and west that would make this place seem like a child's dollhouse."

"Indeed?"

"Suffice to say, though, Patrick's station is as big, maybe bigger, than Camelot."

And it would be bigger still were O'Donnell to combine the two properties, Tony mused. By wedding himself to an heiress O'Donnell would increase his holdings, and all it would cost him would be a gold ring and spoken vows. A cheap price to pay for part of his share of Cedric Chambers's legacy.

Annie felt her eyelids grow heavy. "You'll have to excuse me," she said. "It's past my bedtime"—she yawned—"and I want to get started on something to-morrow."

"What?"

Annie stood up. She didn't want to confide in Tony about her attempt to write for publication in case the experiment failed miserably and she was left with egg on her face. "A personal project."

Tony sliced her a direct glance. "That sounds very mysterious."

"I didn't mean it to be," she countered, wondering what his face would feel like were she to caress it as he'd done hers.

"So, you won't tell?" Tony rose, picking up the lamp he'd used to light his way from his bedroom.

"I can't."

"Won't," he retorted.

"Have it your way, Mr. Chambers," Annie said softly, rising also.

If I did, Tony mused silently, then it would be here,

right now, you and I on this stone floor—and damn the consequences.

Tony led the way to her door, standing there until Annie turned the glass handle. He was within inches of her; all he had to do was bend his head and capture her brandy-flavored mouth.

Tony stepped back. "Sleep well," he said, his baritone husky with unfulfilled desire.

Annie closed the door, her room in almost total darkness save for the light of the fire behind the wire screen. Trembling, she removed her robe and hurried to her bed, pulling the sheet and blankets up over her, snuggling deeper into the warmth and comfort to be found there, the sound of "Sleep well" echoing in her ears.

Tony shut his own bedroom door and extinguished the lamp.

Shucking his robe, he quickly removed the rest of his clothes, not caring that they landed haphazardly in the direction of the wingchair.

Naked, he slipped between the cool sheets of his solitary bed, his last thoughts before sleeping of Annie Ross's captivating face by lamplight.

Chapter Ten

Uneasy tension permeated the days that followed until Sunday.

After two days of chill and rain, the sun rose brightly Sunday morning and promised some measure of relief. The day was still brisk, but Annie didn't care. Just getting out of the house, if only for a little while, was heavenly.

She walked to the rose arbor, then down the brick path past the hedges and flowering shrubs that lined one side of the property. Annie walked slowly through the garden, Fallon by her side. She wanted to gather some fresh blooms and greenery for the table, hoping to add a festive touch to what promised to be an otherwise strained meal.

She carried a sharp pair of scissors in her wide, flat wicker basket, which already contained some clippings of holly and ivy.

"How about this, Mama?" called Fallon, investigating a bright yellow flower native to Australia, the Cootamundra wattle. The little girl stroked the fluffy balls of color with her fingertips. "Uncle Patrick would like this."

"I think that Uncle Patrick isn't the only one," Annie said with a smile in Fallon's direction, whipping out her scissors and making quick work of her task. She piled some of the cut flowers into her daughter's matching, albeit smaller, basket.

"Mr. Tony would like them too," Fallon insisted.

"I'm not so sure about that, sweetheart," Annie responded. Somehow she doubted that Tony Chambers would count the unsophisticated flower as one of his favorites. Annie herself admitted to liking the plant, but it couldn't compare to her deep fondness for roses. All kinds. All colors.

She imagined that Tony gave roses to his ladies. Or maybe camellias. He probably drenched his mistresses with whatever flower they favored. Dozens and dozens until the lady melted in gratitude.

"Mama, is something wrong?" Fallon asked, her head cocked to one side.

"Just daydreaming, nothing more," she explained, shaking her head slightly to clear the image of a room filled with flowers, red roses and baby's breath, and of a tall man with light brown hair, a wicked smile on his beautiful lips.

Chiding herself for such foolishness, Annie added a few more items from the assorted flowering shrubbery, including some violets, daphne, viburnum, and white japonica until their baskets were filled almost to overflowing. "This should give our house a lovely smell and a delightful look," she told her daughter, who skipped a few paces ahead on the brick walkway, Lady at her side.

Annie watched Fallon at play with the dog as she took a seat on a parsons bench, her teeming basket alongside her.

She turned her head and looked out over the land, saw the scattered olive and cypress trees upon a nearby hill. They would look as wonderful with a light dusting of snow as they did in full bloom in spring.

From the capacious pocket of her apron, Annie pulled out a few of the roasted almonds that Mary had been baking this morning. They were coated with sugar, and tasted divine. The harvest had been especially good this year in the neighboring state of South Australia, and Annie loved adding the flavorful nut to many of her winter dishes.

Even Tony had helped himself to a handful when he came into the kitchen earlier that morning requesting that Mary brew him another pot of tea.

Instead of returning to the station's office, he'd lingered, watching Annie through narrowed lids as she sat at the kitchen table, going over the menu for dinner. She'd caught his hooded eyes on her when she looked up. That acute glance of his sent a flash of heat through her body, warming the pit of her stomach.

Disconcerted, she'd been forced to drop her gaze from his.

Moments later, their hands had accidentally touched over the almonds as both had reached for a helping.

Startled by the sparks that tinged her fingertips, Annie had withdrawn her hand immediately. She waited for Tony to take another helping before she risked reaching her hand out again.

It was the slight curve to his full, bow-shaped lips as he picked up the mahogany tea tray that made Annie want to remove that glimmer of a smile with a well-placed slap of her palm. Odious pig, she'd thought. How dare he gloat at her discomfiture?

A male voice uttering a muffled curse brought Annie back to reality. One of the hands, carrying an armful of wood for both the homestead's stove and the fireplaces, had stumbled. He was bending down to retrieve the logs that had fallen when he spied Annie. He nodded his head. "G'day, and I'll be beggin' your pardon, Mrs. Ross."

She smiled her acceptance of his apology and of his friendly greeting, warmed by the goodwill the men of the station continued to show to her. It was another measure of her desire to hold onto the life she had here.

Annie removed from the other pocket of her apron a small notebook, covered in leather. A tiny pencil was contained in a slip hole on the inside. She flipped open the pages, some filled with writing, others with minute drawings. She proceeded to jot down her thoughts about the winter scene as she cast an occasional glance in Fallon's direction to see that all was well with her daughter. In at least one way, these past few days had been a boon to Annie. Confined to the house by the inclement weather, she had taken the time to begin some of her stories. Vignettes of life on the station, of the people who toiled day in and day out, retellings of the stories that she'd heard told, all made their way into her notebook, or onto the typed page. She'd carefully removed the typewriter from Cedric's office and placed it in her bedroom, hidden beneath her bed, practicing upon it so that she could communicate her thoughts with a modicum of speed. Rather than waste the precious supply of quality paper that Cedric had purchased along with the machine, Annie made use of sheets of plain brown wrapping paper.

Slowly, Annie was getting the hang of the instrument. Only at odd times would her concentration quit her. It was at these unsettling moments when images of the man who shared her house intruded that Annie felt unnerved. Since that night in the kitchen, they'd been unfailingly civil to one another, polite and correct.

But there was an undercurrent of something else running through their lives that she couldn't quite name. She only knew that it existed, keeping her slightly off balance where Tony Chambers was concerned.

Fallon's squeals of excited laughter, along with Lady's bark, caused Annie to raise her head in their direction. She saw her daughter jumping up and clapping her hands as Lady ran to fetch the red rubber ball that had been tossed in the air.

Tony Chambers stood nearby. What was he doing playing catch with her child?

Annie quickly put down her writing materials. Rising from her seat, she went to investigate what was happening.

Tony tossed the ball in the dog's direction once more, enjoying the sound of the little girl's laughter as she clapped her gloved hands in delight at the antics of the animal. He'd be damned if this child wasn't slowly working her way under his skin. There were even times when he thought of her completely as Annie Ross's child alone. Other moments, like now, he wondered who'd fathered the girl. Could it have been, as he suspected, his great-uncle? Was this imp somehow part of his own family, linked to him by blood?

He saw nothing of Cedric in the child. But then, that wasn't always a barometer of the truth. He and his older brother were nothing alike, either in temperament or in looks.

The dog's wet nose pressed into Tony's hand as the

animal deposited her toy, eager for another toss of the ball. He bent down and retrieved the ball, tossing it further this time, and the dog took off, Fallon following, cheering her on.

He observed the antics of dog and girl until he heard the soft footfalls along the walkway. Looking up from his crouched position, Tony watched Annie approach. Coming to his full height slowly, he let his gaze roam over her features, from the top of her head, covered by the hood of her dark blue wool cloak, to the soles of her booted feet. She looked so prim and proper, her gloves hiding her hands, the cloak masking her seductive shape from his view. All he could recall was how she'd looked when he'd entered her bedroom that night. Soft. Sweet. Unguarded. Fresh as a newly budded rose.

And like any good rose, he understood that she had thorns as well. Thorns that poked, prodded, and pricked, protecting the flower.

Luckily for him, he'd never worried overmuch about obstacles in the past, and he wasn't about to start now.

"Good day," he said politely.

Annie returned his formality. "Good day to you as well, Mr. Chambers."

Ah, he thought, we are back to that again, are we?

"I hope Fallon isn't bothering you?"

Tony cast a quick glance in the girl's direction. She and the dog were happily playing off by themselves some yards away. "Nonsense," he said, giving Annie an appraising look. "I'm enjoying it. It takes me back to when I was a child and my older brother and I played on the grounds of the country house with our own dogs."

Annie considered his words, the pictures they

evoked of a carefree childhood gamboling amidst the charms of an English countryside. Happy. Content. Without a care in the world. Exactly what she wanted for her own child. Yet, before her stood the man who had the power to eradicate her vision should he ever discover the extent of the truth she kept from him.

"Where was that?"

"Did Cedric never tell you what part of England he was originally from?"

"Cedric spoke little of his family," Annie responded, "except for you. He held you in very high regard for some reason." After she uttered the words, Annie realized how they must have sounded. "I'm sorry, I didn't mean that as a criticism."

"None taken, my dear," Tony assured her. "And my family is from Dorset."

"It's just that Cedric didn't dwell on people so much as places he'd been, things he'd seen. I do know that he kept up with his family by means of letters from a Mr. Whiteside in London."

"Jonas Whiteside?"

"I believe that was his name, yes."

"He's one of my godfathers," Tony said, surprise in his voice at the unexpected piece of information. "He and Cedric were quite good friends."

"Mr. Whiteside sent regular letters to Cedric."

"Fancy that," Tony mused aloud. "The old boy did keep tabs on us."

"He loved you like a son, that much I know for certain," Annie declared. "Whenever Mr. Whiteside wrote about you, he would read that portion of the letter aloud."

"Awfully decent of you to share that with me," Tony stated, drawing closer to her.

Annie's tongue slipped out to wet her lips. The action froze Tony's gaze on the curves of her mouth, on the delicate natural color there. His immediate physical response was purely masculine, brought on by the nearness of her. After all, she was a damned fine looking woman. He couldn't dispute that very evident fact, no matter what.

"It's the truth," she responded.

His voice low and soft, Tony asked, "Are you a believer in the truth, *Mrs.* Ross?"

Nervously, Annie wet her lips again before answering, "I try to be."

"Very commendable," Tony stated, his face wearing a slightly questioning look.

"Though I've often thought," she ventured, "depending on circumstances, that truth itself has many faces."

"How so?" he asked, intrigued.

"Apparent truth is one aspect," Annie said, removing her eyes from his face, giving herself time to proceed. "The truth that one believes one sees." She paused again, sweeping one of her gloved hands along the bark of a bare birch tree. She turned and faced him once more. "Then there is instinctual truth, that which we feel but cannot rationally explain." Like, Annie thought with anxious concern, why she was so drawn to this man, above and beyond anyone she'd ever known. "Lastly," she pointed out, "there is actual truth, that which simply is."

"What an interesting theory," Tony ventured, intrigued by her words in spite of himself. He couldn't believe that he was actually having this conversation: Here, in the midst of a winter garden, he and a beautiful woman, who increasingly stirred his physical passions, were engaged in a philosophical discussion on the esoteric topic of what was truth. Staggering, he mused, his eyes taking in every small movement of her body. He couldn't imagine that such a talk would ever have happened in England, leastways not amongst the majority of the women he knew, especially when there were other, more pleasant ways to pass the time. Impossible.

Yet here he was, doing exactly that with this American emigré.

Tony wondered if he would ever discover what was the real truth behind Annie Ross. Or was that truth buried deeply under layers upon layers of lies and half-truths?

"If you'll excuse me," Annie said as she took a step back, needing to put some space between them, "I should be getting my cuttings inside." She turned in her daughter's direction. "Fallon," she called. "Time to come along."

"Will you be using any for the table tonight?" He reached out his hand and gently touched her arm.

"I thought something fresh would be nice," she answered, intensely aware of his hand on her arm. His touch was light, yet strong. "Winter doesn't give one as much to work with, so finding just the right mixture can make all the difference."

"I'm certain that you will succeed admirably," he quickly assured her, reluctantly removing his hand. Since his arrival, Tony had taken note of the way Annie arranged flowers and other materials within the homestead. Bows of ivy were draped along a mantel. Wreaths of holly wound around a silver candlestick. Crushed rose petals placed in a simmering pot filled the air with scent. Bunches of dried flowers filled silver and glass vases. They were touches his London home had been woefully empty of, only he hadn't realized it until recently.

"Can we play again sometime?" Fallon begged Tony, holding the rubber ball in her mittened hands.

"Of course we can," Tony assured the little girl, bending down once more so that he'd be easier for her to talk to. "I'd like that." Funny thing was, what he said was true. He had enjoyed spending time with the child. Through her eyes, he'd recaptured some fond memories of his own childhood.

"So would me and Lady," the child insisted, giving him a beaming smile.

"Then it's settled." Tony reached out to stroke Fallon's long hair.

"Promise?" Fallon asked, her blue eyes wide and serious.

"Cross my heart," he responded solemnly.

"Hope to die?" the child prodded.

"Fallon!" Annie protested.

Tony winked conspiratorially at the blond child. "Hope to die," he repeated. He glanced up at Annie. "Your daughter drives a very hard bargain."

"Mama told me that a promise made ought to be a promise kept," the child stated candidly.

"And your mama's right," Tony remarked as he rose, watching as Fallon slipped her hand into her mother's. He'd promised himself that he would find out everything there was to know about Annie Ross, and he wasn't going to abandon that idea until he was satisfied. Now, it was more important than ever. Especially as another piece of the puzzle was coming to dinner this evening. Tony fully intended to be prepared.

His voice when he spoke was low, pitched seduc-

Gail Link

tively to Annie's ears, sounding itself like a promise. "Until later, then."

As she turned and walked away, Annie had the strangest sensation that she could feel the direct impact of Tony's eyes on her back, as if he'd easily penetrated the cloak and clothes she wore. It was an odd, tingling feeling that persisted until she reached the door to the kitchen.

Inside the house, Annie peeled off her gloves and cloak, Fallon's as well, intending to lay them aside for the moment when Alice came in and took them from her.

"I'll see to these for you, Mrs. Ross," the other woman offered. "The silver's been polished and the table set exactly how you requested," she reported in a cheery tone. "I brought out the one bowl you asked for and put it there on the sideboard, ma'am."

Annie saw that the bowl was half filled with water as she'd instructed. "This'll do," she stated as she put some of the cuttings from her basket and Fallon's inside the bowl, mixing colors and textures, her daughter helping her.

Finally, Annie stood back and smiled. "Yes, this will do rather nicely indeed," she proclaimed. "What do you think?" she asked Alice.

"Fair dinkum, I'd say, ma'am."

Fallon nodded. "That's what I'd say too, Mama."

Annie hugged the little girl as she laughed. "Oh, you would, would you? What say that you do your mama a big favor now and go and take a nap?" she asked. "That way when Uncle Patrick comes, you can spend some time with him."

Fallon's blue eyes grew huge. "Can he tell me a story about the wee folk?"

"If you ask him nicely, then yes," Annie answered, "I think he'd be happy to tell you about the fairy folk, sweetheart."

"Goody." The child skipped to the door, her dog trailing behind her.

"Now," Annie said, addressing the other woman, "if you wouldn't mind putting that back on the dining-room table, I shall see to the arrangements for the parlor." Annie took an appreciative sniff of the air coming from the direction of the large iron stove with its double ovens before she quit the room. "If I stay here a moment longer I'll be tempted to sample whatever's been baking," she admitted, snatching a handful of toasted almonds from the bowl, "and that'll do me no good whatsoever."

An hour later, Tony was languidly soaking in a hot bath, a glass of tawny port in one hand. The soft glow of a fire warmed the bathroom with light and heat.

Tony had chuckled when he'd first seen the bathtub. It was huge, big enough, should the need arise, for two. A sybarite's dream come true. His great-uncle must have loved the experience of bathing in such luxury.

Another form rapidly replaced the fleeting image of his kin. Had *she* shared this bath with Cedric?

He glanced down at the wide stone tiles that made up the floor. Had water sloshed noisily over the smooth oak rim of the tub? Had it soaked the floor completely?

Tony closed his eyes, his left hand gripping the oak lip as a picture slowly came to life in his mind. He could see the action as if it were unfolding just then.

It was a day like today, with a chill in the air. The

fire was burning brightly. He could smell her perfume as she entered the room and stepped nearer to the tub. Instead of port, he was drinking champagne, a bottle nestled in a silver bucket filled with ice on a round table just inches from the warm bathwater. Another crystal glass was close at hand, waiting for her. She bent down to retrieve it, tasting the bubbly liquid, letting it slide down her slender throat, a captivating smile on her face.

Done, she put the glass back on the table, then unloosened the tie to her robe, pulling it off. The cord floated to the floor, followed quickly by the deep blue wool that had concealed her body.

He gasped at the sheer perfection of her shape. His own responded instantly.

Reaching up, she gave a tug on the ribbon that held her long hair in place. She gave her head a slight shake, the movement causing her thick waves to tumble about her body, obscuring some of her flesh from his view.

"Come here," he whispered, his voice husky with rising need.

She did so, leaning over him to lightly touch her lips to his broad temple, feathering her fingers through his damp hair.

He snaked one arm out and grabbed her, gently tugging her into the water. Water splashed as he lifted her body, adjusting it over his own, her thighs wrapping around his slim hips.

Gasping, she took a deep breath, bracing herself with her palms on the rim of the tub as she moved to the rhythm their bodies created, her face flushed, head thrown back, her hair trailing in the water.

He reached out, his left hand cupping the weight of

one of her breasts, teasing the nipple into a tight bud.

She returned the gesture, doing the same to him, her right hand sliding through the soft whorls of hair on his chest.

Water sluiced over the sides of the tub, created by the whirlpool of desire unleashed inside the bath, splashing the terra-cotta tiles below with the rapidly cooling soapy liquid.

Tony's eyes snapped open. He could feel the definite heavy ache in his flesh. His graphic imagination had ignited the stirring reality.

Exhaling deeply, he tried to calm his racing blood, forcing an iron control over the situation.

Damn!

What the bloody hell was going on?

He stepped from the tub; water dripped from his lean body onto the soft white lambskin rug. Picking up the fleecy towel, Tony proceeded to dry his skin, all the while her image inside his head, a sensual specter he couldn't seem to shake loose.

He dropped the damp towel to the floor, tunneling his hands through his hair, pushing it back away from his face.

The door opened and Alfred walked in. "Your robe, sir."

"Thank you, Alfred." Tony slipped on the garment, the silk clinging to his body, caressing his skin softly, like the light touch of a woman's hand.

"I think that you'll agree with my choice for your wardrobe tonight, sir. Simple, yet elegant. Suitable for the occasion."

Tony shot his valet a questioning glance. "Which is?"

"Why, meeting one of the notable locals. Judging

159

the competition, as it were."

"Competition?"

"Excuse me, sir," Alfred offered in a seemingly modest manner. "That might be too strong a word. Perhaps I should have said one of the minor players in this antipodal opus."

Tony laughed softly at Alfred's comment. "It remains to be seen what Mr. Patrick O'Donnell's role is in this drama. But," he promised, calmly walking through to his bedroom, "I fully intend to know by this evening's end one way or the other. Count on that."

Chapter Eleven

"G'day, Annie," Patrick said, leaning over to give her a soft kiss on the cheek. "You're looking lovely, me darlin', as always."

"God love you for that silver tongue, Patrick O'Donnell," Annie replied, greeting him with a warm smile and a welcome embrace. She didn't care that Tony was standing right beside her, watching the proceedings with his sharp eyes. Let him make of it what he will, she'd decided, for she knew that he would anyway. Patrick was her friend, and she couldn't pretend otherwise, even if it were to put Tony Chambers's aristocratic nose out of kilter.

"Here's a little something I saw in a shop whilst I was in town the other day." Patrick removed a small box from the pocket of his dark brown oilskin drover coat and handed it to her. "I immediately thought of you."

Annie opened the white velvet box and sighed with delight. Inside was a pair of earrings. Opals set in gold.

"Oh, Patrick," Annie sighed, "they're exquisite."

"And one of a kind, the shop owner informed me. They were cut from one blue-green stone." Patrick grinned. "I know it's a trifle early for your birthday, but I couldn't resist."

She reached out and squeezed his hand. "I shall treasure them always."

"So long as they make you happy, me darlin', that's what counts most," Patrick assured her.

Aware that she still hadn't introduced the men to one another, Annie snapped the lid on the box and turned to Tony.

"Mr. Chambers, may I present Patrick O'Donnell of Broken Hill station," she said agreeably. "Patrick, this is Cedric's grandnephew, and part-owner of Camelot, Mr. Anthony Chambers of London."

Patrick held out his broad, square hand, which Tony took.

"How do you do?" Tony inquired more politely than he was feeling at the moment. Inwardly, he bristled at the audacity of the man in giving Annie so personal a gift. Quite bad form, Tony thought.

"I do pretty bloody well, bucko," Patrick answered. "How about yourself?"

Annie bit back the laughter that threatened to erupt from her throat at Patrick's quick rejoinder.

Tony was silent for a moment, considering the man before him. O'Donnell was a youth, and looked it. Tony willingly conceded that the boyish face could possibly win the favor of certain women. The blue eyes were sharp, missing, he suspected, nothing. A good five to six inches shorter than Tony himself, O'Donnell was hardly the dashing seducer he'd pictured. Yet there was something between the other man and Annie Ross that rankled him. Some kind of bond. Just what, he wasn't quite certain. But he would find out. And soon.

"I suspect that I could say the same, if I were of a mind to," Tony quipped.

162

Annie stepped between the two men. "We should go inside," she said. They'd been standing on the veranda, the front doors to the house ajar behind them. Even though the sun was out, the wind was cold.

She led them into the parlor, where a cheerful fire blazed. "Would either of you care for a drink?" she offered.

"I'll take a whiskey, Annie girl," Patrick said as he removed his long coat and wool hat, handing them to Alfred, who stood at the ready.

As the parlor door slid closed behind Alfred, Patrick asked, "Who's he?"

"My valet," Tony answered.

Patrick accepted the glass of neat whiskey from Annie's hand. "A valet," he mused, making the word sound just slightly questionable. He shot a glance in Annie's direction. "Perhaps I should get me one of them too," he remarked casually, as if discussing a pet.

Tony poured a glass of champagne for himself and Annie. "Gentlemen consider it a necessity."

"The implication being that a man such as myself wouldn't?" Patrick demanded.

"Terribly sorry, old man, if you took my comment in the wrong manner," Tony said in a silky, disingenuous voice.

A beseeching look from Annie halted Patrick's verbal rebuttal. Instead, he tossed down the contents of his glass. "My mistake."

Annie breathed a sigh of relief. There was a tense feel to the air in the room, as if she were witnessing two brumby stallions defending their respective territory. That had never been the case when Cedric and Patrick were together; they'd gotten along famously.

"Champagne?" Tony offered.

163

"Swell's lush? No thanks, I'll stick to whiskey," Patrick replied. He saw Annie start to rise and he waved her back down. "No need to stand on ceremony on my account, darlin'," he said, stressing the last word as he crossed the room and picked up the decanter, refilling his short glass. "As you're well aware, I don't mind serving myself."

Tony's nostrils flared slightly. He assumed the slightly barbed words were meant for him.

"So," Patrick asked the other man, taking a seat on the settee next to Annie, "how long are you planning on staying here?"

"Past the required length of time that I'm obliged to stay here, I presume you're wanting to know?" Tony inquired, easing his tall frame into a wing chair opposite.

Patrick's thin lips curved into a smile.

"I hadn't really given it much thought," Tony remarked, taking a sip of the bubbly liquid.

"Now, that surprises me," Patrick responded. "Most Englishmen I've met can't wait to get back to England."

"Is that so?" Tony asked in a drawling tone.

Patrick readily answered, "Yes."

"I wonder why?" Tony mused, holding his glass of champagne before him as if he were interested in examining the contents.

"Lives to go back to, I would imagine," Patrick stated, his gaze still focused on the other man. "Aren't *you* anxious to resume your life there?"

"I'm in no particular hurry," Tony replied.

Patrick's mouth settled into a thin line. "You're not?"

"No," Tony repeated.

164

"Then you're quite different from the majority of your fellow Englishmen," Patrick insisted.

"So I was always led to believe," Tony asserted dryly.

With that remark, Annie chuckled, breaking the tension.

"My apologies for excluding you, my dear," Tony said, realizing that he and Patrick had done just that.

"Think nothing of it," Annie replied.

"Yes, Annie girl," Patrick interjected, "forgive me as well. If me mother was to hear my lack of manners, well, I'd be getting a tongue-lashing for sure."

"Followed by an even bigger warm embrace. I know that you're the darling of your family," Annie pointed out. "They would forgive you anything, especially your mother."

"Ah, so it is with mothers," Patrick stated.

At the quick flash of sadness that passed over Tony's face, Annie asked, "Don't you agree?"

"It's far too general a statement to give it my total approval," Tony commented. "I'm familiar with other scenarios." He thought of his cousin's mother, who'd willingly cut herself off from her own daughter because that child had chosen art as a profession, and who'd further compounded the distance from her child when she discovered the details of a shocking attack Georgie had suffered. Instead of offering comfort to Georgie, his aunt had rebuked her daughter, claiming that the bohemian life-style she'd chosen had precipitated the savage attack. Tony had personally declared his aunt a "cold bitch" to her face, shocking his family. He hadn't regretted his words then. He still didn't.

Compassion for Tony tugged at Annie's heart. How awful it must be to have experienced such an aberration, either directly or indirectly. That he had was evident in his eyes, if visible only for a second. There was a vulnerability there that she was amazed to see. Had they been alone, she might have probed for the cause, but as they weren't, Annie let it pass, wondering if there would come a chance at some other time.

Picking up her glass, she sipped slowly at the champagne, the taste of the liquid stirring up old memories of her own. It had been her first glass of champagne, with more to follow, that had given her the courage to act on her impressionable feelings all those years ago. It had proved false courage, but by then it was too late to turn back the clock.

Mentally snapping out of the past, Annie saw the door to the parlor open a crack, and a small face peered into the room. She put down her libation, smiling in her daughter's direction. "Come on in, sweetheart," she urged the child.

Fallon scampered into the room, heading straight for Patrick.

He stood up and swung Fallon into his arms for a hug and a kiss. "And how's me darlin' angel doing?" he asked teasingly, sitting back down with the child on his knee.

Fallon giggled. "I'm no angel, Uncle Patrick," the child insisted, enjoying the familiar game.

"By all the saints, Fallon Ross, are you calling your Uncle Patrick a liar?"

"Oh no," the little girl said with a smile.

"Then if you're not, what are you?"

Fallon giggled again. "An angel," she admitted with a grin.

"And don't you be forgettin' it," Patrick said with

mock severity. "All good angels get presents, you know."

"I've been real good," Fallon insisted, her eyes sparkling.

"Perhaps we'd best ask your mother about that." Both heads looked in Annie's direction.

"Tell him, Mama," her daughter pleaded.

Annie reached out and touched her child's knee. "She's been the best angel possible."

"You can ask Mr. Tony too," the child informed Patrick. "He'll tell you that I've been ever so good."

"Fallon," her mother admonished. "That's Mr. Chambers to you."

"No harm done," Tony acknowledged. "I told her to call me by my Christian name. And," he continued with a devastating smile, "I can vouch that she's been a perfect angel, ever so good." He repeated the phrase the child had used, giving Annie an idea where her daughter had picked it up.

Patrick smiled. "Then you deserve a present." He stood up and handed the child to Annie. "I'll be right back as soon as I find what your valet did with my coat."

Annie spoke. "It'll be in the hall, as usual."

Patrick nodded gratefully as he slipped out, returning moments later. He stood in the doorway. "Close your eyes," he instructed Fallon.

Fallon did as he bid and Patrick closed the distance between them.

"Hold out your hands," he directed.

Fallon eagerly complied, closing her fingers around the soft object.

"Now you can open them," Patrick said.

167

Fallon laughed in delight. "Look, Mama, my own lamb."

It was a baby jumbuck, skillfully sewn to resemble the real thing, surrounded by lambs' wool, the fleece soft and white, with a pretty pink ribbon around its neck.

Annie prompted, "What do you say?"

"I'll love her forever, Uncle Patrick," Fallon stated with the certainty of a child. "Thank you." Fallon threw her arms around the young man's neck and hugged him tight. "Mamma, can I play with it now?"

"Of course, sweetheart," Annie said, giving her daughter a kiss. "Run along and get ready for bed. I'll be there to tuck you in soon."

Fallon asked, "Will you tell me a story, Uncle Patrick, before you go?"

"I'll look in on you before I leave, darlin'," Patrick promised, "and if you're still awake, then I'll tell you a tale of the leprechaun and the kangaroo."

Fallon scampered off with her new toy, leaving the adults alone once again.

Annie glanced at the tall grandfather clock that stood against one wall of the parlor. "I think dinner will be ready for us, gentlemen," she stated, rising.

Two arms were extended for her to choose the one to escort her into the meal.

Annie stood there, surprised by the duplicate gestures. When she and Cedric had dined with Patrick, it was always Cedric who'd escorted her in. Tonight, she'd assumed that she would walk alone. Obviously, the men had other plans. She hesitated briefly, knowing that whomever she picked, the other would be mightily affronted.

It would serve them both right if she walked ahead

by herself as she'd intended.

Smiling, Annie held out both of her arms, inviting each man to take one.

"Very prudent, my dear," Tony whispered to her as he took her right arm in his left.

Patrick registered surprise as he watched Tony take what had been Cedric's seat at the table when they entered the dining room. Glaring slightly, he took his own regular seat opposite Annie, who looked exceptionally lovely with her long hair swept back by a sapphire velvet ribbon. She'd borne so much tragedy in her life—the death of her husband, the loss of her benefactor and friend. She shouldn't have to lose anything else.

And, by God, Patrick vowed silently, she won't have to.

Annie waved off the red wine Tony would have poured into the crystal goblet, preferring to keep a clear head. Instead, she picked up the other glass filled with water, sipping at the cold liquid, washing away, she hoped, the glow from the champagne.

Mary and Alice brought in the first course, a hearty winter soup, followed by two small baskets of warm bread, sliced thickly, and then the main course, the roast of lamb, served with a large bowl of glazed onions, currants and almonds mixed.

As they ate, Annie observed each man, reflecting on how different they were in looks, manner of dress, and comportment. Patrick was pure Australian: He was dressed in a plain white shirt, creamy-colored moleskin trousers with a wide braided brown leather belt. He wore polished knee-high brown boots and a plain brown wool jacket.

In contrast, Tony was pure English: His dinner out-

Gail Link

fit consisted of an elegantly styled coat of fine black wool, with matching trousers. His immaculate shirt was white, silk to be sure, and his cravat was burgundy. His waistcoat was burgundy also, a rich-textured moire. He was, without a doubt, the personification of sophistication. A man who knew who he was and what his place was in the world.

Annie much preferred the look he had worn several nights before, when she'd discovered him in the kitchen. Relaxed, his white shirt loose at the throat, approachable. A man she could be comfortable with. Conceivably, even become friends with.

But friendship meant trust.

She sliced a piece of the succulent lamb, bringing it to her mouth, chewing slowly. She trusted Patrick, yet she hadn't told him all there was to know about her. There never seemed to be an appropriate time to tell O'Donnell the reason for the lie about her "widow-hood." She believed that when she eventually explained it to him, Patrick would willingly accept her reasons for doing so. With Tony Chambers, Annie didn't have that basic element of trust or certainty. She feared that he might use the truth as a weapon against her.

Right now, that was a chance she couldn't take.

Annie tilted her head in Tony's direction and met his gaze.

Patrick observed the exchange of glances between the two, unsure of what it meant. A slight flush of color rose in Annie's cheeks, but with Tony's head turned away from him, Patrick couldn't see what kind of look the Englishman was giving her. It was obvious to him there was an undercurrent flowing between the two. Of what kind, he wasn't certain. He wished that

Mei were here. He was sure she'd know.

Tony shifted his focus to his left, fixing his gaze upon Patrick. "I've been told your station is rather large, Mr. O'Donnell," Tony said as he poured each of them another glass of the robust red wine. "Sheep, I believe?"

"Best wool in Australia," Patrick responded proudly, sampling another taste of the excellent vintage.

"Not to mention some of the best meat in Australia," Annie added warmly. "We're eating some of Patrick's lamb tonight."

"It's quite good," Tony agreed.

The bland statement pricked Patrick's pride. He retaliated. "Coming from such a small island as England, all this land must seem overwhelming to you, eh, Chambers?"

Tony inhaled sharply at the well-placed dig at his native land, his eyes narrowing slightly.

Annie shot Patrick a sharp look, trying to warn him away from pursuing this subject further.

"Having just come from America, I've obviously seen bigger," Tony quipped smoothly, smiling as he did so.

"But not better?" Patrick asked.

"That remains to be seen," Tony drawled, finishing the last morsel of meat on his plate, "though it may, of course, depend on one's standards of judgment."

Sensing disaster looming ahead if this wasn't nipped soon, Annie picked up the small silver bell near her right hand, her signal to Mary that they were done with this portion of the meal.

Mary and Alice entered unobtrusively and cleared away the remains. When Mary entered for a second time, she approached Annie. "Shall I serve the sweets now, Mrs. Ross?"

"Give us about twenty minutes," Annie instructed, her glance flicking quickly from one man to the other, "then bring them, along with coffee, into the parlor."

"As you wish, ma'am," Mary responded.

Annie pushed back her chair, rising; the men followed suit. "Patrick, I think that we should see to Fallon first, if you don't mind?"

"My pleasure, Annie girl," Patrick said, waiting for her to join him.

Annie addressed Tony. "If you will excuse us for a short while?"

Tony nodded agreeably.

"Would you be so kind as to wait for us in the parlor?" she asked him politely. "I promise that we won't be long."

"I'll hold you to your word," Tony responded.

As soon as they'd left the dining room, Annie demanded of Patrick, "Heaven help us, Patrick, just what where you trying to do in there?"

Patrick smiled audaciously. "Get a rise out of him, me darlin'."

Annie groaned softly. "Why?"

Patrick replied, "To see what this pommy prig's made of."

"Flesh and blood, like you and me," Annie responded.

"Do you really think so?" Patrick questioned, the look in his blue eyes telling her that he had his doubts on that score.

"Don't be silly, Patrick, of course I do."

"That's just it, me darlin'," he insisted, "this Englishman isn't like you or me. He's different. He'll always *be* different." Patrick paused and reached for her hands, taking them into his own. "Do you know why? Because he'll always think of himself as better than us."

"I might have agreed with you only a few weeks ago," Annie confided, gently removing her hands from his, "but I don't believe that's quite true now."

"Then you're being fooled, my girl," Patrick persisted. "His kind won't ever change. It's born and bred in him. Once a toff, always a toff."

"It was born and bred in Cedric, also," Annie pointed out as she moved toward her daughter's bedroom, Patrick at her side. "You were fond of him."

"Cedric Chambers was different."

"Because," Annie offered, "you saw him as a man, Patrick, not part of a larger nebulous"—she made a small movement with her hand—"enclave."

Patrick's voice was soft. "Is that how you see Tony Chambers, Annie, as a man?"

"Of course he's a man," she said, ignoring the deeper meaning of her friend's question. She carefully opened the door to Fallon's room. The little girl was already in bed, the covers tucked up to her chin, the newly given lamb in her hands, sound asleep.

"She'll be so disappointed that she missed hearing your story," Annie said as they backed out of the room, shutting the door as quietly as she could.

"Bring her to Broken Hill for a visit this week and I'll make it up to her," Patrick said in earnest. "In fact, would you like it, Annie girl, if I was to invite you all over for a visit? Maybe an overnight?"

Annie looked Patrick square in the eyes. "Do you mean Tony as well?"

"Of course I mean his lordship, Mr. High and

Mighty Anthony Chambers."

"Patrick," Annie said in a mildly rebuking voice, removing the sting by her softly pitched tone. "Behave yourself."

"For you, me darlin', I'll try, though I can't give you my promise."

The selection laid out in the parlor was delectable: fruit and cheese, along with slices of warm pie, bursting with thick chunks of apple.

"What will you have?" Annie inquired of Patrick, who sat in the wing chair this time. Tony was beside her on the intimate couch.

"A large piece of that pie, Annie girl," he replied.

Annie handed him a small dessert plate with a precut slice and a silver spoon.

"And you?" she asked Tony.

"I'll have the same, though add some cheddar to it," he responded.

When she handed Tony the plate, their fingertips touched. Frissons of excitement danced along her nerves. Annie swallowed nervously as she selected a piece for herself. As she tasted the cinnamon-sweet mixture, the inside of the pie oozing fruit, she kept her eyes demurely downcast on purpose, afraid to tempt whatever joss was present.

Annie thought of the other nights she had spent here in this room with Cedric and Patrick; relaxed, happy evenings filled with conversation and laughter that her open heart had soaked up like a sponge. Each hour in this house brought her more firmly into this present life and increased the distance from her old.

"If you'd be wantin' to see just how a sheep station

is run," Patrick said, "then I propose that you visit Broken Hill."

Tony accepted Patrick's offer. It was the perfect opportunity to see what kind of place the other man had, what type of operation he ran, and how he lived.

"Come and spend the night," Patrick suggested. "And if you do," he said, glancing at Tony's much more formal dress, "leave the fancy rig here. We do things in a different manner at Broken Hill. No need to waste the good gear on my plain hospitality."

"There's nothing about your hospitality that's ever been plain, Patrick," Annie insisted, putting her half-empty plate aside so that she could have some coffee while it was hot.

"When?" Tony asked.

"I leave that for you and Annie to decide," Patrick said. "Whenever you choose, just send a rider to let me know." He put his own empty plate back on the table. "I'd best be getting back home now," he said, standing up.

"So soon?" Annie queried, her voice riddled with disappointment. Gray eyes met blue. "Would you like a brandy before you go?"

"Not tonight, Annie girl."

"It feels like you've just arrived."

Patrick smiled at her. "I know."

"Let me see you out," she offered, rising from her seat.

"As shall I," Tony insisted, all the better to keep a sharp eye on them. He couldn't help but notice that Annie had been avoiding him since they'd momentarily touched over the sweet. Had she felt that acute sexual spark as well? That brief encounter had produced

175

a fire in his belly—a fire, that, while banked, still burned.

She had no hesitation whatsoever in touching the Australian, he noted as they walked outside on the wide veranda. She readily embraced Patrick O'Donnell, both with hands and lips.

Tony tried to read something deeper into their ease with one another, but it didn't strike him as the intimate gesture of long-term lovers.

Perhaps they were cleverer than he gave them credit for?

Or maybe there was nothing there to be clever about? an inner voice mocked. It might be just as she said, they were friends only.

Tony asked himself the question: Could any man willingly remain *just* friends with Annie Ross?

"Come inside," Tony said as Annie stood there watching her friend leave, riding off into the night. "It's far too cold for you to be out with naught on but what you're wearing."

She turned her head and glanced up into his face. Was his concern genuine? Annie couldn't really tell as his face was bathed in shadows. All she could feel was his presence, far too close for her peace of mind.

She refused to scamper inside like a scared rabbit, no matter if she was feeling trapped. She made her exit calmly, her voice strong, though softly pitched. "Good night."

"I can't interest you in joining me for a brandy?"

"Thank you, but no," she stated firmly, slipping back through the front doors.

Tony followed her. "Pity," he said under his breath, shutting the double oak doors behind him, his mouth quirking slightly as he recalled the absence of a lock.

Thrill to the most sensual, adventure-filled Historical Romances on the market today...

FROM  LEISURE BOOKS

As a home subscriber to Leisure Romance Book Club, you'll enjoy the best in today's BRAND-NEW Historical Romance fiction. For over twenty-five years, Leisure Books has brought you the award-winning, high-quality authors you know and love to read. Each Leisure Historical Romance will sweep you away to a world of high adventure...and intimate romance. Discover for yourself all the passion and excitement millions of readers thrill to each and every month.

Save $5.⁰⁰ Each Time You Buy!

Each month, the Leisure Romance Book Club brings you four brand-new titles from Leisure Books, America's foremost publisher of Historical Romances. EACH PACKAGE WILL SAVE YOU $5.00 FROM THE BOOKSTORE PRICE! And you'll never miss a new title with our convenient home delivery service.

Here's how we do it. Each package will carry a FREE 10-DAY EXAMINATION privilege. At the end of that time, if you decide to keep your books, simply pay the low invoice price of $16.96, no shipping or handling charges added. HOME DELIVERY IS ALWAYS FREE. With today's top Historical Romance novels selling for $5.99 and higher, our price SAVES YOU $5.00 with each shipment.

AND YOUR FIRST FOUR-BOOK SHIPMENT IS TOTALLY FREE!
IT'S A BARGAIN YOU CAN'T BEAT! A Super $21.96 Value!

LEISURE BOOKS A Division of Dorchester Publishing Co., Inc.

GET YOUR 4 FREE BOOKS NOW — A $21.96 Value!

Mail the Free Book Certificate Today!

Get Four Books Totally FREE — A $21.96 Value!

PLEASE RUSH
MY FOUR FREE
BOOKS TO ME
RIGHT AWAY!

Leisure Romance Book Club
P.O. Box 6613
Edison, NJ 08818-6613

AFFIX
STAMP
HERE

Annie had explained that to him right after he'd first arrived—here in the country locks weren't a necessity.

"Pardon?"

"Nothing," he insisted, wishing he could reach out and touch her hair. Was it as soft as it looked? He imagined her stroking a brush through its length every night before she went to sleep.

Bloody hell! He didn't even have to try hard to imagine his own hands doing the task.

"Good night then," he said abruptly, leaving her there in the hall as he strode through the door to the parlor, putting a room and a closed door wisely between them.

Chapter Twelve

Tony watched the dying embers of the fire, a snifter of brandy in one hand, a slim cigar in the other. He sat on the brown velvet settee, left leg casually flung over the right, his mind replaying the events of the evening.

Damn, he reluctantly agreed, thinking upon the matter, but O'Donnell was right. The opal earrings would look exquisite on Annie. The stones had a core of fire within them, much like the woman herself. Seemingly cool on first examination, then glowing brighter, hotter from a deeper source. A decidedly perfect choice.

But was it an innocent choice?

Tony wondered about that. Men of his social class gave jewelry to mistresses, wives, occasionally mothers, but, for the most part, never to friends. That was far too personal a gift to offer a lady. A book, some flowers, chocolates, these were all *comme il faut*, acceptable.

Since he'd been here in Australia, so many rules seemed turned askew, which didn't make for a comfortable feeling in him.

Tony had sensed the hostility simmering beneath the surface in O'Donnell's manner, as if the younger man was testing him somehow. Was that because

O'Donnell looked upon Tony as a potential rival? Or was it merely because Tony was English? An outsider to this country?

Tony shrugged. If that were the case, then O'Donnell wouldn't have been so close to Cedric, though he had only Annie's words for the truth of that.

And what of Annie Ross and Patrick O'Donnell?

Tony had thought that by tonight he would have had all the answers. What he had instead were still more questions. Heaps of questions. He'd tried to pay close atention to how she'd looked at the other man, gathering clues—but to no avail. Outwardly, Annie gave no sign that there was anything deeper in their relationship than the friendship she espoused. He'd seen no evidence of stolen glances, nor of longing looks. Guessing, Tony would have assumed that they were more like brother and sister.

Which puzzled Tony all the more. How could any man regard this woman as a mere sister? For himself, that was too improbable a scenario to consider.

Tony swallowed the remainder of the brandy, his thoughts traveling back to the notion of a fine-bristled brush and her long brown hair, of sweeping the mass of it aside to find the nape of her neck with his lips, continuing on downwards, past what he knew would be the delicate blades of her bare shoulders.

His hand was curled around the balloon of the gold-edged snifter; he wondered what it would feel like to hold her breast in his palm. As he put his mouth to the rim of the glass, he wondered what it would be like to put it to the curve of her flesh. He imagined nipples tipped in brandy, of what his tongue could do and taste.

Tony groaned. His own flesh ached, stirred to life by his fantastical musings.

Face it, old man, he told himself, you bloody well want her—want her more and more with each passing hour.

Lord help him, he thought, it was going to be a very long night.

In another part of the house, someone else thought the very same thing.

Annie bent over, brushing her hair, which trailed on the floor, pulling the bristles through the strands with an experienced hand. It was a soothing gesture, although it couldn't keep her mind a blank as she'd hoped it would.

Sleep hadn't been the answer either. She'd tried that already. All that had happened was that she lay in bed, tossing and turning, seeing *his* face every time she closed her eyes.

She'd lit the lamp beside her bed and tried reading. That was no use either, for her eyes wouldn't focus on the page. She had stared at the words, the print blurring. Angry, she'd slammed the volume shut.

Shifting up against the headboard, Annie reached for a glass of water from the etched-glass carafe on the night table. Pouring herself a glass of the still cool water, she drank it down, easing the dryness in her throat.

Frustrated, she dragged herself from the warmth and comfort of her bed, slipped on her robe, and attended to her neglected chore.

Flinging her head back up, Annie brushed the hair away from her face. The lamp on her dressing table was adjusted low, bathing her face in a golden glow as she glanced into the mirror before her. Her own familiar features were reflected there, although with a subtle difference. She examined her face in closer detail. It was there in her eyes. A soft, dreamy look. Not the starry-eyed look of a child, but the deeper, hungrier look of a woman. A woman, moreover, who wanted to dream again. Who needed to dream again.

Annie lowered her head, momentarily closing her eyes as she took a deep breath.

She'd hoped that seeing Tony and Patrick together tonight would give her a sense of balance, of perspective.

It hadn't. Only more questions were raised. Questions she wasn't comfortable with acknowledging, even if only to herself in the privacy of her own head.

Annie extinguished the lamp, rising from her softly padded needlepoint seat. She walked to the long window-doors, pushing aside the lace curtains, placing one hand against the chilled glass for an instant, then to her heated cheeks, all the while gazing outward. A host of stars filled the sky.

Outside, all appeared cool and calm. The seeming serenity of the night fascinated her.

And what about inside? she wondered.

It was warm and teeming with confusion; at least it was, she figured, from her perspective.

Sighing, Annie turned away from the door and padded back to bed, extinguishing the lamp. She had to get some rest. Morning would come soon enough, and with it endless questions she daren't ask.

Sliding beneath the sheet and quilt, she closed her eyes, her last thoughts before sleep invaded by a pair of mesmerizing green eyes and a seductively handsome mouth.

Gail Link

* * *

She was waiting for him when he arrived home.

Patrick walked into the parlor, his heart that much lighter for seeing Mei there. She was sewing, her fingers working a canvas with threads of color, back and forth with skilled dexterity. She reminded him of a fine piece of porcelain with her creamy-gold skin and hair as black as jet in a single thick braid over one shoulder. Mei wore a cheongsam with matching trousers of brocaded satin in deepest wine, splashed with gold; the garment molded itself to her delicate body.

What Patrick wanted to do at that precise moment was carefully unhook and remove her garments so that he could see all of Mei in the light of the fire that burned so brightly in the hearth. He longed to kiss her, starting with her small mouth, then across her face, along her neck, around her breasts, then continuing downwards, slowly, until he made his way to her tiny feet.

Patrick's body stirred with unfulfilled longing and desire, knowing that he would never act upon his wishes. Honor and respect for Mei demanded otherwise. Still, his honorable intentions aside, he couldn't help but ache for what couldn't be.

Mei looked up and saw him standing there. "Patrick," she said, happiness echoing in her tone.

Patrick strode in, taking a seat in the chair opposite hers.

Mei put down her work, carefully placing it back into her lined basket and closing the lid. "Can I get you anything?" she asked, noting the weariness in his face.

"Tea would be lovely," he answered. "And fix a cup for yourself as well, me darlin'."

Mei's heart leapt, as it always did, with his endearment. She knew that it did not mean for him what it did for her, but she didn't care. At least not so very much, she told herself.

She hurried to the kitchen to prepare the tea, heating the water in a copper kettle while she placed two delicate china cups, along with a small jug of milk and a bowl of sugar, on the silver tea tray. Then she looked around for something else to add, should Patrick be hungry.

Smiling, she found what should please him, depending on whether he wanted a sweet or something heartier—a thick slice of gingerbread on one side of the plate, and a slice of buttered wheat bread on the other. That, she decided, should ease any pangs of hunger he might have.

She wondered how the dinner had gone. Had Patrick been able to keep control over his rare temper, knowing how much he already disliked the Englishman? Mei suspected that Patrick was only waiting a respectful period before he declared his intentions to Annie. It must be hard, she thought, for him to see Annie sharing her house with another man when he wanted to be the one she leaned on, the one she turned to.

They each deserved some large measure of happiness. Both were young and healthy. To expect either to live forever alone was ridiculous when they could give comfort and joy to one another. Annie's daughter deserved a father. Mei understood how important that could be to a child. She'd worshiped hers. Patrick had come from a big family. To deny him children would be to condemn him to a half-life.

She loved them both, and because of that, wanted

only what was best for each. She shoved aside her own hurt, buried it under a layer of calm acceptance of what was and what could never be.

What hurt Mei sharpest of all was thinking of Patrick and Annie as lovers. Imagining them lying in each other's arms in Patrick's bed upstairs, of Patrick's solid muscular body taking possession of the other woman's, and bringing them both to the kingdom of sheer ecstasy.

A solitary tear rolled down Mei's cheek; she brushed it aside. There could be no room in her heart for jealousy or regret.

The boiling kettle removed her thoughts from their melancholy path. Pouring a small amount of hot water into the teapot, Mei swished it around, setting the kettle down for a moment as she emptied the excess water in the teapot into the sink. Next, she spooned the leaves into a silver infuser and set it inside the pot, filling it with the remaining hot water.

Adding the pot to the large tray, Mei carried it down the hall to the front parlor.

"Let me lend you a hand, me darlin'," Patrick said as he leapt from his chair, rushing to take the heavy tray from Mei's hands. He set it down on the round table nearest one of the couches.

Mei fixed his cup, handing it to Patrick, offering him a choice of the cake or the bread.

"I'll have the gingerbread, but only if you'll have half as well."

Mei agreed, and Patrick picked up the cake and split it in two, giving her half. She nodded her head in acknowledgment. Crumbs from the gingerbread floated down onto her clothes.

"Now that you have met the Englishman, what do

you think of him?" she asked, taking a dainty bite of the cake.

"That he's a pompous, self-centered, egotistical bastard," Patrick replied mildly, washing his portion of cake down with almost half of the cup of Indian blend.

"You cannot mean that," Mei protested.

"I can and do, darlin'," Patrick insisted. "You should have seen him, Mei, an English swell to his toes. Well, I let him know right away that he wasn't my mate, nor ever likely to be." Patrick slid his arm about the low back of the couch, turning to face Mei, one leg loosely folded onto the seat. "Smug, he was. There be no doubt about that."

Her dark eyes reflected her concern. "Was he deliberately rude?" Insulting a guest under one's own roof was an unforgivable sin. It was most definitely bad joss.

Patrick cleared his throat. "Not exactly."

Mei was puzzled by his response. "Did he offer insult in any way?"

"Not exactly," he repeated.

Mei held her mild exasperation in check. "What do you mean when you say 'not exactly'?" she asked, curious to learn what had infuriated Patrick so about the other man.

"It was his bloody superior attitude. He didn't have to say it outright, but I could tell what he was thinking, as if I was a copper-tail. His type are so filled with their own self-importance that all other opinions cease to matter."

Mei listened while she poured another cup of tea for Patrick. "How was he with Annie?" she asked, concern for her friend evident in her voice. "Did he treat her with respect?"

185

"Odd about that," Patrick mused.

"What is odd?" Mei prodded, her eyes lovingly memorizing all the details of Patrick's face. For her, there would never be another man in her heart. She would rather die a maiden untouched than give herself into another's arms. For her, heart and body were irretrievably linked, there could be no giving of one without the other.

"Sometimes he watched her like a hawk," Patrick responded, "weighing her every move with those sharp eyes of his. Other times, he was cool, almost disinterested, as if what she did was of little consequence to him."

"And what of Annie?"

"She was quieter than usual." Patrick shifted in his seat. "As if she wanted to remain in the background." He thought again of the color that had flushed Annie's cheeks during dinner, the result of Tony Chambers throwing a glance in her direction. Patrick didn't mention it to Mei because he didn't know what to make of it himself. Like trying to explain a platypus to someone who's never seen the creature—you could do it, but it would be better if they were there to see it for themselves.

"I've invited them here to Broken Hill for a visit," he announced.

"What made you do that if you dislike him so?"

"To see if he'd come, for one thing, though mainly for Annie's sake. I want her to see him for what he is, which is, bluntly, not Cedric. And, if truth be told, perhaps to rub his toff nose in the dust just a little. I want him to see that it isn't only the *merinos* that thrive here. His kind come and go with the turn of the seasons. Mine endure."

Patrick reached over and lifted Mei's chin with his index finger. "I'll be doubting that he'll come. In fact, I'd lay odds against it."

"Perhaps," Mei ventured her opinion, "this Englishman might fool you."

"Not bloody likely," Patrick shot back.

"He might want to save face, especially in front of Annie," she stated softly.

"I'd be surprised to learn that 'saving face' plays any part in Chambers's schemes, me darlin'," Patrick insisted. "No, I think he'll make up some excuse and fail to show." His thin lips curved in a deep grin. "Especially after I told him that it would be better if he came looking less like the lord-of-the-manor, shall we say?" Patrick snorted. "Do you think he'd ever go into a local shop and get outfitted like the rest of us? No. He'd be affronted at the mere thought of that. He might consider buying clothes in Melbourne, but only after he's first properly vetted the establishment, and they followed his fashion."

"Still," Mei countered, "he might do it just to please Annie. That is a possibility." Or, she thought, to take Patrick up on what she was sure was a challenge issued. Men, she'd learned, did not suffer insults to their manhood lightly.

"We'll see," he said, placing his empty cup on the tray next to hers. "It's getting late, Mei girl. You go off to bed and let me put this away for you."

"It is most kind of you," she said, agreeing. Arguing with Patrick would have proved a futile waste of time. He simply would have taken the tray from her. Another man might have considered it beneath him to bother about her comfort, about her ease. Not Patrick. She sat there while he got up and muttered a "good night" and then left the room.

Rising, Mei glided softly across the rug, checking to see that the fire was properly banked for the evening. She remained there for a few moments, contemplating Patrick's invitation. She and Annie had discussed the possibility, though each was aware of Patrick's blind dislike of the English. Patrick, Mei knew, was a good man; beneath the sometimes blustery mask he occasionally put on, he was kindness itself, generous to a fault. She wondered if one could say the same about Anthony Chambers.

Alfred handed Tony his jacket, watching as the younger man stood checking his reflection in the mirror.

"Something amiss, sir?" Alfred inquired. As always, Tony looked impeccable. It made Alfred's job so much easier to have a man for whom clothes were an expression of personal style, as opposed to a nitwit who couldn't fathom what color went with what. His last charge had been a brilliant actor, but an idiot regarding his wardrobe. Alfred ofttimes wondered what horrors the man had gotten into when he left his employ. Tony, thankfully, was a high-stepper, always spiffy.

"It would seem that my mode of dress is somewhat formal for this venue, or so I've been told."

"By whom, sir?" Alfred was personally affronted by this remark. "Certainly not by Mrs. Ross?"

"No. She's never mentioned my wardrobe at all."

Except, Alfred noted with a smile, to admire it in silence. He'd caught the young widow surreptitiously giving his employer an appreciative glance every so often. Tony Chambers had a strong, fit body; the kind of inborn grace that tailors adored. He was, after all, a forever gentleman. Alfred thought of the current leader of fashion in England, the Prince of Wales, a portly man who at best, kindly speaking, altered the look of the clothes he wore.

"You'll recall the gentleman who came to dinner last evening?"

"The *Irishman?*" Alfred spoke the word as if that said it all.

"Actually," Tony said as he adjusted his cravat, "he's a native Australian, though from Irish stock. It was he who made the observation."

"Consider the source, sir."

Tony chuckled, turning his back on the mirror. "He did get me to thinking, though."

"About what, if I may be so bold to inquire?"

"Diversifying."

"Come again, sir?"

"Adding some other items, old man, to what I now have," Tony responded. "I've seen the clothes that pass for regular work apparel here. When I first arrived on these shores, I wasn't sure that I would have to adhere to the tenets of my great-uncle's will. Now it would appear that I have no choice but to, and since I do, the clothes I brought along, even the ones I purchased in Melbourne to supplement, will not suffice.

"Besides, O'Donnell actually threw down the gauntlet to me last night," Tony confided to his valet. "He invited Mrs. Ross and myself to his station for an overnight visit, slyly insisting that I adapt my wardrobe so as not to stand out in this more informal setting."

"He's got some nerve."

"There's no denying that fact," Tony responded with a sardonic gleam in his eye. "But he's a scrapper, I'll give him that."

Gail Link

Alfred raised his eyebrows just slightly. "Did you like him?"

Tony shrugged his broad shoulders. "I don't know that I'd go so far as to say that," he admitted. Tony put his hand on the older man's shoulder when he saw the perplexed look on Alfred's face. "I've decided to ride into Mansfield and have a look at what passes for clothing there."

"When do we leave, sir?"

"So, you'll go then?"

"Of course I will, sir. I'm curious as well to see what passes for fashion out here in the country."

"After breakfast, then," Tony replied. "That should give us enough time to ride there and back by late afternoon, early evening." Tony checked his gold pocket watch. "It's eight-thirty now. Before the next hour unfolds."

Alfred nodded. "Do you want me to bring something to you in the office, sir?"

Tony considered the offer and promptly rejected it. "No bother. I shall have it in the kitchen."

"As you wish, sir. I'll just go and inform Mary about your plans."

"Fine."

The valet headed in one direction as Tony went to the office to get the money needed for their excursion. Pausing at the desk, Tony absently fingered the silver monogrammed money clip he had taken from the front drawer.

He hadn't slept much. It was still so strange for him to be up this early in the morning. He'd heard the distinct call of the kookaburra, known around here as the settler's clock. Funny thing was, Tony admitted, he was finding it easier to get up earlier since he was

190

keeping such different hours from his London routine. Everyone around the station was up when he rose, including some that were awake before the dawn broke. The household was afoot and about its business, he discovered. Annie and her daughter were up and about, as were Mary and Alice. Even Alfred seemed to be adapting to the change in schedules without any lingering difficulty.

Tony smiled. It reminded him of his time in Texas, which also reminded him that he should have written a letter to Rafe by now. Tony promised himself that he'd attend to that when he got back from the shopping expedition to Mansfield. It might amuse Rafe to know just what was going on here. At the very least, it would take Rafe's mind off his broken heart. On the voyage from England to America, Rafe had confided the entire story to Tony, sharing, finally, all his secrets. For his American friend, Tony knew there could only be one true love in his life.

Tony wasn't certain he could ever believe in that for himself.

A perfect wife?

Perhaps.

A perfect love?

It didn't seem probable.

Chapter Thirteen

The atmosphere in the kitchen was relaxed and convivial when Tony entered. He paused for a moment and took it in. Alice was polishing some of the silver used last night, humming a tune under her breath; Mary was stirring a pot of oatmeal, along with watching thick strips of bacon sizzling in the cast iron skillet. Fallon was sitting at the table, a pencil in her small hand, working on copying her name, printing the letters over and over in a copybook, her dog munching contentedly on a bone at her feet. Alfred was sitting to the right hand of Annie; both were enjoying their morning meal, and Alfred appeared to be regaling her with humorous tales of his time with the acting troupe.

All in all, Tony mused, it was a very contented scene, with an almost familial air about it.

"Good morning to you, Mr. Chambers," Mary said with a smile, removing the oatmeal from the stove. "Your breakfast is almost ready if you'd care to have a seat."

Tony gave a slight nod to Mary's greeting. From the corner of his eye, he caught Annie's head rising as she fixed her glance on him. He turned toward her, a casual smile on his face as he pulled out the chair at the opposite end of the table and sat down. "Good morning," he said, accepting the cup of tea from Mary's hand. Squeezing a slice of lemon into the tea, he added a heaping teaspoon of sugar. "I trust that you slept well?"

Didn't she just wish? Annie was damned if she'd tell him otherwise. "Perfectly," she responded, the white lie popping out of her mouth with ease. She was caught off guard at having Tony there at the other end of the long table; it wasn't as if his sitting down to breakfast with her was an everyday occurrence. "And you?"

Tony sipped his tea. "Like a babe," he answered, knowing that was an absolute falsehood. He'd been up half the night, smoking and thinking, restless, erotic thoughts running rampant in his brain. If he'd been in London, Melbourne even, he would have put his pent-up energy to good use and visited a brothel. At least that way he would have eased the continuing ache in his loins, relaxed, and been the better for it. Instead, he'd brooded all hours upon this slip of a woman, and what she was doing to his carefully ordered life.

"I understand from Alfred that you're going into Mansfield this morning," Annie said, scooping some warm scrambled eggs onto her fork. "Would you mind if I rode along with you? I've some errands to take care of in town." She lifted the forkful of eggs to her mouth while waiting for his response.

Tony buttered a slice of toast from the silver rack in front of him, spreading some apricot preserves upon it, while he mulled over her request. After last night, he wasn't sure it was wise to be spending the day in such close proximity to her, yet he found himself saying, "I plan to leave as soon as I've had my breakfast."

Gail Link

"That's fine by me," Annie assured him, getting up and refilling her large cup of coffee from the well-used graniteware pot.

Mary set a bowl of oatmeal in front of Tony, who added a large helping of dark brown sugar to the top, along with a splash of fresh cream. "I thought you might like some hot porridge in addition to your cooked breakfast this morning sir, as you'll be needing it before you set out on that long ride into Mansfield. It's certainly a cold one out there today."

Tony flashed the older woman a charming smile. "How thoughtful of you, Mary."

The woman blushed slightly, returning to her task.

Annie observed the scene silently. One more indication that he obviously had a way with women. He knew how to flatter and cajole without raising a sweat. How would he survive out here, she wondered, so far away from the bright lights of the city, away from the hectic social whirl, and more importantly, away from the company of the women he was used to? He was a young man who'd no doubt sown many a wild oat in his time. Probably, she suspected, enough to reap a harvest for an entire farm. What was he to do with nary a prospect around here? Didn't he miss the sparkling gaiety of the life that late he'd led? The costume balls and the various routs; nights at the theater; the hunting weekends on vast estates; the glorious and endless rounds of parties. Always something to do and somewhere to go—and many available someones to be with.

Every so often, Annie herself yearned for the life she'd had in Philadelphia. One of her favorite pastimes had been attending concerts at the Academy of Music, either with her family or alone. Sweet angels in heaven, how she did miss that. Music was a passion to her. She loved the sound of a chamber orchestra playing Vivaldi or Mozart. Annie wanted that world for her daughter as well.

Perhaps later, when Fallon was older, she would take her into Melbourne. Show her what the world had to offer.

Who knows, she thought, maybe someday they could even go back to Philadelphia and attend a concert together at the Academy.

If Annie longed to recapture some of what she'd given up, how must Tony feel?

Picking up her cup, Annie raised her eyes and met Tony's gaze. Annie was struck yet again by the pull he exerted without any apparent knowledge on his part. It was simply there, between them.

She blinked, breaking the contact.

My God, what was happening to her?

Tony couldn't help but stare at Annie Ross. There was an innate grace about her, obvious in everything she did. Every movement of her body was made with a winsome appeal, enhanced by those wide gray eyes fringed by dark lashes.

She was wearing shades of blue today.

Blue, he decided, was rapidly becoming his favorite color.

"Would you like anything else, Mrs. Ross?" Mary inquired.

"No," Annie replied, handing the other woman her empty plate. It was getting easier each day to fall into the comfortable routine of having someone else fix the meals. In so short a period of time, Tony Chambers had effected a change in her. How many more might he orchestrate the longer he remained?

195

Annie wiped her mouth with the linen napkin. "I'd best be getting ready if I'm to go with Mr. Chambers and Alfred."

"Can I come too?" Fallon asked, excited at the prospect of a trip.

"I'm afraid not, poppet." Annie hated to disappoint her daughter, but this wasn't the kind of journey that Fallon could easily make. "Maybe another time."

At the crestfallen look in her child's eyes, Annie rose swiftly from her chair and hurried around the table to Fallon. Bending down, her skirt and petticoats brushing the stone floor in a wide circle, Annie gave a playful tug at one of Fallon's blond braids. "How would you like to go and visit Uncle Patrick at Broken Hill?"

"Can we?" the little girl demanded eagerly.

Annie's mouth kicked into a smile. "Tell me when."

"Right away?"

Annie laughed softly, caught by her own words. "We'll have to give him some notice first, sweetheart," she explained. "Would two days from now be all right with you instead?"

Fallon worried her lower lip, considering. She pointed in Tony's direction. "Can he come too?"

Annie's gaze met Tony's over Fallon's head for a moment before she posed another question to her daughter. "Would you like that?"

Fallon nodded her head vigorously.

It appeared to Annie that Tony had made yet another female conquest. Her child had fallen under his arresting spell, giving her affection without reservation.

Annie sighed. Trust was so easy for a child. They operated on instinct and blind faith. Once, so had she.

"I think that can be arranged," Tony stated with a

half-smile in Fallon's direction.

Fallon clapped her hands in delight and Lady barked in accompaniment.

"That's settled then," Annie remarked.

Mary took a few steps closer to the table. "I'll be happy to keep an eye on your little girl whilst you're gone," she volunteered. "Fallon can help me make a cake if she's of a mind to."

Fallon's eyes lit up at that prospect.

"I'd be happy to keep watch over the lass as well," offered Alfred, throwing Mary a conspiratorial look. "That is, if you wouldn't mind me giving this trip a pass, sir?"

Tony fancied that his valet had only planned on coming with him to see for himself just what Tony intended to purchase in the way of new clothes and vet the same. Now that Annie was going, Alfred seemed quite content to forgo the experience.

Tony shrugged. If he was any judge, his valet had a fancy for the widow Dunmartin. "Do as you will."

"Thank you, sir." Alfred suggested to Annie, "Perhaps a few tales from the Bard will keep the little one amused."

"As long as it's the Bard, and not the bawdy," Annie instructed, a glimmer of laughter in her eyes.

"Heaven forbid, ma'am," Alfred stated dramatically, grinning. "Only the best."

"On second thought," Annie said, gathering Fallon up into her arms and hugging the child close, "perhaps she's not yet ready for Mr. Shakespeare, considering some of his stories. I think perhaps a selection from Mother Goose, or some of Miss Alcott's work will be much better for her tender years."

"Whatever you'd like, ma'am," Alfred agreed.

"Mama Goose it shall be if that's what you will."

Annie returned Fallon to her seat at the table, bending down once again, one of the little's girl's hands cupped between her own. "Now, you're to mind what Mrs. Dunmartin and Alfred tell you, understand?"

Fallon nodded eagerly.

"Don't forget that Lady is to be taken for a walk and all your toys picked up before your nap."

"I won't, Mama," Fallon promised solemnly.

"I'm counting on you," Annie said, rising. "And I'm looking forward," she added with a chuckle underlying her voice, "to seeing what kind of cake you and Mary can make. Now, I'd best go and change my clothes," Annie proposed, meeting Tony's glance. "I shall meet you by the stables. I won't be long."

Tony watched Annie turn and walk away, her hips swaying gently beneath the navy blue wool of her skirt. Her long brown hair was fixed in a single braid flowing down her back, the ends of which caressed her bottom. He swallowed heavily, his mouth suddenly dry, as if he'd eaten raw cotton instead of creamy oatmeal.

Mary placed a large plate filled with thick strips of bacon and several once-over eggs before him. Tony dug into the meal with gusto, his appetite suddenly increasing twofold.

This should prove quite an interesting trip indeed.

She had to be crazy, Annie thought as she unfastened her skirt, sliding it down her hips with a push of her hands. Next came the two petticoats, one of cotton, the other of thin flannel. Standing there in her flounced drawers, she deftly untied the ribbon that held them in place, kicking free of them as well.

Grabbing the thin pair of plain white cotton drawers from the bottom of the bed, she pulled them on, buttoning the fly. They extended to her ankles, having been made originally for a boy. Next came a pair of wool socks, followed by the dungarees she'd purchased almost a year ago and hadn't yet worn.

With her pale blue shirt tucked in, a vest of brown suede buttoned over it, and the pants, she looked almost boyish. Turning slightly, Annie amended that statement. She could never pass for a boy. Too many curves to her form.

Shrugging into the brown tweed riding jacket, she hoped that it would hide some of the more obvious aspects from view. Satisfied, Annie pulled on her knee-high leather boots, tucking the pants into them.

She gathered her discarded clothes and piled them onto the bed for sorting later. She didn't want to keep Tony waiting any longer than necessary.

Sinking onto the dressing-table chair, Annie wondered why she was doing this. She could have given the packages she wanted posted to Alfred. He would have seen to their sending, no questions asked. Why had she suddenly gotten the overwhelming urge to go along as well?

What was she trying to do? Or what was she trying to prove?

She would be alone with him. She hadn't expected Alfred to change his mind. It was too late to back out. Changing her mind now would look like the act of a coward. As if she had something to fear from him.

And she didn't.

Or did she?

Ridiculous, she mentally chastised herself. She was being foolish over a trifle. He probably couldn't care less that she was riding with him. And, since she was, there was no need to pull one of the station hands from his duties to show Tony the way into Mansfield. Annie knew the quickest route, having traveled it with Cedric and Jim several times.

Annie glanced at the two slim, brown-paper-wrapped packages on the dressing table. One was addressed to a newspaper office in Melbourne, the editor of which had been a good friend of Cedric's. She enclosed a note asking if he could make time to look at her work and tell her truthfully if she had a chance at selling it. The other package was addressed to her parents in Philadelphia. Along with letters to her family, she was including some of the pieces that she was sending to the editor in Melbourne. On both manuscripts, she had used the name A. E. Ross, hoping no one would link it to her directly. She could have used another name, but pride forbade it. She wanted to succeed on merit, but she also wanted the satisfaction of seeing her own name in print, not that of a stranger.

She'd copied the words carefully, making sure her handwriting was legible. Still not as proficient with the typewriter as she would have liked, Annie decided it would be better to send it out regardless. After all, her expectations were low. This was simply a trial run. Besides, if she waited any longer, she might lose her nerve. Better to get it over with.

Tony stood talking to Jim as he waited for Annie.

"I was planning on sending Billy along with you to show you the way, but seeing as Mrs. Ross has decided to go along, you'll not be needing anyone else," Jim explained. "She's a crack rider," he reminded Tony, "and knows the area fairly well."

"Still, I'm glad you added the rifle as a precaution."

Jim nodded. "Right as you requested, Mr. Chambers. Checked and cleaned it myself."

"Good man," Tony replied. He wasn't so foolish as to ride away from this station without the means to handle any situation that might occur, especially with a woman by his side.

The stable boy led out two horses, holding them steady. Tony's stallion Merlin was snorting, his head bobbing, eager for a run. Annie's mount was prancing delicately, puffs of air frosting in front of her.

Tony spoke to his animal, calming the horse down with his evenly pitched voice. He noted that along with the rifle in the scabbard, on the other side was a long, coiled whip.

"What's that for?" he asked Jim.

"For whatever it needs to be," the foreman responded. Jim easily uncoiled the whip and removed the rifle, stepped away from the horses several feet, and demonstrated. "Hold this," he said to Tony, handing him the rifle.

Tony stood there, the rifle in his hand.

"Relax," Jim said, working his wrist, the tip of the nearly seven-foot braided kangaroo whip moving slowly back and forth along the ground. Then, striking with the swiftness of a snake, he snapped the whip, ripping the rifle from Tony's hand.

"I see what you mean," Tony conceded.

"Jim's one of the best."

Tony spun around when he heard Annie's voice. She was covered by the same sort of long coat that Patrick O'Donnell had worn, and which he'd seen almost every worker on the station wearing as well. It was brown, as was the wide-brimmed, low-crowned wool felt hat she wore. Beneath the coat he could see dark boots and trousers, of a sort.

She could have almost passed for a boy but for her face. It was that face which had continued to haunt him. A face whose appeal he couldn't explain. Hardly sophisticated—though compelling nonetheless.

Snapping his gaze away from her, Tony focused on the station boss. "You're a marvel with that thing, Jim."

Jim shrugged. "No matter. Comes with living hereabouts, I suppose."

"You're being far too modest, Jim," Annie insisted.

"Mrs. Ross is right. You've a gift for handling that whip well. I'd like you to show me how later."

Tony's statement surprised Annie. She had half expected him to make some sharp retort dismissing the station foreman's skill with the lethal whip. Instead, he seemed genuinely interested. Why? It was hardly the tool of an English gentleman.

She watched, fascinated, as Tony took back the whip, giving it a few quick snaps with a deft flick of his wrist.

"With some practice, you'll get it right enough," Jim stated. "You've got the hands for it."

Annie dropped her gaze to those hands, covered by soft-as-butter leather gloves. She guessed that they cost more than the average station worker made in a year, yet it was what was contained in the gloves that held her interest. Strong hands. Skilled hands. Hands that were capable of so much.

Tony replaced the whip on his saddle and faced the awkward contraption. Australians used riding equipment similar to the Americans, so getting used to this gear was going to take some time. Since he'd, perforce, have to be here for the stipulated time, he would have to look into getting some English tack if it was available. For pleasure riding, he much preferred what he was used to. He doubted that Mansfield would have what he needed. An inquiry would have to be made, he assumed, in Melbourne.

Melbourne. He'd have to put a visit there on his agenda soon. If for no other reason than pleasure.

He sliced a glance at Annie as she mounted the chestnut horse. Should he ask her to join him on the proposed trip to Melbourne? And if he did, would she? Or would she make up some excuse? Pretend indifference?

He mounted the stallion, easing his weight into the saddle. There was one way to know for certain—ask her.

As soon as they got beyond the boundaries of the homestead, Annie, riding alongside Tony, flashed him a grin and put her heels to her horse, bounding ahead.

Tony took the challenge, letting Merlin have his head. They raced across the valley, through streams, up and down hills, through meadows, trees, and shrub until each reined in their mounts near a large snow gum with twisted branches.

There was a flush of color in Annie's cheeks as she patted the mare's neck, taking in a deep gulp of air. "Morganna was feeling rather frisky," Annie explained, "so I thought a good run would expunge it from her system."

Tony arched a brow as he, too, took a deep breath, his wide chest rising and falling beneath the wool coat he wore. "Indeed?"

"Are you doubting me?"

"Far be it from me, my dear," he drawled, "though

I suspect you wanted it just as much as the animal."

"You may be right," she said, laughing lightly.

Like the horse she rode, Tony thought, Annie was spirited and full of life. Contrasted to her usual—what? he mused. He couldn't say reserved or constrained self. She was completely—neither. Cool. Hot. Proud. Shy. Gentle. Strong. Passionate. Quiet. She was all of these together.

But was she also liar, cheat, whore, schemer? Unprincipled seductress? User?

Tony didn't know for sure. All he did know with a certainty that twisted in his gut like a knife was that he wanted to bed her.

Annie walked along High Street in Mansfield toward the large mercantile store. She'd pointed it out to Tony when they entered the town. They'd stabled their horses, which would be fed and cared for by O'Malley & Sons while they completed their respective business.

It hadn't taken very long for Annie to dispatch her packages and pick up some mail for the station. She half expected Tony to question her when she removed the oilskin pouch that hung over her saddle horn. He'd departed instead, questions unasked.

The tingling bell over the double doors announced her arrival into the wide shop. Whatever a settler could want, he would find it at Baker's Emporium. Clothes, tools, equipment, foodstuffs, geegaws, knick-knacks, toys, seed, flowers, magazines, books. You name it, and Baker's probably had it in stock, or could get it for you.

A flash of color caught Annie's gaze and she wandered over to the bolts of fabric. She reached out and stroked the softness of the deep blue velvet.

"Tempting, isn't it?" a familiar male voice whispered in her ear. "Go on, give in," Tony urged.

"I can't."

"Why not?"

"It isn't practical."

"So, who's to know?"

"I would."

"Your secret's safe with me," he promised.

"Would that I could believe that," she retorted. "Still," she said on a sigh, "it would make a lovely dress for Fallon. For Christmas."

"It would look better on her mother."

Annie's pulse pounded in her throat. She swallowed nervously.

"Go on. Take it."

"For Fallon." She leaned over to pick up the bolt. His hands were quicker.

"For yourself."

"G'day, Mrs. Ross," came the friendly voice of Sally Baker. A big-boned, tall woman, Sally was undisputed queen of her establishment. Sally made it her business to know as much about everyone else's as she possibly could, though there wasn't a malicious bone in her body.

"Hello, Mrs. Baker," Annie said. "I'd like a length of this that would do for a child's dress."

"Ah, something for the wee one, eh?" Sally asked as she deftly took the fabric from Tony's hands. Slapping it down onto a pine table, she removed scissors from the drawer and proceeded to cut the material.

"And add enough for a lady's dress, as well," Tony instructed.

Sally ceased cutting, her gray head lifting, sending

a sharp glance from one to the other. "For you, Mrs. Ross?"

"That's correct," Tony put in before Annie had a chance to object.

A sharp kick to his shins would be childish, Annie thought, fuming inwardly, but it would be oh-so satisfying. Trouble was, she did want the material. It was an impractical desire, for she had no real place to wear something made from it.

"Add a few pieces of this also," Tony said as he handed Sally a smaller bolt of tea-stained lace.

"Very good, Mr. Chambers." Sally had already made his acquaintance, profiting handsomely by his trade. She liked his selection, with an eye for style. Chambers had brass, he did, along with the charm of a real born-to-the-manor gentleman. She suspected that Annie Ross wouldn't remain a widow for much longer. Not with the likes of that sleeping under the same roof. Quality, coupled with the leanly muscled body of a young god, could be a sweet combination. Just what the doctor ordered. Or, as the case may be, what nature saw fit to bestow.

That he was blood kin to Cedric Chambers didn't hurt either. In fact, Sally thought as she cut into the bolt again, he had a look about him that made her think of Cedric himself. Not physically; more so in manner.

Annie pulled a hastily scribbled list from the pocket of her dungarees. "Have you some dried fruit?"

"Over in those barrels, lovey," Sally replied, pointing to several stacked against a side wall.

"Then I'll take a look." Annie wandered in the direction of the barrels.

Tony watched as Sally smoothly wrapped the bundles of velvet in tissue paper and then in brown paper.

"Cut the same amount in the dark goldish brown velvet, and the red." He selected two other patterns of lace for trim, tossing in a few pieces of French ribbon also. "Don't tell her."

Sally nodded. "I understand," she said with a wicked gleam in her eyes.

The salesgirl, Sally's granddaughter, was scooping a quantity of dried figs, peaches, and pears into deep paper bags.

"Give me some gumdrops, too," Annie requested, thinking Fallon would like the treat. "And," she considered, her head tilted to one side, "some of the chocolate."

The girl filled a small bag with the assorted flavored gumdrops, and then another bag, this one slightly bigger, with chunks of chocolate.

Annie's mouth watered as she handed over the coin to pay for the sweets and tucked them away in her coat pocket. There was no room for the bags of dried fruit.

"I'll add these to your other order, ma'am," the girl offered, gathering the paper sacks and placing them inside larger woven bags already stuffed with items.

"What say we get a bite to eat before we head back?" Tony asked.

"The hotel serves a rather good meal," Annie stated.

"Then the hotel it is."

"Have you finished your purchases?" She gave a quick glance to the stack of bags and parcels.

"I've gotten what I needed from here, yes," he said, his baritone sounding deeper and darker to Annie's ears.

"Shall we come back for it then?" How would they ever get it all back to the station? she wondered.

"No," Tony replied, taking her arm and escorting her to the door, a nod of his head in Sally's direction. "It's being sent to the station tomorrow, or so I've been promised."

"Whatever did you buy?" Annie asked, curiosity getting the better of her manners.

"All in good time, my dear," he assured her. "All in good time."

Chapter Fourteen

He was definitely an enigma.

Just when Annie thought she had all the clues to who he was, Tony went and changed the components of the game.

She sliced a sharp glance in his direction. He was riding just a few feet away from her. The sun was playing tag with the scattered clouds, popping in and out. Fallon rode in front of Tony; one of his gloved hands held her securely in place. Her daughter was enjoying the experience; Annie could tell that by the laughter that erupted from the little girl's mouth every so often.

They were on their way to Broken Hill, taking Patrick up on his offer of hospitality. So that they could make the journey unencumbered, their satchels, containing changes of clothes and personal items, had been sent ahead yesterday, along with a side of freshly dressed beef for Patrick's larder.

If she hadn't seen the wagon loaded with packages arrive yesterday from Baker's in Mansfield, Annie wouldn't have believed all that had transpired since they'd returned from town. Luncheon there had actually been a most pleasant meal. She and Tony had shared a private corner table in the hotel dining room, along with a bottle of crisp local white wine—she found herself beginning to enjoy the taste of wines more and more with Tony as her guide—and a selection of fresh fish.

Time had sped by as they lingered, finding, surprisingly, myriad things to talk about. Relaxing with Tony over a meal in public hadn't been as hard as Annie had thought. He made it easy, or maybe it was the wine. He seemed genuinely interested in what she had to say, which made Annie open up slightly, albeit cautiously. Then it was her chance to discover what she could about him. She wanted to find out if there was more to him than simply a man for whom the pursuit of pleasure was the sole object of life. Cedric had often claimed that there was starch in the boy, underneath the *bon vivant* exterior. Once or twice, Cedric had hinted that it would only take the right woman to bring it to the foreground.

After meeting Tony, Annie had wondered what type of woman Cedric had had in mind. Certainly not a complacent society wife, content to sit idly by while her husband did as he pleased, leaving her to a barren existence in his shadow. A woman without spirit or pride would never see beyond the outer layer of the man. A meek mouse wouldn't bring out starch. Neither, she judged, would a shrew. This man might be tamed to an extent, but he would never be dominated.

Annie thought of her own parents' long-term marriage. They had been partners, both giving to and accepting from each other. Rare it was, but that was the kind of marriage she'd once hoped to have as well. A lifelong partner to see the years through with; someone to share both the pleasure and the pain of life. Someone to count on, to trust. A man, it could be said, for all seasons.

Did such a man exist?

Oh yes, she'd had proof of that—her father, for one; Cedric, for another. She'd loved them both—one as a father, the other as the truest kind of friend. She even imagined that Patrick might be that kind of man if only he would open his eyes and see what was right under his nose.

Spunk. Mettle. Those were the terms Cedric had used. Tony's wife would have to possess those traits, he'd said. A woman of courage and passion who could meet his grandnephew more than halfway.

Such a woman, Annie decided, would more than have her work cut out for her.

With a sigh of exasperation as they rode across the starkly beautiful winter High Country landscape, Annie recalled what had happened when the items they'd ordered from Baker's had arrived.

Foodstuffs aplenty were unloaded from the large wagon, including triple the quantity of dried fruits she'd purchased. Barrels one-quarter the size of those in the general store were loaded with figs, peaches, raisins, apricots, pears, and more. They were taken from the flatbed wagon into the kitchen, to be stored in the pantry for use as needed. Several similar oak barrels were taken to Jim Winters's cottage so that Nora could use them for the meals she fixed for the men. Glass jars filled with assorted candies were divided between the main homestead, the Winterses', and the bunkhouse.

Tony had remembered the station hands and the staff also. Presents for Mary, Alice, and Alfred emerged from the wrappings of brown paper. Lengths of pretty fabric for new frocks and a bright silk shawl for each sister and for Jim's wife. For Alfred, he'd purchased a new gold watch and fob. Jim Winters received a new hat, along with a bottle of vintage Scotch whiskey. The station jackeroos got tobacco and tea.

Tony hadn't neglected Fallon either, surprising Annie with his choice of a gift. He'd picked a white china music box, decorated with painted pansies, that played "Greeensleeves." Fallon had instantly adored it, winding the key and listening to the haunting piece of music, insisting that everyone else listen as well.

For Annie, the biggest surprise had come when she unwrapped the bundles that contained the fabrics. Tony had carried them into the parlor, placing them on the velvet settee. Annie followed, as did Fallon.

"They're not all mine," she'd insisted, frowning at the assorted packages. By her reckoning, there should have only been two. "There's been some mistake."

"Open them," was all he said.

Annie was flabbergasted by what she saw as she untied the string of the first bundle. Inside were several lengths and colors of ribbons. The next small package contained various pieces of lace trim.

"How pretty," Fallon declared, handling a piece of dark blue gros grain ribbon.

Annie opened the rest of the packages, the selection of the velvets a shock to her. In addition to the blue she'd chosen, there was a shade in deepest wine, and one in golden brown, a color similar, she thought, to Tony's hair.

"I didn't choose these," she protested mildly, unable to stop her fingers from stroking the soft material, nor her imagination from picturing the finished garments. Each color included a length for Fallon as well.

"I did."

She regarded Tony, gazing at the curve of his lips as he smiled. "Why?"

"Quite simply because I wanted to."

"I can't allow you to—"

Tony interrupted her. "Why ever not? You let O'Donnell give you earrings without a by-your-leave."

"That was different," she insisted.

"How so?"

She wet her lips and lowered her lashes. "Because it was."

"Not quite good enough, my dear." Tony stepped closer to her. "Call it selfish of me if you will," he commented with a shrug. "I adore seeing women in fine clothes." He lowered his voice so that Fallon, sitting close by on a tapestried footstool, playing with her music box, wouldn't hear. "Do you think I had an ulterior motive?"

Annie shot him a glance, her eyes meeting his. "I don't know what you mean."

"Oh," Tony drawled, "I think you do."

"If I'd wanted to purchase more material," she declared, "I would have."

"I doubt that," he countered. "I saw how you looked at it, how you responded to the feel. Don't deny what we both know is truth—you wanted it, yet something held you back."

"I didn't need it," Annie insisted. "That's the only reason."

Tony arched a thick brown brow. "Is it? Truly?"

"Of course," she stated.

Tony took her hand, gently pulling her from her chair, scooping the two lengths of velvets from her. He led her to the gilt-edged mirror on the wall.

"What are you doing?" Annie demanded.

"Hush," he said in a soft voice, draping a length of the wine velvet over one of her shoulders, then the other. "Now, see what that color does for you."

Annie stared at her reflection. The claret hue brought out the color in her cheeks, and deepened the gray in her eyes. Her right hand caressed the texture of the material, her fingertips idly stroking it.

"Now try this," Tony urged, whisking that piece of fabric from her with a gentle tug, replacing it with the brown.

She stood there as he arranged the other hue in the same manner as the previous. The color blended well with her hair and her skin, giving both a golden glow. It evoked a softer, gentler mood.

Tony leaned close to her, bending slightly; their faces were caught in the mirror, framed together momentarily, as if they were the only two people in the world. He whispered, his tone dark and seductive, "Beauty needs no other reason for adornment than that it exists." His hands lingered on her shoulders as he stood behind her. "Accept what I've given you in good faith."

And Annie had done just that. But now she wondered if she'd done the right thing in keeping Tony's gifts. Standing there in front of the mirror, the fabric around her like a web of dreams spun by a far superior hand than hers, she'd glimpsed another side of herself. A side richer and deeper than ever existed before; a side aching with unknown feelings churning inside her.

"We'll soon be there," Annie called out as they sped across the open expanse of land, a large flock of sheep grazing less than a half mile away.

Tony nodded in acknowledgment of her words. Good thing, too, he thought, as her daughter had drifted off to sleep some moments ago. A trusting child, Fallon had closed her eyes and put herself completely into his care. His responsibility, as it were.

Responsibility. From a man with none but what time to rise in the morning, or which offer to accept for a dinner or a party, he now had heaps, the list growing longer every day, it seemed. Funny thing was, it was like a new coat. It fit as though tailored to his form.

He pulled back slightly on Merlin's reins, slowing the stallion to a brisk canter. He sliced a glance at Annie to his left. She was an able rider, moving as one with her animal, confident. He admired that in a woman, loving riding as he did.

And that was not all he admired about her. He couldn't help but recall how she'd looked last night when he'd enfolded her body with the soft velvet. The deep claret heightened the color of her eyes, giving her the appearance of an ancient temptress. How much more would the color have done for her if he could have draped it over the hills and valleys of her bare body? His flesh tightened with the thought. The golden-brown hue brought to mind visions of autumn, leaves aplenty, a late-day tryst upon the earth, surrounded by color and texture.

Tony forced his ill-advised thoughts aside as they rode through the gates of Broken Hill station, shouts of "G'day" from sheepmen echoing in his ears.

As Patrick's homestead came into view, Tony's eyes widened slightly. Expecting something less grand, he was taken aback by the size and design of the house. It was bold and impressive, from the colors used to the way it rose above the surrounding area.

"Beautiful, isn't it." Annie's statement was rhetorical, though Tony chose to answer as if she'd posed a question.

"Rather interesting, I would say."

"Interesting?" She threw him a puzzled glance before a suspicion leapt into her brain. "Ah," she said, dismounting and giving the reins to the carrot-headed stable boy, "you thought Patrick might live in less than first-rate circumstances?"

Tony leaned over and put Fallon into Annie's waiting arms, then dismounted from his huge horse with practiced ease. "I will admit that I wasn't expecting something like this," he responded, waving in the direction of the house, "ambitious, if you will."

Annie smiled. "You're in for quite a few surprises then." She was curious as to what Tony would make of Mei, praying that nothing untoward would come of the situation for all their sakes. Since the subject had never been broached, she didn't know how he felt about a woman of another race. She knew how many in this new country treated the Chinese, brought over to labor in the mining fields. The legacy of the Celestials had been fraught with prejudice and derision. Many returned to China. Still others remained in the new land, looking for what Annie had wanted as well, shelter and a new beginning. A place to make a new life, away from the old.

Fallon awoke and rubbed her eyes, blinking in the sunlight. Annie hefted the weight of the child until Tony said, "Here, let me," and picked Fallon up, holding her against his chest as Fallon curved her arms about his neck, snuggling close to him.

Annie remained rooted to the spot, her eyes drinking in the sight of her child and the tall man who held Fallon so protectively in his grasp, as if she belonged there. It brought to mind the inescapable fact that Fallon was a child in need of a father, or at least a strong male figure in her young life. As Fallon had responded to Cedric, now she responded to his grandnephew in much the same way. Annie watched as Tony whispered something that made the little girl giggle. How was it that he, rake that he surely was, looked so right with her daughter, as if they were bonded by blood rather than circumstance?

Or was that simply her own fanciful imagination running wild, seeing things as she wished them to be, instead of how they really were?

Annie sighed, quickly following them up the steps as the door to the house opened and Patrick stepped onto the vernada.

"Welcome to Broken Hill station," he announced.

"Get away!" Patrick exclaimed. "He bought all that?" His small mouth curved in speculation. "Trying to bribe his way into being 'boss' of the station, is he?"

"That wasn't the reason, I'm sure," Annie insisted, finding herself defending her partner from Patrick's suspicions.

"Oh, and aren't you taking a lot on faith, me darlin'?" he observed keenly. "Perhaps a wee bit too much, I'm thinking."

"Nonsense," Annie protested. "You're much too cynical, Patrick."

"With regards to that pommy, you'd better believe it."

"So, here's the perfect chance to win him over."

"And what would I be doing that for?" he asked.

Quietly Annie responded, "For me."

"And why would that be so important to you all of a sudden, my girl?"

"I have to live with him for a year," she explained. "Do you think I want us all at odds for that time?"

"While he's beneath my roof, I'll keep a civil tongue in me head, darlin'," Patrick assured her, "providing he does likewise, but don't expect me to embrace him warmly all the same."

"That's all I ask. That you give him a chance. Let him get to know you as I have."

"Are you giving him a chance, too?"

"Haven't I indicated as much?" Annie moved aside, walking around the parlor, pretending an interest in the objets d'art in a corner curio cabinet.

"Annie, me girl, what's wrong? And don't be lying to me and saying nothing, because I'd know the truth of the matter."

She wrung her hands. What could she say? That the sight of her daughter held in Tony Chambers's arms had melted something inside herself, flooding her body with an ache deep in the pit of her stomach. A haunting longing for something that she couldn't define.

"It's nothing, really," she answered her friend. "Just a mood."

"Look at me," Patrick insisted. When she did, Patrick could see the truth in her eyes. "You're fibbing to test the patience of the saints, me girl. Why?"

"Not on purpose, I assure you."

Patrick closed the distance between them, taking Annie's hands in his. "I'd help you if I could."

Annie gave him a weak smile. "I know you would. It's just that I don't know what it is, actually. All I know is that I feel slightly off balance," she confessed, laying

218

her head on Patrick's chest, feeling his strong arms close about her.

Tony stood in the open doorway, watching them, unable to hear their words distinctly because they'd spoken so softly. All he could see was that Annie was in O'Donnell's arms, her eyes closed, seemingly content in the embrace. He doubted that a breath of wind could get between their bodies, so close did they appear to be. And one of O'Donnell's broad, square hands was tenderly stroking Annie's long hair and back.

Tony's nostrils flared as his eyes narrowed; anger, hot and passionate, rose within him; his hands balled into tight fists at his sides. If he'd had that stock whip in his hands, he might have been tempted to use it on O'Donnell right now, hoping to ease the unexplained raw pain that ripped through his middle.

In another man, he might have suspected jealousy as the cause for the mixture of rage and hurt churning inside him. But for him, he'd have to care deeply first for the woman involved, and he knew that wasn't the situation. At least Tony told himself that it wasn't the situation in which he found himself.

Tony took a deep breath and unballed his fists. When he spoke, his voice dripped with chilly politeness. "Am I interrupting a private moment? If so, I can come back later."

Annie's head jerked back from Patrick. Her eyes snapped open. A guilty flush rose in her cheeks. Oh God! she thought, what must this look like to Tony, already suspicious as he was of her relationship to Patrick? She glanced anxiously at Tony's face and found no clues there. An impassively polite social mask had settled over his features.

219

Gail Link

"No, you aren't," she hastened to say, leaving it at that, fearful that if she tried to explain further, it would only complicate matters. She noted that Tony had changed from the clothes that he'd worn on the journey to Broken Hill. This morning, when they'd left Camelot, Tony had dressed in some new gear, which she assumed he'd purchased in Mansfield. What was referred to as a "Colonialist" style shirt had graced his upper body. The four-button, long-sleeve shirt was of soft cotton chambray in a blue and white stripe, and he wore it with ivory moleskin trousers which had hugged his slim hips, long legs, and powerful thighs. A new wool felt hat had sat upon his head, similar in style to what everyone hereabouts wore.

Now he stood in the doorway to the parlor, a commanding presence in the clothes he'd chosen to wear tonight. They were not quite so formal as he wore at their station, though a decided cut above the average. A bottle-green wool jacket was impeccably tailored to fit his tall frame, beneath which he wore a white silk shirt, the cut exactly like the one he'd worn earlier, definitely Australian in design. Matching trousers of the same dark green covered his legs.

Patrick was more informal in his mode of dress, with a white cotton shirt, buff-colored trousers, and riding boots.

Annie had changed clothes too. She wore a long-sleeved, high-necked blouse of cotton, its masculine styling contrasting to her very feminine form. Her sweeping skirt was navy wool. Tonight, her hair was pulled back from her face with a new ribbon of dark blue silk. On her ears she wore Patrick's opals.

Patrick broke the silence in the room. "Whiskey?" He'd seen the slight flare of cold anger in the other man's eyes before Tony hid it. He'd be damned if he'd apologize within his own house for comforting a friend. If Mr. Chambers's long English nose was out of joint, then so be it. Devil take him for a fool.

"Neat," Tony answered, his eyes monitoring Annie's movements as she took a seat on one of the two Chesterfield sofas in the room.

Patrick handed Tony his drink, fixing one for himself as well. "What'll you have, Annie?"

"You know, I'd love a glass of apple cider, if you have any." It was also, Annie reckoned, a way to get Patrick out of the room without arousing Tony's suspicions. She'd felt the chill that had settled over the parlor after Tony had caught them like two naughty children with their hands in the cookie jar. Explanations would be futile and serve no purpose, except to raise even more questions.

Patrick smiled in her direction. "I think that can be arranged, me darlin','" he responded. "Let me go and see if there's any in the kitchen, and while I'm at it, I'll see if Mei's got supper about ready."

After Patrick left the room, Tony asked, "Who's May?"

"Patrick's housekeeper-cook," Annie answered, adding in a no-nonsense tone, "and my friend."

He tossed back a large swallow of whiskey. "May. An interesting name." Tony expected a large, hearty Irish woman, with a cheery face and a sharp eye, one who would take no guff from anyone, rather like the Irish cook his mother had employed when he was thirteen. A stolid soul, one who would probably provide a meal of unsurpassed boredom.

Tony took another drink of the Irish whiskey, wondering what he had interrupted between Annie and

O'Donnell. He didn't believe her lame excuse for a minute. There was something going on and he meant to discover what it was before he quit this house. He'd have it out with O'Donnell soon enough.

He glanced at Annie sitting quietly in her seat, hands folded primly in her lap. He watched her tongue snake out to wet her lips. Hunger for her mouth, to trace the same path as her tongue just had, ate at him. Did he have the patience to slowly unbutton that blouse, from neck to waist, taking his time with each detail, or would he rather tear it quickly, exposing the treasures that it hid? Could he wait for the skirt to come off, or would he simply toss it up, along with however many petticoats she wore and take her there without waiting?

He imagined the soft cries that would come from her throat as he slid into her tight dampness. Would she lie there passively, moaning softly as he filled her, or would she scream and claw like a wild cat in her abandon?

"You don't know the half of it," Annie remarked with a slight chuckle.

He almost choked on the remains of his drink at her words. She was referring to her earlier comment, and he was still entertaining fanciful thoughts of bedding her.

"Don't I?" One of Tony's thick brown brows arched ever so slightly.

Annie raised her chin, her mouth curving into an I-know-something-you-don't smile. "No, but you will, soon."

Patrick walked in, in his hand a large glass of cider. Annie took the cold beverage, sipped it, and pronounced her approval; "Marvelous." She glanced in

Tony's direction. "You really should try some of this."

Tony put down his empty glass. "May I?" he asked, extending his hand toward her.

Annie blinked. He wanted to taste the cider from her own glass. She found herself handing it to him, watching as Tony put his mouth to the same spot where hers had been, feeling odd at so intimate a gesture.

After sampling the drink, Tony extended the glass to Annie. "Quite good," he remarked, his tongue skimming softly over his lips. "Reminds me somewhat of the cider from the farms in Somerset. Sweet," he said, his eyes making direct contact with Annie's, "with the hint of a bite." *Like you*, he wanted to say.

Their hands touched briefly when Annie took the glass from him. Annie swallowed, cognizant of the same heat flowing between them that she'd felt before. It frightened her because she didn't understand it. Sweet angels in heaven, what did it mean? She'd touched the hands of other men in her life, and no one had affected her as his touch had. But then, no one she'd ever met had been like Tony Chambers. He was unique in so many ways. She mentally searched for a Latin phrase her father had taught her. *Sui generis.* Tony was that, all right. One of a kind.

The mahogany grandfather clock in the corner chimed the hour.

"Supper should be ready," Patrick announced.

And not a moment too soon, Annie thought, rising. She needed Mei's calming presence more than she cared to admit.

"Gentlemen, if you will excuse me, I'll just go and collect Fallon and meet you both in the kitchen as soon as I can."

Annie watched them walk away, each man keeping

223

to himself. She took a deep breath, letting out a long sigh.

Was her life ever going to return to some semblance of normality? Or was she to be forever lost in this limbo, without hope of a reprieve?

Chapter Fifteen

The beautiful young Asian woman standing in Patrick O'Donnell's kitchen was a confusing sight to Tony Chambers, who'd been expecting an entirely different sort of woman. Thrown for a loop, Tony recovered quickly, extending his hand in greeting, which the woman took.

"Tony Chambers."

Patrick stepped in and made the formal introductions. "Mei, this is Annie's partner in the station, Cedric's relative, Anthony Chambers." Patrick moved closer to Mei, his arm casually about her slender shoulders, a wide, impish grin on his small mouth. "Mr. Chambers, I have the honor to introduce to you Miss Mei Thomas."

"My pleasure, indeed, Miss Thomas," Tony offered, studying the girl before him. She couldn't be more than eighteen, he judged. And a definite beauty, with her dark, sloe eyes and creamy skin. Her chosen costume was new to his experience: a long-sleeved, slim black sheath in brocaded satin, with swirling patterns of gold and red in a dragon motif. The garment hugged her contours and fell to past her knees; it was split up both sides, revealing black silk trousers, white stockings, and flat black slippers. Her shiny ebony hair was pulled back in a knot at the nape of her slender neck, anchored with long ivory sticks. She was tall, Tony suspected, for a woman of her race, matching O'Donnell in height.

Housekeepers were generally older women in the world Tony inhabited, certainly not young girls barely out of the schoolroom. He assumed that there must be more to this unusual situation than met his eye. Annie had told him that O'Donnell was a bachelor, yet he lived in the same house—platonically?—as this delightful-looking creature. Was O'Donnell feathering his nest with a bird of exotic plumage while actively pursuing another?

"If you will both take your seats," Mei requested in a gentle manner, a bit unnerved by all the attention being paid her, "I shall begin to serve."

Patrick indicated the large round pine table in the center of the room.

Tony strolled over, taking a chair. It didn't seem to matter which one as the arrangement of the table was very informal, cozy even. He remained standing while Patrick hefted a platter containing a roast of beef, half sliced, onto the table, making room for the heaping bowl of roasted vegetables that Mei placed next to the meat, followed by a small gravy boat. A wicker basket lined with a linen napkin held slices of warm Irish soda bread.

Annie walked into the big kitchen, Fallon holding her hand. She crossed the room and went to the place next to Tony without thinking.

"There is something here," Mei said, taking a brown and cream-colored afghan from the back of a rocking chair, "that you can use to add height to Fallon's chair."

Accepting the folded-over plump afghan, Annie

placed it on Fallon's chair, lifting the little girl and settling her in before taking her own chair.

Tony held it out for her, pushing it in when she was seated. Annie murmured her thanks, watching from the corner of her eye as he sat down next to her. They were close. Very close. She could detect the scent of the soap he used and the cologne he wore, the aroma of the woods overlaced with a hint of lime.

"I hope you don't mind eating in the kitchen," Patrick said to Tony as he passed the plate of meat to Mei on his right. "We do have a formal dining room, but we've only ever used it when my family came here last Christmas." He helped himself to the steaming vegetables before passing them along. "I don't set much with all the trappings, not like some hereabouts with their overly grand ideas," Patrick added with a trace of sarcasm in his tone. "We live as we live and like it that way."

Tony understood that he was being baited by the Aussie; he chose to ignore it, mainly for the sake of the two women at the table. Engaging in a verbal slanging match here would be a waste of time and energy, not to mention a breach of good manners. Tony knew he was perceived by O'Donnell as a snob, one who couldn't pass muster in this environment. Did O'Donnell expect that he would turn up his nose and demand that they eat in the dining room, or not eat at all, like a sulky child having a tantrum? Good God, if O'Donnell thought that this was the worst he could heap upon him, then he was in for a surprise. Yes, Tony readily admitted preferring elegance in his surroundings. What fool wouldn't? But, if needs must, then he could adapt. He'd taken meals in his share of country inns and taverns, by camp fire even.

O'Donnell had a lot to learn about who Tony was and what being a Chambers meant. The family motto was "Forge on."

Tony accepted the platter from Mei. After selecting several slices of beef for himself, he held the plate for Annie so that she could pick what she wanted for herself and Fallon.

The circle of light overhead cast a warm glow upon Annie's skin. There was a touch of color in her cheeks; a hint of her perfume wafted into his nostrils, tantalizing him. Delicate and expensive, not cheap and tawdry as he might have expected once upon a time.

"Thank you," she said softly, indicating that she was done.

Even the sound of her voice stroked something inside him. Wondering what it would be like to hear that voice expressing passion was becoming a never-ending source of mental scrutiny. Would it be soft and low, warm with need, or louder, with a hungry demand?

"Are you quite finished?"

O'Donnell's voice broke the chain of his thoughts. Tony realized he'd been holding the platter, daydreaming right there at the table.

"Sorry." He passed the meat back to Patrick, taking the bowl of vegetables in its stead while Annie shot him a bemused look.

Tony returned Annie's glance with a small smile as he helped himself to the assorted vegetables before passing them along to her. The meal was simple, but tasted surprisingly good. The addition of several spices to the meat and rich brown gravy convinced Tony that Mei could hold her own in the province of the kitchen, much as Annie had proven to him.

These women were, indeed, worlds apart from the women of his experience.

Tony sipped at his glass of cider, O'Donnell having informed him earlier that he didn't keep a wine cellar in his house. Whiskey and brandy, however, O'Donnell had at the ready. Conversation floated around him as Annie and Patrick caught up on local gossip, neighbors, and news. Tony remained silent for the most part, watching. He realized he wasn't the only one, either. Mei was silent as well, eating her meal without uttering a word. She appeared somewhat shy to Tony, content to keep to her place, though he did observe one glance she aimed in Patrick's direction that seemed briefly clouded in pain.

"Are you as in the dark as I am?" Tony asked Mei, leaning closer to her, his voice a whisper.

Mei put down her fork and turned her head in Tony's direction, speaking softly. "I am used to it," she replied forthrightly. "It was even more"—she paused as if searching for the right word—"animated when your great-uncle graced this house with his presence."

"So, you knew Cedric as well?"

Mei nodded, a fond smile upon her lips. "He was a kind and gentle man, much loved by all who knew him."

"So I've been told."

"It is always gratifying to hear good spoken about one's family, is it not?"

Tony frowned, thinking about the recent troubles within his family—how many an unkind word had been bandied about in recent months.

"Have I said something to disturb you?" Mei asked, anxious. "If so, please, I humbly beg your forgiveness if I have given offense. I would not knowingly insult a guest in Patrick's home."

Tony hastened to reassure the young woman, whose distress sounded genuine. "It's nothing. Really. And you're correct, sometimes it's quite refreshing to hear good things said about one's relatives. I only wish," he added thoughtfully, "that I could have known Cedric as well as others seem to have."

Choosing her words carefully, trying to help her friend in the best way possible, Mei hoped to make this man see Annie in a new light. "Annie loved him so. She was devastated when he died."

"Was she?" Tony asked, glancing in Annie's direction.

As if she could sense that Tony was looking at her, Annie momentarily halted her conversation and turned her head, smiling at Tony before continuing what she'd been saying.

"Oh yes," Mei insisted, "there must be no doubt in your mind about that. He was like a father to her, and she mourned him."

But, Tony wondered, had Cedric also been more than a father? Had he crossed the boundaries of accepted familial duty and been a lover to Annie Ross? And what about the man at whose table they now ate? Had O'Donnell been her lover, too? And if so, was he her lover still?

Annie suddenly realized that she and Patrick had rambled on so that they had, in effect, excluded both Mei and Tony from their conversation. Ashamed of her lapse of manners, she hastily apologized to them.

"It's of no consequence," Tony acknowledged matter-of-factly. "I can hardly comment on the price of sheep or beef when I know little or nothing about them. Nor can I appreciate the merits of local gossip since I don't know the parties involved; but, should you consider discussing politics, or plays, maybe music or art, ah, then," he drawled, "I can most assuredly hold my own and then some."

Annie flushed with embarrassment at his politely phrased rebuke.

"You're quite right," she said. "I didn't realize that I was being rude."

Tony was amazed at her sincere apology. In truth, he'd been annoyed at what he perceived to be a deliberate attempt to keep him at a distance, as if he were only on the fringes, where he belonged. She'd readily taken the blame for what hadn't been her fault alone. Nor, he judged, had she precluded him on purpose. He could read the truth of that on her face—she was really sorry for any slight she might have committed.

Damn. She was making it bloody difficult to distrust her.

Annie stole a glance at Tony's wary face. Lord, but he was making it harder and harder to keep the barriers in place between them. Slowly, surely, Tony Chambers was wearing away at the doubts she harbored. The momentary vulnerability that Annie had glimpsed in his eyes had almost made her want to throw caution to the winds and draw him to her bosom in comfort, as if he were a child in need.

Reason stopped her.

Once, she recalled, when she was little, a traveling circus had come to Philadelphia. It featured a caged mountain lion from one of the southwestern territories. She'd been frightened, yet oddly captivated by the big tawny-gold cat; she'd watched as it prowled restlessly about its confining cage. For one moment, Annie had glimpsed the look of unguarded anguish in its green eyes before it regained its ferocity when a young boy yelled taunts.

Tony, she realized, reminded her of that animal.

Don't let him in, a voice inside her warned. *He is dangerous. Much too dangerous.*

"Mama, can I be excused?"

Annie turned to her daughter. "Are you tired, sweetheart?"

Fallon nodded her head, her eyes drooping.

"You've had a very long day, my dear," Tony commented, pushing back his chair. "Would you like to go to bed?"

Fallon nodded again.

Tony was out of his chair, scooping up the little girl into his arms, where she snuggled against his wide chest as if she'd been doing it all her life.

Tony looked down at Annie. "What say we put her to bed?"

"I'll clear the table while you settle her," Mei proposed, rising from her seat. "When you return, we can have dessert."

Annie led the way up the stairs to the second level, down the hall until she reached the room she shared with her daughter. Opening the door, she stepped inside. Tony followed.

"Just put her down on the bed and I'll get her things," Annie instructed, scooping up the child's nightgown from the chair where it lay next to hers.

Tony's gaze shifted from the child on the bed to the mother picking up the child's change of clothes and stuffed lamb. He noticed that Annie had brought along the same nightgown that she'd worn the night when he'd entered her room. Soft cream-colored flannel, all prim and proper. Still, his flesh quickened with the thought of Annie slipping the gown over her bare body, the material enfolding her from neck to ankle.

"Uncle Tony?"

He snatched his glance away from the forbidden realms into which it had wandered so effortlessly.

"Yes, sweetheart?" he answered.

"Can I give you a good night kiss?"

Tony smiled, cupping his hand around the little girl's blond head as he sat down on the edge of the bed. "You may indeed, my lady fair."

Fallon wrapped her arms about Tony's neck, squeezing it tight, kissing his cheek with a resounding smack. Her tiny fingers skimmed the brown mole along his jawline. "What's this?"

"Fallon!"

"But I want to know what it is, Mama," the child protested.

"It's an angel's kiss," Tony explained.

Fallon blinked, examining the brown dot closer. "Really?"

"My grandmother told me it was," Tony answered with a straight face, although Annie could see the glint of humor in his eyes as they met hers over the child's head.

"I wish I could be kissed by an angel," the little girl said with a sigh.

"Who knows," Tony replied, "you just might be one day."

Fallon lightly touched the mole again, tilting her head in consideration. "Do you think so, Mama?"

"Perhaps," Annie said, coming closer to the bed, her own eyes focused on the mark.

"It only happens when you're asleep," Tony said.

"Really?" the little girl asked, excited at the prospect. "I'm going to sleep right now," she declared.

"Not without changing your clothes, young lady," Annie insisted, "which we can do as soon as *Uncle* Tony leaves."

"Ah," Tony said, "my cue for an exit." He bent over and kissed the child on the forehead. "Sleep well, my lady fair." He rose and quit the room, waiting outside for Annie.

"Angel's kiss indeed," she said a few minutes later, her hands resting on her hips as she closed the door to her bedroom behind her. "Are you sure it's not you that has a touch of the blarney, Mr. Chambers?"

Tony laughed. "Sorry to disappoint you, but I'm resoundingly English, my dear, although my grandmother was half French."

"That must explain it. She sounds delightfully imaginative."

"Oh, that she was," he said with a devilish glint in his eyes. "A regular Original. She was barely eighteen when she married my grandfather, who was forty-one."

"Are you joking?"

"Not at all," he responded. "They were, from all accounts, devoted to one another."

"Unusual, wouldn't you say?"

"Do I detect a note of surprise in your voice, *Mrs.* Ross?"

"Perhaps, although I didn't mean it to sound censorious."

Tony closed the space between them, standing in front of her, trapping her against the door. "Don't you think there can be great passion within a marriage?"

"I wouldn't—"

"What?" he interjected, hands on either side of her head, holding his weight as he leaned closer still, his voice low and intimate. "Know?"

Annie wet her lips. He'd caught her. She was about to admit that she had no real idea if there could be a great and all-consuming passion in a marriage. Having never been married, how would she be privy to such information? And what was so important about passion anyway? It was another fancy name for lust, and hadn't she already seen that side of folly masquerading as love?

". . . care to comment." She finished the sentence with a defiant look upward into his face.

The corners of Tony's mouth kicked up in a smile, deepening grooves on either side of his lips.

Annie lowered her eyes. Damn the man! Why did he have to smile like that? It was the kind of smile that would have a woman forgiving him for just about anything because it held traces of the boy he must have once been. Sweet. Carefree. And totally disarming.

She ducked beneath his spread arms. "I think we'd best be getting back downstairs before Patrick and Mei wonder what's happened to us."

"Yes, it wouldn't do to upset our host, now would it?" Tony inquired with a raised brow. He held out his arm. "Shall we?"

After the sweets course, which consisted of selections of cheese, apples, and a creamy rice pudding, Patrick offered Tony what he knew was the preferred gentleman's end to a long day: brandy, cigars, and a game of cards.

That left the two ladies on their own in the confines of the kitchen, where they lingered over tea and coffee.

Gail Link

"I think it went rather well, don't you?" Annie asked, sipping from an oversized granitewear mug. A half-eaten bowl of rice pudding sat in front of her.

"If you mean that the two of them didn't get into fisticuffs, then, yes, it went well," Mei replied.

The picture that sprang to mind of Tony Chambers engaging in a brawl was almost too unbelievable. Granted, Annie could imagine him at a gentlemen's club, sparring with a seasoned pro, but bare-knuckled in an alley, outside on the lawn, scrabbling in the dirt, or in the confines of a home was too ridiculous a prospect. He would use words as weapons. They were part of his arsenal. Or a glance. Those proud eyes could condemn or show disdain, wounding, she suspected, as deeply as any bullet could.

"Annie?"

"Sorry," she murmured. "I was just thinking about something."

"Don't you mean someone?" Mei drank from her cup of tea, refilling it from the small teapot. She'd inherited her father's fondness for an Indian blend rather than her mother's preferred green tea. Drinking her papa's favorite always brought her closer to his memory.

Annie rested her elbows on the table, her chin supported by her two overlapping hands. A deep sigh escaped her lips. "What did you think of him?"

There was no need to further identify "him." Mei knew about whom Annie spoke. "That your Mr. Chambers is a most pleasing man to the eye. Handsome. Very charming."

Annie swallowed a spoonful of the rice pudding, loaded with plump raisins and sprinkled with cinnamon. "You'll get no argument from me."

"There is a gentleness about him that I hadn't expected."

"Gentleness?" Annie tilted her head and stared at Mei.

"Yes. I saw it for a moment in his eyes when you first walked into the room with Fallon. It was there again when he lifted your child into his arms."

"He does seem to like Fallon very much."

"He likes Fallon's mother."

Annie could feel heat gathering in her cheeks. "I don't think he knows what to make of me."

"He knows what he'd like to make of you," Mei stated quietly.

Annie stared at her friend. "And what's that?"

"*His.*"

Annie's eyes widened in shock. "No. You must be mistaken." Annie repeated.

"I think not," Mei stated quietly. "Most times, his eyes appear to be like pale jade, beautiful and cool; then they warm with a heat that blazes hotter than any fire when he looks upon you."

Annie denied her friend's words again, shaking her head back and forth.

"I have seen the look of want on many men's faces when I was in the House of the Golden Lotus. Any woman would have fulfilled their needs, they were hungry only for a body. This man's pride, his soul if you will, burns only for you."

"You must be mistaken." Annie repeated.

"Do you not feel it?" Mei asked.

Annie's thoughts flew back to the encounter in her bedroom at the station, and to the other night when he'd draped the fabric over her shoulders and they had looked into the mirror together.

237

Mei read the answer in Annie's expressive face. "So, you have? I thought as much. I could tell that something has changed in you. It's there in the way you speak about him. The way you say his name, even. Your eyes express what your heart will not."

Annie was almost afraid to ask. "Which is?"

"That you are learning to love this man."

Annie sat stunned by Mei's words. *Love?* Tony Chambers?

It couldn't be true.

It mustn't be true.

Tears slipped down Annie's cheeks. Oh God, she thought, the realization searing her heart. What Mei said might just be true after all.

Chapter Sixteen

Thin reams of cigar smoke floated about Tony's head as he examined the hand that he'd been dealt. He and Patrick were playing for small sums, nothing like the amounts he was used to wagering in exclusive London establishments. This was what his friend Rafe would have laughingly called penny ante poker. Still, Tony played it with all the finesse he was capable of, since he loved the challenge of the game more than the actual wager. This past hour his bets had been conservative while he took stock of his opponent's mettle.

"I'll open," he drawled, tossing in a few coins from the stacks in front of him to the center of the round table.

Patrick flicked an equal amount in, plus an additional four shillings to liven the action.

Tony matched him, calling for three cards to replace the same number discarded. He swept the cards into his hand, adding them to the pair of jacks he held.

His face remained blank while his mind churned with questions that refused to go away. Would he get an honest answer to any he posed from the man sitting opposite him? Or would O'Donnell's mouth spew forth only lies to protect the good name of the woman he'd been cavorting with?

Tony paused to take another puff on his cigar,

blowing the smoke upwards. "I do believe I'll have to raise your raise," he informed Patrick, pushing all of his assorted coins into the center of the table. Tony was growing weary of waiting to discover what he had to know. The time for games was at an end. He wanted the truth. Now. Nothing else would suffice. He'd cautioned himself to have patience, but that was no longer an option.

Patrick glanced over the width of the card table and locked eyes with the other man. He wondered if the Englishman was bluffing. By all the saints, he couldn't tell, for the man opposite was a study in composure. Nothing marred the coolly presented look on Tony Chambers's face.

Picking up his glass of neat whiskey, Patrick downed it in one hearty swallow.

He pushed his own pile of money to the center, adding a pound note from his trouser pocket. He couldn't refuse the challenge, bluff or no bluff. "Call."

"Three gentlemen of the realm." Tony laid down his hand, three jacks prominent in the five-card group.

Patrick tossed his own cards upon the table, two queens alone in the crowd. "Congratulations," he said evenly. "It would seem that tonight you've the luck that people often say is reserved for the Irish alone."

"The 'Devil's Own,' eh?" Tony inquired, drinking the remainder of his brandy, the winning pot still in place. He made no move to rake in the money when he set down his glass. Instead, he picked up a single coin, flipping it back and forth between his long, nimble fingers.

Patrick observed, a trace of irony in his tone, "So it would seem."

"But are things always as they seem?" Tony asked,

blowing another ring of smoke into the air.

Patrick's brow furrowed at the other man's enigmatic question. "What do you mean?"

"Simply put, appearances."

"Such as?" Patrick wondered where this was all leading to. What in the world was the Englishman blathering about?

Tony tapped the ash on his slim cigar into the china tray. "Your close friendship with Annie Ross, for example."

"What of it?" Patrick demanded, belligerence rising in his voice.

"Just how close is it?"

"I'd be saying that's none of your damned business, Mr. Chambers. There's an end to it."

Tony replied, "I beg to differ."

"Differ all you want, pommy," Patrick shot back. "It's not something that I care to discuss."

"Why?" Another puff of smoke wafted in the air, though this was directed across the table at the other man. "Guilt, perhaps?"

"What would I have to be feeling guilty about?"

"The nature of your *friendship* with Mrs. Ross."

"You stiff-arsed bastard!" Patrick swore. "Just who the hell do you think you are?"

"I know who I am," Tony replied, his words delivered with the chill tones of ice. "That's not the point."

"Then what is?"

"To discover if you and she were playing my uncle for a fool."

"What's Cedric to do with this?" Patrick demanded. "He was my friend."

"Friends have been known, upon occasion, to betray friends over a woman," Tony stated. "It's happened before. It will happen again."

"Maybe where you come from it does, boyo, but not with me," Patrick retorted.

Tony's gaze never wavered from the other man, even as he continued to work the coin nimbly between his long fingers. "I'd like to believe that."

"No, I don't bloody well think you would," Patrick protested. "Because, if you did that, then you'd have to admit that you were wrong. That, God forbid, your precious English judgment was impaired in some way. Your kind will never own up to that."

Tony inquired blandly, "And what kind is that?"

"Pompous. Arrogant," Patrick replied scathingly, forgetting his position as host. He was beyond caring about politeness to a guest, especially this guest, now. "You think the world is yours for the asking, and be damned to anyone who stands in your way."

"Interesting," Tony drawled. "Wrong, but interesting." He was trying to keep himself from blurting out the question he wanted answered desperately. To do so would be to give the other man the upper hand, and it would mean admitting something to himself that he wasn't sure he could cope with at the moment. "But we digress. I think, on my great-uncle's behalf, that I have the right to know if you were playing Lancelot to his Arthur."

Patrick stared at him blankly. "What are you talking about?"

"Were you sleeping with his Guenevere—Annie Ross?"

Patrick froze in shock; moments later his anger was evident in the set of his face and in the fists that banged the card table. "No," he snarled. "And if you knew your uncle and Annie better," he retorted, "you'd never even think that ugly thought. Annie Ross is every inch a lady, not a whore, easily tumbled for the taking; if you weren't so much of an ass, Chambers, you'd see it plainly for yourself."

Patrick rose hastily, almost knocking over his chair, his face livid with temper. "My God, man, you're living with the woman. Are you so blind as not to see what's under your very nose? By all the blessed saints, she's quality. Cedric recognized that."

Tony realized in that instant that O'Donnell was telling him the truth. It was there in the indignation plainly stamped on his features, in the rigid set of his muscles, in the flare of anger in the blue eyes. A sense of relief spread rapidly through Tony's body.

But if what the younger man said was true, Tony speculated, where did that leave his suspicions?

The answer came rapidly: crumbling, like pillars of sand washed away by the tide.

Patrick came back with a question of his own for Tony. "Are you jealous?" he demanded. "Is it that you've tried to woo Annie and she's turned you down?"

"Don't be ridiculous," Tony said, fumbling with the coin as it slipped through his fingers and clattered upon the table. "I just needed to know what kind of person I'm dealing with, that's all."

Patrick's tone was contemptuous. "Haven't you the sense to figure that out for yourself? Or are you so caught up with your own narrow ways that you can't render judgment by what's in your heart? That is," he mocked, "supposing you have one. Being the English prig that you are, I'd be doubtin' that."

Patrick huffed, anger boiling inside him. "For insulting Annie, I ought to throw you out of my house this very minute and beat the bloody hell out of you for good measure," he snarled. "If I didn't think it would hurt and humiliate Annie to realize her partner thinks so little of her to believe that she's a strumpet, I would."

"You might try, O'Donnell," Tony warned, "but don't be fooled into believing that you would win." Tony slowly came to his feet, his taller height and broader body a contrast to Patrick's. "I could stop you."

"You might be thinkin' you could," Patrick retorted, unafraid, "but there's no knowing for sure."

Tony had to admire the younger man's determination and guts. O'Donnell had the cocky self-assurance and brass of a scrappy bantam rooster. He was loyal and fearless when standing up for a friend. These were traits Tony considered worthy of his respect.

He offered what he thought was an olive branch. "Let's forget we had this talk and chalk it up to the air needing to be cleared," Tony suggested.

"Cleared, is it?" Patrick asked, dumbfounded by Tony's blithe dismissal of the words that had been spoken. "Muddied is more like it, I'd be thinkin.' " He moved closer to the taller man. "Next I suppose you'll be wantin' to know if I love Annie.

"Well," Patrick declared pugnaciously, "I do."

Tony inhaled sharply, as if struck by a blow to his midsection. He hadn't been expecting that bit of information. "You do?"

Patrick heard the subtle change in the Englishman's voice. He smiled slightly. He'd scored a point in their verbal battle. "Yes, I do, and so did your uncle. He wouldn't have left her the station if he hadn't wanted to see Annie taken care of as she's a right to expect. And before your mind takes another step into the gutter, he wasn't sleeping with her either. Cedric Chambers was too honorable a man to take advantage of a woman like Annie in so base a manner. If he'd known her that way, then he would have married her, you can believe that. Unlike your kind," Patrick scathingly pointed out, "who's probably bedded more women than he can recall."

"And are you going to tell me that you've wanted to marry every woman you've bedded?" Tony retorted cynically.

At the unexpected flush of color in the younger man's skin, Tony's green eyes widened with surprise at the unforeseen notion that abruptly invaded his brain. By God, was it actually possible?

Tony voiced his thought aloud. "You're a virgin still?"

Patrick flushed deeper, replying honestly to the blunt query. "So what if I am?"

Tony didn't quite know how to react to that bit of news. He'd never met a man over the age of sixteen who hadn't been with a woman at least once. This was most unusual, to say the least. It certainly knocked his ideas of a romance between O'Donnell and Annie for a loop. It had to be true. No man would claim it otherwise to another if it weren't.

Patrick saw the change that came over Tony's face. The incredulity as Tony listened to the words, doubting the veracity. Then the pity as he accepted.

"Don't you dare to judge me!" Patrick exclaimed.

"I'm not," Tony replied.

"That's a bloody lie and you know it, Englishman. You're thinking that I'm not quite the man that you are. Well, I'm not," he admitted. "When I take a woman to my bed, she'll be sure she's loved. Can you say the same?"

O'Donnell had neatly turned the tables on him. Tony had been passing fond of most of the women who'd shared his bed, or he theirs, but as for love? No. He couldn't claim to have ever loved a woman he'd slept with. He'd never lied and pretended that he had, either, as did others he knew.

Yet Patrick had also said that he loved Annie. Was he hoping to have a flutter with her? To have her teach him the ways of the world? Tony wanted to press O'Donnell for an answer.

Before he could, however, O'Donnell struck first. "Cat got your tongue?"

Tony took a deep breath. "I find that your honesty deserves more of the same. No, I've never loved a woman in the way I think you mean. Love, I've found, shouldn't be a part of one's *amourettes*. That only leads to unavoidable complications when the affair has run its course. Better for all parties to stay uninvolved and remember the rules of the game."

Now it was Patrick's turn to give the older man a pitying glance. "You're really quite the coldhearted bastard, Chambers."

"Think what you will."

"I'm not after needing your permission for that." Patrick helped himself to another whiskey from the bottle on a nearby table, tossing it down in one quick swallow. "Do me a favor, pommy. Get out of my sight, would you?"

"This conversation will remain between us, I trust?" Tony asked.

Patrick leveled the other man a withering glance. "I should by rights tell Annie just what you think of her. She ought to be warned that you're a callous beggar who's out to ruin her."

246

Tony denied that remark. "That's not true."

"Oh, isn't it?"

"No. If Annie Ross is who and what she claims, then she has nothing to fear from me."

"Who died and named you bloody king of the world, Mr. Chambers?" Patrick demanded. "What right do you have to judge her? Or anyone, for that matter?"

"Whether you believe it or not, I have a duty that I owe to Cedric's memory."

"Which you willingly debase by your continued suspicions about Annie. Why don't you just go back to England where you belong? Leave everyone here alone."

"You'd like that, wouldn't you? Then you'd have the rich widow all to yourself."

Patrick's eyes sharpened. "So, you'd be thinking that I'd marry Annie just for her inheritance?"

"It's a tempting proposition."

"So's the lady herself, without the trappings," Patrick retorted. "Not that it's any of your business, boyo, but I'd not be wedding a woman I didn't love."

Tony pointed out, "You just a few minutes ago said that you did love her."

"Yes, I do, though it's not," Patrick admitted, "the 'till death do us part' way God intended for a husband and wife. Annie's me friend, like another of me sisters, and that she shall remain." Patrick walked the distance separating them. "You see, some of us take marriage seriously. When we pledge our vow before God, it's for keeps. For love. Not for property or the expectations of the family. I'll wager that you can't say as much."

Tony remained silent. What could he say to refute the Aussie's statements? Nothing. They were true.

247

When he married, he expected that it wouldn't be for love. That was too silly a prospect to even contemplate. Social considerations, breeding, money—they were what mattered in his world. He had responsibilities to meet, expectations to heed. Why, the idea of tossing aside what he'd been brought up to accept as ordained was ridiculous. Months ago in England he'd told Rafe that only a virgin bride would be suitable to him. A woman he could mold to what he wanted, what he expected. A woman who'd already be aware of her place in his life, her role. To entertain ideas of anything else was folly.

He ignored the younger man's questions. "Do we have an agreement that what's been said between us in this room remains here?"

Patrick considered the proposal. "For now. But I'll be watching you. If you hurt Annie, in any way, then all bets are off. I promise you that I'll make you regret it. Don't doubt it."

Tony didn't. He saw the determined spark of truth in the other man's blue eyes. O'Donnell appeared a man of his word, willing—almost eager—to keep a promise, especially *this* promise. Tony nodded, turned on his heel, and walked out the door, closing it softly behind him.

Pouring himself another whiskey, Patrick tossed it back, then threw the empty glass into the small hearth, where it shattered against the burning logs.

Patrick sank back into his chair. He glanced at the money that still lay in the middle of the table in a messy pile. With the back of his hand, he sent the money scattering about the floor. His elbows on the table, he rested his forehead against the heels of his

palms, his eyes closed. Had he made the right deci-
sions?

Mei found Patrick in the same position when she
opened the door to the office almost a half hour later.
The lamps were low, their light barely illuminating the
room. She saw the coins strewn across the carpet and
the bare floor.

Since Patrick hadn't bothered to bid her and Annie
good night, Mei assumed that the men were still playing cards. After Annie retired for the evening, Mei decided to see if there was anything Patrick or Tony
might want before she did likewise.

Crossing the room as quietly as she could, Mei bent
down and started to pick up the money.

"Leave it," Patrick said, his voice weary.

Mei's heart ached for him. He looked so forlorn, as
if he'd lost something precious. She immediately went
to him, kneeling at his feet, taking one of his strong
hands in hers, hoping to ease whatever was troubling
him.

"Tell me," she whispered coaxingly.

"I came near tonight to thrashing him, Mei," Patrick
declared. "I wanted to. Oh, saints be blessed, you don't
know how much I would have enjoyed putting my fist
in his handsome face, knocking that superior attitude
to kingdom come."

"Why?"

"For Annie's sake. The English bastard thinks he
knows it all."

"What did he say to you?" Mei stroked his hand with
her fingers, soothing the tension away gradually. It always came back to Annie. Should she tell Patrick her

suspicions regarding Annie's feelings for the Englishman?

No, she realized, now was not the time to do so. It could only serve to upset Patrick further. Maybe push him into acting in a way that would bring hurt to himself as well as others. Later would be better for all concerned.

"He had the gall to ask me if it was true that Annie and me were. . . ." Patrick's voice faded as he realized what he was about to say. It wasn't fitting talk, he knew, for a lady's ears.

Mei understood what he'd left unspoken. "He wanted to know if you and she were lovers?" The word didn't hold the shame for her that it did for him.

Patrick looked away from Mei.

"That's what he wanted to know, isn't it?" she asked softly.

Patrick turned his head and looked down at the woman whose every gesture was a comfort. God, but she was the most beautiful creature. He reached out and touched her cheek, his fingers trailing across the smooth golden flesh. Mei leaned into his caress, as if seeking to prolong it. "Yes, that's exactly what he wanted to know, as if he had the right to demand such simply by asking. He didn't care that he offered offense to her honor or mine."

"He is a man adrift, who seeks the anchor of the familiar," Mei rationalized. "Where he comes from, pride and place are everything. Arrogance for him is like the color of his eyes. You cannot change what molded him. Only love can do that."

"Love?" Patrick scoffed. "Tony Chambers doesn't know the meaning of the word. He admitted as much to me tonight."

"Then do not hate him for what he cannot help," she counseled. "His chance will come. Perhaps sooner than he knows."

Now it was Patrick's turn to be bewildered. "What, my girl, are you talking about?"

"Does not the Bible say, 'Pride goeth before a fall'?"

Patrick nodded. "You think love will humble him?"

"It is the force that bends and shapes all our lives. Anthony Chambers is no exception."

Patrick gave a short bark of laughter. "He wouldn't agree with you at all."

"That doesn't matter."

"It does, Mei. I should have tossed him out of my house."

"That would have served no useful purpose."

Patrick stated, "Except to give me satisfaction."

"Temporary only."

"Better than nothing, my girl."

"It might have cost you dearly had you done so. Annie would have felt bound to follow."

"I'm not so sure about that."

"I am."

"You are? Why?"

Mei weighed her words carefully. "Because he is her destiny."

Patrick frowned. "What?"

Mei gripped his hand in hers, squeeezing tighter. "Fate. He is hers. She is his. Tonight, I have seen it in their eyes."

"No." Patrick hastily denied the statement she'd uttered. "I refuse to believe that."

"It is not for you to accept," Mei pointed out. "It is for them."

"You're wrong."

She wanted to spare him the pain, but couldn't. "Think what you will. It shall not change the outcome."

"Chambers thinks she's a whore," he blurted.

"He knows that to be a lie."

"He did after I told him so."

Mei smiled. "I think he knew the truth of it before you spoke. He may not have understood the message, though, until you said the words he needed to hear."

"Still, should I have told Annie? Warned her?"

"There is no need."

"Are you certain?"

"As much as I can be."

"By all the saints, Mei, I believe you've more than a touch of the fey within you."

"Mama said that came from my Welsh father."

"Ah, the Welsh. Good folk. Like the Irish, they're not overly fond of their English overlords." Patrick sighed. "And that's what Chambers thinks he is. Overlord to us all."

Mei reached up and feathered her fingers across his brow. "You must not dwell on this. Please. Despair and anger will only tear you apart."

Patrick wondered again how he'd ever existed before meeting Mei. She was the light in the darkness for him. The only light he was ever likely to need. The only one he wanted.

Tony paced around the confines of his spacious room. He'd left O'Donnell and gone upstairs, parts of their conversation still buzzing about in his brain.

O'Donnell hadn't been with Annie. Neither, O'Donnell had declared confidently, had Cedric.

Tony stood by the window, gazing out into the

night. Stars filled the sky. In the distance, he could see smoke rising from a camp fire. If he were to open the window, the night sounds here in the Victoria High Country would be so much different from those surrounding his London digs.

He turned in the direction of the room next door. Was she awake as well?

He had only to turn the handle of the connecting door to find out. Odd that they'd been given adjoining rooms, given his host's barely concealed hostility. It had to have been the work of the housekeeper, Mei. Maybe she had been used to this arrangement when Cedric and Annie had stopped here.

Tony glanced at the door. There was a lock on his side, unbolted. Was there one on her side also? And if so, had she shot it home?

He padded softly across the floor, his bare feet making no sound as he twisted the glass knob slowly. The door gave way, opening. Cautiously, he peered inside the other bedroom.

He crossed the threshold, knowing that he shouldn't be there. It was an invasion of her privacy.

Unfortunately, he couldn't resist.

He stood at the foot of her bed. Light from his room spilled into hers. Annie lay sleeping, one arm curled protectively around her daughter.

Minutes passed as Tony simply gazed down at her. Some of her long brown hair spilled over the white blanket that covered her body. Her breathing was slow and even.

Abruptly, he turned and retreated back into his own room, leaning against the door, palms flat against the wood, his breathing ragged.

In the other room, Annie opened her eyes. She

253

hadn't been imagining it. Tony had been there, watching her.

Why?

She lifted her head from the pillow, glancing at the pool of light beneath the closed connecting door. He couldn't sleep.

Somehow, that made her feel better.

With a smile on her lips, she closed her eyes.

Chapter Seventeen

Breakfast the next morning was a somber affair; the only exception was Fallon, who was her usual bright and cheery self, plying all who sat round the table with questions.

Annie observed that a cool distance existed between Tony and Patrick. Neither man spoke freely, limiting their responses to simple declarative statements whenever possible.

"Can I go out and see the sheep now, Uncle Patrick?" Fallon entreated the man. "I promise I'll be careful. Please?"

O'Donnell glanced in Annie's direction. "Are you fine with that?"

"Certainly," Annie said, laying her hand on Fallon's head, softly stroking the child's long blond hair. "I know she'll come to no harm so long as you're around."

"Then let's go now, me darlin' angel," Patrick said, pushing back his chair. "The day's gone colder, so mind that you dress properly. I wouldn't want them sheep of mine to be thinkin' you're a frozen lump of sugar that I'm after giving them for a treat."

Fallon giggled at his teasing remark as Tony leaned over and lifted the child down from her chair. "Will you come with us, Uncle Tony?"

"I'm not sure that's—"

"Oh, please," the little girl pleaded. "It will be heaps of fun. And the sheep are real nice, too. They won't hurt you."

Tony shot Patrick a glance as if to say, *I can't refuse Fallon this request, so live with it.*

His green eyes reflecting his amusement at the child's assumption that he was afraid of the animals, Tony bent down to put himself closer to her eye level. "All right, my lady fair, I shall accompany you, and trust that the sheep are on their best behavior today."

"Mind you wear your gloves, Fallon," Annie stated, "and don't forget your hat and scarf."

Tony hefted the child into his arms, standing. "I'll see that she's outfitted properly. Trust me."

Annie gazed up into his eyes. She realized that she did trust Tony, with not only her own life, but that which was even more precious to her, her daughter's. He was genuinely fond of Fallon. She could tell that by his actions, by the way he talked to the little girl. Sweetly. Caringly. As if she mattered very much to him. He wouldn't allow harm to come to her.

For the briefest instant, Annie felt as though she had a window into which to gaze, allowing her to see what it would be like if Fallon had a loving, caring father. A man who would cherish and guide her, protect and even spoil her upon occasion. All the things Fallon would never receive from the man who had been responsible for her conception.

Tony returned Annie's look, his glance focused and smoldering so as to send warmth flooding into her skin. Beneath her pale blue-striped blouse and camisole, her nipples puckered with a sweet ache against the weight of the two fabrics. Her lips parted; her breathing deepened momentarily.

The exchange had lasted only seconds but it seemed like an eternity. Time hung suspended, as if the world had stopped on its axis, and then it returned to its proper rotation.

Tony gave a short nod and strode briskly out of the room, Fallon clinging to him.

Patrick, his thin lips set in a stern line, grabbed his long oilskin overcoat from the rack on one wall of the kitchen. "I'll be outside," he mumbled to no one in particular. He opened the door and let in a blast of cold air—almost as cold as the atmosphere had been between the two men in the kitchen.

"I fear that things did not go well with them at cards last evening," Annie confided as Mei refilled their teacups. "Did Patrick say anything to you?"

Mei hesitated. She didn't want to betray what she felt was a confidence from Patrick about Tony, nor could she reveal what she thought she knew to be the truth—how Patrick really felt about Annie.

Annie saw that something was amiss; she read the conflicting emotions in the other woman's face. "Is there something he told you that you feel you cannot repeat to me?" she asked. "If so, then I'll understand, don't worry. It's just that I'd hoped they could have met on neutral ground and resolved some of the hostility between them. I thought this trip would have been the perfect opportunity." Annie gave a slight shrug of her shoulders. "Wishful thinking, I guess."

"I think they will never be close."

"I wasn't expecting them to be," Annie replied. "Given half a chance, I had wished maybe, just maybe, they would put aside their differences long enough to realize that they could do so much for each other. Patrick could help Tony adjust to life here. Show him what Australia has to offer. Give him the benefit of his knowledge and a fresh perspective.

"Likewise, Tony could share some of his more sophisticated, cosmopolitan tastes with Patrick. Open up new horizons and give him a chance to see England, and what it represents, in another light."

Mei wanted to tell Annie that that wasn't possible so long as both men wanted her. She was the obstacle that could never be scaled, or forgotten. Annie would always remain between the two men.

But Mei couldn't burden Annie with that knowledge, so she kept her thoughts to herself. "Perhaps," Mei ventured, "it's too soon."

"Give them time, you mean?"

Mei nodded.

"You could be right," Annie conceded. "Perhaps it is better to let things progress as they shall." She sipped the warm tea, hardly noticing the flavor. "Oh, I almost forgot," she said, switching abruptly to another subject, "I've an enormous favor to ask of you."

"You know that I would do whatever you wished," Mei replied.

"Could you possibly make time to sew a dress for me and one for Fallon as well?"

Mei gave Annie a beaming smile, signaling her acceptance of the task. "I would be most happy to do so. Have you a pattern in mind?"

Annie returned Mei's smile. "In the last issue of *Godey's* there was a dress that I particularly liked." She described it.

Mei nodded. "I think I can do that." She patted Annie's hand. "I'm so glad to see that you've finally given yourself a treat. Something new for a change that you so well deserve."

Annie blushed. "Actually, I didn't."

Mei asked, although she felt she already possessed the answer. "Then who?"

The name was uttered softly: "Tony." Just speaking his name conjured up his image in Annie's mind, vital and compelling, alive for her in a way no one had been before.

"When did this happen?"

Annie snapped out of her reverie. "In Mansfield the other day. We went shopping for some things, and while I was looking at a length of velvet for Fallon, he instructed—rather high-handedly I might add—Mrs. Baker to cut some for me as well. Little did I guess he'd also ordered two other lengths in different colors, along with ribbon and trim. It was a total surprise when I opened the packages the next day after they'd been delivered."

"Obviously," Mei observed, "quite a pleasant surprise, from the look on your face."

"I didn't know what to think," Annie disclosed. "I'm not used to receiving such items from a man. At first, I thought I should send them back to Baker's. Refuse them politely outright."

"Why didn't you?"

Annie replied truthfully. "Vanity, I suppose."

"You?" Mei laughed softly, shaking her head. "No."

"You wouldn't have thought that had you been there when I held the fabric in my hands," Annie said quietly. "It was beautiful. Blue. So rich a shade, like a sapphire stone. Then the next bolt was the warm golden brown of a jar of honey. And lastly, the third length of velvet was the dark color of wine. He insisted

259

that I see what they looked like next to my skin. When I did, I couldn't send them back." Annie turned her head slightly and looked into Mei's face. "It was like seeing someone else in that mirror. A woman I wasn't quite familiar with. Someone privy to secrets I wasn't."

Annie glanced away from her friend, staring at the bottom of the teacup as she revealed one more important piece of information. "He put his hands on my shoulders; I could feel his touch in every part of my body, like magic." She wet her lips. "Does that shock you? God knows, it did me."

"No." *How could it*—Mei wanted desperately to confide to her friend—*when every time Patrick touches me I feel the same way?* "It is most natural."

"Natural?" Annie scoffed. "I'm not so sure. When I recall how I felt when Fallon's father touched me, there is a world of difference. With him, there was a pleasant kind of excitement at first. This," she confided, "this is much deeper. So much so that it frightens me."

"Why?"

"Because Tony Chambers might easily make me forget who I am, what I am."

"You are a young woman," Mei pointed out. "There is life yet to be lived. You cannot let one man from the past hold you back from experiencing all that there is to be with another man."

"I will not be any man's whore," Annie declared, her voice soft, yet firm.

"Neither would I," Mei replied. "Had not Patrick saved me that night, I would have taken my own life rather than be forced to submit to someone who thought of me as only a piece of property that he had purchased. But"—she paused—"that is different from wanting to share a man's pleasure, to be all the lover that he requires. My mother taught me that there was a great difference in being taken in lust from being taken in love. She was always my father's lover, as he was hers, no matter what anyone else said or did. She was never his whore."

Mei paused, some of the memories painful. "Her own family, she told me, rejected her when she became the companion of a white man, a 'foreign devil.' They considered her dead from then on. It hurt, but she bore it for love. Even after my father died, when she needed help the most, they would not relent from their position."

Annie risked tearing a rent in the friendship between herself and Mei when she asked in a gentle, curious voice, "Would you become Patrick's lover if you could?"

Mei stared at her friend, confused. Had Annie guessed her secret?

"Tell me."

Mei discovered she couldn't lie about her feelings any longer. "If Patrick would have me, then yes, I would be his, gladly, proudly."

"What's stopping you?"

"Another woman."

"What other woman?"

Mei declined to give Annie a name.

"Patrick's a fool to look elsewhere for happiness when he has you. Is he so blind as not to know you love him?"

Mei replied with a touch of sadness, "I think that his eyes are for her only. He cares for me, yes, I know this.

But as for love. . . ." Her words held both sadness and resignation.

"Why won't you tell me her name?"

"It is of no importance."

"I beg to differ."

"Please," Mei stated, "I have long ago accepted this. I would see Patrick happy, for he deserves to be. That is what matters most to me. Unfortunately, I do not believe that this woman loves him in the same way. In the end, he will be hurt."

A thought struck Annie, like the blinding flash of a light in the darkness. "You think Patrick is in love with me, is that it?"

"He is," Mei replied calmly.

Annie took a deep breath, choosing what to say carefully. "Yes, I believe that Patrick does love me, Mei, in much the same manner as I love him"—Annie stressed the words—"as a brother only. No more. No less." She hunched her shoulders and bowed her head. "Perhaps I should have spoken up long before this. I truly believe that Patrick cares about you, Mei. And not just simply as the woman who keeps his house. Don't fear to show him whatever you feel because of me."

Mei asked softly, "Will you take the same advice?"

Annie understood that Mei was speaking about Tony. "I can't," Annie admitted sadly. "Along that path lies only heartache. I cannot risk the consequences again."

"There are ways to prevent having another child, should you wish to know them," Mei offered, willing to share her knowledge, "if that is what is stopping you from reaching for what I think you want."

Annie blushed. "How do you know about that? Or need I ask?"

"What my mother did not tell me, the women of the House of the Golden Lotus did. They were experts in many things."

Annie shot Mei a shrewd look. "I can just imagine."

"They made pleasure an art."

"What pleasure can be found in coupling save for the man's?"

Mei tilted her head, probing into Annie's past after hearing the tinge of bitterness in her friend's words. "There was no happiness for you when your child was conceived?"

Annie shook her head. "None. Drink had befuddled my brain, and when I realized where he was leading me, I couldn't find the energy to push him aside." Her gray eyes narrowed slightly with the memories. She couldn't bring herself to use the man's Christian name, preferring to keep him an anonymous pronoun.

"I'd fancied myself in love with him, you see, and I thought he felt the same for me. He swore with each glass of the bubbly wine that he cared for me, that he loved me. I was thrilled. Excited. I was with the man who I thought wanted to marry me. The scenario unfolded like a dream that turned into a nightmare."

Annie rose from her chair and wrapped her arms about herself, moving about the kitchen slowly. "There was no one home that day. His mother and father had gone out to visit friends. They'd taken his brother and sister with them; I was governess to his younger siblings, having been hired only four months before. Each day when he chanced to smile at me, or asked how I was, I rejoiced. *He'd* noticed me. Being so young, I suppose I flattered myself that he cared for me beyond my station.

"Though we came from different rankings in society, I believed he didn't care about that.

"That afternoon, snow fell lightly. I was going to walk a few blocks to the bookshop to get a Christmas gift for my father. He insisted that I couldn't go alone. That I needed his help and protection.

"He walked with me, his arm supporting mine down the slippery streets. He made small talk about his family, about the upcoming holidays, about how he wanted to go ice-skating again, and would I like to go along with him?

"I couldn't believe my luck. Here was the man I believed I loved, spending time with me, asking me to go places with him. My world was getting bigger and brighter. He carried my purchases back to the grand house that he lived in, and where I worked. It was growing darker, and I'd realized that I was supposed to visit my family later. When we got inside, he insisted that I have a hot toddy and that he would hire a cab to take me to my parents' house. That I couldn't possibly walk the streets of Philadelphia on a night like this. No decent gentleman could allow that.

"He had Cook fix up some of her special toddies, and we had them in the library. A roaring fire had been lit, and we sipped the drinks. I'd only ever had a taste of wine, mainly watered. The rum went straight to my head and I felt slightly woozy. Next, he opened a bottle of champagne, to celebrate. I'd made him so very happy by letting him be a part of my day. He said he hoped it would be the start of many more. 'Come on,' he insisted. 'One glass of champagne can't hurt. You'll crush me if you refuse.'

264

"How could I be responsible for that? I thought after all his kindness. Foolishly, I went along." Annie paused, gathering her composure. "Several glasses later, I'd forgotten all about going out. I was all warm and cozy there with him. We were sitting on the couch, side by side. I recall giggling over something he'd said. He leaned over and kissed me, his mustache tickling me. I was shocked by his lips. Then happy. It must mean that he cared." Annie cast a glance in Mei's direction. "Naive, wasn't I?" She retraced her steps. Walking seemed to make her words flow easier. It was as if, once undammed, she couldn't relent. The tide of her words was too powerful. The need to expiate the memories was all pervasive.

"One thing, as they say, led to another, and before I knew it, I was flat on my back atop the leather Chesterfield, with his eager hands pushing at my skirt and petticoats. I asked him to stop.

"He laughed. 'Why? You want this as much as I do,' he insisted. 'Don't be coy and pretend that you don't. What's wrong? I love you.' He repeated that, and somewhere in my mind I thought he must love me if he wants to touch me, kiss me.

"Then, when he went even further, I begged him to stop. He told me in a voice I almost didn't recognize, 'Too late.' My head was spinning so fast that I felt as if I were going to faint. I tried to raise my arms, but they were pinned down. Moments later, my skirt was pushed up to my thighs, and I felt his hands upon my legs, squeezing me roughly as he shoved them apart. 'No,' I repeated, begging him once more. 'Please no.'

" 'It's all right,' he whispered. 'I love you.' "

Tears rolled down Mei's cheeks as she listened to her friend. She dabbed the linen napkin at her eyes.

In a soft, understanding voice, she said flatly, "He didn't stop."

"No," Annie replied. "Pain shot through my body in the next instant. Pain like a knife, sharp and quick. I felt as though I'd been torn in half. He put one hand over my mouth to stifle my scream. Then his body was forcing its way deeper into mine. Seconds later, though it seemed like hours, I heard a grunt and then he collapsed on top of me, his weight crushing the breath from me momentarily.

"A minute later, he got up. I lay there, confused, then I tried to sit up. I felt sick.

"He smiled at me. Actually," Annie said, her tone flat and uncompromising, "it was more of a smirk now that I think about it. He picked up the bottle of champagne and poured another glass for both of us. 'Now, that wasn't so bad, was it?' he asked me.

"Not so bad?" Annie's voice reverberated with her anguish. "I wanted to die."

She returned to her seat at the table. When she turned to look at Mei, Annie saw compassion in her friend's dark eyes. It was almost her undoing. "All I could think was that he'd said he loved me. Somehow, that was supposed to make it right. He would do the honorable thing, now that he'd anticipated our wedding night. He was a gentleman, after all.

"I sat there, refusing the glass he offered, waiting for the words to come that would ease my conscience and make me forget the pain he'd caused.

"I waited in vain.

"Finally," she said, taking a deep breath, "he did speak. 'You'd better get to your room before my family returns. Wouldn't want them to guess our little secret, now, would we?' "

" 'Secret?' I asked. What was he talking about?

" 'Of course,' he said, finishing off the glass of champagne. 'This must remain between us.'

"I didn't know what to do, so I just sat there, thinking I was in some kind of bad dream. My body hurt, and I could feel something wet between my legs.

" 'Well,' he said, looking at me as if I were some naughty child to be sent to bed without its supper, 'what are you waiting for?'

"I stared at him. He just sat there as if nothing had happened, as if he hadn't just taken from me that which was mine to give only once. Suddenly I realized that he wasn't going to bring up the subject, so I thought that I must. I had to know, so I asked him about marriage.

"It was then that he laughed. Laughed as if I had made a splendid joke. 'Why would you think I'd want to marry you? Just because we've enjoyed each other? Oh no, my dear. This is between us. No need to drag in formalities.'

" 'You said that you loved me.'

" 'So?' I saw the look on his face then. As if it had suddenly dawned on him that I accepted his words for the truth. 'You believed me?' He laughed again, mockingly this time. 'Silly fool. A man always says that, don't you know?'

"Obviously, I didn't know.

" 'I'll be up later, after my family's asleep,' he said. 'We can continue then. After all, you've already lost your innocence, so why waste time crying over it? A pretty piece like you was bound to lose it sooner or later.'

"I had to get out of there. I forced myself to stand up and walk away as best I could, though my legs were wobbly. Climbing those stairs to the third floor was the hardest thing I had to do. Each step was agony, but I was determined to get my things and leave that house as soon as I could.

"I couldn't believe I'd been so stupid as to swallow his lies. I fell for his pretty words like a mouse caught in a trap loaded with cheese.

"When I got to my room, I took off my dress. As I removed my torn pantalets, I saw the blood, and something else, something sticky on my inner legs. My stomach churned so much I thought I would be sick right there on the spot, but I told myself that I couldn't waste the time. The water in the jug was cold, but I didn't care. I washed the stains away, hoping that no one would be the wiser.

"When I was done, I gathered my things and waited until the family was at dinner. I crept down the stairs and left the house, walking home.

"I told my parents that I'd left my position there, and that I couldn't go back. All I wanted to do was forget that it had ever happened. I thought if I pretended that it hadn't, then that would make it all right. I could cope.

"I was wrong," Annie said in a dull voice. "Six weeks later, I was so sick that I couldn't keep my breakfast down, and my monthly hadn't come. It was then that I told my mother what had occurred at his house and begged her not to tell my father, for fear that he would do something rash. They were powerful, well-connected people, and we weren't. I would speak to my child's father, I told her. He would surely do the right thing once he knew about the baby.

"The next day I waited outside his house until I knew he was alone. Then I knocked on the door and the housekeeper let me in. I waited in the hall until he agreed to see me. In the library, of all places. Perhaps that was a good omen, I thought. Our child had been conceived there.

"When I gave him my news he just sat there, silent for a moment, then he said, 'So, what would you like me to do? It's your problem. If you need a name of someone who can get rid of it for you, I'll see what I can do.'

"At first, I couldn't accept what I was hearing. And then, do you know what he asked me?" she said bitterly. "If he was the father.

"'How can I be sure? You might have been with plenty of other men after I broke you in. In fact, I could probably get a few friends of mine to swear they've had you as well, if you think you're going to blackmail me.'

"'Blackmail,' I said, astonished that he could think so little of me. 'No,' I told him, 'I thought you'd want to do the honest thing. If we don't marry, your son or daughter will be born without a name.'

"'So?' It didn't matter to him in the slightest.

"I didn't think, Mei, that I could feel any more hurt and humiliated than I had before. He'd insinuated that I was a whore and that the baby I was carrying wasn't his, when he knew all along that it was no one else's.

"I couldn't let him see me cry. I wouldn't give him the satisfaction of knowing how much he'd wounded me again. I ran out of the room and out of that house as fast as I could. I ran and ran until I couldn't run any more and the tears came."

Annie paused, taking a moment to collect herself, sitting straighter in her chair. "I wasn't crying so much for me as I was for my child. To be tossed casually aside as if you have no worth, denied a birthright. My baby deserved better. It was innocent.

"It was then that I met Cedric Chambers. God had seen fit to give me and my child a way out, a way to keep our secret and for me to protect my daughter from scandal and the stain of bastardy. Cedric suggested that I become a 'widow' and relocate, far away from prying eyes. He made sense. So I followed his advice, inventing a 'husband' and 'father' that Fallon could be proud of."

Annie folded her hands. "The rest you already know."

Tony leaned against the wall with a sigh. He'd listened to the whole story, aware that he was eavesdropping on what was a private conversation, but unable to tear himself away. He'd come inside the house by the front door, anxious to tell Annie that they would soon have to leave as the skies were darkening, threatening snow.

When he heard Annie tell O'Donnell's housekeeper how she really felt about the man, he'd been unable to interrupt, wanting to know more.

And now he did.

He'd heard all the details of how Fallon had come into the world. Heard that he'd been right all along in suspecting that Annie Ross wasn't actually a widow. Heard, also, that he'd been wrong in his initial judgment of her.

It was just a matter of time before he'd discover the truth. The Pinkerton agent he'd hired in Los Angeles would no doubt be wiring him the particulars about her background. Secrets had a way of exploding if one was persistent enough.

But this. He hadn't expected that she'd been the victim of a cad who'd played her false.

She'd been seduced by a silver-tongued lout who had taken the gravest advantage of her, a man who'd treated her like a serf, exercising his *droit du seigneur*.

Admiration for Annie's courage in building a new life leapt within him. It took strength and pride to overcome the obstacles she'd been faced with. She'd done it, and managed to love the child as well.

If he could have that man for just a few moments, he'd have gladly taken the stockman's whip to his back, flaying him within an inch of his life for what he'd done to her. Meting out what he considered a just punishment for the actions of a pig. After all, it wouldn't be the first time he'd had to defend a woman's honor.

The urge to hold her in his arms almost overwhelmed him. But he couldn't let Annie know he'd been listening at the door when by rights he should have either left immediately or made his presence known. Embarrassment would only be served by walking in on them now. Emotions were still too raw, he judged.

Tony initially had wanted to sleep with Annie to prove a point: that she was a harlot. Easy and eager to tumble.

Now he wanted to sleep with Annie to show her that not all men were such inept lovers; that women could, and did, find pleasure in sharing a bed with a man, in expressing passion.

Some women had taught him well, and he was eager to return the favor to her.

To see those gray eyes glimmer in ecstasy, to hear

that soft voice splinter in abandon. Ah yes, that would be sheer delight. She deserved to know that there was infinitely more to passion than fumbling and pain.

He could show her.

Part Two
You and No Other

Chapter Eighteen

Spring had finally arrived in the High Country after a severe spell of heavy snow, which had forced the occupants of Camelot station to get to know one another better while confined to the homestead.

Annie breathed in the warm air as she strolled through the garden, enjoying the scent of the various flowers in bloom, especially the roses. She stopped and sniffed one particular rose bush; it was one of Cedric's favorites, an old rose, pink and fragrant, imported from England. She stooped along the brick walkway, inhaling the aroma.

She wondered if Tony would like some roses for his office. Cedric had favored them as much as she did, and Annie had seen to it that there were roses on constant display throughout the house, including the bedrooms.

Would he like roses in his bedroom too? Since the day that Tony first arrived, she'd never set foot in there, respecting his privacy. Alice took care of the cleaning; it was she who saw to the upkeep of Tony's room. Annie made a mental note to fill two of the Waterford vases with an assortment of roses, along with several other flowers that were indigenous to the area.

The warble of a bird sent her glance to a nearby tree. Blossoming leaves sheltered the bird from view.

Gail Link

Annie continued along the walkway until she came to the arbor. She sat down, the warmth of the sun streaming through the white roses that surrounded the trellis on the top and sides, thinking of how grateful she'd become to Cedric for his having chosen Tony as co-heir of the station. If he hadn't added this stipulation to his will, they might never have met.

And, if that hadn't happened, Annie realized that she might never have discovered what it was like to fall in love. Deeply, completely in love. What she'd once believed to be love had only been a girlish infatuation. A blind, stupid fancy for a handsome, shallow figure of a man.

In contrast, Tony Chambers was real. Excitingly so. There was nothing shallow about him. He was genuine. Stubborn—yes. Opinionated—very. Sometimes infuriating. Damnably arrogant. But, she thought, sighing, she loved him for all that he was. More and more with each passing day, with each new thing she found out about him.

A growing respect, a camaraderie, had sprung up between them since their return from Patrick's house several months past. They talked about all manner of things, surprising each other with their range of topics and interests. An occasional difference in opinion was more readily tolerated by both sides now. Sharp words had been pushed aside, replaced by willing compromise and conciliation. Slowly, surely, some measure of confidences were exchanged. Each new day, another link in their personal bridge was formed, growing stronger.

Although total, absolute trust hadn't been achieved, it was no longer unimaginable to Annie to hope that one day, it very well might be.

Maybe she was being overly optimistic, though she prayed she was not.

Things between them had progressed to such an extent that Annie felt free in telling Tony about her ongoing project, the stories she was writing and illustrating, especially after a newspaper in Melbourne requested more of the same, and she'd also had interest from an American publisher offering her a contract for a collection of her observations on life in Australia. Tony shared her joy at the news and even suggested that she also seek a publisher in London, promising to write to a friend whose family owned a Fleet Street daily.

There was a new intimacy to their private mealtime as well. Each night, dinner was a languid affair. They relaxed and used the time to enjoy each other's company, to talk about whatever they wanted, for as long as they wanted. Often, laughter rang out in the dining room, much to the amusement, Annie was sure, of the household staff. Moreover, Annie learned, under Tony's careful tutelage, to appreciate the finer points of wine, discovering that she now had a much better head for the odd glass or two than she'd had several years past. Even the smell of his after-dinner cigar brought her pleasure as they shared an occasional glass of brandy or port.

It was during these sometimes quiet, sometimes not, evenings that the sensual awareness between them grew. Annie could feel the heat of Tony's gaze, or the warmth in his smile, as never before. Still, neither broached the subject of the attraction. Yet, it was there. Steadily increasing. The blood flowed hotter in her veins; the beat of her pulse raced even faster.

At first, she'd been apprehensive about these new

and deepening feelings for Tony, afraid that she would betray what she held locked inside either by a look or a word. Annie guarded her heart as well as she could. And she knew that it was her fear of the unknown he represented which was a major factor in her reluctance to admit her true emotions. Yet there were times that her fancy took flight and she imagined what it would feel like if Tony kissed her, if he held her in his arms. If ever he did, would she be able to put aside the bitter memories of the last man who'd kissed her in feigned passion? Would her stomach remain calm, or would it revolt again at the invasion?

Or, having experienced the myriad of female lips that Annie was certain Tony had kissed, would he be bored with her lack of ability?

Mei had talked about pleasure. Was that really true? Annie wondered. Could a woman find pleasure in the taste and feel of a man's lips upon hers?

So intently had Annie beem focusing on her own private thoughts, she hadn't heard the sound of booted feet approaching her shelter.

"Ha'penny for them," said the deep, masculine voice.

"Pardon me?" Her head snapped up. Tony Chambers was standing there. Her eyes lifted from the taut muscles of his thighs outlined by the snug fit of the white moleskin trousers he wore, up and over the broad expanse of his chest, covered by a linen shirt, all the way to the brown wool flat-crowned hat that shaded his head from the sun.

"You looked so lost in thoughts that I wondered what could Annie Ross have to ponder on so fine a day as to give her a frown." Tony stepped into the arbor, moving closer to her, taking a seat.

Annie's heart beat in a quicker tempo as she side-stepped the complete truth. "Actually, I was remembering how much Cedric loved this time of year. And," she said, raising one hand and laying it upon a bloom, "roses. He loved roses."

A trait that we share, Tony thought, with the loveliest rose of all now beside him. A true American Beauty.

He extended his hand. "Come with me."

"Where?"

"A picnic."

Her head tilted in his direction, a quizzical look on her face. "A what?"

"Certainly you've heard of a picnic?"

"Well, of course I have," Annie answered with a curve of her lips. "They're not unknown in Philadelphia, you know."

Amused, Tony's lips curled. "Good. Then let's go."

"Now?"

"Why not?"

"Where?" she repeated.

"To a perfect spot that I found when I first arrived here," he replied.

When he looked at her the way he was doing now, with that trace of a boyish gleam in his eyes, as if it meant all the world to him that she accompany him, Annie couldn't refuse. "I'll go and get changed."

"No," he said, placing a hand on her arm, restraining her with the lightest of touches. "There's no need."

"You're sure?"

He quickly dropped his gaze down the length of her body, leaving warmth in his wake. "Positive."

"All right," she murmured.

"I've already seen to Fallon. Alfred and Mrs. Dun-

279

martin will look after her. A hamper is packed. The horses are saddled."

Annie slanted him an arch glance. "You were so certain that I'd come?"

"Let's say that I was prepared for a positive response and leave it at that, shall we?"

Right now, if he'd asked her to ride with him across the breadth of Australia, from the harbor at Sydney to the interior of the Outback, then on to Perth, Annie would have been sorely tempted to answer yes.

"Well then, I'd be most pleased to accompany you, Mr. Chambers, on this planned excursion. I will, however, want to see Fallon before we leave, and procure a hat."

"Then," Tony said, rising and offering Annie his arm, "I suggest that we don't delay."

"What a delightful hamper. Where did you get it?" Annie asked as she unbuckled the straps that held it closed.

"Melbourne," he replied casually. "In a little shop there."

Tony'd gone to the city on a business trip, or at least that's what he told Annie when he left a fortnight ago for almost a week. Five days, actually. Annie had missed him terribly. The house seemed empty, the days longer without his presence. She realized just how much she missed Tony as she found herself listening for the sound of his voice, or longing to see his tall frame command a room with just his entrance.

Tony uncorked a bottle of white wine, producing a surprise for Annie from the picnic basket. Smiling, he handed her a gaily wrapped small package. "Go on, open it."

She did so, exclaiming in delight over the collapsible drinking cup. "It's like yours."

Tony laughed. "I ordered it from a silversmith in Melbourne. Beauty and practicality in the same package. I bought one for Fallon as well."

Annie chuckled softly as she unfolded the cup to its proper size, and Tony promptly filled it with wine.

"To spring," he proposed.

Annie echoed his words. "To spring—and all its promises," she added.

She'd removed her hat, her long hair blowing gently in the breeze. It cascaded down her back and over the plain blue shirt she wore, trailing along the quilt upon which they sat. So warm a brown, like the pelt of a beaver, Tony thought, sleek and shiny in the afternoon sun.

God, those five days he'd been absent from Annie were abominably lonely. How surprisingly she'd engaged his affections. Slyly, without warning, she'd taken root. It was while he was in Melbourne that Tony realized that he cared for her, deeply. When he'd gotten word that the report from the Pinkerton man was waiting for him at the solicitor's office in the capital city, he'd informed Annie that pressing business forced him to make the trip.

Once there, this time catching a train directly into Melbourne, he'd pored over the file, finding facts and data that told him the bare bones of her story. Tony also learned the name of the cad in Philadelphia, promising himself that one day that situation would be dealt with as it deserved. It might take time, years maybe, but it would be done to his satisfaction. Hadn't someone once said, "Revenge is a dish best served cold"? He'd see to it for her, although it never crossed his mind to ask her permission, or even if she wanted revenge. This was something he wanted to do for Annie's besmirched honor.

Linen-wrapped sandwiches were laid upon the quilt between them, with fresh fruit and a thick slice for each of vanilla cake.

"This is a beautiful spot," Annie said, watching the splash of water as it moved rapidly along the rocky stream. It was clear and cold, coming from a mountain source. All around her was greenery, from shrubs, bushes, ferns, trees, and grass. Nature rejuvenating itself after a long winter's sleep.

In a way, Annie felt like that as well. Awake and overwhelmingly alive for the first time in years. And it was all due to the man who sat on the quilt beside her. As she lifted a sandwich, carefully unfolding the linen, she glanced in Tony's direction. He was staring across the creek at a lone female kangaroo with a joey peeking out of her pouch. The animal stopped to drink, giving careful regard to the humans on the other side. Moments later, a big male, obviously the "boss" of the herd, came up beside his mate, drinking as well before urging her on.

"My family back home can hardly believe it when I describe what a kangaroo looks like," Annie said between bites of her sandwich, "especially one with a young one in her stomach. I've tried to sketch them, but don't know if I quite capture the sense of them."

Laughter erupted from Tony's throat. "I know what you mean. I've written to my friend in America, Rafe, and attempted to put into words just what the wildlife is like here and I'm sure he wonders at my sanity. It's often hard to convey just *how* very different all this is." He glanced up as a brilliantly hued lorikeet flew by. "And," he remarked, "the birds. Their splendid colors." He picked up a sandwich for himself, peeling back the napkin, revealing slices of white-meat chicken between pieces of hearty wheat bread. A wedge of farmhouse cheddar was wrapped in a smaller square of blue and white striped linen, along with a tiny sharp knife for slicing the cheese.

"The seasons," he continued after devouring half of his sandwich, "will take some getting used to, being topsy-turvy as they are. It all seems so unreal, having a picnic when we'll be celebrating Christmas in little over a month."

"Yes, for us," Annie agreed, "I suppose it does. For Fallon, it's perfectly natural. My daughter was born here, so it's the only way of life she's known. It's the same for Patrick and Mei. They're native Australians."

Tony cut a slice of cheese for her, holding it out on the blade of the knife. Annie picked it up and bit into it, savoring the taste before finishing off the chunk.

"Did it take you long to adapt?" he asked, eating a piece of cheese himself.

"A bit," she confessed. "It was all so new and exciting, every new day an adventure."

"Would you ever go back to Philadelphia?"

Annie answered him without hesitation in a strong, confident voice. "Someday, to have Fallon meet my family there, but to live again, no." She looked away, resolve coming through her words. "My home is here now." She swung her glance back in his direction a moment later. "But what about you? I guess you're just counting the days until you can return to England?"

Tony considered before answering. Months ago, he would have said yes, without hesitation. Now, England, as much as he loved the country of his birth, was slowly becoming a part of another life. Since coming here, he'd discovered a purpose, one which challenged him. Overseeing the financial empire left him by his great-uncle was no task for a dilettante. In London, Tony realized, not much had ever really been expected of him. Only that he do the proper thing and eventually produce a family to continue on the Chambers name; otherwise, his life was his own, to do with as he pleased.

From Rafe, Tony had learned the value of a man's pride in what he did, in building something that would last beyond one man's lifetime. He'd seen that here as well.

He'd also learned about personal involvement. In getting to know the men who worked on the station, in listening to what they had to say, he discovered who and what they were, as they did him.

Sorting through Cedric's holdings and keeping abreast of all the developments was a keen mental task, one Tony found himself enjoying more and more. And, he was learning every day about the running of a successful horse and cattle station. Neighbors called. Invitations to races, parties, and other social functions were now constant. He could finally see what it was that had made his great-uncle fall in love with this place.

Of course, Tony could still, if he wished, chuck it all and return to England. Hire a manager, or sell off his holdings, if he chose. As soon as his tenure was up here, he could leave, if he wanted.

If he wanted.

No, that wasn't an option any longer. Not since he'd determined that he was beginning to care about this woman, care in a way that he hadn't experienced before. He certainly wanted her more than he'd wanted any other woman. And he'd waited longer to have her than any other woman.

But she was worth the wait. He'd bet his life on that.

"Are you deliberately ignoring my question?" she asked.

"Sorry," Tony responded. "Actually, I'm not. There are ever so many things to keep me busy here that I haven't given returning to England much thought." He arched a thick brow. "Why? Anxious to see the last of me?"

Never. The response she couldn't utter aloud came straight from her heart.

"Once," Annie answered honestly, brushing crumbs off her skirt, "I might have said yes, but I've come to realize that this is as much your home as mine. Maybe more so." *Once, I could have let you go with a fare-thee-well, a complacent smile, and a whole heart. Now, it's too late.* "It's what Cedric would have wanted."

"What about what you want, Annie?"

She shot him a quick glance. "I don't know what you mean."

"You don't?"

"No."

"Then let me show you," Tony whispered, moving closer to her, pushing aside the food.

Her eyes widened as he inched nearer. "What do you want?"

"You."

Annie blinked slowly. That one word hit her with the force of a blow.

"Yes, you," he repeated. Tony's voice was low and soft, caressing her with its velvet tone. He hadn't meant to be quite so blunt, but it couldn't be helped. This was the perfect opportunity to begin the next step in his campaign to woo her to his bed.

She wet her lips. "I don't think. . . ."

"Shhh," he murmured, "don't think." He traced his index finger along the sleeve of her blouse, gently, up and down. "Feel."

Annie did feel—the increased pulse of her blood, the quick intake of her breath when the warmth of his fingertip touched her, penetrating the layer of fabric.

"That wasn't so awful, was it?" Tony asked, edging closer.

"No."

His fingers slid down past the cuff, skimming along the soft flesh of the back of her hand, covering it with his much larger hand. It remained there for a few seconds before Tony lifted it to brush back a lock of her hair. "Beautiful."

"You think so?" she asked, surprise in her voice.

"Without a doubt."

Annie had never thought of her hair as beautiful. It was just plain brown hair. Yet, from his lips, it sounded special. Her daughter's—now, that was beautiful, so blond it looked like spun sugar. And Tony's own—lightened by the Australian sun so that streaks of gold blended with the light brown. She was sorely tempted on many occasions to run her fingers through it.

They were close. So close that Annie could see just how thick the lashes were that surrounded his oh-so-very-green eyes. She could get an intimate look at the brown mole that graced his jaw. Suddenly, Annie was struck with an ache deep in her belly; she desperately longed to put her mouth to that special mark. It was followed closely by the thought: Did he have others on his body? And if so, where?

Where indeed. Where had that shocking thought sprung from? she wondered. It wasn't as if she was ever going to find out. Still, Annie's curiosity was raised, as was her temperature. She knew it wasn't from the clear, warm day or the sun. It was him. The nearness of him. The scent of him.

Tony could see that her misty gray eyes were filled with questions. He had to warn himself to keep the pace slow so as not to frighten her. It was awkward. He was used to going after what he wanted when he wanted where women were concerned. The ladies he'd dallied with knew the rules. Annie wasn't a virgin, and yet, in many ways, she was. Remembering that was making everything so damned complicated.

He backed away, giving them both a fraction of breathing space. Time to think. Time to try something else.

A moment later, Tony lifted his hand and placed his middle finger against her mouth, outlining it. Slowly her lips parted and his finger moved deeper along the fleshy core inside.

Abruptly he withdrew the digit, replacing it seconds later with a slice of cheddar. He fed her the cheese, watching as she took it into her mouth.

Next he offered her a cupful of wine, which she duly accepted.

Intrigued and emboldened, following an instinct she didn't fully understand, Annie whispered, "Let me."

Tony acquiesced, leaning back as she broke apart a piece of cake and fed it to him, putting the morsel up to his mouth, to those handsome bow-shaped lips that were beckoning her without speaking a word.

Tony responded by devouring the piece, sucking the tips of her fingers gently into his mouth also.

A deeper flood of warmth shot through Annie when he did that.

Their eyes met. Each knew what was to come.

Their lips touched—and nothing would ever be the same.

Tony's mouth brushed Annie's in a sweetly gentle kiss that lingered before he pursued it further, deepening the contact as his hunger for her came to the fore. Like a man deprived too long of water, he drank from her lips as if from an oasis, quenching his thirst.

Annie's arms automatically lifted and circled Tony's neck, drawing him even closer, if possible, to her. What he was doing took her beyond herself. She was there, yet she was somehow floating free, like a bird soaring on the wing. Her mouth obeyed his, opening freely at his insistence. She felt the glide of his tongue on hers, like a swirl of silk.

She clung tighter to him as his hands spread across her back and waist, upwards into her long hair, clasping her to the warmth of his body, her breasts softly crushed against the hard wall of his wide chest. Sensation rioted within her, moving rapidly from her head to her toes.

When Tony broke the kiss, Annie blinked in confusion, then locked gazes with him once again. She lifted one hand to her lips, fingertips tracing the swollen contours in wonderment, proof positive that she hadn't imagined the encounter. It had been real. As real as could be. Wonderfully, achingly so.

She waited to see triumph in his eyes. To read gloating satisfaction in his face at having attained his goal.

Annie would have waited in vain.

Instead, what she saw there was surprise, genuine warmth, and concern.

Tony offered no excuses for his actions. "I won't apologize."

"I wasn't asking you to," she responded as she tried to comprehend all that had happened. He'd effectively shattered all her long-held beliefs that in a man's embrace she would feel absolutely empty. That whatever starry-eyed dreams she'd once had had been buried so deeply under the rubble of that one night that they could never be revived.

Tony Chambers had proven her wrong.

What talent did he possess that the mere touch of that mouth could transform what she thought was the truth into a lie?

"And I won't pretend that it didn't happen."

"Neither will I." Annie couldn't, even if she wanted to, which she didn't.

Her voice was huskier than normal. "What happens next?"

Tony cradled her chin in his palm. His green eyes were direct. "What do you want to happen, Annie?"

"I don't know."

"Then," he said, his baritone low and seductive, "we'll leave it at that, shall we? Let's finish what we started first, the picnic. The rest can be sorted out later." He shifted slightly, giving her some space, resuming his portion of the meal as if that were of major importance.

Annie thought she wouldn't be able to eat, but she followed Tony's example, finding that her appetite had actually increased. As she lustily attacked the food, she realized that she felt alive and invigorated, tinglingly aware in a brand new way of her surroundings and of the handsome man who shared them.

But she wasn't fooled. The reckoning was yet to come.

Chapter Nineteen

Annie picked up the blue glass bottle of perfume, lifting the silver stopper and dabbing it on her neck, behind her ears, and on each wrist.

"Can I smell, Mama?" Fallon asked, standing by her mother's chair.

Annie smiled at the little girl. "Of course you can, sweetheart. Here, let Mama put some on you." She held out the bottle so that the child could take a sniff of the perfume, then dabbed a bit behind Fallon's ears.

"Now I smell just like you do, pretty," Fallon said with a big grin. She was wearing the same color as her mother, the deep blue velvet, fashioned into a dress, with lace around the high-buttoned collar and cuffs. Fallon's petticoat of starched white lace peeped out from the hem of her outfit. Her blond hair was left long and flowing, a matching blue ribbon holding it back from her face, while her mother's hair was artfully wound into a chignon, held in place by several mother-of-pearl pins.

A soft knock sounded on the door and Fallon eagerly went to answer it.

Alfred stood outside in the hall, leaning in with his upper body. "I've got something here for you, ma'am."

"You do?" Annie inquired as she put the perfume back in its place. "What?"

"A gift," he stated. "It's from Mr. Chambers. He wanted you to have it before you greeted your guests." Alfred bent down and gave Fallon a tiny wrapped box. "If you don't mind my being quite so bold, ma'am, you're looking exceptionally stunning this day."

Annie lifted a hand to her throat. "Thank you, Alfred. It must be this dress. Mei created a wonder."

"If you'll pardon me, ma'am, the dress is lovely, yes, but it's the woman who's wearing it which makes it special."

Annie smiled. "I do most humbly accept your compliment, kind sir," she said with a mock-formal tone.

"I do hope that this will be a most happy holiday for you and the little one, ma'am."

"It's beginning to look as though it will be, Alfred," she commented with a note of anticipation. "More so than I might have imagined."

"Can I go and help Mrs. Mary, Mama?" Fallon dutifully handed the gift to her mother.

"Mind that you don't get in her way, Fallon."

"I won't," the little girl swore. "She promised me that I could put some icing on the cupcakes."

Annie noted that that task rated higher in her daughter's world than sticking around to see just what her mother had received. She pretended sternness in warning her daughter, "Make sure that the icing gets onto the cakes, and not all in your mouth."

Fallon snickered. "Cross my heart."

"And watch that you wear an apron," Annie cautioned. "I don't want you spoiling that beautiful dress before our guests see it."

"I'll be careful, Mama."

Annie dropped a kiss on her daughter's cheek. "Then scoot."

Gail Link

Alfred piped up, "I'll see that Fallon's properly togged, ma'am, before she wields a spreading knife upon the sweets."

Alfred shut the door, leaving Annie alone with Tony's gift. She wondered why and what as she held the package in the palm of her hand.

Open it, a voice inside her head insisted. *It won't bite.*

Can I be sure? she demanded.

Inquisitiveness won out and Annie tore open the blue flocked wrapping paper. Inside was a plain white box with gold lettering, marking it as coming from one of Melbourne's most exclusive jewelry shops. She hesitated in removing the lid. Instead, she read the card that accompanied the gift.

Wear this today, I insist. The letter **T** was scrawled boldly on the bottom of the heavy cream card. With a fingertip she traced the initial before sliding the card into her leather-bound journal.

Annie lifted the lid. What was inside the box took her breath away. She removed the item, holding it up, the slender gold chain threaded through her fingers as she examined the stone. It was an opal, blue, shot through with flashes of green fire.

Annie held it up to the dangling earrings she wore. It was an almost perfect match. She slipped the chain over her head, letting the opal pendant fall to just above the swell of her breasts revealed by the lower-cut neckline of the two-piece dress she wore. Her fingers touched the stone softly as she wondered again about wearing the velvet outfit. Ordinarily it wasn't something she would have even considered, but as the party was expected to last into the evening, she made an exception. Perhaps she was being too brazen?

292

Would Tony think so?

It was made from material he'd bought for her. Thankfully, rain had come two days ago and brought with it cooler temperatures, or wearing velvet would have been unthinkable anyway.

Still . . .

Annie gazed into the mirror over her dressing table. Higher up on her throat she wore a gold cross that had been her mother's.

She stared into the looking glass for almost three minutes before opting to remove one of the necklaces while keeping the dress on.

"You mark my words, they'll be seeing in the New Year with a wedding," Alfred crowed triumphantly to Mary as they set up food on the long trestle tables beneath the tents erected to give shelter from the elements. When Alfred saw that no one was looking in their direction, he boldly gave the widow Dunmartin a quick kiss upon the lips. Mary blushed to the roots of her graying hair.

"Get on with you now," she chided him, arranging the platter of fresh-baked ham just so as Alice trotted over with a plate of cooked eggs. Mrs. Winters, accompanied by her son, carried bowls filled high with biscuits. The aroma of beef simmering upon the huge spit wafted through the air.

"Isn't it just grand to see Camelot station coming alive?" Mary Dunmartin observed with a keen eye. "And taking its proper place amongst the folks hereabouts?"

"It's about time," Mrs. Winters replied. "These are quality people, and it's long past due that everyone around here knows it. My Jim is fair bursting with pride at it all."

"We're all proud as can be," Mary assured her, grabbing Alfred's arm as it slid around her ample waist. She was fiercely loyal to the master and mistress of the station, having come to love them as family. They'd given both her and Alice not only a new life, but for herself, a new love. Mary'd been smitten by the English valet, whose saucy actions caused her to regain the feelings she'd thought had long ago been put away upon the shelf. And if her widow's heart could be bowled over by so lusty a man, then why not Mrs. Ross's by Mr. Chambers? There was no denying that Anthony Chambers was a handsome fellow, bound to be fawned over by the ladies coming today. He well deserved their attention.

Mrs. Ross, in Mary's opinion, could do no better than the Englishman if she was in the market for another husband. Why search further than under one's own roof?

"Jim and some of the jackeroos can't wait for the races to start," Nora Winters remarked. "It was flat-out generous of Mr. Chambers to put up the money for the purses."

"He's hoping, of course," Alfred stated, "that our lads take all the prizes."

"I hear," Alice said, carrying a large glass-domed cake server in one hand and a pitcher of lemonade in the other, "that he's going to ride in one of the races himself."

"That he is," Alfred disclosed. "On Merlin."

"Perhaps I'll be laying a wager on that," Nora Winters said with a knowing smile. "My Jim says that our Mr. Chambers is an all-out demon when riding that big black. All power and grace."

"That he is."

The collective group swiveled their heads around at the other female voice that added its weight to the discussion.

Annie smiled, placing the silver tray she brought from the kitchen upon the white tablecloth. It was easy to see which cupcakes her daughter had done, the icing a tad lopsided on several. To Annie, they looked perfect.

"I'd lay a wager on Tony Chambers as well," Annie said. "I doubt that there's anyone who could beat him."

"What if Mr. O'Donnell should challenge him?" Nora Winters asked. "He's a good man on a horse himself, or so I've been told."

Confidently Annie replied, "Tony will win, no matter who goes against him. I'm that sure."

"Mrs. Ross is right," Alfred said, a gleam in his eye. "What Mr. Chambers goes after, he gets. If he's set his sights on a prize, then it's his for the claiming."

Mary gently nudged him with her elbow, her glance falling on Annie Ross to see if she took Alfred's words to heart.

Annie's face remained calm and collected, her smile in place and her eyes focused. She hadn't missed the undercurrents in the valet's words. Was it a warning— or a promise?

That afternoon at Camelot station the grounds were bursting with people laughing, mingling, eating and dancing. A roast lamb cooked over one pit; in another, a side of beef. Drovers mixed with owners; hands from different stations got into friendly competition with one another in games of chance and feats of skill.

Some women sat on the veranda watching the events, others moved closer to cheer on favorites or gathered to gossip and catch up on local news.

Annie strolled around the homestead, searching for Tony. The party had been in full flower for over an hour and she still hadn't caught sight of him. Nor had she seen Patrick arrive. She'd invited him, insisting in a personal message that he come and join them. She'd invited Mei, too, knowing that the other woman wouldn't accept. Since she and Tony had stayed at his homestead, Patrick had come to Camelot only once. The bad weather was his excuse, but Annie suspected that it wasn't the only reason. Even after winter had turned to spring, he hadn't come as before. Now, with summer only a few weeks away, and this, the first party held at Camelot, she wanted him to be a part of their lives again.

"My, but he's a striking devil, isn't he?"

Annie overheard two women talking as she came around the corner of the house and she wondered who they were speaking about.

She should have guessed. *Tony.* He looked utterly dashing in his tailored wool coat of dark green, worn over a pair of matching trousers, a white shirt, a silvery-gray cravat, and a waistcoat of green moire satin. Had it only been a few weeks ago that they'd shared a kiss? If she closed her eyes, Annie could swear she could still feel the imprint of his mouth on hers. In the interim, he'd been circumspect, but the knowledge was there between them. It vibrated through every touch, every look they exchanged.

"What a temptation for any woman, let alone a widow so young and lovely."

"I can tell you, Grace," the older of the two confided, "that I'd be very happy to warm his bed if he has need of a companion. Old Tom isn't the man he used to be," she said with a hint of sadness, "and this one looks to be long and strong, if you catch my meaning." They both snickered with laughter.

"G'day, ladies."

Grace and her friend Maude turned pale at the interruption. "Why, Mrs. Ross, how good it is to see you again. Maude and I were just talking about the race between your partner and my husband."

Annie arched a brow. "Were you?"

"I think that young Mr. Chambers has a better than good chance of beating him. What do you think?"

"I agree."

Grace heaved a slightly exaggerated sigh. "I feel the need for a glass of that wonderful lemonade you're serving today. Coming, Maude?"

The other woman nodded and they walked away, leaving Annie alone. She walked to the paddock fence, where Tony was feeding carrots to Merlin.

"Hello."

Tony swung his head around and saw Annie standing there. She was breathtaking. He couldn't believe how beautiful she looked. That shade of blue made her skin seem the color of cream. The velvet molded her body, showing off her slim waist, rounded hips, and especially the curves of her breasts. The lower neckline afforded him an opportunity to view their rounded fullness better than the clothes she normally wore. Each tiny gold button that held the jacket closed was a bewitching enticement to his eager fingers to slide the object from its moorings so that he could see what lay beneath.

297

Pleasure made him smile. She was wearing his gift. "I knew it was made for you."

God, but he wanted to kiss her again. Take that soft, sweet mouth and feed upon it.

"You shouldn't have, you know."

"Nonsense." Tony scoffed at her remark. "I wanted to. Besides, it complements the dress." He let his gaze drift downwards over her frame, slowly, as if memorizing every detail, before working his way back up again to her eyes.

"You make it difficult to refuse," she admitted.

"That's the object."

"Oh, I'm not quite sure if that's true."

They exchanged glances, each taking the measure of the other.

"However, it's beautiful, and I thank you for it."

"You're learning."

"What?" she demanded softly.

"To accept graciously without being quite so prickly about it."

Annie opened the gate and stepped closer to him. "Prickly, is it?"

Tony inhaled her perfume. "Precisely."

She lifted her hand and stroked it down Merlin's neck. "Mmm, perhaps." Yes, she could have refused the gift. Sent it back unopened, or failing that, acknowledging it and telling him that for propriety's sake, she couldn't keep it. She should have. However, since it came from Tony, that made the gift all the more special in her eyes, and therefore, hard to part with.

Damn his arrogant soul.

Tony checked his gold pocket watch. "I think the first race is about to begin." He had to get away from here. Being alone with her right now was dangerous. Too tempting. "What say we go and watch, cheer our boys on?" He offered Annie his hand.

She slipped her arm around his, her tongue wetting her lips. "I'd like that."

Tony stifled the groan that was about to escape his throat. "Then, by all means, my dear."

Patrick O'Donnell had just ridden up, tethered his horse, and searched the property for a sign of Annie. There were certainly plenty of people about the grounds, all in a happy holiday mood. A section of the station had been marked off for a race, another for events. He gave a cursory glance at two men performing tricks with their mounts, pausing to watch momentarily.

He scanned the crowd. Still no Annie. Exasperated, Patrick began to question some of the guests. Eventually, after having no luck, he met two women from Ruranga station who suggested that he try the paddock area, so off he went.

That's when he saw them, Chambers and Annie, walking arm-in-arm, laughing together as if sharing some private joke, his head bent close to her face. Looking to all the world as if they were happy together; perhaps more importantly, as if they belonged together.

Had Annie succumbed to the pommy's brand of charm? Had she bitten into the forbidden fruit?

Patrick stood unobserved. He'd been tempted to disregard the invitation to this gathering. Mei had changed his mind. She told him that he couldn't ignore Annie's friendship, no matter what the consequences of her partnership with Tony Chambers. That he owed it to himself to go see with his own eyes if Annie was happy or not.

Grudgingly, Patrick had to admit that they made a most handsome couple.

"G'day, boss."

Patrick returned the greeting from one of his men.

"They put on a fair *corroboree* here," the jackeroo offered.

Patrick recognized the term his herdsman used, the aboriginal word for a dance or celebration. "That they do," he agreed.

The older man fixed himself a cigarette, rolling up the paper and lighting it. "Are you going to enter the race?"

"What race?" Patrick asked. "It looks as though they've already begun."

The sheep hand laughed. "The big one between the station bosses. Chambers put up a thousand pounds."

Patrick considered this. Taking Chambers's money would be fun, though for the satisfaction of racing against him, he wouldn't have cared if the purse were a single pound. "Yes, I'm thinkin' that I will." His mountain brumby could outrun almost anything, except perhaps Cedric's—no, Chambers's—animal. He'd seen that big black run before. A close match. It was worth the risk.

"Patrick."

He swung around at the sound of the sweet, American-accented voice.

"Annie, me girl. I've been looking for you."

"And I you." She left Tony's side and hurried over to Patrick. "Did you just arrive? I've been waiting for you to come." Annie's eyes met his, searching for a sign as to Patrick's mood.

He stepped back and looked her over. "My, but you are grand, me girl. Just grand. As fine as ever any lady could hope to be." He stepped closer, holding out his arms. "Come here."

Annie went willingly, kissing his cheek. "I've missed you, you know."

"Have you now? Even with your fancy man?" He glanced at Tony, who glared back, a slight frown on his face.

Annie's smile faltered. "Don't be that way, please, even if he can't hear you. There's room in my life for you both."

"So," Patrick inquired, giving her a sharp look, "is he *in* your life, Annie? Truly? And if so, for how long?"

"I honestly can't answer that, Patrick."

"Do you love him?" He hadn't meant to ask.

She met his direct question with a direct response. "Yes, I do."

Patrick sighed. "Do you think he can give you the life you want? The life that you and Fallon deserve? Be a proper husband to you and a father to your daughter?"

"Honestly, I don't know since we've not discussed the matter at all."

"You mean he hasn't a bloody clue as to how you're feeling, my girl?"

"No."

"You're afraid to tell him, aren't you?"

Annie lowered her eyes. "It's very complicated, Patrick."

"Why?"

"Because it just is."

He heard the sadness in her voice. "Are you holding back something?"

"I'd rather not get into it here. We've guests aplenty and I'm neglecting my duties as hostess." She shot him a glance. "Can I trust that there'll be no unpleasantness today?"

"Word of honor, Annie girl."

She gave him a generous smile. "I really did miss you." Annie linked her arm through his. "Come on. Let's watch the races."

The afternoon's activities progressed, with a good time had by all concerned. Tony and Patrick maintained a polite veneer toward one another, for Annie's sake.

When it came to the last race of the day, a longer run over two miles, five men were mounted and ready to go.

Delight flooded through Annie's body. Tony Chambers was one who could hold his own against this hardy breed who were practically born into the saddle.

She noted that Tony was using the lighter English equipment that he'd ordered through Baker's. Merlin, his reins held by a groom, his coat gleaming like polished coal in the sun, tossed his head, eager to get on with it.

"Wish me luck?" a voice whispered in Annie's ear.

Startled, she almost jumped. "Do you have to ask?" she countered.

"Since I'm racing against O'Donnell, yes, I do."

Was that apprehension she heard in Tony's voice? Annie lifted her head, looked into his eyes. He stood there, outwardly radiating masculine confidence. His eyes and lips, however, told her a different story. It was as if he was waiting eagerly at the gate himself, holding back, reining himself in when all he wanted to do was let go.

"You represent Camelot. Of course I'm cheering for you to take the prize. I'd do so against anyone."

"Anyone?"

There was no hesitation or pretense when she spoke. "Yes, Tony, anyone." She reached out and took his hand, feeling its warmth.

Fallon skipped over to them as they stood by the starting line. "Can I give you a kiss for luck, Uncle Tony?" she begged.

He bent down and scooped the little girl up into his arms. "A kiss is it? Wherever did you hear that?"

"Mrs. Winters asked Mr. Jim if she could when he raced earlier. And he won, so it must have brought him luck. I want you to win, so I thought you could use a kiss and then you'd win too."

Tony laughed at Fallon's logic. "Kiss away, my lady fair."

Fallon giggled as she gave him a big, smacking kiss upon his sun-warmed cheek.

"That ought to be all I need to ride to victory," he said, "though if I want to be sure, I should have a token from my lady to keep with me."

"What's a token?" Fallon asked.

"A favor," Tony explained. "Like a ribbon." He looked at the one she wore in her hair.

Fallon pulled it quickly from her head. "Here it is."

"Let's have your mama tie it around my wrist, shall we?"

"Yes, Mama," the little girl insisted, "you must so that he can win."

Annie took the ribbon and tied it around the wrist that Tony held out, her fingers lingering on the warm

Gail Link

skin. Golden hairs stirred as she bound the ribbon into a bow.

Tony handed Fallon over to Annie's waiting arms and stood there briefly, giving her one last intense glance before he strode away and mounted his horse.

Alfred, with Mary on his arm, came up beside her.

"Alfred, what's the wagering?" Annie asked.

"Odds-on favorite seems to be split between O'Donnell and the Ruranga station man."

"Who's holding the bets?"

"Jim Winters."

"Tell him that I want a hundred pounds on Tony."

"Oh my," Mary Dunmartin remarked.

"Done," Alfred said, walking back toward where the foreman of Camelot station stood. He returned to his place in less than a minute.

"All taken care of, Mrs. Ross."

Annie smiled. "Good. Thank you, Alfred."

"You're quite welcome, ma'am, and may I add that I've taken the liberty to wager a sum upon Mr. Chambers as well."

"Then for both our sakes, along with the honor of Camelot, let us hope that he wins the race."

"The people who doubt are the fools, ma'am."

Tony was on the outside. Next to him was Patrick. The two men had barely exchanged more than a few civil words. "You've made Annie happy by coming, O'Donnell," Tony stated, keeping a grip on Merlin's reins as he admitted the truth as he saw it. At first, when he'd seen the two of them together, jealousy had stirred within him once again, stronger than before. He wanted to toss the Irish Aussie out on his ear, with instructions never to come back. But then, reason took over. O'Donnell was Annie's friend. He would have to accept that fact whether he liked it or not. O'Donnell was part of the life she'd rebuilt for herself here.

Patrick threw the other man a skeptical glance. It was on the tip of his tongue to caution the Englishman to take good care of Annie, but he held his thoughts inside. That she cared for the man was easy to read. Her gray eyes shone with it. She fairly glowed with her regard for the upstart interloper. Hell wouldn't be enough of a punishment if he hurt her in any way. Patrick promised himself that he'd see to that.

Tony held out his hand. "May the best man win."

"I'll be thinking we both know who that is," Patrick answered, shaking the Englishman's hand.

"Nice of you to acknowledge it, old man." Tony smiled. "Not so many as can get the upshot so quickly."

Patrick threw him an arch look. "By all the saints, you're in no doubt of your worth, are you?"

"No," Tony said, glancing away from the man beside him to the woman and child who stood a few feet from them, "nor that of others."

Patrick followed his eyes. "See it stays that way and we'll have no complaints."

"Gentlemen, on the ready," Jim Winters called out.

The horses pawed the ground, anxious to be off, as were their riders.

Tony leaned low over his mount. "Let's show them all what we're made of," he whispered to the animal.

A pistol shot rang out and the race was on, amidst cheers and shouts of encouragement from all assembled.

Tony held Merlin back, letting several others pass him by as he took the course, keeping pace as the animals traveled beyond the boundaries of the homestead, across the valley and upwards. Making the halfway mark, he could tell that two of the other horses were tiring, their heaving sides flecked with foam. Merlin was eager to go, yet Tony still held him in check. The time wasn't right.

"What's happening?" Annie demanded.

Alfred shrugged. "I don't know." He looked toward where Jim was standing, a mounted rider coming quickly into the gathering. He stopped long enough to say something to Jim and then rode out again.

Jim Winters held up his hand. "Halfway mark passed. Ruranga and Broken Hill stations in the lead."

Cheers from those from the two stations erupted. Jim threw a cautious look in Annie's direction.

"It's not over yet, ma'am," Alfred said consolingly.

"You've no need to tell me, Alfred," Annie insisted. "I know upon whom I've placed my faith." She didn't care a fig about the wager. That had been done solely for appearances. Annie wanted there to be no doubt as to where her loyalty was placed. She hugged Fallon. "You'll see, sweetheart. He'll win."

The riders had passed the three-quarters mark. Another horse was losing the pace set by the two leads.

"Now," Tony whispered as he let Merlin take the race, "it's our turn." The stallion shot past three others and took over as co-leader with O'Donnell's mount.

They were making their way across the valley back to the homestead, the crowd cheering.

Annie wanted to scream and shout as well. Decorum held sway until Alfred removed the child from her arms, perching the little girl upon his shoulders so that she could get a better view as she clapped her hands and yelled for "Tony."

Annie moved closer to the finish line, already thronged on both sides with people. She could see the horses coming faster as they raced across the ground and around the trees, the last hurdle a small stone fence to be jumped.

Tony's and Patrick's horses sailed over the obstacle. They were neck and neck. As they approached the flag, Merlin put on an extra burst of speed and rushed past Patrick's horse.

Acting purely on instinct, Annie sped across the dirt until she reached Tony's side.

He heaved a deep breath and when he saw her, reached down and scooped her up into the saddle in front of him.

"I claim my prize," he whispered in a deep growl, taking her mouth in a quick, hungry kiss, uncaring that all eyes were on them.

Chapter Twenty

"He kissed her right there in front of everyone, bold as you please. Just swept her up into his arms and gave her an embrace that's sure to keep the gossips happy until well into the New Year."

Mei sipped her tea thoughtfully as she listened to what Patrick had to say regarding the party at Camelot station. She could tell by the tone of his voice and the expression in his eyes that he was confused by what had happened between Chambers and Annie. She wished that she could have seen them for herself, that way she could have judged Annie's reaction to Tony Chambers's kiss.

"What did Annie do?"

"What could she do?" Patrick retorted.

"Shown her dislike of the situation in some manner," Mei pointed out. "A slap. A scream. Did she struggle?"

"No. Annie's too much of a lady for any of that."

"Or," Mei commented dryly, "she wasn't as upset as you think."

"What are you implying, my girl?" Patrick asked, his eyes sharp. "That she liked being picked up like a sack of grain and hoisted into the air in plain view of all her neighbors?"

Mei lowered her lids, studying the carpet in the parlor for a moment. She knew how she would feel if it were Patrick who was doing the sweeping gesture. She would love it, no matter who was watching. Hadn't he been so bold once before, when he hauled her off the block at the brothel?

"She might have enjoyed it," Mei at last replied. "Did she show any signs of distress?"

Patrick's mouth twisted as he pondered that question. He admitted with a shrug and a sheepish look, "Not really."

"Then perhaps she was pleased." Mei suspected that Annie had been. After all, she cared for the man, more than she was willing to admit. A public display of affection between them would have to mean something. At least Mei hoped so. "What happened next?"

"Chambers was officially declared the winner of the race."

"That isn't what I meant." She held aloft an empty teacup in Patrick's direction. "What happened between them?"

"Oh." Patrick declined Mei's offer of tea with a shake of his head; instead, he poured himself a large Irish whiskey from the decanter. "He set her back down and joined her. Plenty of people mobbed them, offering congratulations." Patrick took a hearty swallow of the liquor, then continued. "Chambers asked one of the men who'd brought instruments to play a tune, then he and Annie waltzed alone in a victory dance right there on the grounds."

"How did she look?"

Patrick took another long swallow of his drink before answering. "Now that I think back on it, Annie looked"—he paused for a moment—"happy. As if she was well pleased, actually."

Gail Link

"Then perhaps," Mei counseled, "you should trust her feelings."

"I trust Annie," Patrick stated. "It's Chambers that I've my doubts about. He's out for himself."

"How do you mean?"

"Women, to put it bluntly, are fair game for his kind," he said scathingly. "They're all just plain sheilas to him." He bit off the rest of what he was going to say for fear of being far too blunt.

"You still see Chamber as a *kind?*" Mei feared that Patrick's dislike of the Englishman was far too personal.

"Until he proves otherwise, yes."

"And what kind is he?" she asked, draining her cup.

"Selfish and spoiled," Patrick said contemptuously. "When all is said and done, he'll still be what he is—a member of the English upper crust. The gentry."

A bittersweet smile curved Mei's lips. "I think it is you who may be the snob, Patrick."

"Snob?" he asked, disbelief in his tone.

"Yes," she responded. "You aren't willing to give Anthony Chambers the benefit of the doubt."

"What doubt?" Patrick shot back. "He's going to hurt Annie."

"Maybe," Mei said, "maybe not. You cannot know for certain what he will or will not do. Love can change many things, many people."

"Love? What's love got to do with him?"

Patiently Mei explained, "The same thing as it does with everyone."

Patrick gave her a questioning look. "I don't understand how you can be so accepting of the man."

"Perhaps because I can see him as just a man, no better or worse."

Patrick worried over that last remark. Had Mei fallen for the Englishman's brand of charm? Here he was worrying about Annie when perhaps he should have been looking closer to home.

Mei saw the disconcerting look that came over Patrick's face; she believed the cause was still his overriding concern about Annie's involvement with Chambers.

"What you need is a hot bath to soothe away some of your worries," she suggested. "Why not let me fix one for you?"

That idea appealed to Patrick. He could use some time to relax and think. Besides, he was tired. Riding to and fro and engaging in a race was enough for one day. "It's a grand idea, Mei girl. I'd be happy if you'd do that for me."

Mei removed the tea tray and deposited it in the kitchen. Normally, she would have seen to washing it up and putting away all the items, but tonight something else weighed on her mind. Patrick was upset—how hard it must be, she thought, for him to watch the woman he loved with another man. To wonder if they soon would be lovers. His hurt must be overwhelming.

She could ease that ache.

She loved Patrick enough to do that for him.

Tonight. It must be tonight. If she waited—if she thought too deeply, then she might lose courage and he would be all alone.

Patrick eased his body into the large tub, the warm water soaking away the knots in his muscles. He'd ridden his horse hell-bent today, once during the race, then again when he'd come home.

The bloody race. He'd almost beaten the pommy.
Almost.

Almost, he reckoned, was not quite good enough. If nothing else, he did have to grudgingly admire the Englishman's handling of his horse, holding Merlin in check until the race was damned near over. Careful and cool. Biding his time until he was within sight of his goal.

Was Chambers planning on handling Annie in the same manner? Winner take all?

And what if he was? There was nothing Patrick could do to stop it. It was, as Mei so rightfully said, Annie's life. He couldn't tell her what to do. She was a grown woman. With, as it so happened, more experience of life than he himself had. She was no lemming-like creature, easily led astray.

God, what a Pandora's box Cedric had let loose upon them all when he'd insisted that his grand-nephew come to Australia. Patrick could only think that it would have been better had Cedric never made it a condition that his relative actually come to Victoria and claim his inheritance in person. How much better off they might all be if Tony Chambers had remained in London, doing what he most likely did best—being one of Society's top "darlings," a rake amongst rakes.

Patrick ran the bar of hard-milled lavender soap across his chest and down his arms. The smell of the soap reminded him of Mei. Delicate. But never weak.

Mei. His bright angel of compassion and understanding, his shining star in the darkness.

His one and only love.

* * *

She waited for him.

Candles bathed the room in a soft mellow light. Tonight wasn't the time for harsh, cold illumination. Things that needed to be expressed here in this room needed gentleness, warmth, and the feel of a temple, a place where souls worshiped freely, as they should, without guilt or care.

She was oddly calm. In her heart, Mei had made the only choice she could have, given the circumstances. Love, and faith in that love, had guided her, shown her the way to proceed.

She turned her head when she heard a sound in the corridor outside; her hair spilled over the shoulder of her white silk robe like a black curtain.

Patrick turned the handle and walked into his bedroom, surprised at the myriad candles that banished the darkness. His bed was turned down, inviting.

She stepped out of the shadows, near one window.

Patrick sucked in his breath. Was he hallucinating, or was that really Mei standing there, clad only in a silk robe, her bare feet testament to the fact she was most likely bare beneath the fabric?

He licked suddenly dry lips. "Mei, what are you doing here?" he demanded softly, certain he was in the throes of a dream, praying that he might never wake.

"To give to you what you bought; what I thought you might have need of this night." She stepped closer, coming around the four-poster bed until she was standing in front of him, her dark eyes taking the measure of him as he stood there, his compact, muscular body smooth and damp from his bath, a towel wrapped loosely about his hips. "It would be my honor to serve you, to pleasure you in any way that I can." Warmth curled through her belly.

Patrick knew he wasn't a saint. He could feel the change coming over him, a tightening in his groin, a stronger beat of his heart, an urge to pull her to him and kiss that beautiful mouth, to touch that lovely skin. "Mei . . ." Her name came out in a low groan.

"Let me ease your ache," she said softly, her words a gentle invitation. "Let me soothe your wounds and see to your comfort."

"Wounds?" Confusion clouded his thoughts. "By all the saints, what are you talking about?"

"I know how much seeing Annie with the Englishman has hurt you."

"So, you're offering yourself to me as a substitute?" he asked incredulously. Patrick couldn't quite understand what was going on here. Was she truly proposing to sleep with him to take his mind off of Annie? And if so, why?

"If it would make you happy and remove the pain from your heart, then yes."

Patrick's blue-green eyes met hers. "I respect you too much, Mei girl, to use you in that way."

"So, you would refuse my gift?" Mei tried to keep the pain she was feeling from her voice.

Patrick was beginning to get a glimmer of an idea. Somehow, someway, Mei thought he was upset about Annie and Chambers for a different reason—that he was jealous. Or lovesick at the notion of Annie in another man's arms.

Holy saints, Mei felt sorry for him.

Hopes newly risen within him dashed on the rocks of despair.

"I don't want your *gift* out of some imagined pity that you feel for me."

"I sought only to give you comfort—to ease your

pain," she explained. "No pity was involved."

"No pain exists," Patrick assured her, wondering how much longer he could stand there and not take what Mei was willing to bestow, "so your sacrifice would be in vain." Temptation had never come in so wonderful a package. Realizing that, he moved away, his back to her.

Mei wouldn't drop the subject. "You are angry that she has chosen another, are you not?"

Patrick sighed. "I realized that it's Annie's decision to make where she will find her happiness. I cannot dictate terms to her. I may not approve her choice, if indeed she chooses Chambers, but it's hers to make, as it should be."

Mei lifted her chin, a glimmer of hope rising in her breast. "So, you are not broken-hearted."

Patrick turned back to face her. "Over Annie?"

"Yes," Mei replied. "Do you not love her?"

Another suspicion was wedging aside the former in Patrick's brain. "Of course I do," he said softly, "as a sister." He emphasized the last word, praying that Mei would understand the differences in his love.

Mei couldn't believe what she was hearing. Was Patrick saying this to keep his pride? Or had she been wrong all this time about how he felt? "Truly?"

Patrick nodded, taking a few steps in her direction.

"You would swear to that?"

"I would so swear, by all the saints in heaven, if that would make you happy, Mei girl."

"I thought—"

"That I was in love with Annie Ross?"

It was her turn to nod.

"I'm not." Patrick took a step nearer to her, their bodies almost touching. "So, if you want to come to my bed, it must be because it's where you want to be. That it's what *you* want," he stressed, his voice husky with the desire he was experiencing. "No other reason will do for me."

Mei loosened her robe, letting it fall open.

Patrick gasped at the perfection of her body. He looked slowly, deeply, taking it all in, from her head to her toes: small, high breasts crowned with rosy-brown nipples; a waist that he could easily span with his hands; a black delta of hair that he longed to explore; a pair of slender legs and arching, delicate feet. She was the dream of a thousand lonely nights, the hauntingly lovely reminder that God was the creator of all life.

Color rose in Mei's cheeks, giving her creamy-golden skin a blush of pink. "Do I please you?"

"More than I could ever say," Patrick replied.

"Then let me give you what is mine only once to share."

Mei's words were a vivid reminder to Patrick that they were both virgins. He had no skill to dazzle her with, no depth of knowledge from which to draw upon to show her the way. All he had was the love that threatened to overwhelm him to act as his guide. Would it be enough?

He reached out his hand and touched the sheen of her black hair. "Silk," he whispered.

He was nervous. Mei could read that in his honest eyes, endearing him to her all the more. He didn't bother to hide or pretend that he was other than what he was.

Patrick touched his lips to hers, a sweet, gentle salute.

Warmth, sunshine, and laughter, the beginning of

the best yet to be. That was what his kiss meant to Mei, who willingly surrendered her mouth to Patrick's when he sought to deepen the kiss.

When his arms slid around her back, pulling her closer, Mei broke the union of their lips. "Please," she said, "let me show you the pathway to the garden of delights."

"What?" Patrick was confused. His body was reacting visibly and strongly to the nearness of her, to the softness of her skin, to the sweetness of her mouth.

"I have been well schooled in the arts of pleasure," she confessed, "for my mother, and later the women of the House of the Golden Dragon, taught me well. This knowledge I possess, and have never used before, is for you alone. Allow me to do what I have wanted to do since the night you entered that place and bought me, saving me from certain shame."

Bloody hell, he thought, pain slicing through him. She was grateful. Just that. "I've told you before, Mei, you don't owe me."

"Oh, but I do."

"No," he insisted, wondering how he was going to make it through the night if he had to turn her away now.

"I owe you the love I have inside my heart," she explained. "It was you who taught me this love, Patrick. Without you, I would be like a river forever frozen, never knowing the joy of life, never realizing my true purpose. It is right for me to show you my love."

"You love me?" he asked, humbled by her words.

"I would not be here tonight if I did not."

"Then I've a confession of my own to make." Patrick couldn't let her think that love was only on her side. "I've loved you since that first night, as well. When I

317

Gail Link

entered that place and saw you there, I thought it was my lucky day indeed. Then, when I heard whispers of the auction, and saw that they meant to sell your maidenhood to the highest bidder, I knew I couldn't bear to see you go to anyone else. I would have paid any price to spare you from that."

"Yet you never once sought to collect upon your investment."

"I didn't want to buy your love," he explained. "If it wasn't given freely, then it wasn't mine to have."

"It is yours," Mei assured him, sharing her own fears. "I believed that you cared for me, though only as one cared for a friend, a companion, never as the woman you wanted."

Patrick smiled. "How wrong we both were. I thought you saw me only as your benefactor, the man who was your employer."

"You are the man," she whispered, sliding her hand down his cheek and around his neck, "that I would give my life to—and for."

"No man could ever want more."

"Then will you permit me to show you my love?"

Patrick's eyes locked with hers. "Please."

Mei took his hand and drew him to the bed. "Lie down," she instructed.

Patrick complied with her request, sliding in between the sheets. He smelled the essence of flowers in the fresh linen. "Will you join me?" he asked.

Mei smiled. "Not yet." Mei pulled her robe closed, tying the belt securely about her waist.

Patrick watched in fascination as she glided about the room, examining items she'd obviously brought in with her. Finally, she held one small glass bottle over

318

the flame of a candle for a few seconds. Satisfied, Mei returned.

She sat down upon the bed, her eyes daringly focused upon Patrick's body. Mei poured some of the contents of the bottle into her palms, then eased her hands onto his flesh, smoothing the heated lavender oil into his skin, around his neck and shoulders.

Patrick sighed from the sheer delight of the combination of her hands and the warm, fragrant oil. Like the soap, it reminded him of Mei.

"You like that?"

Like? He could be damned to hell for all eternity for liking it so much. "That I do, my girl," he replied.

Mei dribbled more oil onto him, working her hands carefully along one arm, soothing the muscles downward, kneading his palm, then each finger separately. That arm completed, she did the same to the other.

Tension fled from Patrick's body. He relaxed under her ministrations, enjoying the feel of being pampered.

When she moved on the bed, her hands next upon his thighs, Patrick sucked in his breath, tension of another sort rising within him. Slowly she stroked, massaged, kneaded, soothed down one leg, across his knee and around his calf, all the way to his toes. Each toe came under special consideration of her adroit fingers.

When Mei switched to his other leg, Patrick thought he was losing his grasp on reality. He hadn't known a man could feel so much from the touch of a woman's hands upon his body. Sliding, caressing, her fingers worked magic.

Mei smiled at the look on Patrick's face. His lids were closing; his hands were finding it hard to remain

319

still; his breathing grew deeper. She wet her lips as she poured more lavender oil into her palms, rubbing them together. Her hair slid across his skin as she placed her hands upon his smooth chest.

Patrick's eyes flew open.

Mei guided her fingers along a sensual path, back and forth, around and over, caressing each particle of skin, circling the masculine nipples. She bent her head and, like a cat feeding at a bowl of cream, licked them lightly.

Patrick groaned. "Enough."

"Not yet," she replied, moving down his flat stomach until she reached the towel that was still hooked about his waist. Deftly she pulled it aside.

His response was true and undeniable.

She slid her hands over the length of him, watching as he grew even bigger. This was power and life, and she worshiped at its altar.

Patrick ached with want, so much that he thought he might explode. His hands reached for her, pulling at the sash of her silk robe, eager for their joining.

Mei removed the robe herself, sitting back, letting him look his fill, enjoying the pleasure she saw mirrored there. Then, realizing the time had come to end one lesson and begin another, she shifted, moving her body until she rested upon his swollen member. Sinking slightly, she took a deep breath and sheathed him completely, biting back her cry of pain at the piercing of her maidenhead.

Patrick reached up and grasped her hips, moving to the rhythm their bodies set, nature taking sway over their emotions, teaching them both the wonder of the first time when love was partnered with desire.

* * *

Patrick was glad that he'd waited to experience this. He hadn't wanted his first taste of love to be with a whore. He wanted to share that with a woman he loved—and he had. Satisfied, Patrick wanted a repeat performance, though he knew that depended upon Mei.

He glanced at the woman sleeping in his arms, her breathing deep and even. He couldn't believe how blessed he felt at this moment. It was as if God had personally given him a glimpse of heaven. Love like this couldn't be a sin.

Tears of happiness clouded his eyes.

Mei stirred. She whispered words in Chinese.

Patrick sealed her mouth with a kiss. "What are you saying, my girl?"

Yawning, she replied, "That I love you."

"Teach me to say it."

Mei repeated the words, louder this time. Patrick worked them around his tongue, giving them back to her.

She laughed at his pronunciation, happy that he tried.

He joined in the laughter. "No matter what the language, I love you, Mei." He kissed her, holding her close to his heart. "I'll be quick about getting a priest to wed us," he promised. "Today, if I can find one who'll waive the banns."

Mei cried.

"What's wrong?" he asked, afraid that he'd somehow botched things up. "You do want to marry me, do you not?"

She brushed the tears from her eyes. "To be your wife is all that I want."

"Then we'll see it done. The sooner the better."

Mei smiled, her last thought before drifting back to sleep that this was how it was meant to be. Joss had showered her with its blessing. She wished the same for Annie.

Chapter Twenty-One

"It was a huge success, ma'am," Mary said as she stirred the batter for the holiday cookies. She showed Fallon, who was standing on a chair so she could reach the bowl on the wooden counter, how to slowly pour in dried rasins and nuts to the mixture.

"Yes, it was, wasn't it," Annie agreed, thinking back on the day before. The event had gone well, with much goodwill spread among the other stations. Many who'd come had gone home with good memories of the party, and of Camelot's co-owners, which pleased Annie very much.

Rising from her seat at the kitchen table, Annie poured herself another cup of coffee from the granite-ware pot, smiling as she scooped up a few nuts from the copper measuring cup Fallon held so carefully in both her tiny hands.

"Mama!" the little girl protested, giving Annie a mock-cross look.

"You won't miss these, sweetheart," Annie said with a laugh. "You've got more than enough for your cookies." At her daughter's slightly pouty expression, Annie confessed, "I just couldn't resist."

She popped the pecans into her mouth and took her seat, the household accounts book open and waiting for her perusal. Annie sipped her coffee, her mind

Gail Link

wandering. She happily recalled the events of the afternoon in vivid detail; especially of the race, the thrill in seeing Tony win, even if he had to beat Patrick to do so. The utter delight in being caught up in his arms and kissed soundly before everyone there, even if it was only for a instant—or at least what seemed like an instant. His kiss had been all too brief, but wildly satisfying nonetheless. Filled with heat, it scorched her mouth with the force of a brand, burning into her memory.

And then she remembered being held in Tony's strong arms as the band played a waltz. It didn't matter that it wasn't a grand ballroom in some magnificent estate, that they weren't gliding across a floor of marble or polished oak underneath a grand set of chandeliers blazing with light. All that mattered was that she was in Tony's embrace, held close to his body as the music played on, as the people on the sidelines cheered while they danced on the grass.

Annie'd felt like a fairy princess, especially when he'd whispered, "You are by far the loveliest woman here." The look in his eyes as she'd raised her head had momentarily stunned her. It was hot and hungry, frankly, intensely male.

All too soon the music had come to a halt. Men crowded around Tony, wishing him well, heaping praise upon his riding skills, and asking for the chance to use Merlin as a stud for their own mares.

Even Patrick had offered his hand in congratulations to the winner. Annie was thankful for that gesture. She imagined she knew just how much it had cost Patrick to make it.

Annie had found herself surrounded by women, all eager to chat and make observations about the handsome Englishman as they walked toward the tents for the early supper. They oohed and aahed about this and that, some even dropping sly hints about upcoming weddings.

Her thoughts back in the present, Annie took another sip of coffee. She couldn't dwell on that, not when other things weighed heavily on her mind. What she was feeling was all so new to her, all so intoxicating, that she feared to examine it too closely.

Where did she and Tony proceed from here? she wondered. What exactly was on his mind? There'd been no time for them to be alone yesterday after the dance. Too many other things to attend to, namely the guests. Many hadn't left the station until late; some had stayed over, leaving this morning. Breakfast this morning had been a noisy, cluttered meal. Luncheon was catch-as-catch-can, Tony having ridden out with Jim and some of the men to search for a herd of brumbies reported close by. At least at dinner they could be alone. Hopefully. Time then to talk.

But was talking all she wanted to do?

Annie couldn't help recalling the feel of his mouth on hers. How it made her quiver with excitement as it brought a warmth to her skin, along with a sharp, tingling sensation deep in her belly. Had the kiss meant something to him as well? Or was it simply another female mouth, no different from any other? One kiss out of hundreds in his life so far?

Lord, she wished that she knew.

Annie was afraid of the feelings he stirred within her. Afraid of the way Tony had come to mean so much to her in such a short time. Afraid that in some way he'd be like the other—a man bent on only one thing, getting what he wanted, who could blithely walk away without looking back.

Could she ever trust him?

Could she ever trust herself?

"Look, Mama," Fallon crowed with pride, "I'm making one big cookie for Uncle Tony and another for you." Lady sat on the floor a few feet away from Fallon, her head cocked, watching the child, every so often giving an encouraging whoof.

Annie watched as Fallon dropped batter from a large wooden spoon onto a tin sheet that would be slipped into the oven. "That's nice, sweetheart," Annie replied with a smile, happy that Fallon cared so much for him. "I'm certain that Tony will be pleased that you made it especially for him."

Fallon, her fingers tipped with batter, looked at her mother, her wide blue eyes huge and innocent in her honesty. "I love Uncle Tony, Mama. Don't you?"

Mary coughed abruptly, almost dropping the bowl she was holding. "Excuse me, ma'am."

Pink flushed Annie's cheeks. She avoided a direct answer to Fallon's question by saying, "He's a good man, sweetheart. One that Cedric would have been very proud of, I'm sure."

Not quite the answer that her daughter may have wanted, but it was all that Annie felt willing to give at that instant. How could she explain to a child of Fallon's age just how many varieties of love there were? Some soft and sweet, others mild and soothing. Then there was the deeply intense kind that shook your world upon its foundations, reshaping your life, altering your perceptions. It was the latter that she'd come to feel for Tony Chambers.

And loving, for Annie, involved expressing that love, giving of herself. But how could she when the hardest thing demanded of her would be that which she was afraid to bestow?

How easy it had been, once upon a time, to declare that one would stay as far removed as one could from love, from passion. To remain cloistered, like a penitent seeking absolution for a past sin.

Annie had thought she could.

Tony Chambers had proved her wrong.

Now, she knew what it was to care again, to emerge as if from a darkened cave into the sweet, dazzling brightness of daylight. Exhilarating. Frightening.

Tony rode slightly apart from the others.

They'd been successful in capturing five mares from the brumby stallion's herd. The agile, slightly wild mountain horses would make an interesting mix with Merlin's blood, Tony decided. Crossing pure-bred with lesser stock was risky in some instances, but from what he'd read of Cedric's journal in which he kept careful notes on the breeding of his horses, it could prove to be profitable to the station. His great-uncle had wanted to try the experiment, but died before he could see his plan come to fruition. Two of the mares they'd caught had borne foals, proof that they were capable breeders.

Galloping across the spectacular expanse of countryside made Tony think about the race yesterday. It wasn't quite like winning the Derby, but for him, close enough. What he'd really enjoyed was beating O'Donnell. Tony couldn't pretend otherwise, especially not to himself. Some might call it petty, but he didn't care. Satisfaction brought a smile to his lips and a sense of triumph to his soul. Annie had been cheering him on as he'd crossed the finish line. He'd heard her call his name through the din. Heard her over everyone else and seen the joy on her face as he'd come across first.

Nothing had seemed quite so important right then as wanting to share the moment with her.

Instinct had guided him. When he saw her, his first thought was to hold her. His next was to take possession, no matter how temporary, of those inviting lips.

He'd cursed the fact that they'd been surrounded by so many curious pairs of eyes, all, it seemed, looking in their direction. He would rather have taken her somewhere private to continue the moment, building on it. That hadn't been possible. The next best thing had been to dance with her. There, in his arms, Annie felt real, and somehow a part of him.

Circumstances had forced them apart, curtailing his desire to spend the rest of the day with her. She'd already gone to bed by the time his amiable card game had broken up. His luck had held there as well, winning more games than he lost. Most, in fact. A streak of good fortune. It was a wonder since his mind wasn't really focused on the cards—rather, it was on the woman who more and more filled his every waking moment.

Tony could no longer pretend that he didn't have deep feelings for Annie. He did. Strong, intense feelings, unlike any he'd heretofore experienced. Passionate. Tender. Razor-sharp. And, he suspected, long-lasting.

When had this happened? When had she snuck so effortlessly into his heart? How had she managed to burrow through what he thought was the hardened shell of his cynical presumptions?

And not only her—her daughter, this land, the people, the way of life. It had all become a part of him.

When he woke in the mornings, he had a sense of accomplishment, of doing something right, of continuing his great-uncle's dream.

He realized, with an insightful clarity, that in England—which of course he still loved—he'd been bored. Drifting from one thing to the next without an anchor. Enjoying the life he led, unaware that he needed more. Needed the challenge that this change in venue had provided him, in more ways than one.

What he needed especially was *her*—his greatest challenge.

"Fine day's work, Mr. Chambers," Jim Winters said, coming up beside him as they rode through the summer-awakened valley. "These are good animals. Hardy mares who'll give you foals worth the time and trouble it took to secure them."

"I hope you're right, Jim," Tony said over the din of the pounding hooves.

"Your uncle would have been right proud of you, carrying on with what he never lived to do."

Tony flashed the foreman a grin. "I'd like to think so."

"And," Jim continued, "he'd likewise be proud of how you and Mrs. Ross have come along. He cared for her like she was his blood."

"I think I can understand now why he did," Tony said, more to himself than to Jim.

The foreman heard the remark and approved the sentiment. He'd kept a watchful eye on the situation, feeling he owed it to the old man's memory, and because he and the men were fond of Mrs. Ross. It eased Jim's mind to know that there'd be no divided loyalties on the station. Things would continue to run smoothly. "She's a grand lady who'll someday make some man very lucky." With that observation, Jim pulled his horse away from Tony's and rode back to rejoin the men riding behind, his words echoing in Tony's ears.

Lucky.

Some man.

What Jim meant was some *other* man.

Not bloody likely, Tony thought, pressing his heels gently into Merlin's ribs. Not if he had anything to do about it. And he did.

Tonight.

All the guests had left. Things would be back to normal, so they'd have their private time at dinner. Alone. With no interruptions. Nothing to divert their attention from one another. Time enough then to see where things stood and where they went.

He certainly knew where he wanted them to go.

Tony understood that they couldn't continue to wander aimlessly any longer. Something potent existed between them. Powerful. Exciting. It was long past time to explore the possibilities.

Tonight.

The doors that opened onto the veranda had been left ajar to let in the air. The evening was pleasant, with the hint of a warm breeze wafting through the room.

Tony and Annie had finished their meal. Instead of moving to the parlor for coffee and dessert, they'd chosen to remain where they were, replete and content. Mary had brought in the silver service so that Annie could pour their coffee at the table. Mary had also brought in bowls of rice pudding, loaded with thick, plump raisins and topped with a generous dash of cinnamon.

"Would you be wanting anything else, ma'am?" she asked.

Annie smiled. "No, this will be quite fine, Mary. Thank you. Dinner was, as always, wonderful. Adding the chunks of pineapple to the roast chicken was a marvelous touch."

Mary beamed at the praise. "My pleasure, ma'am. Being's as we got it, no sense wasting it."

"I would add my compliments to those of Mrs. Ross, Mary," Tony stated, accepting the cup of coffee that Annie handed him.

"Thank you, sir," Mary replied, making her exit back to the kitchen.

Tony sipped his coffee. "Have you noticed that she and Alfred are spending a fair amount of time together?"

"It has come to my attention, yes," Annie said, pouring herself a cup. "They seem quite content with one another."

Content. A mildly agreeable state of being, Tony observed silently. He suspected that Alfred would put it rather more strongly if he was to ask him.

"As content as any man can be who knows his affections are reciprocated, I assume," Tony observed, slanting a glance in her direction.

Annie tasted the pudding, savoring the flavor, her eyes deliberately downcast. All through dinner she couldn't help but feel a certain tension rising between them. It was here now. Left over from yesterday, and growing increasingly strong. It was all Annie could do to simply eat, pretending there was nothing untoward happening when she knew with every part of her body that a great deal was happening.

Tony thought the pudding very good, but it couldn't compare to the flavor he'd found in her mouth. Annie's lips were sweeter than any dessert, more potent than any wine. She'd carefully avoided his eyes tonight whenever possible. Why? Because she knew that the reckoning was upon them? If not now, then soon.

"Would you care to take a stroll in the garden when you're finished?" he inquired, trying to maintain an even tone.

Annie wiped the traces of the creamy rice pudding from her mouth. She should say no. If she answered yes, then she'd be tempting fate, pushing hard at the boundaries she'd tried to keep in place.

"I'd like that," she replied, cracking the foundation of the borders with her own words.

"Best take a wrap," he said, glancing at her outfit, knowing that the weather could always change here in the High Country, summer or not. She wore a high-necked white cotton and lace blouse with leg-o'-mutton sleeves, tucked into a skirt of navy blue and white striped taffeta, which crinkled as she moved. A dark blue sash wrapped around her slim waist. The only jewelry she wore was his pendant and the earrings from Patrick. Her hands, he thought, needed a ring to show off their slender beauty. Several, perhaps, but most definitely of his choosing. One was in his possession now. He'd bought it when he purchased the pendant.

Annie rose. "I'll return in a moment," she promised, leaving him to fetch her shawl.

Tony rose also, reseating himself when she vacated the room, poured himself another cup, adding cream and a cube of sugar. Desire rose steadily within him.

A want so strong that he could feel it in his bones. A yearning so fierce that it was like an ache deep in his soul.

All for her.

Annie drew out a dark blue cashmere shawl and wrapped it around her shoulders. She stood there for a moment, her thoughts hearkening to Tony. These days she found that he was never far from them. Either awake or asleep, he was there, filling her mind with his image, constantly.

Tony.

Women yesterday had flocked to him, reacting just as she expected they would. He was charming, winning over most of the people who'd come. The perfect English gentleman. Witty. Sophisticated. Blatantly self-assured. Oh, there were still some few who remained skeptical, withholding their full-out approval until they determined he'd earned it. They, however, were in the minority. Certainly, there were no women in that contingent.

The other men, in her opinion, couldn't compare to him. It wasn't that they lacked anything; rather, it was that Tony possessed something else, something extra.

Favor.

From God, from fate, from other men, from women—most especially from women. Fortune smiled upon him, gracing him with all manner of gifts. He had but to reach out and take.

But he wasn't a user or despoiler.

She knew that now.

The other thing she knew was that she wanted him. Wanted him in a way completely foreign to her before he'd arrived. Heart and body. Flesh and spirit.

When Tony touched her, she trembled, though she felt stronger. When he looked at her, it was as if she'd fallen through a deep tunnel, while soaring above the clouds.

Confusing.

But she loved him.

She now understood that line from one of Mr. Poe's poems, "We loved with a love that was more than love." It was how she loved him. More than she realized it was possible to love.

Tony stood in the open doorway, waiting for her. He'd shed his jacket, wearing only a white lawn shirt, open at the throat, and black trousers tucked into high black boots. Handsome as sin and twice as tempting.

Annie took the arm he offered as he led her into the night, lanterns hanging to light their way along the garden path. It was like walking into a fairyland, escorted by a handsome prince.

They walked in companionable silence for almost a quarter hour, strolling along the stone walk until they came to a wooden bench. An iron and glass lantern hung overhead, illuminating the encroaching darkness.

Annie glanced at the fixture, the smell of vanilla coming from the candle burning inside. "Where did these items"—she pointed to the lamp—"come from?"

Tony smiled as he sat down next to her. "I had the station blacksmith make them. I knew you liked walking here. I've seen you do it often, at dusk. Now, you may do it at any time without fear."

His thoughtfulness touched her. "How kind of you to think of me."

Kind. She thought he was being kind. Annie had no

idea that it was actually a selfish act. He'd discovered that her pleasure gave him pleasure. Making her happy by such a small token was easily within his power. The joy on her face was as if he'd given her an estate and an army of servants to run it smoothly, or a chestful of jewels. With Annie, Tony found he gave gifts because he wanted to, not because he had to, or it was expected. Her favors weren't for sale; they couldn't be bought with the price of a trinket. He'd learned that. Far from being the greedy, grasping whore he'd expected to find upon his arrival, he'd discovered she was one of the most genuine women he'd ever met. Engaging, intelligent, soft-hearted, strong, and stubborn. So much more than he'd bargained for. Another woman might have fallen apart had what happened to Annie befallen her. Annie hadn't.

Tony reached out and cupped her chin. Her skin was soft. Leaning over, he took her mouth with his.

His lips were tender and persuasive, melting her reserve. Annie closed her eyes, languishing in the feelings Tony evoked within her. He had skill aplenty, weaving a spell of magic over her, taking her on a spectacular journey into the uncharted realm of the senses.

He broke the kiss and they gazed into each other's eyes. Long and lingering. His, to her, were no longer shards of polished green glass, cool and sharp. They were now flames that burned with a pale olive fire. Hot and fervent.

Hers, to him, ceased being the misty gray of a Cotswold lake in winter; now, they burned with the underlying spark of smokey charcoal. Smoldering.

Annie lifted her hand and placed her index and middle fingers against the fullness of his mouth, touching it gently, giving in to the temptation she'd been experiencing. She'd dreamed about doing this. She traced his mouth slowly, lovingly, as a child would, wonder in her movements.

Next, her fingers skimmed along his square, angular jawline until they reached the brown mole.

Tony tried valiantly to maintain some control of his emotions as her fingers slid over his skin. "Some consider it a flaw, you know," he whispered, his voice husky.

"Nonsense," she insisted, so close that she could feel his breath upon her face. "How could anyone?" Certainly not she. It made him even more attractive, if that were possible.

"It doesn't bother you?"

"Why should it?" Annie demanded. "It's part of you." She smiled. "A kiss from an angel, didn't you say?"

Tony grinned.

"Perhaps," Annie mused in a light-hearted vein, "a fallen angel?" Yes, she thought, like Milton's Lucifer, Tony was proud and no man's second.

"Forever banned from paradise?" he retorted. "Is that what you think?" And what was, he wondered, for him, paradise? He wasn't sure he even believed in its existence.

"Temporarily at best," she replied, her hands dropping to her lap. "No one could keep you from what you wanted, or where you belonged, I'm sure."

Ah, one person could, he reckoned. Annie Ross. He wanted her. And as to where he belonged, it was in her bed. Or she in his. Simple as that.

Tony stretched out his hand and found the combs that held her brown hair in place atop her head. He loosened them, letting them fall to the ground. Her hair tumbled down in long waves and he gathered a fistful into his hand, bringing it to his lips. It was like touching raw silk.

"I . . . we should be getting back," Annie suddenly said, her voice low and laced with urgency. If she stayed out here with him any longer, she despaired of the outcome. She ached with the newly discovered want she felt for this man. An aching so deep, so intense that to deny it its full expression was painful; yet, to surrender was to find herself in unknown and dangerous waters.

His voice, his look, his touch, were all so captivating and persuasive, that she could feel panic rising within her breast. A man's overwhelming passion had once hurt her so badly it had almost crushed her spirit and brutalized her senses so that she wasn't sure she could allow that to happen again.

Trust. It all boiled down to trust.

Tony captured her mouth with his again, this time his arms resting loosely at his sides. He didn't want her to feel trapped in his embrace, so he let his lips alone show her how much he wanted her. They hungrily devoured hers until she withdrew from the kiss.

Annie put out her hand again, resting her fingers across his mouth. "I can't," she said. "Please understand. Not here. Not now."

He sighed, need burning through his body. As much as he wanted to pursue further what was between them, Tony respected her wish to call a halt. At least for the moment. He'd never taken by force what he felt certain to win by other means.

Besides, Annie was right. Here wasn't the place. Now wasn't the moment. He wanted privacy and time

337

to show her the delights of making love, neither of which this place afforded.

"I understand," he said.

"Do you?"

"Yes."

Annie rose, the feel of him still fresh on her lips, on her fingers. She moved, her feet mechanically taking the steps that would lead her away from him and back to sanity, back to safety.

Then, abruptly, she halted, turning toward him.

Tony sat there watching her, those hooded eyes fixed on her, sharp as a hawk's.

Without thinking, Annie dashed the short distance back to Tony.

He stood up.

Annie stopped mere inches from him.

Then she did something which took them both by surprise. One hand on his shoulder to steady herself, she raised on tiptoe and kissed him.

Not on the lips, as Tony might have expected. Instead, she lightly touched his mole, brushing her lips across it.

Before Tony could react, she was gone.

A smile curved his mouth, kicking up the corners.

An angel's kiss indeed.

Chapter Twenty-Two

Almost an hour had passed.

Annie paced around her room, unable to settle down. All she could think about was the walk in the garden, the closeness that existed between her and Tony. The touch of his hands, the feel of his lips, the heat in his eyes. She'd responded to it all, wanting more, though apprehensive of that want, so strong was it. Almost overwhelming. She couldn't be sure if this was right. If it was true. Nothing in her life had prepared her for this.

A knock sounded.

Grabbing her lightweight robe, she slipped it on and opened the door.

Alfred stood there holding a pouch. "Excuse me, ma'am, but a rider from Broken Hill just arrived and asked that you get this as soon as possible. Since I saw the light beneath your door, I thought it was all right to deliver it now, rather than wait till the morning."

Annie took the pouch. "Thank you, Alfred."

"With pleasure, ma'am. Good night."

"Good night," she said, closing the door. Annie untied the string that held the oilskin together. Inside were two letters addressed to her. She walked back to her dressing table, sat down, and broke the wax seal on the first. The delicate handwriting she recognized as Mei's.

My Dear Annie:

It is with great joy that I write to you to share my happiness. Today, Patrick and I are leaving for Sydney, there to spend Christmas with his family, who are gathered at his sister Mary's house. It is there that we plan to marry, if we can find a priest to waive the banns.

Yes, marry. It is sudden, but what we both want. I was so wrong in hiding my true feelings from him. I know this now. I should have been brave enough to tell Patrick before what he meant to me. So much time wasted when we could have been together.

Do not, my friend, make the same mistake.

If you will but reach for your dream, I think you shall find it within your grasp. Do not allow the past to stop you from having what you want—who you want. Take the risk.

May the gods grant you your heart's desire, as they have mine.

Your loving friend,
Mei

Annie couldn't believe what she'd read. Mei and Patrick. Finally together. And to be married. A sigh escaped her lips. How she wished she could be there to witness their richly deserved joy. She was so happy for them.

And what of Mei's advice to her? Annie reread the letter. Mei urged her to grasp happiness while she could. Annie knew just what, or rather whom, Mei was referring to—Tony.

She broke the seal on Patrick's note.

Annie girl,

I'm just wanting to tell you that I'll be away, in Sydney, for about three weeks. Celebrating the holidays with my family, and taking care of something else—my wedding to Mei.

She's done me the honor of consenting to marry me. Ain't that grand? I'm the luckiest man in Australia, or so it seems to me. I love her more than I can say, and to think that I almost let her get away. Foolish pride could have cost me dearly. God in his wisdom saw fit to grant me what I wanted most— and I'm not letting the chance pass me by.

My only regret is that you won't be there to stand witness for us. I pray that you'll forgive me and wish us both well.

I trust also that God will see to it that you get all that you deserve and more. All I wish for is that you find what Mei and I have together.

I remain your devoted friend,
Patrick O'Donnell

Tears filled Annie's eyes, threatening to spill over at any moment. She reached into her drawer and pulled out a pale blue handkerchief, dabbing at the moisture. How strange that she should hear from them now, now when she was facing an important decision. It had to be fate. What Mei called joss. Both letters urged her to find happiness, to take a chance.

Could she? Should she follow her instinct, which prompted her to trust that Tony wouldn't hurt her?

Could she trust him with her heart and not regret the action? She had no proof. All she had was faith.

Was it enough?

It had been for Patrick and Mei.

Annie left both letters on the dressing table when she arose, walking to the doors. She opened them, letting the air waft over her body. Like the stroke of fingers, it ruffled her hair, her clothes. She shed her night robe, flinging it aside. She closed her eyes, her imagination taking flight as the breeze became his fingers, feathering along her skin, molding her nightgown to her body. Gentle. Possessive.

She blushed, but not in shame. Shame had no place in what she felt for Tony. Though she'd removed the opal earrings, she still wore the pendant, *his* pendant. Her right hand clasped it tightly, as if by doing so she could summon him to appear.

His name fell from her lips in a whisper of longing. "Tony."

Tony sat in the comfortable wing chair in his bedroom, a glass of brandy in his hand. The room was in almost total darkness save for the light of a single branch of candles.

"Could I get you anything else, sir?" Alfred asked, wondering why Tony was simply sitting there staring at his drink instead of consuming it. He seemed in a strange mood this night, almost as if he were weighing options, or making an important decision.

"Nothing, Alfred," Tony said. "Don't let me keep you from your bed."

Alfred turned and was halfway to the door when Tony called out softly, "Wait."

The valet-cum-butler turned. "Yes, sir?"

342

"How do you feel about old boots?"

Alfred looked perplexed. "I beg your pardon, sir?"

"Old boots," Tony reiterated. "Things that generally have seen wear before you've had them."

A flash of light went off in Alfred's head. He thought he knew now what Tony was hinting at. *Old boots.* A slang term for a woman who'd been with another man previous to the man she was with now.

Tony brought the brandy to his lips and drank. He'd always believed that when one was in the market for a wife, one didn't even consider used goods. A gentleman always went for the new item, preferring to see it marked with his stamp and no one else's. Hadn't he had a similar conversation with Rafe some months back whilst they were both in England? He'd been so damned sure then of what he wanted. He'd told his friend that only a virgin would do for him as a bride. A malleable, pure, pretty puppet who would do his bidding and stay out of things that didn't concern her, like his life.

"Breaking in something new has always been a bit tricky, sir," Alfred responded. "Me, I like comfort. Being the first isn't always best in some cases. Sometimes there's more value in being the last to have something. One appreciates the design and purpose better, I think."

Tony smiled, silently blessing the day he'd engaged Alfred to work for him. The man was a straight talker whose words made sense.

Tony put down the half-full glass of spirits on the low, round table next to his chair. "Thank you, Alfred."

"Happy to be of service, sir, for what it's worth."

Tony flicked a glance in the valet's direction, as if imparting a confidence. "I may sleep in tomorrow, so don't bother waking me at my usual time."

Alfred couldn't repress his delight. "As you wish, sir."

"Enjoy the remainder of your evening, as well."

Alfred's lips kicked up into a sly smile. "That I will, sir. And you yours."

It was Tony's turn to grin. "I'm planning on it."

As soon as Alfred shut the door behind him, Tony was out of his seat. He glanced at the clock on the mantel. Gone ten P.M. She might already be asleep.

So what if she was? He'd wake her if he had to. Tony had a distinct feeling that this encounter couldn't wait any longer.

So much had changed. Months ago he'd come to this country, journeyed halfway round the world, determined to catch what he thought was a scheming, lying tart.

Instead, he'd been caught himself—by the softness of a smile, the goodness of a heart, the beauty of a face. Caught and snared by the grayest of eyes, the brownest of hair, the creamiest of skin. Hoisted, one might say, by his own petard, his certainty of mind.

He thought he'd had all the answers.

Until meeting her, he had. Now, the questions were different.

Still, they remained to be asked.

Did he love her?

Yes.

Did he want her?

Yes.

Did he plan on showing her, telling her?

Yes.

* * *

Annie was dozing and instantly came awake at a sound outside her window. As her eyes adjusted to the dark, she saw a tall figure silhouetted behind the white curtains.

Slowly she threw back the linen sheet covering her body. Her breathing quickened. Her feet touched the ground and she stood, moving, as if commanded by an unseen force, to the door. She turned the brass handle.

Tony stood there.

"If you don't want me, tell me to go."

Annie heard his words, uttered in that dark, sensual voice. He was leaving the decision up to her. She could shut the door, lock him out of her life with the quick slam of the glass in his face. She wouldn't have to speak a word. It would be obvious what her choice was.

If she did that, it would be an end to whatever was between them. She knew that for certain.

She looked into his eyes. She expected arrogance, the cool, assessing look of the man who could, and did, get what he wanted.

Rather than that, there was a hint of vulnerability there. As if he were uncertain, like a child waiting to get a promised treat, not sure it would materialize.

It was that window into his soul that cleared away any lingering doubts on her part.

Annie reached out her hand and clasped his. "Stay," she whispered.

It was all Tony needed to hear. He stepped into the room and gathered her into his arms, pulling her close to his body. His mouth was on hers, probing, finding the willing responsiveness of hers. He yielded to the desire to taste and discover, kissing her as deeply, as intimately as he could.

Annie was swept up in the whirlwind of his mouth, surrendering to the demands he was making. Her arms slid around his waist, grasping his shirt, clutching it as she succumbed to the hungry desire he elicited.

It was all Tony could do to restrain himself from taking her then and there. He had to keep reminding himself that she had no experience of love, or desire. All she'd had before was lust and disappointment. No tenderness, no caring, no tutoring in the art of love. There would be time later for heat and wild abandon. All that had gone before in his life was so that he could show Annie that wanting was mutual, that love was a duet, not a solo piece.

His hands skimmed her shoulders. His lips followed, feathering across her skin, down her neck, to the hollows of her throat.

Her small gasp brought a smile to his face.

Annie's head rolled back, giving him greater access to her flesh. The smooth touch of his hands, the magic in his fingertips, awakened something new inside her. Tremors of need erupted under her skin.

Slowly he undid the first four tiny buttons of her gown, exposing the skin beneath the white cotton. He slid his fingers inside the flaps, spreading them.

She gasped again, slightly louder this time.

His mouth met hers, drinking in her sighs. He coaxed it open, his tongue seeking entrance.

Annie's head swam with delight, savoring the sensations he evoked. One minute floating, the next soaring higher and higher.

His hands caressed and conquered, allowing her to

346

get used to their touch. The nightgown was unbuttoned almost to her waist, giving him better access to her skin, to the fullness of her breasts. He cupped one, the nipple budding beneath his palm, tightening to a stiff point.

She felt the cool air from the open door on her skin. Her eyes flashed open, watching as he stepped to the bed and grabbed the quilt that was folded at the foot. He snatched it in one large hand, spreading it across the floor with an elegant toss. Next, she watched from bemused eyes as Tony removed his shirt, pulling it from his trousers and tugging it open, scattering the buttons in his haste to shed it.

He had the long, leanly muscled torso of a Greek statue. A superb build, without an ounce of superfluous flesh. A wide, magnificent chest, a dusting of golden-brown hair across the broad width of it.

Tony took her hand and brought it to his chest.

Annie wet her lips. His skin was warm to the touch, the hair crisp. She let her fingers explore the foreign territory of his body, until she heard his own low gasp.

"What's wrong?" God, had she hurt him in some way?

"Nothing," Tony assured her, his voice husky. "Pray, continue."

She did so, at first tentatively, then becoming bolder, enjoying the feel of his skin.

"You like this?" she asked, anxious to please.

"Very much."

There was beauty in his body. More than she could have imagined.

"My turn again," he murmured, bending slightly to scoop her up into his arms. He knelt on the quilt, gently laying her down before joining her there. He slipped still more buttons undone, both breasts completely bare to his gaze.

Inhaling sharply, Tony bent his head and put his mouth to the crest of one.

Annie whimpered softly. His ministrations were creating an ache deep within her, centering low in her belly, warmth spreading. Her defenses were lowered, welcoming the seductiveness of his masterful touch.

Tony's mouth took hers once again, as if he couldn't get enough of it. Kisses upon kisses, each one longer, deeper, hotter than the one before.

Annie wrapped her arms around him, fingers sliding slowly up his broad back. On his right shoulder blade, her hand encountered a raised bump, another angel's kiss. She clasped him closer, giving in to the need coursing through her blood. His weight wasn't a burden—rather it was a joy, an acceptance of his power and strength. The feel of his chest upon hers sparked odd sensations as his crisp hair rubbed against her skin, against her sensitive nipples.

He gazed into her eyes. "Do you want me to stop?"

"No," Annie whispered, almost not recognizing her own voice, so raw did it sound to her ears. "I want—"

"What?" he cut in, nibbling her neck.

"I don't know," she replied. She couldn't put her feelings into words because she didn't understand all that was happening to her, within her. It was all new, unchartered territory for her. His navigational skills must lead them both.

With a smile, Tony answered, "You will. Trust me."

"I do." She trusted in the love she had for him, trusted that he was worthy of the price.

Tony slid his left hand down past her waist, then

down further still. He heard her moans, low little sounds of the pleasure she couldn't deny. Deliberately, he skipped the area he most wanted to touch, saving that for later. Slowly he ran his hand down her leg, then pulled it back up, bringing along the hem of her nightdress.

Annie felt the breeze flow over her skin when he lifted the cotton. It was like another caress of his fingers, doubling the awareness. Then she tensed, recalling the last time a man had pushed up her clothing. Pain had followed.

Tony could feel her stiffen. "What's wrong?"

Annie couldn't tell him. Not yet. Not now. "Must you?" she asked, her hands reaching down in an attempt to halt his progress.

"I want to see you, Annie," he explained. "All of you. Just as I want you to see all of me."

"All?"

"All." He had to break through the fear he saw in her eyes, show her that what was taking place tonight was natural, that it was right. He cursed that selfish bastard to hell for what he'd done to Annie. "Let go."

Annie dropped her hands to her sides, clutching instead the quilt, tightly.

Tony continued, feathering his fingertips along her thigh, inching ever higher. He'd pushed the gown up to the apex of her legs. Moving slightly, he said, "Let me remove it. Please."

She hadn't realized that he'd want her completely bare. She trembled.

"Sit up," he commanded gently.

Annie complied, raising her hands over her head to facilitate the removal of the garment, which he tossed aside. She crossed her arms over her breasts, her long hair hiding the rest of her body, offering her some form of shelter from his hot, avid gaze.

"You've nothing to be ashamed of, Annie. You're beautiful." He pushed aside a length of her hair, placing a kiss upon her shoulder as he did so. Rising, Tony unbuttoned his trousers, pushing them, along with the fine linen drawers he wore underneath, down his legs.

Annie was unable to tear her gaze away as Tony stripped. Her eyes widened, then widened further still when he was completely naked. He was beautiful. Michelangelo could have carved him from marble, so much did he resemble the master's best work. Color tinged her cheeks as she gazed at that part of him that rose hard and high from a thick nest of golden-brown hair. She'd seen male animals about the station before, bulls, horses, but never a man; at least not like this. She wet her lips, awestruck.

"I can't hide my desire for you, nor pretend that I'm indifferent," he confessed as he joined her once more on the tangled quilt. "I want you, Annie. All of you, and not for a quick tumble. Know that. Believe that."

Tony tenderly pushed aside her hair, then unlocked her arms. "You've no need to hide from me. Ever. Come," he coaxed, "kiss me. Let me know what you want."

"You," Annie whispered softly, her eyes on his. "I want you." She wrapped her arms about his neck and offered him her mouth.

He took her gift as they floated down, the quilt against Annie's back. Tony continued to kiss her as he stroked her body with his hands, cupping, fondling, bringing her to a feverish pitch. When he feathered his fingers across the brown curls at the juncture of her legs, he felt her immediate reaction. When he slowly slid one finger around, then inside, she bucked slightly. "Easy," he whispered.

Annie was almost over the edge, her body feverish and waiting. For what? she wondered, her mind adrift in all the feelings he was drawing out of her. Where before she'd felt violated, she now felt cherished, as if on the brink of an important discovery.

Tony resisted the need to taste her there as well. Later, when she was ready for all the lessons of love. Now, he'd determined, she was ready for the next, the crucial as it were, lesson.

Tony moved, positioning his body up and over hers, bringing himself to the portal of her feminine temple. "Annie, look at me."

She did, their eyes and hearts connecting in the same instant that their bodies did.

Annie waited for the pain, and found none. Tony was joined to her, his powerful body moving in and out, setting the tempo, all the while his green eyes gazing deeply into hers. They closed when he kissed her, their mouths blending just as harmoniously as their bodies.

Her hands latched on tight to his back, short nails finding an anchor in his flesh, clinging as she rode the storm, becoming part of it, a tempest that tossed and twirled, sending sparks of fire through her body. The deeper he thrust, the higher she flew, until finally, her senses ablaze, Annie burst into a fiery conflagration.

Tony joined her a moment later, his body exploding in rapture so intense he thought he'd truly died, only to be reclaimed. His seed spilled into her as he collapsed, his mind adaze, his spirits still soaring.

It was as if he'd been in an emotional quagmire for

far too long—almost his entire life. Here was love just within his grasp.

And to think that he might never have known this. If not for a quirk of fate, he might have been forever cut off from his greatest joy.

Yes, he believed in paradise now. He had firsthand knowledge of its existence. And having tasted paradise, he knew beyond doubt that he could never lose it. No matter what, he would hold it safe.

Tony pulled her to him, cradling her in his arms. He could never let her go. He knew that. Annie Ross was his as surely as he was hers. Emotion this strong couldn't be denied or mocked. Love had made a believer of him.

Annie couldn't halt the tears that spilled from her eyes. She wept from the beauty of what Tony had shown her. Everything that came before dissolved in the heat of his passion. Like a flame burning clean, this night she was reborn from the ashes of her past.

God, that she might have lived her life alone, never knowing, never experiencing this rapture, was almost unbearable. This was what Mei tried to tell her about, and what she hadn't wanted to hear.

Her head rested on his chest, inhaling the scent of him, one arm thrown about his lean waist. She never wanted to let go. This, she realized, was where she wanted to wake up every morning of her life. In Tony Chambers's strong arms, held close to his warm body.

"I love you, Annie," Tony murmured in his deep baritone voice, made even huskier in passion's aftermath. "And," he paused, kissing the top of her head, "I want to marry you."

Her heart raced with his words. She couldn't believe she was hearing this. Then, like a splash of cold water, her past rose up before her eyes. She owed him the truth. Chances were, he might never find out. But Annie couldn't live with herself if she wasn't honest. It was a risk; one she had to take. She loved him too much to lie.

Annie removed herself from his embrace. Suddenly shy, she located her nightgown and pulled it back on, quickly fastening the buttons as best she could.

Tony watched her, wondering what was on her mind. God, but she'd been beautiful, all giving and accepting. He loved her quiet strength, her tenacity of spirit. "I don't make this offer lightly, nor," he reassured her, "have I ever made it before."

She turned and faced him. He still lay on the quilt, though he'd pulled an edge of it over his waist. More for her modesty than his, she thought.

"I'm flattered," she replied, searching for the proper words, "but I won't hold you to it if it isn't what you truly want."

"I'm not asking as a sop to your ego or mine, nor because I feel guilty about what we've shared."

The depth of that sharing still rocked Annie's emotions. "It's just that I have a daughter. I have to think about Fallon's happiness as well as my own." And, she added silently, your own, my love. She wouldn't trap him.

Tony shifted. His chest rose and fell with every breath he took, making Annie remember the feel of it.

"What is the problem?" he inquired. "I want to marry you. I fully understand that she comes with you. Truthfully, I wouldn't have it any other way."

"You wouldn't?"

"No," he said, a smile curving his lips. "I'm quite fond of Fallon already."

"As she is of you."

"Then there's no problem, Annie. I will treat her as my own. You've my promise on that."

"Will you?"

"I love you, Annie." It was easy to say the words because they were true. "I love you," he repeated, "and she's a part of you."

Annie swallowed nervously. "And of someone else."

"That doesn't matter to me." For Tony, Fallon was all Annie's child as far as he was concerned.

"You're certain?"

"Without a doubt. If you'd like, I'll see to it legally. There should be no problems as he's deceased." Tony waited, wondering if she would tell him about her child's father now. He'd given her the opening. It was important for him to discover whether he could trust her to share her secrets with him, for in doing so, he would know beyond a doubt that she trusted him as well.

"That's just it," Annie admitted. "He isn't."

"What do you mean?"

"He's alive."

Satisfied by her honesty, Tony made a confession of his own. "I know."

"What?" Annie's eyes grew wide, her face drained of color. Had she heard him correctly?

"I said, I know."

"How could you?" she demanded, stunned.

Now it was time for Tony to reveal facts. He couldn't tell her that he'd overheard her conversation with Mei. He'd spare her that embarrassment and hurt. He owed her pride that. "From the Pinkerton detective agency."

"Pinkerton?" Annie had heard of them. They were famous in her country. Oh God, she thought, wrap-

ping her arms about her waist as if in pain. Why hadn't
he said anything? "How long have you known?"

"Not long," he admitted.

"You had me investigated?" She felt naked, except
that this time it wasn't a lack of clothes; instead, it was
her soul that had been laid bare.

"I felt I owed it to Cedric," he explained. "I didn't
know what kind of a woman you were. I suspected
you to be, in point of fact, a whore, out for the easy
opportunity. I believed that you'd taken advantage of
an old man, beguiling him with your wiles so that you
could live a life of ease in exchange for your favors."

"I could never do that," she protested. No wonder
his eyes had been cold, his manner chilly, when he
arrived here. His accusations of a love affair between
herself and Patrick made more sense, too. Still, it hurt
that he'd thought her a whore.

"I know that now." In a fluid motion, Tony rose,
draping the quilt around his middle until he reached
his trousers. Turning his back to her, he hastily pulled
them on.

Annie averted her eyes from the sight of his lean
body while he dressed. "This report, it said what?"

Tony walked over to Annie and gently turned her to
face him, his hands cupping her face. "That you were
never married when you left Philadelphia in the company of my great-uncle, nor had you ever been married. You'd been a governess and abruptly left your
employ, without references." He told her the family
she'd worked for, along with the name of the eldest
son. "Am I correct in assuming that he might be Fallon's father?"

Annie nodded her head, her shoulders sagging momentarily before she stood upright, squaring them,

her eyes raised, connecting with his. "He is."

"So, you made up the dead husband." It was a simple statement, one laced with compassion for her plight.

"Yes," she said. "Cedric suggested that it would solve the embarrassing problem of being alone and having a child out of wedlock. A simple solution. No one need ever know the truth here, unless I told them."

"Does anyone?"

"Only Mei."

"Not Patrick?"

Annie thought she detected a small reserve of jealousy in Tony's voice. She shook her head. "No. I was introduced to him as a widow. We never discussed my *late* husband. Cedric told him that it was too painful a topic for me to speak about, and Patrick respected my privacy. Later, when we became close, I just couldn't tell him. I was afraid," she confided, "that he would think ill of me." Just as she'd harbored fears that Tony might.

"I doubt that O'Donnell ever would," Tony replied honestly. He might not be close to the Australian himself, but he didn't doubt or deny the deep bond of friendship the man had with Annie.

"So, you know the truth and you still want to marry me?" she asked, her voice barely above a whisper. Annie knew Tony for a man of pride, a man used to being first in all that mattered. It was the way he was, the way of the world he was used to. She was also well aware of what kind of wife his heritage demanded. She wasn't it. Not by a long shot.

Tony pulled her into his arms, sealing her mouth with a swift kiss. "More than anything I've ever wanted in my life," he answered her. "And as soon as possible.

I don't want to wait much longer to make you my wife."

"Your wife," Annie said, the words sounding glorious to her ears. All the dreams that she'd packed aside and put away were now coming true, but better than she could have ever wished for. All she had to do was say one word—yes—and she would be Mrs. Anthony Chambers. She would have the man she loved as her husband, and Fallon would have a father she could love and respect.

"Yes."

Tony lifted her chin in his hand. "Excuse me, ma'am," he said in a formal tone, "but I don't believe I quite heard your reply."

"Yes!" Annie said, louder.

He swung her up in his embrace, carrying her to the bed. "Comfort this time, I think." With nimble fingers he helped her rid herself of the gown. "No need for this, my love. From now on, you'll have me." He deftly removed his own recently donned apparel also.

"Promise?" she asked, her hands drawing him to her as she wound them around his neck.

"Always." Tony's voice was deep and dark with desire. His pale olive green eyes stared deeply into Annie's luminescent gray ones as he swore, "Upon my honor, for me, from this day forward, it's you and no other."

Annie surrendered to his intoxicating kiss and to his thrilling, magical possession. For her, as well, it was Tony, for all the days to come.

Epilogue
A Dream Renewed

Camelot Station, New Year's Eve, 1888

Today was her wedding day.

What a wonderful way to see out the old year and welcome in the new. Actually, it was a double celebration for it was also Tony's twenty-sixth birthday.

Annie stared at herself in the mirror, dabbing perfume behind each ear and in the hollow of her throat. She wore her hair pulled away from her face, anchored with two mother-of-pearl combs. It cascaded down the back of her ivory silk and satin wedding dress.

It never ceased to amaze her how fast someone could sew. The morning after she'd accepted Tony's proposal, he'd sent Alfred to Melbourne to hire a seamstress and get the material. He'd returned within two days with three women from an exclusive shop in Melbourne, happy to be outfitting the wedding of the year, or so it was being described among the locals. The women had completed the work yesterday, and were back on their way to the city, their pockets very well compensated for their time and effort.

Annie wore Patrick's earrings, Tony's pendant, and on her left hand she wore the magnificent diamond and opal ring Tony had placed there. It was a lovely oval stone of blue shot with green, surrounded by diamonds. She held out her hand, admiring the ring. What mattered about it most was that it represented Tony's pledge of love and the future, their future. Together.

When they'd made the announcement to Alfred, Mary, and Alice, there were hugs, handshakes, and best wishes all around. Several bottles of wine were opened in celebration, and Alfred was so frank as to admit that he'd seen it coming. He just wondered what had taken *them* so bloody long to discover that they loved one another.

Annie's heart was light and carefree, filled with hope. She smiled as she rose from her dressing-table chair, an old, faded photograph in her hand. All this had been made possible by one man—Cedric Chambers. *I wish that you were here to see this, my dear Cedric,* Annie thought as she gazed down at the picture. *I can't ever thank you enough for all the things you've given me, the most precious being this man, your grandnephew. Did you believe that we were meant for each other? Was that why you arranged this? If it was, my thanks for all eternity, dear friend.*

Annie tucked the small, well-worn photo into the carefully hidden pocket of her skirt. She knew that somehow, in spirit, he would be there with them today.

Fallon, Lady at her side, came scampering into her mother's bedroom. Annie's daughter was wearing a new dress also. In her hand she held a basket of flowers, consisting mainly of roses. "I'm to carry this, Mama," she said proudly.

"And you'll do a fine job, sweetheart." Annie bent down to hug her daughter close. Gently she touched

Fallon's cheek, her eyes meeting those of the little girl. Although she and Tony had already discussed their upcoming nuptials with Fallon, and how it would affect her life, Annie wanted to be sure, at least one more time, that her daughter was content with the change to come. "You're happy about this, aren't you?"

"Oh yes, ever so much, Mama," Fallon said with enthusiasm. "Uncle Tony said that he's going to be my papa now, and that I should begin today in calling him that. He also said that I would be the oldest of his children. That's important, isn't it?"

"Very," Annie agreed. "It's a very great responsibility, my angel. He wouldn't have said that if he didn't have confidence in your ability to carry out the position." At the self-important look on Fallon's face, Annie smiled tenderly. If she didn't already love Tony, she would all the more. He'd made good on his word to include her daughter in their new family.

"Are you looking forward to seeing Melbourne?" she asked, adjusting the ribbon in Fallon's blond hair.

Fallon smiled. She knew a secret that Uncle . . . Papa had made her promise not to reveal. He wanted to surprise Mama with the news himself. They were not only going to Melbourne, but to Papa's own country, England. Then, on the way home, they would visit with Mama's family in Philadelphia; maybe even go and see Papa's friends in Texas. She crossed her heart and swore that she wouldn't tell, even though she desperately wanted to. It was Mama's present.

"Yes, Mama, I am."

"So am I," Annie confided. "There are so many things we can do and see there, sweetheart. You'll be amazed."

Mary knocked on the door.

360

"Come in," Annie called.

"Just thought I'd see if you'd be needing any more help, ma'am." Mary had been in earlier to give Annie a hand getting into her wedding costume.

Annie rose. "Maybe with the veil, if you wouldn't mind."

Mary carefully picked it up from the bed. She adjusted the veil of white lace, edged with robin's egg blue satin, upon Annie's head. Then, she stepped back, eyeing the younger woman. "Your mama," she said to Fallon, "looks just like a princess, don't you think?"

The little girl nodded and Lady whoofed her approval as well.

"What time is it?"

Mary checked the watch pinned to her dress. "It's gone noon, ma'am."

Annie took a deep breath, a radiant smile curving her lips. "We'd best be going then. I don't want to keep Tony waiting."

Tony checked his gold pocket watch. She'd be here soon, he thought as he snapped the monogrammed lid back in place, replacing the watch into his vest. Today he was dressed in full formal regalia: a black frock coat and trousers, formal white shirt and studs, gray satin neckcloth, and silver brocaded vest.

Alfred stood at his side, his best man, while the minister, from Mansfield, chatted with Jim Winters and his wife. They'd chosen the garden for the wedding, deciding on a more private ceremony, with only the station's people in attendance.

Tony smiled, thinking how improbable this would have seemed to him only a few months ago. Ah, he thought, what a difference time makes in the scheme

361

of things. Rafe would find this turn of events amusing. Tony had written to his American friend yesterday, informing him of his soon-to-be-married status, adding a postscript that Rafe had been right about love. It did change one's life. Forever.

He thought about the words the minister would recite—the vows that he and Annie would exchange. *Better or worse. Richer or poorer. In sickness and in health. Till death do us part.* More importantly—*Forsaking all others.* That had never meant much to him before, except in terms of his wife's fidelity. Now Tony knew it was meant for him as well. He would keep that vow because he loved Annie Ross. And because she was now the most important person in his life. He'd forsaken his old world to find her, and been rewarded tenfold with a better, brighter one.

"Here she comes, sir," Alfred whispered dramatically. "May I say again, sir, that you're quite the lucky man."

"Don't I know it?" Tony focused on the woman walking slowly toward them. God, but Annie was beautiful. He ached to hold her, to have her stand beside him, where she belonged. To proclaim proudly, this woman is mine.

Tony winked at Fallon, walking in front of her mother, her tiny face wreathed in smiles as she trod along the brick walkway, her ever-faithful border collie Lady beside her. Amusement curved Tony's lips. The dog was dressed for the wedding as well, with a garland of flowers woven around her neck, like a collar. Mary walked behind the little girl, having agreed to stand as witness for the couple with Alfred.

Annie glowed. There was no other word for it. The sun was bright today, but no brighter than the look in

Annie's gray eyes as she joined him. She slipped her gloveless hand into Tony's, feeling the warmth of his.

"Dearly beloved," the minister began.

"I love you," she said softly to Tony.

He squeezed her hand. "And I love you," he answered, keeping his voice low, pitched for her ears alone, "from now through eternity, I promise."

Within a short time, the minister concluded, "You may kiss the bride."

Tony grinned, lifting her chin up. He dipped his head, and his mouth captured Annie's, hungrily demonstrating his ardor.

Uncaring of the witnesses, Annie flung her arms about his neck and returned his kiss with equal fervor.

Cheers and whistles exploded from the station's hands as corks were popped on bottles of champagne and toasts were drunk to the happy couple.

"It's but a sample of what awaits us tonight, Mrs. Chambers," Tony declared a moment later. "Tonight and all the nights of our life together."

"That sounds wonderful," Annie murmured.

Tony flashed a deep smile. "It does, doesn't it?"

And it was.

TIMESWEPT

THERE NEVER WAS A TIME

Gail Link

"Gail Link was born to write romance!"
—Jayne Ann Krentz

Sitting alone in her Vermont farmhouse, Rebecca Gallagher Fraser hears a ghostly voice whisper to her. But not until she stumbles across a distant ancestor's diary do the spirit's words hold any meaning for her.

Drawn by inexplicable forces, Rebecca journeys to the once resplendent Southern plantation where her forebear loved and lost a Union soldier. And there, on a jasmine-scented New Orleans night, she discovers that passion unfulfilled in one lifetime can defy fate and logic and be reborn so much sweeter in another.

__52025-7 $4.99 US/$5.99 CAN

DEBRA DIER
LORD SAVAGE
Author of *Scoundrel*

Lady Elizabeth Barrington is sent to Colorado to find the Marquess of Angelstone, the grandson of an English duke who disappeared during an attack by renegade Indians. But the only thing she discovers is Ash MacGregor, a bounty-hunting rogue who takes great pleasure residing in the back of a bawdy house. Convinced that his rugged good looks resemble those of the noble family, Elizabeth vows she will prove to him that aristocratic blood does pulse through his veins. And in six month's time, she will make him into a proper man. But the more she tries to show him which fork to use or how to help a lady into her carriage, the more she yearns to be caressed by this virile stranger, touched by this beautiful barbarian, embraced by Lord Savage.

___4119-7 $4.99 US/$5.99 CAN

A Quest of Dreams — DEBRA DIER

Bestselling Author Of *Shadow Of The Storm*

To Devlin McCain, she is a fool who is chasing after moonbeams, a spoiled rich girl who thinks her money can buy anything. But beneath her maddening facade burns a blistering sensuality he is powerless to resist, and he will journey to the ends of the earth to claim her.

To Kate Whitmore, he is an overpowering brute who treats women like chattel, an unscrupulous scoundrel who values gold above all else. Yet try as she might, she cannot deny the irresistible allure of his dangerous virility.

Hard-edged realist and passionate idealist, Devlin and Kate plunge into the Brazilian jungle, searching for the answer to an age-old mystery and a magnificent love that will bind them together forever.

_3583-9 $4.99 US/$5.99 CAN